MOST WANTED

"A Dying Life" by Fiona Patton—in which a young bodysnatcher is caught between a vendetta and a hard place.

"My Claw Is Quick" by Simon Hawke—in which Catseye Gomez tracks down a young damsel in distress in the seamy underworld of the Southwest.

"The Quick Way Down" by P.N. Elrod—in which undead detective Jack Fleming cracks the gangland case of a prizefighter's death.

"Cycle of Horror" by Mickey Zucker Reichert—in which a hitman's many-lived career of murder comes to an end.

"Saint Al" by Dennis O'Neil—in which the spirit of Al Capone indoctrinates a naive novice.

This is just a partial list of the crimes herein, where gangsters and molls, detectives and demigods ply their magical craft in the cosmic syndicate of

MOB MAGIC

MOB MAGIC

Edited by
Brian Thomsen
and
Martin H. Greenberg

DAW BOOKS, INC.
DONALD A. WOLLHEIM, FOUNDER
375 Hudson Street, New York, NY 10014

ELIZABETH R. WOLLHEIM
SHEILA E. GILBERT
PUBLISHERS

First Printing, November 1998
1   2   3   4   5   6   7   8   9

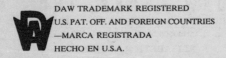

DAW TRADEMARK REGISTERED
U.S. PAT. OFF. AND FOREIGN COUNTRIES
—MARCA REGISTRADA
HECHO EN U.S.A.

PRINTED IN THE U.S.A.

ACKNOWLEDGMENTS

Introduction © 1998 by Brian M. Thomsen
The Faerie Godfather © 1998 by J. Robert King
Odie and The Zoo © 1998 by Jeff Grubb
Saint Al © 1998 by Dennis O'Neil
Money Well Spent © 1998 by Janet Pack
A Dying Life © 1998 by Fiona Patton
Solo © 1998 by Robert Greenberger
Cycle of Horror © 1998 by Mickey Zucker Reichert
My Claw Is Quick © 1998 by Simon Hawke
The Quick Way Down © 1998 by P. N. Elrod
A Bird for Becky © 1998 by Max Allan Collins
The Dream Job © 1998 by Heidi E. Y. Stemple
Power Corrupts © 1998 by Jody Lynn Nye
Whaddya See? © 1998 by Randall G. Thomas
Sashimi © 1998 by Brian M. Thomsen
Live Bait © 1998 by Roland J. Green
Stan © 1998 by Mike Resnick & Ron Collins
With a Smile © 1998 by Tom Dupree

For
Francis Ford Coppola,
Robert De Niro
&
Martin Scorsese,
who make their own kind of
"mob magic"
on the silver screen

CONTENTS

DONS & THE DAMNED

CRIMES & CORPORATIONS

INTRODUCTION

Originally the word "mob" was meant to mean an unruly mass or throng of people subject to spontaneous whims and demands. Both the Old and New Testaments make reference to mobs having influence on various significant events, and no less a writer than Shakespeare himself made frequent references to the psyche of the mob (eg., Mark Anthony winning over the mob at Caesar's funeral in "Julius Caesar," the Duke's address to the mob of Capulets and Montagues in "Romeo and Juliet," etc.). Mobs were usually destructive and were often used as a weapon by a persuasive orator or a charismatic leader.

Today when we say "mob," we are usually referring to "goodfellas," "wiseguys," "gangsters" or "hoods," or, as the less colorful refer to them, the practitioners of organized crime.

From Damon Runyon to Mario Puzo, the mob has been a subject of major fascination for most Americans, who seem to harbor an innate need to romanticize these outlaws of society. Some gangsters become folk heroes, pop icons no different from the latest rock star or sports hero. Fellows with nicknames like "the Teflon Don," "the Chin," and "the Bull" make the cover of *Time* magazine and are played by award-winning actors in big-money movies.

For twentieth-century U.S.A., the mob is every bit as American as baseball, and its presence in civilization itself is older than our country and the Holy Roman Empire combined. The first primate who realized that he had something that someone else wanted—and was willing to kill for—sought "protection" from the first primate who was willing to give that protection for a price (an extra banana a week or perhaps just a favor to be redeemed at some later date).

Thus civilization began with the social contract while organized crime began when the first social contract included interest (or, in the vernacular, "juice").

Gods & Godfathers

"Hey, Godfather! You owe me a favor."

Mario Puzo's Corleone family has become the seminal archetype for most people's conception of what a crime family is really like—close-knit, immigrant ethnic, and moral and religious in their own way. The now often used moniker of "godfather" is ripe in its own irony as both the title of a male sponsor in the sacrament of baptism and the title for the spiritual and authoritative head of an organized crime family.

The authors in the following section exploit this irony in their stories. Rob King's tale of a slightly different Camelot features a decidedly non-Christian godfather, while Jeff Grubb has a bit of fun with a pair of old Dons in quasi-retirement. Denny O'Neil and Janet Pack, on the other hand, focus on surrogate higher powers whose angelic assistance may not always be in the best interest of their clients.

THE FAERIE GODFATHER

by J. Robert King

The bishop rode his tiny gray donkey into the shadow of the city walls and reined it to a stop. Camelot. He'd never seen anything like it. He was used to Rome—sacked Rome. Crumbled buildings, scurrying rats, burned shacks, twisting catacombs—age and decay. There was nothing like that here: white turrets, snapping red pennants, cleanly cobbled streets, ladies in silken gowns, knights in shining armor, walls that fairly glowed with life. . . . Everything was new. Even the horses were brave.

The bishop sat there a moment before the main gate as other travelers filed past along the rising dirt road. He scratched his uneven tonsure, straightened a robe the same color as his donkey, and stared, astonished.

The pope was right. This *was* the New Jerusalem.

"Bishop Niccolai?" said a shining knight beside the gates. He had stood so still and shone so brightly that he had seemed a silver statue. Now he strode over to meet the meek-mannered bishop. "Welcome. I am Sir Kay, Seneschal of Camelot and stepbrother to King Arthur. I am pleased to learn that the beautiful metropolis of our king is known even to Rome."

Niccolai gave the knight a pleasant smile. Here was a beautiful creature, a veritable angel on earth. Beneath a planished helm, Kay's blond hair was delicately coifed, and enough lines creased his high brow to make him appear intelligent but not brooding. His blue eyes glimmered with wit, his teeth were perfectly white, and his smile was ready. A neatly trimmed mustache and goatee showed his dedication to grooming. "Yes, well, as the scriptures say, 'A city on an hill cannot be hid,' and then again, 'For nothing is secret, that shall not be made manifest; neither any thing hid, that shall not be known and come abroad.' "

Sir Kay laughed a little at that. "No, indeed. But the exact reason you have 'come abroad' is, I confess, still a mystery to me."

With a gentle nudge of his heels, the bishop headed his mount toward the gates. "Let us walk as we talk, for I am eager to see your beautiful city." Sir Kay happily fell into step beside the donkey and leaned in, somewhat conspiratorially, as they passed over the drawbridge and beneath the first of two portcullises. Niccolai continued. "There is considerable pressure on the church of Rome—especially after the move of the capital to Constantinople and the plague of pretender popes spreading across the land—to come up with some definitive sign of God's approval—"

"If you are interested in signs from God, perhaps you are looking in the wrong—"

"And many among the laity and the clergy themselves feel that the Second Coming is overdue. Some wonder if we've missed it. After all, no one has seen John the Beloved in centuries, and he is supposed to remain until Christ's return—"

Kay's laugh this time was explosive. "I've heard tales of a Joseph of Arimethea hereabouts, but no Beloved Disciple—"

"And so, a number of us have been dispatched to cities such as this, likely candidates for the New Jerusalem—"

"New Jerusalem?" Kay asked, wonderingly.

"Yes. And I quote:

'Behold, I come quickly: hold that fast which thou hast, that no man take thy crown. Him that overcometh will I make a pillar in the temple of my

God, and he shall go no more out: and I will write upon him the name of my God, and the name of the city of my God, which is new Jerusalem, which cometh down out of heaven from my God.'

"Quite possibly, your Arthur is 'Him that overcometh.' Surely he has held fast his crown through the great tribulation that has come upon the world, and perhaps this earthly kingdom of his is the New Jerusalem, come down out of heaven from God."

The smile that crossed Kay's face was rueful. "Camelot, come down out of heaven? Ha!" He slapped a hand on the bishop's back as the two men entered the courtyard beyond the gate. An open-air market stood beyond, bright pavilions riffling beneath a gentle breeze. "I fear you've wasted your journey, Eminence. Arthur won this land through blood and battle. He was born a child of fornication—what would have been adultery except that the cuckold was a few hours dead at the time of conception—was raised by a meddling wizard, and he fathered a child by his half-sister. In fact, as Arthur has grown to embody all that is noble and good, his very son has grown to embody all that is wicked. It is as though the man you have heard of is split in half.

"No, Your Worship, if half of this grand city descended from heaven, the other half arose from hell. Above ground it is all Christian virtue, but below ground, its foundations rest upon wild paganism. Its glorious knighthood is matched by its underworld of extortion, bribery, smuggling, counterfeiting, and murder. Arthur may be King of Britain, but then his son and nephew, Mordred, is its kingpin."

Bishop Niccolai did not seem to hear. "Ah, here is a clue, just here." He pointed to a mark upon a foundation stone of the gate they had just passed.

Sir Kay crouched down beside the stone, where some hoodlum had scratched his name. "Ah, you see?

If this were the New Jerusalem, would there be defacing graffiti on the walls?"

"But, look what it says—'IAKOBVS.' Jacob—the name of Israel, father of the twelve tribes. Or it might be the name of James, the brother of John, or James the Less, brother of Jesus."

Kay could not contain his dubiety. "So?"

"The New Jerusalem—and I quote—

> 'had a wall great and high, and had twelve gates,
> and at the gates twelve angels, and names written
> thereon, which are the names of the twelve tribes
> of the children of Israel. . . . And the wall of the
> city had twelve foundations, and in them the names
> of the twelve apostles of the Lamb.'

"So, you see, this foundation contains the name of one of the twelve apostles—James," said Niccolai, his voice tinged in excitement.

"The James that wrote this—that is, the Jacobus— if I have it right, is no apostle of the Lamb but one of Mordred's crew. He is a strong-man, a bit of muscle used by fey racketeers. I suspect that, since his name is carved into this stone, this gate is his territory. He's got a list of folk, such as Arthur and his knights, from whom he does not extort a toll for safe passage, but anyone else who seeks entry must pay dearly."

"Such gate guards, too, were prophesied in the New Jerusalem, for:

> 'There shall in no wise enter into it anything that
> defileth, neither whatsoever worketh abominations,
> or maketh a lie; but they which are written in the
> Lamb's book of life.'

"Your king, you, and the other knights must be written in the Lamb's book of life, whereby Jacobus allows you passage. All others must pay dearly—must give away all they own and follow the Lamb—to enter the city."

Kay grew chagrined, and he removed his helm in order to scratch a tousled crown. "You don't seem to understand. These followers of Mordred do not believe in the Christian God, and Mordred is no divine ambassador. You would make him God, but he is more a hoodlum godfather. He rules this city from below as Arthur does from above. I would not be surprised if his coffers held more coin than Arthur's, so effective are Mordred's 'tax gatherers,' his 'water bearers,' and his illicit 'entertainers.' He is not even human, this Mordred—did you know that? Though he is Arthur's son, he is also the get of a witch woman, a pagan creature known in these parts as a faerie."

Blinking, Bishop Niccolai drew a deep, contented sigh, and reasoned, simplistically, "There are many pagan deities that the church has discovered in fact to be saints and angels." He reached into his pack and drew out a map of the countryside. "Now, by my rough calculations, the whole of Arthur's realm—including Eire, the Scottish Highlands, Northumberland, Snowdonia and Surrounds, Central Briton, Anglia, and Britanny—falls within a square that is twelve thousand furlongs, which is about five thousand leagues or fifteen thousand miles. That fits the prophecies exactly.

'. . . and the length is as large as the breadth: and he measured the city with the reed, twelve thousand furlongs. . . . And he measured the wall thereof, an hundred and forty and four cubits, according to the measure of a man.'

"And this wall here, if we count also the great earthwork upon which it is raised, measures one hundred forty-four cubits in width—one hundred sixty of my own armlengths, but I am a small man. Now, as to the gates, there are only four, one in each cardinal direction, though Revelation speaks of twelve total. Even so, I noticed an outer gate and two portcullises here, which makes three eastern gates—and if each of the four cardinal directions holds three such gates—"

"Look," Kay interrupted, "you can calculate and interpret yourself into believing that anyplace is your New Jerusalem, but once you've seen Mordred and his gang at work, you'll know this couldn't possibly be an earthly heaven. Come with me." Kay rather forcefully drew the bishop off his stamping ass, tied the mount to a nearby post, and led him toward the open market. "I do this, Eminence, because I am a pious man. I do not want a bishop of the church to be shamed by misapprehension."

"Where are we going?" asked the bishop somewhat nervously.

"Through one of the sorcerous portals that leads into Mordred's underworld," Kay said, distaste clear on his features. "Beyond those portals, fey gather, flaunt their pagan ways, practice magics, entice mortals, bottle intoxicating waters, hatch plans for confidence games, arrange 'hits.' You'll see what I mean. This is no heaven on earth."

The shining knight led the bishop among flapping awnings and particolored tents—Camelot's main market. Everything was for sale here, from Chinese silks and Persian carpets to African black wood and Icelandic cod. Here were penned sheep dogs from the borderlands, and there serpents driven recently from Eire by a certain priest of shamrocks. The lively banter of merchants and buyers filled the spaces between leaning poles and guy ropes. They spoke in tongues as varied as the wares they hawked.

Bishop Niccolai was mesmerized by the chanting sound of it all. "Again, the prophecies are fulfilled, as was said of old:

'And it shall come to pass in the last days, saith God, I will pour out my Spirit upon all flesh, and

your sons and your daughters shall prophesy, and
your young men shall see visions, and your old
men shall dream dreams.' "

Sir Kay's spirits visibly slumped, and he caught up
his drooping frame against a lamp post. "These folk
aren't Pentecostals 'speaking in tongues.' They aren't
drunk with the Spirit of God, Your Eminence. If they
are drunk with anything, it is with the very stuff Mordred and his minions bottle in their realm and smuggle
into Camelot."

"You cannot tell me," said the Bishop, gesturing
excitedly about him, "that all this vitality, all this
bounty, results from anything but the abundance of
God. After all, in the book of Acts, God told Peter
to embrace the gentiles and their strange ways, saying,
'What God hath cleansed, that call not thou
common.' "

In exasperation, Kay flung his hands into the air.
"But that's just it, Your Eminence. The beauty and
perfection you see in this city comes only half from
heavenly Arthur. The other half of it comes from vulgar, common, earthly Mordred. This can't be the New
Jerusalem unless Satan is as much its founder as
God."

The bishop made the sign of the cross. "I think I
understand your hesitation. Don't worry, Sir Kay. If
this is indeed the New Jerusalem, Arthur will be fully
compensated."

"Compensated for what?"

"Well, if this is the New Jerusalem, the city and its
inhabitants will, of course, become immediate property of the church," said Niccolai easily. "And by the
city, I mean the great square that encompasses Arthur's kingdom, from Orkney in the north to Brittany
in the South. Rome will reimburse him, if that is required, though I would think a good Christian king
such as Arthur would be eager to grant the whole of
his holdings to the pope."

Fury flared bright in Kay's face. "Neither Arthur nor Mordred would ever relinquish Camelot, let alone Britain. Not to the pope. Not to anyone."

"Then Arthur would be excommunicated and the church would be forced to take the land by might of arms, as it is written:

'From the days of John the Baptist, the kingdom of heaven suffereth violence, and the violent take it by force.' "

A growl mounted up in Kay's throat, and his eyes narrowed to slits. His hand strayed to the sword at his belt. This man threatened Camelot with invasion. With war—holy war! Even so, Kay knew he could never slay a bishop of the True Church. He would have to convince this man. "But this *isn't* the New Jerusalem."

"Take me to Mordred's underworld, and let me judge for myself."

"Fine," replied Kay as he shouldered through the crowd toward a tangled maze of shops in half-timber and fieldstone.

"Fine," agreed Niccolai. "And by the way, how is it that a Knight of the Round Table—the Seneschal of Camelot himself—should know the whereabouts of these outlaw portals, let alone be allowed passage through them?"

The knight's eyes flashed with a warning for discretion—and a secret delight. "Because Arthur understands the improvements worked by Mordred's corruption, and so do I. While officially outlawed, Mordred's various industries are unofficially tolerated, occasionally promoted." So saying, he turned to a certain cellar door that crouched at the base of a leaning building of brick. Kay set his left foot upon a panel in the door and said, "My, but the king looks well hung this morn!"

A quizzical, scandalized look screwed itself into the

bishop's features. Without further comment, Kay pointed at his foot. The panel beneath it, though painted to look like woods, was in fact a cleverly fashioned pane of glass, through which a baleful eye now stared out, bulbous and yellow as a pealed onion. The eye withdrew, and there came a furtive sound of bolts drawing back from brackets within. Kay paused a moment more before stooping to heave upon the handle and reveal a flight of stairs descending into a dark cellar.

"After you," Kay said with a sweeping gesture.

Bishop Niccolai stared into the glowering darkness as if peering into Perdition itself. "You may proceed."

A smile quirked across the knight's face. "You are beginning to glimpse the true, infernal origins of this heavenly city of yours." So saying, he descended into the swirling dust motes of the cellar.

Niccolai hesitated a moment, fearful of following; then, more fearful of being left behind, he hurried after.

The stairs let off on a dirt floor awash in Tophet gloom. Ahead, on the far side of the room, a rectangle of golden light leaked past a closed door. Kay moved toward that door, and Niccolai padded nervously in his wake. Undeniably, there were others in that space, hushed and waiting in the darkness, steel drawn.

Kay reached the door, and his knuckles rapped out a complex rhythm. A slide in the door drew back, and bright light glowed out the gap. A pair of eyes presented themselves, almond-shaped beside a knife-thin nose and luminous cheeks. The voice that spoke had a queer, elfin timbre, but was at the same time strangely gruff. "What gives?"

"Speak easy, Friend," replied the knight, giving the secret password. "It is I, Sir Kay."

"Ah, another knight. Sheesh. Can't spit without it landin' on one of youse guys. Ain't you got your own gods, knight?"

"You know I have the open invitation of Mordred," replied Kay smoothly. "Now let me in."

"Peachy," came the snarled response. "How long you gonna stay? We've had it up to here with youse guys expectin' a day to last a minute and suchlike. We ain't gonna screw up time anymore for youse guys. Better make it quick, or you'll wake up in a couple centuries."

"Aye," replied the knight, considering this threat. He stood briefly aside. "And I have brought a guest. He is under the impression that Camelot is heaven. One sip of Avalon's nectar and his sacred mind will be riled with a thousand Pagan things."

"Jesus Christ!" said the voice irritably. "Come down here for a look see, Father Holiness? Youse guys're worse than the friggin' knights. Preachin' against sorcery while the whole time you got our pan-pipes jigglin' your willy. Ah, well, the goddess ends up turnin' most of youse missionaries into moles." With that, the slide closed, and the door opened. The elf—a mere suggestion of crossing light and whirling dust—held out a luminous hand: "Cover charge. Gold then, eh?"

Kay handed over one moderate-size bag.

"Ahem, which one of you ain't a man, that I get shorted a bag?"

Jaw clenching, Kay surrendered another bag.

"Thanks, gents. Enjoy your stay in Avalon. The food's terrific, the water's chock-full of intoxication, and the floor show's something to see." With that, the scintillating figure moved aside to admit the two.

Side by side, Kay and Niccolai stepped forward into a land of wonders. The place was impossibly large. It could not have been secreted beneath the entire city, let alone a single building of brick. Instead of cob-webbed floor joists overhead, there was limitless blue sky. Instead of mold-encrusted walls of stone and mor-tar, there was a green and rolling horizon line. Instead of a grub-strewn floor cluttered with wax-sealed pots of pickled and questionable content, there was a great green meadow, and here and there glades of flowering apple trees, beech, oak, and elm, and thousands of fanciful creatures streaking and dancing and cavorting across the hillside.

Some were tiny, like the wild-haired brownies who patiently tended dandelion patches, tricking from the flowers their golden nectar, or the Ellyllon sprites that flitted insectlike among the blossoming apple trees. Others were enormous, such as the giant hag Caillech Bheur, visible only in the lightning and circling clouds that shrouded her home in a deep wood of oak, or the kelpies that herded among the waves of the blue bay below. Many of the beasts were hard at work, such as the blue caps that trundled bags of pyrite out of a gopher-sized mine they had delved in a mountainside. Others were hard at play, dancing in the sunshine or sipping the intoxicating waters of wellsprings that bubbled up across the land.

The elfin guard closed the door behind them, and it and he sank into invisible air.

Accustomed to such departures, Kay glared at the scene. "You see? This is the foundation of Camelot. Not the heaven of a moral god, but the rollicking pagan hills of Avalon. That is where we are, you see—the apple trees should have given it away: Avalon means 'Place of Apples.' This is the heart of fey, the realm where the Tuatha Thay of the Seelie Court rule. Here, beneath our grand Christian Camelot, reachable through a hundred secret portals, is this unChristian land of intoxication and debauchery, sorcery, treachery, gambling, and foolishness." He turned, expecting to see despair written across the bishop's face.

But the look there was nothing of the kind—beatific, hopeful, ecstatic. "It is written:

'The foolishness of God is wiser than men; and the weakness of God is stronger than men.' "

Kay was incredulous. "But, look there upon the hills! Do you see these pagan spirits cavorting, Mordred's mob of henchmen—the bogarts and bugaboos, the firbolgs and ogres, the pecks and redcaps, the trows and mermen?"

Niccolai gave a thrilled shout, "These cannot be any but God's own angels,

> 'For by him were all things created, that are in heaven, and that are in earth, visible and invisible, whether they be thrones, or dominions, or principalities, or powers.' "

"These aren't angels! They are fairies, pagans, outlaws! Running numbers on the jousting matches, heading out to bag extortion money, bottling intoxicating waters for black-market sale, pawning off arcane magics, selling their bodies in prostitution, digging pyrite for counterfeit coins, getting orders for killings in the city above," Kay said, striking his own forehead. It had begun to occur to him that this bishop was not just mistaken but deluded, that nothing could dissuade him about Camelot being the New Jerusalem. If he returned to Rome with that assessment, there would be a second Roman invasion of Britain. "Look more closely. These are not just fey down here. Yonder are Bedevere and Gawain, gambling! See those bended backs beside that stream of faerie water? There are Lancelot and Mark. The very Round Table is hereabouts, corrupted by pagan delights!"

Niccolai only shook his head wonderingly. "It is heaven, of a certain, for,

> 'Eye has not seen, nor ear heard, neither have entered into the heart of man, the things which God hath prepared for them that love him.' "

Teeth grinding, Kay drew his wide-eyed companion forward into the decadent place. "You leave me no choice. I will take you to meet the ruler of it all, the godfather of this underworld. Then you will know that this is not any court but a hellish one." To himself, he added, *Then you will know that much, or know nothing ever again. I may have scruples against slaying a bishop, but Mordred will not.*

Sir Kay marched up the hillside, tugging the wondering bishop along behind him as a parent pulls a reluctant child. They strode across grasses and gorse that simply swarmed with faerie folk—pinpricks of light that danced away from each footfall only to whirl back into place in the very shadow of their lifted soles. Some of these underworldly creatures swarmed angrily about them, shouting derisions that were so tiny and ineffectual as to sound like the buzz of bees.

Kay took no notice of the tiny fairies but was careful to avoid swales where revelers reclined, wine spilled blood-red among them, crusts of great loaves tumbled among half-eaten blocks of cheese. He had comrades lounging in that unseemly torpor, and Kay was not eager to meet any of their eyes. Even so, he hoped the good bishop noted it all.

They entered a brake of trees and began descending a long valley that cut down into the depth of the forest. In the embankments on one side, brownies had dug village burrows; in the trees on the other, hollow boles had become chattering leprechaun towns. Many species of hob trooped in winding columns up vines. Still more sat sunning themselves languidly on leaftops or argued over ant husbandry among the undergrowth. The very air was alive with Pagan spirits. Some of them made a game of diving through the nostrils of the two men, tickling their lungs, and riding out on great sneezes.

Kay tried to remain stoic about these invasions, though he was irritated to notice that the bishop hadn't even enough sense to sneeze the beasts forth, nor the good breeding to bless Kay after each of his aerial exorcisms.

"Where are we going?" Bishop Niccolai asked, a welkin spirit reclining provocatively across his nose.

Recovering from his thirteenth major sneeze, Kay blinked rheumy eyes and said, "Down, to the center of this all. Down to the deepest wellspring in Avalon. Just as, in the world above, the seat of power is in an exalted place, so here, in the underworld, the seat of power is in the lowest place. There, we will find Avalon's so-called 'water of life' bottled in its most potent distillation, and beside it, Mordred."

The bishop nodded, seeming well-pleased, and as Kay gave his fourteenth and fifteenth sternutation, said, "It makes me think of the story of Jesus curing the blind man:

> 'When He had thus spoken, He spat on the ground, and made clay of the spittle, and He anointed the eyes of the blind man with the clay, and said unto him, Go, wash in the pool of Siloam (which is by interpretation, Sent). He went his way therefore, and washed, and came seeing.' "

Kay wondered bitterly which of them was supposed to be Jesus and which the blind man. Who was worse, a bishop who could not see that he stood in hell, or a knight who could not see that he stood in heaven?

With a now-soggy handkerchief, Kay wiped a clinging goblin from his septum and gestured outward. "There it is. The dark heart of Mordred's underworld empire."

Just ahead, the vale ended in a deep, dark place—a black pit that plunged away to unseeable depths through humus and clay and bedrock. Ferns overhung the raw edge of the pit, losing occasional fronds that would circle slowly downward until they disappeared against the blackness. A cold, wet wind sifted ominously up from the pit, and Kay's armor felt suddenly like a suit of ice.

When he spoke, he found himself whispering rever-

ently. "Well, Bishop, this is it. The true foundation of
Camelot. An insatiable abyss. We can turn back now.
I have ventured within before and have the promise
of its Occupant that I shall ever return safely to the
surface world. I cannot promise the same to you. Mordred does not like priests. This is his territory, and,
let's face it, you intend to move in and take over. He
may kill you on sight. He may have his goblins break
your knuckles and knees and send you hobbling back
to Rome with a warning. I cannot tell what Mordred
will do. Shall we go back?"

The beatific delusions that had been crawling across
the face of the bishop were now gone, leaving only
brave resolution.

" 'And the Lord spake unto Moses, after the death
of the two sons of Aaron, when they offered before the Lord, and died. . . . Speak unto Aaron thy
brother, that he come not at all times into the holy
place within the veil before the mercy seat, which
is upon the ark, that he die not; for I will appear
in the cloud upon the mercy seat.' "

Sick to the gills, Kay grabbed the bishop's hand and
leaped into the deep and rushing darkness. Together,
they plunged. For a time, there was only the vertigi-
nous rush of rock and space, the flailing plummet from
a world of light to a world of utter darkness. Then,
all was lost in cold and death. A swallowing chill enveloped them like ice water, and neither man could
breathe.

Then, they were free of it, in a warm, paneled room,
redolent with aromatic smoke and dark save for a set
of dim oil lanterns on side tables and a great mahogany desk. The sense of flailing motion and roaring air
was gone, replaced by absolute, ritualized calm. The
floor underfoot was polished marble covered in thick
woolen carpet. The night-black windows bore long
golden draperies, and the smooth ceiling overhead was

patterned with a subtle painting in maroon and gray and gold. Despite the low lighting, Kay and Niccolai sensed at once that they were surrounded by spectral watchers—the kingpin's henchmen. The singular set of eyes, though, that caught their attention at the moment of their arrival and held it fast thereafter belonged to the man behind the desk. Mordred.

Half-human and half-faerie, he was ageless. He looked young, perhaps thirty, though his tailored suit, the rubies and diamonds glimmering upon his fingers, and his sober, judging eyes seemed to belong to a man twice his age. His thick black hair was well groomed and touched with gray only by the crazings of smoke that wandered up from the rolled leaves clutched in his fingers. He sat in a soft, dark chair and regarded the visitors with a stare that was both impatient and untouched by time.

"Mordred," Kay said with a slight bow, "thank you for receiving me, though I know you received no notice of my visit. I myself did not know I was bound here until after I was on the shores of Avalon. I come because of this man. A Christian. A bishop. He has come from Rome, believing our city here to be the New Jerusalem, an earthly heaven fashioned by the hand of God. He believes the city—and all of Arthur's lands, from the Viking realms to the Gaulish ones—to belong to the church, to Rome. Unless we convince him otherwise, he will return to Rome, and the pope will send armies to take this land." Kay's ominous tones sifted away into the carpets.

Seeming still to be listening, Mordred stared intently at the two.

"I've been trying to show him that this city is not ruled by God but by a man, an imperfect and fallible man—King Arthur. And not just by him, but by you as well. I've been trying to show him that the impossible beauty of the city arises not just from virtue but also from vice, from outlawed, Pagan magic—and that much of what he would call Camelot's heavenly felicity in fact results from Avalon's indulgence of every carnal, greedy, selfish, unChristian impulse. I've led him into this underworld of yours, showed him hoodlums and prostitutes, counterfeiters and confidence men and extortionists, but he sees only angels and apostles. So I have brought him here, begging you to convince him . . . or to offer some other—well, some other solution."

Mordred at last blinked. He pivoted sideways in his seat and drew a long breath of smoke from the thing in his hand. In distraction of thought, his free hand strayed up to the part in his black hair and slid in a smooth line from the crown of his head to the valley behind one ear. Blue and mystic, smoke drifted from slightly parted lips. His voice was equally smoky. "So, Arthur has a problem, and you come to me. It's Rome's problem, really, Christendom's, and you come to me. And for what? To show this man the dark shadow of Camelot? To show him my evil, sinful people? You're happy enough to drink my waters and eat my bread, Kay. You're happy enough to enjoy the fruits of my land, and yet you bring this man here to show him all that is wrong with Camelot? What have I done to earn such disrespect?"

Kay paled. "I respect you, Mordred. I have told this man you are as much ruler here as the king."

"And yet you come here, unannounced, and ask me for a favor, and do not even think to call me godfather." The man seemed genuinely vexed behind his calm face and gently blinking eyes. "I have taken on all the bloodshed that won Arthur his throne. My underworld caters to the lower passions of Arthur and his knights and his citizens so that the upper world can be clean and bright. I make Camelot Camelot, and yet you come here with such disrespect."

Kay dropped to one knee before the great mahogany desk, bowed his head, and said, "I ask this favor in full respect, Godfather."

"Good," said Mordred. "Good. I cannot help you

or your friend until you both understand my true position in this city. Arthur's knights seem a host of angels only because I am here to provide comfort to the beasts within them. Arthur has turned his back on all the darkness in himself and in his people. He has turned his back on me, his very own son. And his people do so, too. The people of Camelot don't accept me, don't even know me, but I'm living here below, making their world beautiful and true. We rule together, my father and I, he in the light and I in the shadow. I provide comfort to the dark regions of men's souls."

At last, Bishop Niccolai moved, going down on both knees, his eyes glistening with tears of joy.

" 'And I will pray the Father, and he shall give you another Comforter, that he may abide with you for ever; even the Spirit of truth; whom the world cannot receive, because it seeth him not, neither knoweth him: but ye know him; for he dwelleth with you, and shall be in you. I will not leave you comfortless. . . . At that day ye shall know that I am in my Father, and ye in me, and I in you . . .' "

Slowly, Mordred rose from his seat and approached the bishop, kneeling there gladly before him. He extended his hand.

Niccolai seized and kissed it. "Godfather!"

Mordred blinked, studying the man. "I will do this favor for you, Sir Kay. Still, it is obvious that I cannot argue with the simple faith of such a one. I cannot convince him to report what he does not believe. Here is a man of truth, and I am a man of truth—even if I am not the Spirit of truth he believes me to be." The faerie godfather took a long draw upon his bundle of leaves. "But you spoke of another solution . . ."

Glancing at the glowing eyes of the bishop, Kay suddenly wished he had not brought the man to Mordred's underworld. "I was wrong, Godfather. You cannot kill him. He is a child, a fool—you can't kill him—"

"No," replied Mordred, a shallow smile on his lips. "I won't kill him. Where's the justice in that? This is a good man, honest and true, a man who sees God in all things. He's a right pagan, no matter what he calls himself. I could use a man like this in Arthur's chapel. I think I can convince him to stay. I am, after all, the Spirit of his god, and this is, after all, heaven. And, speaking of spirits, I have a decanter here that will help him see everything more clearly."

Relieved, Sir Kay said, "I owe you a great debt for this service, Godfather."

"Yes, you do," Mordred affirmed. "And I have in mind a way in which you can pay me back. I'll contact you soon. Until then, I am done with you. The bishop will stay here with me for a time, but for now, I am done with you, Kay."

"Wait," said the knight, trembling and astonished, "what will you have me do?"

And the godfather said, "As your own god said to Saul when he was blinded for persecuting a faith he did not understand,

   " 'Arise, and go into the city, and it shall be told
   thee what thou must do.' "

ODIE AND THE ZOO

by Jeff Grubb

Big Odie slouched into The Zoo's Olympic Cafe. His sweat-covered biker leathers slapped against his thighs as he settled his massive frame on one of the spindly legged, white-enameled, cast-iron chairs. A young woman in a toga, nervous and pale, manifested at his left side almost immediately, order pad held before her like a protective talisman.

"Can I help you, sir?" squeaked the maiden, for Odie was not one of the regular clientele, and particularly not regular for a quiet Wednesday.

Odie regarded the young stripling of a girl with his single baleful eye, and muttered, "Ale."

The waitress gulped and managed, "You mean beer, sir?"

Odie grunted, somewhere between irritation and a guffaw, "Whatever," he said simply.

"We have Sparta, Fix, and . . ." started the maiden, but Odie stopped her, slamming a meaty hand against the glass tabletop. "Ale!"

The maiden vaporized, leaving only the swinging doors back to the kitchen swaying with her passage. That made Big Odie smile. It was good to know that he still could spook the hired help.

Odie looked around and gave a derisive sniff. The café had white stucco walls painted with Mediterranean scenes. Stenciled grape leaves ran around the front window, and a clanking balalaika played from hidden speakers. It was too light and airy for Odie,

34

who preferred smoked-filled bars and firepits beneath the open sky.

From the kitchen came the sound of a rapid-fire discussion in Greek, and the maiden was back with a tumbler filled with pale yellow fluid. She set the tumbler down in front of her muscular customer.

"What's this?" snarled Odie.

"Your beer, sir," squeaked the maiden.

"This?" said the massive, one-eyed biker. "This pig's urine? Ale should be foaming when served, wench, and in a cup carved from the skull of an enemy! My Vals know better than to serve this swill."

A heavy hand touched Odie's left shoulder and he flinched, spinning in place in his chair. Someone had come up on the biker's blind side, the side with the eye patch. Odie wheeled to see the smiling bearded face of The Zoo.

"Is everything to your satisfaction, *sir*?" asked The Zoo, turning the last word into a private joke. The owner of the Olympic Cafe was as large as Odie, but his bulk was soft and old, and his beard was shot with silver.

"You should know better than to do that," snapped the biker, glowering at the restaurant owner. Then Odie added, "You can't get a decent ale in this place of yours."

The Zoo smiled, and the smile crinkled the corners of his eyes. The restaurant owner nodded to the waitress and said, "Clio, bring him a rhyton of my best. And don't bother running a tab. This gentleman here is an old friend."

Big Odie turned back to the maiden but caught only a glimpse of her short toga as she scampered back into the kitchen. He would have laid a deadly curse on her slender form if she had not vanished.

Instead he turned back to the owner. "Zoo," he said simply.

"Please, I go by Jove now," said the owner, settling

his own bulk into the chair opposite the biker. "No one has called me Zoo in ages."

"You'll always be The Zoo," said Odie, "And hiding away in this crap-ass little dago restaurant won't change that."

The broad smile became a little brittle, "I see you haven't changed. Still a silver-tongued bard, you are."

Odie reddened and held up both hands in apology. "Sorry. I speak without thinking."

The waitress returned with an ornately carved drinking horn filled with beer, the foaming head spilling over the rim.

Odie hefted the oversized horn and said, "Big enough. But how do you set it down?"

"You don't," said The Zoo. "That's the purpose of the rhyton. You only put it down when you've drained it."

Odie looked at the horn and let out a chortle. "And I bet it's a lot deeper than it looks."

The Zoo shrugged. "It's carved from the horn of the minotaur. Father's Day present from one of the kids. I think he meant it as a joke."

"You've got quite a brood," said Odie.

Again the large owner shrugged. "When I was young," he said. "How's yours?"

Odie took a deep draft from the drinking horn and rubbed the cascading suds from his red beard. "The usual. He's block-headed, foul-mouthed, and violent. A real nasty little psychopath."

"Well, it runs in the family," said Jove the Zoo. Big Odie grimaced, and the restaurant owner gave a deep chuckle and smiled again. "Sorry. I speak without thinking. So what brings you to my neck of the woods? You're usually up north, instead of around here, parking your eight-wheeler in front of my cafe and scoping my muses. What can I do for you?"

Odie was silent for a moment, then looked up at the other, older being. "I got problems."

"Don't we all," said The Zoo.

Odie was quiet for another long moment, then said, "It's the new kid. He's muscling in on my territory."

The Zoo let out a long, low sigh, the sigh of an old man when all the life went out of him. "Yaweh."

Odie raised the rhyton to his lips, cursing as he did. "The little bastard jew-boy ki . . ."

With a speed that belied his girth, The Zoo lunged forward, grasping Odie's wrist. The benevolent face of moments before was gone, replaced with a storm-clouded brow and eyes that flashed lightning.

"In my place of business," said The Zoo in a voice that had once leveled mountains, "we don't use that kind of language. This is a family place. Remember that, *please.*"

Odie looked around quickly, but the rest of the café was still empty. Still, the big Nordic biker felt the grip around his wrist and the tone in The Zoo's voice, and nodded. "Sorry," he said at last. "I meant no insult."

"None taken," said The Zoo, and he let go of Big Odie's massive wrist. His own fingers had barely spanned the other man's forearm. "I know how you feel. I had worse words for him when he and I fought, years ago."

Big Odie leaned over the table, and the iron legs of his chair groaned from his girth. "So you did fight him?"

The Zoo motioned with his hands to the rest of his café. "I fought him. I lost. You may have noticed that things aren't as busy as they once were." He waved at the vacant chairs in the sunlit café.

Big Odie grunted, "You know, you were once a big fish."

"The biggest," said The Zoo, "back when you were leading your first roughneck gang through the German woods. But those were the elder days, when you moved in on Frey's territory and I was fat and happy from ousting old Lady Ishtar and those Egyptians. But it's different nowadays. I'm still happy," he leaned back and patted his own expansive girth, "though not as fat, believe it or not."

"So what happened?" asked Odie.

The Zoo shrugged. "What always happens. I got lucky. Got cocky. Thought it would last forever. Thought I was too smart to get sideswiped like Ishtar, and Tiamat, and the others. Thought I could conquer the world."

"You almost did."

"I almost did," grunted The Zoo, and his eyes grew misty. "At least the parts that were worth anything. But I didn't take care of business. That's the bottom line. If you don't take care of the day-to-day, you make yourself vulnerable. You got into this because you care about your people. And if you don't do that, fugeddaboutit!"

Odie sat silently for a moment, chewing over what The Zoo had said. Zoo looked at the one-eyed biker and shook his head. "It's a tough lesson," he said. "By the time I realized that it was the little things that mattered, it was too late. The New Kid was firmly entrenched."

Finally Big Odie said, "My first lieutenant went over to him."

"Loke?" said The Zoo. "The weaselly little accountant? Better off without him. Never liked him. Too tricky for my taste."

"Yeah, but I thought he was LOYAL," thundered Odie, and the kitchen doors rattled at the sound of his voice.

"Yeah, I thought my capo, Dion, was loyal, too," said The Zoo. "But when push came to shove, they all bailed on me. Diana, Hermie, Festus, the whole lot. The New Kid had positions all ready for them. Not as good as I was offering, but I was on the way down. They saw it coming, and they bailed. Don't blame them. Not really."

"But you fought him," said Odie. "You went to the mattresses."

"Yeah," said The Zoo, leaning back. "Biggest mistake I coulda made, and I made it."

Odie cocked an eyebrow and took a long pull from the drinking horn, waiting for The Zoo to continue. The restaurant owner let out a long sigh, as deep as the Aegean, and when he spoke again, it was in a soft voice.

"Before we tangled, the New Kid was a punk. Just another hairy thunderer with an attitude. No offense. You and me both, we're like that. Old school. Fling a few thunderbolts, smash a few mountains, and everyone falls into line. So once I woke up to the fact that he was stealing my markets and luring away my people, I tried to fight him that way."

The Zoo let out another long sigh, his mind peeling back the years. "So I did the whole mano a mano thing with him. Expecting him to treat me the same way he treated Baal, or the way I ground down Ishtar. But he was too smart. He kept himself tight, loyal, and dedicated. Worked himself into the fabric, into the chinks between the bricks, until he was supporting a big part of my own activities. And then I made the big mistake."

Another long pause. Odie finally said, "And the mistake?"

"I whacked his son," said The Zoo. "Thought I was pretty damned clever at it, too. Set it up within his own organization. Found the right fall guy. All safe and legal. The boy was hung out to dry. Then, blammo!"

"Blammo?"

"Pulls an Osiris on me!" The Zoo chuckled. "You're too young to remember, but it's an old trick, creating yourself anew, rising from the ashes like a phoenix. But Kid Yaweh puts a new spin on it. He brings back his boy, with more than a little head-nod to the idea that he can do it for anybody. So the New Kid makes the crossover from another street punk to a respected figure. His kid dies on him, and in the

passion of the passing he makes his move. He's got
the martyr, he's got the organization, and he's got the
promise for anyone who throws in with him. I'm still
fighting with thunderstorms, and he's changing the system out from under me. Within a few years, he's got
all of my power bases in the home country, and then
he moves into my big house in Rome." The Zoo
chuckled again.

"You almost sound like you respect him," said
Odie.

The Zoo shrugged. "At the time I wanted to give
him a lightning-bolt enema and mail his body parts
back to Palestine. But yeah, he had me, and I didn't
even see it coming. So tell me, does this sound much
like what you're going through?"

Odie looked into his drinking horn and let out his
own sigh. "So you're telling me I can't fight him."

"I'm telling you he's no backwoods war-god," said
The Zoo, tapping his finger against the tabletop for
emphasis. "I'm telling you he's got organization and
he plans real good. And he's not afraid of making
sacrifices for his cause. He doesn't do things in half
measures."

At the mention of sacrifice, Odie raised his hand to
the patch over his left eye.

The Zoo noticed the motion and said, "If you don't
mind me asking, how'd that happen? You had two of
those the last time I saw you."

"Another sacrifice," said Odie. "You know the
Norn Girls?"

The Zoo nodded. "The Weird Sisters? Yeah, I
know them way too well. They run off of women's
magic. That's another piece of work entirely. Neither
you nor me nor the New Kid have them figured out
entirely. What did you get for the eye?"

"I wanted to know what would happen," said Odie.
"What would happen if I went to the mattresses with
the New Kid."

"And they told you . . ." The Zoo left the question dangling.

"Pretty ugly stuff," said Odie. "Ragnarock and Roll. That's when I thought of you."

"You thought I could find a way around the Weird Sisters," said The Zoo.

"You're older and wiser," replied Odie.

"The Weirds are older than you and me and the New Kid combined," said The Zoo. "But wiser? Well, perhaps. Wise enough to know you asked the wrong question for your eyeball."

Odie blinked at him with his one good eye. The Zoo got up and waddled over to the cash register. He rummaged around the menus for a moment, coming up with a thin pamphlet.

He returned to the table but kept the pamphlet against his expansive chest. "You asked what would happen if you fought the New Kid. The Weirds ran their numbers based on the question. You were still thinking that you could win. When I hired the Norn Girls, I asked a different question."

"And that was . . . ?"

"By the time the Weirds showed up on my doorstep, I was pretty sure how the dice would tumble for me. So my question was, 'How do I keep myself alive once the New Kid wins?'"

Odie thought about it, then nodded. "Yeah, that's the question I should have asked."

"You folded Frey's people into your organization but never let him get close to power again," said the Zoo. "I did the same thing to Ishtar. Nobody, I mean nobody, remembers them except for some dusty scholars. Not the best place to rebuild a power base from. So I asked the Weirds how to keep our names alive in the future."

"And?"

"And this," said The Zoo, and tossed the pamphlet on the table in front of Odie.

Odie shifted the drinking horn to his other hand

and reached out. The pamphlet was a slender volume, covered with garish ink in a variety of colors. He flipped it open to a random page, revealing a portrayal of battle between colorful combatants.

"What is this?" said Odie.

"Salvation, One-eye," said The Zoo. "Look at the pictures."

Big Odie squinted, then said, "Is that supposed to be your boy?"

"Yeah," said The Zoo with a smile, "Lousy representation, but it's him. I'm in there too, but they've taken a few pounds off."

"This is salvation?" said Odie, "What a crock of shi . . . I mean dwarf-droppings. This is some trivial thing, a minor entertainment for the young."

"A tale written for children," said The Zoo. "There are a lot of these tales in the future. The gods of their age, as it were. People who were stronger, faster, and smarter than everyone else. It's a popular culture thing. You can get one too, for you and your boy."

Odie looked at the booklet, then shook his head. "I don't get it."

"This keeps your name alive," said The Zoo, placing a large hand on the booklet. "It keeps you in circulation. Better, it keeps you in circulation with the very target audience that is willing to think about you. Not like a scholar carving up your origin like it was a frog to be dissected. Sure, they don't get everything right, but they get enough to make everything work."

Odie kept his gaze on the book. At last he said, "So what did it cost you."

"The Weirds charge dear," said The Zoo. "You got off easy with losing an eye."

"Meaning?"

The Zoo leaned toward the red-haired biker and said in a low voice, "Let's just say that my boys don't have to worry about anyone else contesting the family estate, if you get my meaning."

Odie leaned back in the wrought-iron chair and let out a low whistle. "That's chill."

"The Weird Sisters always seek to make the cost fit the reward," said The Zoo.

Odie looked at the booklet and said, "So why tell me?"

The Zoo managed a weary smile. "I found a way out. One thing I know about such tales is that there is a need for continual conflict. And you can't talk about the New Kid, that would be sacrilege."

"Sacrilege?" asked Odie.

The Zoo folded his hands across his paunch. "The market would be resistant to such matters. So as a matter of course, we don't have to worry about him horning in on our action."

Big Odie stared at the comic book for a long time, the gears turning beneath his disheveled mane. "So you want competition," he said at last. "Somebody for your boy to fight."

"That's about it," said The Zoo, "like in professional wrestling."

"And just as honest," said Odie, running his knuckles against his beard. "I don't know about this."

"Fine," said The Zoo, "pass on my offer. Join Ishtar and Frey and the rest in oblivion. Join Osiris and Tiamat and the others in the pages of the dry textbooks, reduced to their component legends. Or try to go out in a blaze of glory, fight the New Kid, and have your name burned from the books entirely. Or sit back with me and plan for the future. Listen, the New Kid will eventually become an Old Man, fat and comfortable, and we'll get a chance to start again."

Odie looked up at the owner and said, "Mimir's Blood, let it be done! If that's the best route, let's take it. To the future!" He held out the horn.

"I thought you'd see it my way," said Jove The Zoo.

"I'd like to drink from your endless horn all afternoon," said the biker, rising from the table, "but I have to have a chat with my own boy about this. I think he could beat your brood hands-down."

"I think it would be an interesting team-up," said The Zoo, showing not even the merest trace of a smile.

Odie held out the horn again, "You'd best take this. I don't think I've even drained it an inch."

"It's empty now, One-Eye," said The Zoo, and this time he let a broad smile, as bright as the sun's chariot, show on his face. It was a stage magician's smile, the smile of a man who had expected the comment and was ready for it.

Big Odie turned the horn upside down, and only a few drops spilled out onto the table. The biker goggled, then smiled, and let a laugh spill across his own features. A smile that held hope.

"Thanks, Zooey," said the biker, "I owe you one."

"Yes, you do," said the elder god, "but that will be a matter for another day."

The biker headed for the door, for the eight-wheeled hog he had named Sliepner. "Thanks! See you around, Zooey!"

"Yeah," said the elder god quietly to the biker's back, tapping the small booklet. "See you in the funny pages."

SAINT AL

by Dennis O'Neil

Somewhere between bound-for-heaven and going-straight-to-hell Joel discovered he had been praying to the wrong saints. Although he had been sending his celestial entreaties in the wrong direction for years, since he had been old enough to talk, once the change began, it happened quickly, within thirty-six hours of his coming down to the Coalbin.

A few weeks earlier, he hadn't even heard of the Coalbin, or even *a* (lower case) coalbin, because by his birth date, his father and everyone else in Mountain Meadows had converted to gas heat. So when Monsignor Flotsky suggested he take a leave of absence from the seminary "to get a bit more experience in the world, ya know, lad," and Joel had asked where he might get such experience and the monsignor replied, after what seemed eternal reflection, "I've heard there's a lot of experience down at that Coalbin place," Joel didn't know what he was talking about.

But he asked his brother seminarians and was told that the Coalbin was what locals called a neighborhood at the east end of the city, near the river—a slum, a ghetto, a good area to avoid.

"I'd think twice about this," Sammy Diener said after Mass the next day. "That's pretty rough, that Coalbin, and let's face it, Joel, you're not exactly Clint Eastwood."

Joel rolled his eyes upward and said, "*He'll* protect me."

"Clint Eastwood?"

"No, the Lord," Joel replied, bowing his head.

"I was joking, Joel."

"Oh."

"Well, good luck."

"*Luck* will have nothing to do with it."

Monsignor Flotsky gave Joel the number of a soup kitchen operated by Catholic Outreach and administered by Sister Agatha. Joel called Sister Agatha, who told him to rent an apartment near the soup kitchen and then report to her. So on a sunny day in July, Joel watched Sammy Diener cram his personal belongings into the back of a 1955 Nash his older brother had given him and drove past the suburbs surrounding the seminary, past the business district, past the downtown stores and off the end of any world he had ever known. During most of the journey, his fingers were white on the steering wheel and he struggled with the enormously complicated task of operating the car. Stop lights, holes in the street, other vehicles speeding past, their horns blaring—this was vastly different from his previous experiences with driving, which consisted solely of taking his grandmother to Sunday Mass. But he persevered, feeling brave and, well, darn it, holy. Glancing out the side windows, he saw block after block of brick structures blackened by fire, windows covered with slabs of plywood or, worse, empty holes rimmed with soot, overturned trash cans rolling in the gutters, knots of undershirted men sharing beer bottles, human figures sprawled on the sidewalks— surely not dead, surely just napping? The few undamaged shops all seemed to be liquor stores or pawnbrokers, and even these were covered, like everything else, by mad, swirling, obscene graffiti.

Where were the Lord's nobly suffering poor? Hiding somewhere in this chaotic ugliness? He muttered a quick Hail Mary and an Ave and, just to be sure, an Act of Contrition—not that the Lord would let anything happen to him—and, numb with an emotion he could not name—could this be what St. Thomas

More felt as he walked to the block?—he somehow found the address he was looking for.

He got out of the Nash in front of a five-story tenement and looked around. He saw no people, just broken glass glinting on the pavement. A song in a foreign language—Spanish?—was coming from a storefront across the street. He decided not to lock the car; that would be a sign of distrust of the Lord's poor.

He ascended a small flight of steps, squinted at a row of pushbuttons, and firmly thumbed the one with "supt" scrawled in blue ballpoint on a piece of adhesive tape above it. The door opened, and he was facing a fat man wearing only soiled boxer shorts and holding a wine bottle. "You lookin' for the sooper, you found 'im," the man growled, the words riding a breath full of garbage that made Joel almost gag. "Whachoo wan'?"

"Good afternoon. I'm Joel Terwilliger. I'm here about the apartment. I called—"

"Yeh, yeh. C'mon inside."

Joel followed the man into a dark hallway, and again the smell pulled bile into his throat.

"You got key money?"

"Key money?"

"You gimme a hunner bucks, I give you the key."

"There must be some mistake, sir. Nobody said—"

The man thrust his face at Joel's. "You thin' I give a fuck what nobody said?"

"Sir, I must protest your language. Such talk is the sign of a deficient vocabulary—"

"I shove you 'ficient up you ass, you limp-dick faggot. You got the hunner or not? I ain't got all fuckin' day."

Joel was suddenly aware of the wall against his spine. He had actually reeled under the verbal assault.

"Sir," he said when he could finally speak, "I feel it is my duty to inform you that you are possessed by the devil. But do not despair. I shall return with an exorcist and we will free you of perdition. By nightfall, if all goes well."

The man's mouth was full of wine, which may be why he did not answer. Joel turned, went through the door, down the steps to the car. Something different about the car. Quite different. It took Joel a minute to realize what.

No tires. Trunk open. Windows and headlights smashed. His belongings nowhere in sight. Lost? How? He said a quick prayer to St. Anthony, patron saint of lost things, and was, apparently, immediately answered.

"Looking for something?" Joel turned toward the voice. A thin person was standing in the open doorway of the storefront from which the music wafted. Joel couldn't be certain—the sun's glare was really ferocious—but he thought the person, a young man in jeans and a T-shirt, was smiling. Joel smiled back: a new friend.

Joel's friend motioned and when Joel was near, he said, "Name's Choo-choo."

"I'm Joel Terwilliger."

"You lose somethin'?"

"Yes, actually. I'm missing three suitcases, a Douay Bible, two rosaries . . . oh, and four tires. I don't know where they could have gone to."

"You want 'em?"

"Yes, actually."

"You gotta buy 'em."

"You don't understand, Mr. Choo-choo," Joel said patiently, remembering that not everyone enjoyed the benefits on a Catholic education. "They belong to me."

"Not anymore they don't."

"They certainly do."

"Okay, lemme see 'em."

"They're *missing,* as I believe I mentioned."

"You ain't got 'em, they don't belong to you. You want 'em to belong to you, you gotta buy 'em."

Obviously, there was a misunderstanding. Joel was beginning to formulate a careful, clear explanation when Choo-choo put a bony hand on Joel's shoulder and smiled—*definitely* a smile, now, and a kindly one. "You ain't from around here, right? Lemme tell you what is. You leave somethin' onna street, it belongs to whoever finds it. But I'm gonna help you."

Ah. The kindness of the Lord's creatures!

"That stuff you had inna car . . . the silk underwear, the Donna Karan suit, the Florsheim shoes, them pitchers, the leather case with the gold razor—must be worth a lotta money, right?"

"I suppose. I didn't buy any of it—"

"Trust me. Worth a couple thou, easy. I git it back for a hunnert. Lousy hunnert, a bargain. Whaddaya say?"

Well, Joel had been warned that he'd have to learn strange customs, and he did have the hundred in tens his father had sent in his wallet . . . "You've got yourself a deal, Mr. Choo-choo, my friend," Joel said heartily, vigorously shaking Choo-choo's hand.

"I show you where it is." Joel followed Choo-choo into a narrow space between two tenements. It was out of the sun—cool, pleasant. "Lemme see the money," Choo-choo said, not sounding so friendly.

Joel pulled his wallet from a hip pocket and gave Choo-choo the tens.

"Where'sa rest?" Choo-choo demanded.

"You said a hundred—"

"Ain't you never heard of tax? I need another hundred."

"That's all I have."

"Lemme see." Choo-choo grabbed the wallet and tore it apart. "*Fuck!*"

"When you use that language, you drive nails into the Lord's—"

"Take off your clothes."

"I certainly will not," Joel said, allowing himself

righteous indignation, and gasped, because Choo-choo had hit him in the stomach.

Choo-choo held up a knife. "Gimme the clothes or I cut you." First, Joel did not believe that he meant it. Then he registered the pain from the blow, and the knife, and he did believe it. And then reality ebbed away from him and, for a time, Joel inhabited a vast, gray limbo he never imagined existed. When Joel was again in the world, he was staring at the Nash, which now had no seats or engine block, and he was naked.

A large policeman approached. "Okay, twinkletoes, the sunbathin's over. I'd ask for your ID, but I can see you ain't got any, 'less it's tattooed someplace. Let's go for a ride."

"Sister Agatha," Joel murmured.

"You one'a hers? Figures."

The policeman led Joel to a police car, pushed him into the rear seat, got in the driver's side and turned to another, much smaller, officer, who seemed to be female.

"One'a Ag the Bag's," he said.

"Let's drop him at the kitchen," the second officer said in a definitely female voice. "Save us the fuckin' paperwork."

Joel shook his head. Either the second officer was not, in fact, female, or he had misheard. No woman would use the f-word.

Joel watched the passing scene for a while. *Where were the poor?*

With an officer on either side of him, Joel walked into what may have once been some kind of temple—Protestant or Jewish or maybe heathen Buddhist: definitely not Catholic.

"Ow," he said, suddenly aware of the hot sidewalk on his bare feet.

Inside was a large hall with rows of long tables flanked by dozens of folding chairs. At one end, there was a counter and behind that, several stoves and

ovens, an interior door, a staircase. Joel looked down
at his feet, now cool against cracked linoleum.

"What's this and why should I care?" someone
asked in a voice that reminded Joel of a wheelbarrow
rolling over gravel. A brutal thumb and forefinger
pinched Joel's cheeks and forced his head up, and he
was confronting a face like a cement slab.

"Found him on Sixth Street, sister," said the male
officer. "Says he belongs to you."

"It got a name?" the slab asked.

"Joel Terwilliger," Joel whispered.

"Who?"

"Joel Terwilliger," Joel said, louder.

"The seminarian?"

Joel nodded.

"You want him?" the male officer asked.

"No, but I guess I have to take him," the slab told
the officers. She released Joel's cheeks and said, "I'm
Sister Agatha, in case you haven't guessed."

"I don't know if we should let a nun alone with
such a hunk," the female officer said, and giggled.
"Might make her break her vows of chastity."

"Believe me, with this specimen my vows have
never been safer," Sister Agatha said, inspecting Joel,
and both officers laughed—*at me,* Joel was sure, but
he did not understand the joke.

Then he glimpsed his genitals, screamed and ran
behind the counter.

Still laughing, the officers left.

"You'll find some clothes behind the door to your
left," Sister Agatha said. "Get dressed and get out
here. The dinner crowd'll be coming in soon."

Joel crawled into a dank, musty room the size of
his cell back at the seminary filled with soiled cardboard boxes containing underwear, shoes and various
other garments, all filthy, smelly, tattered. He found
nothing suitable, but he had to wear *something.* He
knelt and prayed for strength to his favorite saint,
Saint Prisca, second-century virgin and martyr. Forti-

fied with her saintly presence, he put on khaki pants
cut off at the knees, a checked shirt with only one
sleeve and two buttons and a pair of plastic beach
sandals.

"*Get out here,*" Sister Agatha shouted from the
other room.

The hall was filled with the kind of people he had
seen on the streets—surly, sullen, soiled men and
women, muttering, growling or staring emptily at the
walls. Some of them were smoking cigarettes.

"I don't believe we should allow smoking," Joel said
to Sister Agatha, who was now wearing an apron, and
standing at the counter near a row of stainless steel
pans heaped with what Joel supposed was food.

"Look, junior, maybe some day I'll ask for your
opinion, but that day isn't today. My regular server
got busted for dealing crack this morning, and that
means it's just you and me. So get ready to dish out
the mashed potatoes."

Sister Agatha pounded the counter with a wooden
spoon and shouted, "Settle down. Let's pray." She
placed her palms together and said, "Lord, we thank
you for the gifts we are about to receive. Okay, come
and get it."

A line formed at the end of the counter.

"Wait a minute," Joel said to Sister Agatha.
"Shouldn't we wait for the poor?"

"The *what?*"

"The Lord's poor."

Sister Agatha gestured at the hall. "Who the hell
do you think these people are, junior?"

Something inside Joel that may have been his soul
threw a tantrum. *No no no no no. These are not the
Lord's poor. These are ghastly and stinky and
awful . . . undesirables.*"

"You gonna serve the spuds or you gonna stand
there pullin' yer pud?" The questioner was a bald
dwarf with huge ears and a string of some kind hanging from his left nostril. He thrust a tin plate up at

Joel. Joel took a scoop from a mound of white stuff in one of the pans, presumably mashed potatoes, filled it half way and carefully placed the potatoes on the dwarf's plate.

"What the shit?" the dwarf shouted angrily, dipping his chubby hand into the mount and slapping mashed potatoes onto his plate.

"One more like that, Benny," said Sister Agatha, "and you're eighty-sixed for a week. You think I'm kidding, you try me."

"You see what numbnuts gimme?" Benny whined. "You couldn't feed a fuckin' canary with that!"

"He's new," said Sister Agatha. "Wipe your nose."

For the next hour, Joel served potatoes. It was boring and stupid work for a fellow with a good Catholic education, and not a single tin-plate holder so much as thanked him. These . . . *creatures* could not be the humble, grateful Lord's poor.

Hours later, Sister Agatha locked the door behind the last diner, Benny, and, untying the apron, said to Joel, "You better eat. There's some stew left."

"I'm not hungry."

"Eat anyway. I'm not asking you, I'm telling you. You're no good to me if you drop dead from hunger."

"I said I'm not—"

"*Eat*, dammit."

Dammit?

Of course. It was clear to Joel now. "You're not really a nun."

"Yeah? How do you figure."

"Your language. The way you hurried through the prayer. That filthy joke you made—"

Agatha strode to within inches of Joel and glared. "Listen to me. I have a hundred and three temperature, I have been on my feet for the last twenty hours, I have been told we're getting no more funding from that hypocrite in the Cathedral, and I am *not* in the mood for criticism from a snotty twerp who couldn't find his ass with a roadmap." She stalked toward the stairs, whirled and said, "Find someplace to sleep. Be ready to work at six. Oh, and maybe you noticed I didn't ask how you lost your stuff. Know why? Because I don't care."

She stomped up the stairs, and the lights went out. Joel crept to the room where he had found the clothing, lowered his eyes, knelt and prayed to Saint Prisca. Prayed hard, desperately seeking the sense that holy Prisca was bestowing her presence upon him.

"Give me wisdom and comfort, dear saint," he implored aloud.

"Ain't never gonna happen, pally."

Had Blessed Prisca answered him? Finally? After years of beseeching? In bad grammar? Joel looked around the room, dark except for a wan glow coming through a single, dust-covered window.

"Saint Prisca?" he whispered.

"You ain't got the word, pally? Them padres figured out what I could'a told 'em, that there ain't no Prisca and there ain't never been no Prisca, on account of somebody made up them bullshit stories 'bout her anna buncha saps like you b'lieved 'em. 'Second-century virgin an' martyr.' Inna rat's ass."

Joel's eyes had adjusted to the darkness; he could, by squinting, discern a bulky shadow near the window, and he was pretty sure he was smelling cigar smoke, which was even fouler than cigarette smoke.

"Go on," the shadow said. "Ast me who I am."

"Who are you?" Joel asked, obediently.

"The boss. Big Al. Alphonse Capone. Yer grampa's old man useta run with me in Brooklyn when we was punks. Yer grampa told you, 'member?"

"Scarface," Joel breathed.

"Watch yer mouth. The last sumbitch called me that's still breathin' the Chicago river." The shadow barked a laugh. " 'Breathin' the river . . .' Thassa good one." Another laugh, more a snort than a bark. "You got any other questions, spit 'em out."

"What do you want?"

"To set you straight. To begin with, this prayin' to
virgins and martyrs is a chump's game, on account'a
even if they existed, which a lotta them don't, and
some that do ain't exactly virgins, what're they gonna
do for you? Not screw? Hell, you got that down pat
already. If you had the brains of a pissant, you'd pray
to somebody like me. Saint Al. I ain't pretty as Teresa
of Avila, though I gotta tell you I boffed a lotta toot-
sies'd make her look like a mud fence, but I'm a can-
do paisan. I mean, Tessy never made no twenny-seven
mil, and them was the days when a million'd buy
more'n three cigars anna used rubber. So yer havin'
grief with this Choo-choo jackoff, right? So ast me to
do somethin' for you."

"I'd like my belongings back. Especially the
rosaries."

"Yeah, the white one with the glow inna dark cross
yer gramma gave you when you made yer first holy
communion—real class. I never had nothin' that swell
when I was a kid. Well, pally, Saint Al's gonna deliver,
an' when I do, maybe you an' me'll make a little deal.
That jake with you?"

"I guess so. But how will I know you kept your part
of the bargain?"

No reply. Joel peered into the shadows and sniffed
the air, seeking the stink of a cigar, but there was
nothing but gloom and mildew.

Then his eyelids were bright and he was shaking—
no, *being* shaken. He opened his eyes and was staring
at Sister Agatha's slab of a face, inches from his. "On
your feet, you lazy sack!"

Joel realized that he had been sleeping and dreaming a strange dream about a Chicago criminal. He
arose and followed Agatha into the hall, which was
even drearier in the morning light.

"The bakery didn't have any leftovers, so it'll have
to be oatmeal for breakfast," Agatha said. "Start making some while I—"

"Making what?"

"Oatmeal."

"I don't know how."

Agatha sighed. "All right, start a pot of coffee—"

"Coffee is a *drug*," Joel said indignantly.

"We'll risk a bust. Get busy."

"It's evil, and besides, I don't know how."

"Mop the floor."

"I don't know how."

"Tell you what. I'll get a postage stamp and you can write me a list of what you *do* know how to do."

"Are you ridiculing me?"

Agatha grabbed two fistfuls of her sleet-colored hair and pulled. "Sit down and stay out of the way—can you manage *that*?"

"Certainly," Joel replied with what he was sure was devastating dignity.

He sat on a folding chair and, for a while, watched the woman scurry around the kitchen area. After a few minutes, reality again ebbed and he was in the gray limbo; he found it comfortable. When he returned, suddenly and rudely, to the world, he was behind the counter, ladling creamy goo onto a tin plate, being called "numbnuts" by Benny, the dwarf.

"Hey, Twinkletoes, done any sunbathing lately?" The male officer he had met yesterday was next to Benny.

"What's on your mind, Willy?" Agatha asked from the sink, where she was spraying water onto a plate.

"Your name's Terwilliger, right?" the officer asked Joel, who nodded.

"The narks busted a crack house last night, found these." said the officer. He had a suitcase in either hand and a third under his left arm. "Got your name on 'em. Bulls say they ain't evidence and that I could return 'em to their owner, which is you." He dropped the cases onto the linoleum.

"Was there a man named Choo-choo?" Joel asked.

"*Was* is right. His ass is cooling in the morgue. Dumb skel pulled a piece and the bulls put him down.

"He's dead?"

"That's what usually happens when you take a load of nine mike-mike slugs in the chest."

"That means he was shot with automatic pistols," Agatha explained.

For the first time since he left the seminary, Joel smiled. "Good. He deserved it."

The officer raised his brows and smirked. "Ain't you s'posed to love your enemies?"

"Yes. But he wasn't my enemy. He was *bad*! He stole my belongings."

"Yeah, that'd make him public enemy number one, all right." The officer touched a forefinger to his cap and walked away.

Joel turned to Agatha. "Could you help me carry my belongings?"

"I don't know how."

"I don't think you're telling me the truth."

"I'll mention it in confession."

Joel dragged the suitcases back to the clothing room, opened them and inspected the contents. Nothing was missing. He lifted the white rosary with the glow-in-the-dark cross, gazed at it reverently—and sniffed. Something in the air. Cigar smoke?

He spent the rest of the morning saying the sorrowful mysteries. Then Agatha entered, pulled his ear, which really *hurt,* and led him to the hall. He ladled stew until Agatha told the diners to go away. As he was carrying an empty pan to the sink, at Agatha's command, he hit the coffee urn with his elbow and knocked it to the floor Agatha had just finished mopping, spilling a mixture of liquid and brown grit onto the linoleum. Agatha moaned and rapped his skull with a knuckle.

Lips trembling, eyes watering, Joel said, "You liked that!"

"I wouldn't say 'liked.' I'd say, 'deeply enjoyed.' I'd say 'got a whole lot of satisfaction.' I'd say 'never had so much fun in my life.' "

"You're not a nun!"

"You got me. I'm actually Satan's little sister."

Joel fled to the door. "I'm going out."

"No," Agatha said in a voice Joel did not recognize, holding up her long skirt and running from the counter to put a hand on his arm. "They'd chop you into dog meat. Just go say your rosary. I'll handle the chores."

That seemed like a good idea. Joel was upset; it seemed wrong, almost sacrilegious, for Agatha to have a good idea. But he remembered what his grandmother had once taught him—"The devil can quote scripture for his own purposes"—and was comforted.

He knelt among the boxes and heaps of clothing and, fingering the white beads, said the sorrowful mysteries, the joyful mysteries, and the glorious mysteries. The familiar prayer solidified into solid objects—no, not objects: *angels,* clean and shining and pure. They carried him to the limbo, no longer gray but now a gleaming place sculpted from golden clouds.

He felt a pain in his knees, and the clouds vanished. He was in the clothing room, kneeling in the rectangle of dirty light from the window, staring at a familiar clump of shadow.

"Did Saint Al deliver the goods or did Saint Al deliver the goods?" Al Capone blew out a jet of smoke that smelled, not like a cigar, but like the sulfur in Joel's high school chemistry class. "Choo-choo's breathin' the Chicago river. He ain't really, but it's a great gag. Tickles me."

"You're real."

"Helluva lot realer than Prisca, an' you can take that straight to the bank. Anyway, whaddaya say, pally? You ready to play the game my way?"

"What game?"

"The game'a life. . . ." Al mumbled another word; it sounded like "numbnuts," but Joel was sure he must have misheard it.

"I don't know how," he said.

"Not yet, you don't, 'cause you ain't had no advantages. But you can learn. Lemme take it slow for you. Ast you a question. Who do you hate?"

"Nobody."

"Yeah? What about this Agatha frail?"

"I don't hate her. I just wish she'd burn in fiery torment for eternity."

"She could keep Choo-choo company."

"You could do that?" Joel asked, rising and rubbing his knees. "To Sister Agatha?"

"Naw. But you could, see? Lemme tell you a story. There was these two rats back in Chi town. They was actin' like they was pals of mine, but they was really rats, see? So I invite 'em to a real swell feed and just when they're gettin' ready to dig into the eats and I get behind 'em with a bat and *bam bam bam* I smack their brains all over the tablecloth."

"You killed them with a baseball bat?"

"They was astin' for it, just like that Agatha frail! What I done was only right! Now, do yourself a favor. Take a gander behind that big box in the corner."

Joel limped on stiff legs to a cardboard carton that had once contained a gas stove and pulled it away from the wall. In the dim glow from the window, he saw a baseball bat standing on its fat end.

"Go 'head," Al Capone said. "Pick it up."

Joel's fingers closed around the tape on the narrow end of the bat and he lifted it.

"Feel good?" Al Capone asked. "Now you gotta ast yourself if you wanna go on bein' pushed around and if that frail in the next room don't deserve what I give them rats back in Chi."

"She does," Joel said, righteousness swelling within him.

" 'The Lord helps them what helps themselves,' " Al Capone said. "I done Choo-choo for you. The frail's yours."

Feeling like St. Louis, like Joan of Arc, even like the Archangel Michael himself—like *all* the mighty

warriors of holiness throughout the ages—Joel shouldered his weapon and opened the door to the dining
hall, dark except for light from the street lamps shining through the front windows. Sister Agatha was sitting at the table nearest the counter with her back to
him, her head bowed, her shoulders slumped. He
gripped the bat tighter and crept toward her. As he
drew hear, he heard a snuffling sound. Was she weep-
ing? Or perhaps just sleeping?

"Go on," Al Capone said from everywhere at once.
"Hit her."

Joel raised the bat over his head.

"*Go on!*"

Trembling, filled with rage and loathing and frustration, Joel dropped the bat and whispered, "I don't
know how."

MONEY WELL SPENT

by Janet Pack

"Isn't this fun?" Theresa di Luna, known as Tesa to nearly everyone, snuggled her chin against her husband's shoulder despite the cloying heat. "I just *love* old stuff, and New Orleans is famous for it."

"Yeah, yeah," Marcello di Luna, called Marc, replied shortly. Unease on several counts wormed down his neck, tandem to sweat. First, he was dressed in off-the-rack short-sleeved shirt and cotton slacks bought by his wife, instead of his usual hand-tailored suits and shirts. He did not appreciate the indifferent fit since it did little for his stocky Italian-American frame. Second, he stood in an unknown place out in the open. Anything could happen. His three personal bodyguards were worried—he could tell by their restive postures and quick eye movements. Third, he was hot. The New Orleans temperature had pushed into the eighties by noon with equal amounts of humidity. Marc hated sweating except for exercise. And fourth, he stood in a graveyard looking at white crumbling stone encasing moldering bones with French names. Graveyards had bothered him since he was five, when Uncle Carlo had been gunned down by a rival family at Uncle Stephano's funeral. Marc and his father Julio escaped with minor wounds, but only because two bodyguards sacrificed themselves.

Graveyards gave him big-time willies. This one was no exception.

Today his nerves were worse than usual. His hands trembled. Perhaps it was the residual stress from that

business deal he'd closed before leaving Chicago. It
had been necessary to snuff the lives of three midlevel
managers who'd proved inefficient or untrustworthy.
An easy job turned messy because one assassin had
allowed his target enough breath to curse his murder's
instigator before he died. That made Marc more wary
than ever. The last thing he'd done before leaving his
office for this vacation was have his big multitalented
personal assistant, Guido, permanently lose that assassin. No one would ever find the body. Marc had tied
up all the loose ends quickly and quietly, traits for
which he'd become famous in the Chicago "business."

Decisive, tough, honest most of the time, determined to do things for the good of his company and
his extended family. His reputation didn't include his
secret credence in hexes, charms, and curses. The thin
voices of his victims, clamoring from beyond the pale,
increased enough to dent the mental barrier he'd built
against them. Grimacing, Marc shut them out and re-
inforced his defenses.

He'd never admitted this superstition about graveyards or ghosts to anyone, not even to Tesa. Di Luna
considered it a personal weakness. He tried to shrug
off the impression of something dire hanging above
his head in the shimmering blue sky and pay attention
to the guide's historical harangue. Tesa had insisted
on a tour of the above-ground St. Louis cemetery just
beyond Rampart Street. He'd paid triple for the privilege of a private tour. What could happen?

"Anything," he muttered, glancing about. Prepara-
tion for the unexpected had kept Marc alive years
longer than anyone predicted, had made him at age
thirty-four the youngest and most dynamic leader in
the annals of the Chicago organization. He intended
to keep his position as long as possible.

Now he stood on a walkway in this seedy garden of
oven-shaped crypts listening to a young black woman
narrate the peculiar burial practices of a city below
sea level. Looking down, he snatched his hand away

from the slat of a worn park bench someone had installed more than a hundred years ago so they could share Sunday picnics with dead relatives. The back of his neck crawled again. His hand ached for a weapon even though he knew his only targets were phantoms.

"Make it short," he growled, interrupting the guide. His baritone sounded as sticky as the humidity.

She stopped in mid-sentence, gave him a penetrating look, and nodded. "This way," she said, turning and leading them to a site that appeared identical to many other graves except that the middle one in the stack of three had little notes tied with red ribbons shoved into cracks in the stone. The bright satins fluttered languidly in the reluctant breeze. In front of the tomb, where grass wilted, there were several baguettes both stale and fresh, plates of rotting beans and rice, and two tall dark-green bottles of sealed French wine. Coins of all denominations littered the area, particularly quarters. A fan of five carefully placed silver dollars had dulled during their sojourn in front of the oven vault.

Marc grunted, estimating the total of the coinage. "Person could get some quick money here. That's a pretty good pile."

"No one would ever do that, Mr. Di Luna," the guide's conviction unnerved him more. "Some of this money, like those silver dollars, has been here for over a year, undisturbed as long as I've been guiding tours. It's never touched because it means the worst possible luck."

"Why?" Marc asked, trying to ignore a peculiar itch between his shoulder blades.

"Because this is the most famous grave in the cemetery. Buried here is Marie Laveau, the renowned voodoo queen. Practitioners believe that if they offer food or money and leave requests, Marie will answer." She smiled as if sharing secrets. "In fact, there were two Marie Laveaus, both buried in this crypt. The daughter took over when the mother resigned her calling as

voudoun leader, returned to the Catholic faith, and
dedicated her last years to healing the sick."

"Voodoo is still practiced here?" squealed Tesa.
"Ooooohh, spooky!"

"That's it." Marc grabbed his wife's elbow and spun
her toward the cemetery's wrought-iron gate as his
tremors exploded into full-blown shakes. "I'm not
gonna listen to any more of this crap."

"But we're only half done," Tesa pouted.

"Sir, I hope I haven't offended . . ." the guide
stuttered.

Marc whirled away from the voodooienne's grave
and stumbled on nothing, falling to his knees against
the gravel walkway. Rising, waving away his bodyguards, he discovered a quarter stuck to one sweaty
palm. Propelled by his need to exit one of New Orleans' historical wonders and desperate get back to
the normalcy of leading the mob in Chicago, he
dropped the coin in a pocket of his slacks and forgot
about it. Shoving through the graveyard's wrought-
iron gates, he pushed Theresa into the cool dark plush
of the waiting limousine. The bodyguards piled in behind them.

"Back to the hotel," Marc ordered the driver over
his wife's protests.

From the relative safety of their double suite, he
directed Tesa to cancel the rest of their reservations
and call the airport to begin refueling of the company's private jet. Opening the private bar in the
room, Marc chose a drink, poured it into a hotel glass,
and tossed it down, ignoring Tesa complaints about
his canceling the rest of their vacation. He followed
the first drink with another, and a third, tasting none.
Despite the dulling edge of alcohol, his shakes
remained.

That night, in his own opulent bed in Chicago, the
dreams began. Balls of gray wax with dark hair like
his coiled inside, studded with bright feathers. Dead
bats, reeking of turpentine and snuff preservative,

sometimes of other, more noxious, smells. A pendant of writhing snake that grew until it crushed him. Marc tossed and turned, unable to rest.

Drums began after the first week, their heavy beat controlling the pace of his heart. Chanting and singing followed two days later in barely understandable French that had an African-Carribean island twang. He began seeing figures, sweaty, gyrating bodies clothed in loud or faded colors, a few not clothed at all, shadows against flickering torchlight. The distinct sensation of power chilled his visions, wild and only marginally controlled, a far different kind from that Di Luna manipulated for the majority of the Chicago underworld.

Marc soon looked haggard from lack of rest. His sense of humor disappeared, his lauded patience with subordinates vanished. On Tesa's insistence, DiLuna visited his doctor. The doctor prescribed sleeping pills, suggesting if they didn't help in a week Marc should make another appointment. The sleeping aids made him groggy but did nothing to stop the dreams. Di Luna threw them away and ignored his doctor's advice.

That night the voices began. They popped in and out of his nightmares, ebbing at what seemed the most intriguing moments of argument. Voices speaking French with a Carribean-African inflection. Two female voices spitting at one another like fur-fluffed cats. Marc fretted about his inability to understand them as well as his inability to banish their presences.

The third night, in the midst of a spate of bullet-like antique French, the language became as clear as most English to Marc.

". . . and what do you propose we do with him since he hasn't heard us? Allow him to continue to ramp about with all that power? He is nearly unstoppable now."

"*Oui*," the older, darker voice replied, turning soft with memories. "He should have been my consort at the ceremonies by the lake . . . at least for a little while." The cold smile implicit in that statement, as well as the unspoken threat of what happened to some of the men after, made Marc shudder.

"Not that you'd return to that life since your reconversion to the Church and your taking up good works," the younger sniped.

"I do not ask for my old life back," the second female snapped. "After all, you usurped me when I halted as voodooienne, adopting everything, even embracing my achievements as your own." Her hands fluttered, punctuating her words. "No place for the first Marie, as if I never existed. Gone like smoke."

"Why let a stellar reputation go to waste? I accepted the burden of everything you did during your reign over the dances. Besides, there was room for only one queen."

"Who are you, and what are you doing here?" Marc thundered within his sleep-darkened mind.

"Ah, the little man has finally awakened," the first voice purred.

"Took him long enough," the second grated. "I'd began wondering if he wasn't completely head-blind."

Marc roared, "Quit ignoring me, witch!"

"*Au contraire*," said the older woman archly, "it is you who've been ignoring us so rudely. I'm not a witch, I'm a queen of voudoun."

"Aha, you finally admit it!" caroled the first voice.

"I meant that in the past tense," the second snapped. "Mind your rebellious tongue when speaking to your *mamman*, child!"

"Rebellious! Who broke with the teachings of the Church and started the voudoun meetings in the first place?"

"If you feel so zealous about the Church, why did you continue—"

"Shut up!" Marc now saw hazy figures in his dream-fog. One woman was definitely older than the other, perhaps by sixteen or eighteen years. Both had strik-

ing features, memorable rather than beautiful. Each
had her own powerful, exotic magnetism that fascinated Di Luna as a cobra does its victim. A strong
resemblance existed between the women—dark skin,
although the younger's shone several shades lighter,
wide noses heralding African descent, snapping dark
eyes under arched eyebrows, high cheekbones, and
cascades of black hair confined beneath elaborate
scarves layered and whorled like confections. They
both wore colorful calico shirts and yards of petti-
coated skirts with discreet peekings of lace, clothing
of a bygone era.

"Why in hell are you bothering me?" He felt as if
he'd finally asked the correct question.

"*Non, non,* Monsieur, you have it wrong. You disturbed us," the older one stated with an assurance
that shook Marc to the core of his being. "And none
of us is in hell. Yet."

"How could I have disturbed you? I've never even
seen you before, much less spent time with you. You
must have died almost a century before I was born!"

The younger woman tilted her head. "You do not
realize? You have visited us both recently."

"And have stolen that which belongs to us. It is our
right to be here, to persuade you to return our property. As promptly as possible.

Marc's outrage and disbelief got the better of him.
"Where? When? I've stolen nothing from you! You're
both crazy."

"You visited the graveyard of St. Louis in New Orleans recently, *non*?" the younger asked.

"And saw there the resting place of the voudoun
queen—"

"Queens!"

"Very well, queens were we both. Eh, you remember, the vault had little messages tied with red ribbon,
and offerings of food and money left before it."

Di Luna wrinkled his nose. The heavy odor of old
beans and rice in humid air suddenly revisited his ol-

factory senses. "Disgusting, particularly in that climate. The place stank of rotting food. A health agency should be called in, should forbid it in future."

The young woman shrugged. "They know this is done. They allow these offerings from my—our—followers and fully understand what will happen if they don't."

Her mother nodded. "And what happened as you were leaving the cemetery?"

The head of Chicago's organized crime syndicate frowned. "I interrupted the guide's speech, turned quickly, and pushed my wife out of there. We got into the limo and headed for the hotel, had a drink, checked out, then went to the airport."

"He has blanked it from his mind." The daughter flung her hands into the air and shook her head at her mother in resignation. "His memory refused to work. *Mon Dieu,* can we do more than we have already done to convince him?"

"Try again," the second woman urged.

"Very well." The first female turned blazing black eyes on Marc. "Do you not recall what came away from that cemetery with you?"

"I—I fell." Di Luna's eyes widened suddenly. "The coin . . ."

". . . belongs to us," the elder nodded. "We are here to secure and return it. But there is one *petit* problem. We cannot carry it ourselves. We are now purely spiritual creatures."

"You mean," Di Luna said slowly, incredulity coloring his voice, "you expect me to cancel everything to return to New Orleans and put that damned quarter back? I don't even know where the thing is! I'll give you a hundred coins, no, a thousand, of the same denomination to replace it. Will that do? No? All right, two thousand! Now let me get some sleep!"

Both ladies shook their heads before the older one spoke. "That we cannot do, at least not until that same coin takes its place again at our gravesite."

"I'll have the housekeeper search it out, and I'll send one of my secretaries back with it. And the rest." He nodded, thinking he'd reached the best solution. "That ought to work."

"But no, *mon cher,* the one who stole the coin must put it back, as acknowledgment and apology," insisted the younger.

"And what happens if I don't?" snapped Marc. "I don't have time for this crap!"

Both ladies recoiled at his vulgarity. The elder recovered first, her head at a regal angle that made Di Luna feel like a recalcitrant child. "We shall invade your rest, make sleep impossible, shape your dreams to bother you much more than now. Much more."

"And since you will find it difficult to lead a normal life, you will go *lunatique*," the daughter finished. "Unpleasantly so."

"So you're leaving me no choice."

"You had none in the first place."

"None at all." The Creoles shook their heads, their hair coverings Marc somehow knew were called *tignons* waggling tendrils of red, blue, and yellow as exclamation points.

Di Luna straightened his dream-form, his six feet not that much taller than the older Marie. "Very well. In the morning I'll cancel my appointments and order the plane readied for a return trip to New Orleans. Does that satisfy you?"

Mother and daughter nodded. "*Bien.*"

"Now get out of my head."

"*Non, mon ami.* That we cannot do," said the elder mournfully, but with a wicked twinkle in her black eyes. "We must stay as reminders and impellers, to make certain you complete your promise."

Marc's roar of frustration woke his wife.

The hazy Chicago morning dawned on the Di Luna household in disorder. Giving no reason, Marc canceled important meetings that had been scheduled for a month, sullying his pristine reputation among business associates. He stalked about the house giving orders in a foghorn voice, brown eyes fever-bright under lowered brows and face pale. He drove the frazzled housekeeper to search every article of clothing in his closet for the coin, then every article of clothing in the house. She finally found the off-the-rack slacks in a sack stored in a little-used cubby which she cleaned only twice a year, intended for donations to the poor at St. Mary's parish. Drawing the coin from a front pocket, she held it out to her employer.

Di Luna snatched it from her shaking hand without thanks, poked it gingerly into a jewelry pouch of Tesa's, then tossed the embroidered satin envelope to a yawning bodyguard. "Keep it safe." His eyes glittered strangely in his haggard face. "If you don't, I'll see to it you'll lose more than your job."

The bodyguard straightened immediately. "Yes, sir."

The drive to the airport was silent and uneasy. Tesa threw furtive "Why me?" glances at her husband while the guards kept watch for danger lurking on the roads or in the skies. The man in charge of the coin touched the breast pocket of his suit often to assure himself of its presence. Marc adopted a stony attitude with arms crossed across his chest and chin down, only surfacing to bustle his wife out of the car and into the plane when the limo stopped at the small airport where the company hangared its two jets.

"I can't believe I'm doing this!" Di Luna's mind sang over and over. Just a hint of African drums, their pace accelerating his heart, answered. He knew the two Maries were still in his mind—he could feel their presence just beyond his internal sight, waiting impatiently for him to fulfill his promise.

His belief in curses now rivaled his fear of graveyards. The last thing Marc wanted to do was to pass through the wrought-iron gates of St. Louis Cemetery and replace the coin at the Laveau oven vault. His skin crawled, bad feelings assailed his mind. "Perhaps I should take ribbon and leave a request with all the others," he thought. Composition of that scathing note occupied his attention until the older Marie whispered, "*Americaine,*" with an inflection that consigned Marc irrevocably to the redolent summer gutters of the old French Quarter.

"Italian-American," he snapped back aloud, startling Tesa and his bodyguards. "Sorry," Di Luna muttered just above the noise of the jets. "Guess I've been dozing."

"Oh, honey, you'll be all right as soon as you get back on your sleeping schedule," his wife said. "Here," she dug in her purse, a tiny but expensive thing just large enough for lipstick, hairbrush, ten credit cards, and a bottle of pills. "Take a Valium. It'll help."

"No." Marc said tightly, remembering at the last minute to tack on "Thank you" so her feelings wouldn't shatter. He didn't want to put up with Tesa's "poor baby" attitude, nor did he dare get groggy now. Anything could still happen.

The little jet touched down just before noon without incident in the sultry southern airport. Di Luna hustled his party into the limo awaiting them, then punched down the air-conditioning. Heat and humidity again, in combination with his own feverish mental state and lack of sleep, made him feel queasy.

The claustrophobia began when the car turned from the freeways onto smaller streets leading to old town, then along narrow avenues designed wide enough for two horse-drawn carriages to pass. The famous Spanish-influenced wrought-iron balconies on many of the brick and stucco buildings leaned heavily toward him despite their airy look. Marc found his breath short, his heart keeping pace to soprano and bass drums that beat African-inspired rhythms through his consciousness. He steeled his resolve. "It'll all be over in a little while," he assured himself silently as the car wound slowly toward its goal on the far side of the famous old settlement.

Past the square, where lines of mule-drawn carriages awaited passengers. Past the Café du Monde, where a brass jazz trio of two blacks and a white were in full roar on the last verse of "Basin Street Blues," the trumpeter's case open to encourage donations from appreciative listeners and offer their latest CD for sale. Past the Rue Royale's coffee, antique, and curio shops where a tourist can buy anything from a praline to Mississippi sternwheeler charms to a Civil War-replica pistol to yard-long strands of bright plastic and glass Carnival beads. Past quiet residential "courtyards," houses built around breeze-catching space open to the sky behind colorful high walls that discourage prying eyes. Marc wondered briefly if one had once belonged to either of the Maries.

The younger of his mind-phantoms shook her head. "Not here. We lived in a modest area. These are town houses of wealthy Creoles, the ones known as free persons of color, such as bank owners and those lucky enough to inherit family money."

"Cottages housed us," the older Marie stated.

"Ah, very much like Chicago for some," muttered Marc.

"*Nothing* like Chicago," both women chorused.

The limo finally turned onto Rampart Street. The proximity of the graveyard made the hairs rise on Marc's neck and arms.

The car pulled to the side of the avenue, next to the gates of the St. Louis Cemetery. Marc exited after two of the bodyguards, hauling Tesa out by her hand. A guide waited at the wrought-iron barrier with a key, glancing at his watch.

"It's very irregular to open up a half-hour early," he drawled.

Marc thrust a hundred-dollar bill into his hand. "I understand, but this is an emergency. Make sure you and the other guides get something good out of this."

"Yes, sir!" Eyes wide, the man unlocked one side of the gate and swung it wide. "There you are, sir, ma'am. Anything special I can show you while I'm here?"

"No," Di Luna said roughly. "I know where I'm going." Careful not to trip, hands shaking with more than his usual spate of graveyard nerves, he headed for the Laveau vault. Planting himself firmly in front of it, he reached his left hand to the bodyguard with the coin. The man pulled the fabric jewelry pouch from his pocket and handed it to his employer.

Marc took out the coin, examined both sides, shrugged, then quickly bent and placed the quarter among the other offerings left for the voudoun queens. It looked no different from the two quarters he carried in his front suit pocket. Rubbing his fingers as if he'd carried something noisome between them, he stepped back from the grave and listened intently.

"What is it, honey?" asked Tesa, worried.

"Shhh," replied Di Luna, searching within his mind for taint of the voodooiennes.

No drums, no Creole-lilted French. No Maries.

Grinning, feeling better now than any time in the last two weeks, Marc thanked the guide and returned to the limo with his wife and bodyguards. In a festive mood, he bought them all dinner at a famous Creole restaurant while waiting for the Lear jet's refueling. He settled deep into the limo's cushions on the ride back to the airport, convinced he could finally sleep. Dismissing the driver with a huge tip and a compliment on her driving when she pulled the car to a gentle stop on the tarmac, Di Luna scrambled out and boarded the plane with his wife, bodyguards front and back. As soon as the jet climbed into the air and headed for Chicago, Marc fell into a deep, peaceful sleep.

Tesa roused him just before landing and handed him an envelope. "This just came for you from the pilot, darling. It came over the radio."

Marc tore open the sealed paper. Screening it from the eyes of his wife, he read the few handwritten lines.

"Situation serious. Must have your decision immediately."

He crumpled the note. "Damn."

"Something important?" asked Tesa.

"Just means I'll have to spend a few hours in the office tonight before I can come to bed."

She pouted so very prettily. "Oh, honey, do you really have to?"

"Sorry." He kissed her tenderly, the first time in two weeks. "I really have to. I'll make it quick as possible, I promise."

They held hands during the limo ride back to their lakeshore condo, even while he was on the phone. Marc kissed Tesa again before she disappeared to tuck in their children, Carl and Julia. Di Luna disappeared into the office he maintained at home, picked up the phone, and dialed a number.

"Di Luna here. What's the situation now? That bad?" He listened for a long time, his expression turning stormy as he settled into his high-backed leather chair. "Sounds like we need the hit squad. No, not all of them, just the best, the top three or four. Yes, I'll see to it. Don't worry. Immediately."

He put down the phone. Disgusting how things could quickly disintegrate when he took a few hours off. This situation had involved a major drug pickup and sale. Somehow the authorities had gotten wind of it, apparently through the flapping mouth of one of the little people involved whom he hadn't been around to approve. No time to delay. He punched a number.

"Guido, Di Luna here. Yes, the trip went fine. Listen, I need your help. Remem-m-m—"

African drums robbed his throat of speech, his mind of thought. Both Maries stood before his internal eye, bright as if surrounded by flames.

"You said . . . you'd get out . . . of my dreams!"

Marc labored to howl. "I returned your damned coin!"

"*Oui,* your dreams," the older Marie spat. "This is not one."

"And you are directing an odious plan again," her daughter stated. "We are here to stop that. To stop you."

"You can't. This is free-enterprise business," Di Luna returned, recovering.

"Oh, but we can, *mon cher,*" replied Marie the First with a feral grin. "This duty was given us by Powers beyond the grave. We do not sit biding our time in Purgatory but are involved in active good works. We've been planning your retirement for months."

"Better than singing hymns to a Being who turns an ear our direction once a century," Marie Fil nodded.

"And infinitely more satisfying." The older voodooienne nodded to the phone squawking in Marc's hand. "That call was routed straight to the police. An individual in your organization, one you trust, has been an informant for quite some time."

Di Luna felt the blood desert his face. "But this line is secure."

"No more," Marie the younger announced. "The authorities are on the way."

Marc roared, "I'll get you voodoo bitches!" Dropping the receiver, he lunged for them, hands clutching at their throats.

And passed right through. The wall of his office brought him up short. Turning, Di Luna dove again, pounding his fists against the edge of the desk when he couldn't reach the Maries.

"Definitely deranged," the daughter said. "But he'll recover in time for a lengthy trial."

"*Oui,*" agreed her mother. "Now, much as I hate to miss a delicious *denouement,* there is that situation with the senator awaiting us."

"Must we go?"

"Only if you're not interested in finishing two dances in the same night."

"You're still determined to make a reputation."

"You're the one so desirous of continuing the one I build." She twitched the flounce of her sleeve into place. "Let us be gone. We are finished here."

They faded, leaving howling Di Luna to the ministrations of the police breaking through the door.

Assassins & Hitmen

"Tonight, he will be sleeping with the fishes."

What's a mob without a hitman? It would be like a politician without a bribe, a precinct without a pad, and a stoolie without an unfortunate and very fatal accident. Whether he's a very close friend of the family or just a very professional hired gun practicing homicide for profit, he's a principal member of the organized crime team, ready with a rod (or some equivalent) to help settle age-old or recently incurred family disputes.

   . . . and what is a hitman but the modern day equivalent of the family assassin of the good old days of medieval and Renaissance vendettas. This is the spin that Fiona Patton and Robert Greenberger take as the new kid in town is forced to earn his bones, while Mickey Zucker Reichert turns the focus to a fellow who has been practicing his chosen trade for an extremely long time.

A DYING LIFE

by Fiona Patton

The city of Cerchicava was growing. The black death had passed, the Mage's War was a distant memory, and a renaissance of culture, both magical and financial, had flowered, swelling the population of the ancient city-state to record numbers. Hundreds flocked there seeking a new life of riches and opportunities. Some found it. Most did not.

The two men who leaned against the tavern wall in the upscale church district that night were after bigger prey then some chance-met country immigrant. One was heavyset, bulky muscles straining the cloth of his patched doublet. He carried a truncheon and a hooded lantern. The other was slight, eighteen or nineteen years old with dark, feverish eyes that seemed to look inward at some danger only he could see.

In the distance the great bell of San Demino began to toll. The smaller man squinted up through the shadows.

"He'll be out soon," he noted.

His companion grunted. "You sure, Coll?"

"Bennie's been setting him for a week. He always goes in, has a dram, and comes out in time to walk to San Lucazi's for evening prayers."

"Priest is he?"

"Yeah, Paulo."

"Is he protected?"

"Not magically."

"Wonder who he pissed off."

Coll just shrugged. He was a "cutter," Paulo, a

"marker." Neither knew more than that their contact had fingered the "mark" and told them to collect tonight. Neither wanted to know more.

It began to rain, and Coll shivered under his thin jacket. He'd been collecting with a marker for over a year now, a sign that his work had been noticed. He'd been moved up to "set jobs": collections of specific items for specific spells. It kept him out of the cemeteries but not out of the rain.

The tavern door opened, and noise poured into the street, interrupting his thoughts. A large man, red robes prominent in the lantern light, emerged and immediately turned south toward the distant row of churches. Coll took the lantern, and he and Paulo fell into step behind him.

They caught up with him swiftly. The priest had barely enough time to gasp his surprise as the marker slammed into him, driving him toward an alley mouth. Coll was right behind, a thin stiletto appearing in his hand.

Paulo's arm came up, there was a distinctive crack and the priest was down. Coll scuttled forward as he fell, flinging the priest onto his back and pressing his ear against his chest. The priest moaned.

"Paulo!"

The big man raised his arm again. The priest's eyes locked on Coll's face, the sudden knowledge of a death too horrible to conceive of sending a shock through them both. The priest cried out and clutched at the smaller man's clothing, trying to throw him off. Unnerved for just an instant, Coll could only stare back at him, and then the jack came down with a crunch. The priest went limp.

The cutter went to work quickly now, slicing through the robe with an experienced motion. The white flesh underneath was soon exposed, and as Paulo held the lantern, Coll pressed his ear to the priest's chest once again. There was no sound.

A quick, deep cut in the dead man's abdomen ex-

posed the soft organs underneath. Coll reached in with
his left hand, lifted the liver, turned it, and sliced an
inch long piece cleanly off with an expertise born from
years of practice. One motion and the urn inside his
pocket was out, opened and the "item" deposited in
the liquid within. Another motion and it was corked,
soft wax pressed around the mouth. Coll pocketed the
urn and, without a word, left Paulo to dispose of the
body.

No one would ever know that Zeno de Podeno,
pastor of San Lucazi, had been marked to die so that
his flesh might be sold to the enemies of his family—
no one but the cutter, the marker, and the necromancer who would make use of the item.

Moving quickly through the alleyway, Coll stripped
off his bloody jacket, using it to clean his hands. He'd
barely flung it to one side before a sudden stab of
pain doubled him over. His stomach heaved and,
stumbling to his knees, he crouched, choking and
retching, in the lee of a dilapidated building.

To many, necromancy was the most heinous crime
that could ever be visited upon the dead. To defile a
corpse was vile enough and called for brutal penalties
in all the city-states; but to use dead flesh against the
living was to attack the spirit of them both and was
punishable by death. It was a gruesome, highly illegal
business but one so lucrative that many were willing
to risk the savage penalties to service Cerchicava's
growing number of Death Mages.

The priests taught that those who served the Necromantic Spellcraft were as dammed as the mages themselves. Coll believed them. Wiping his hand across his
mouth, he waited for the fit to pass, then stood and
straightened his clothes. He'd been corpse-cutting
since he was a boy, starting by holding the lantern
while his master worked. In due time he'd moved up
to crude collections from plague victims and hanged
criminals, then finally to set jobs. It was all he knew.
He was good at it. It had taken him off the streets

and made him safe, and if the faces of the dead came
back to hover about his bedside, there were plenty of
herbs that brought him the insensibility of a drugged
night's sleep. He was alive, that was all that mattered.

Pulling himself roughly together, he continued on
his way.

Gebhard, Coll's contact, maintained an alehouse on
the docks. After a word with the "protector" by the
door, the young cutter was ushered into the back
room. The man was busy scratching figures in a ledger
and did not look up, although the tense set of his
shoulders said he knew who approached.

Used to the aversion of others, Coll still glared at
him. *Hypocrite,* he thought bitterly. Setting the urn
down on the table, he turned to go. He would be paid
later. Whatever Gebhard thought of him, he needed
him.

As he reached for the door, the man looked up.

"I've another collection for you," he said without
meeting Coll's eyes.

The cutter turned back.

"A set job, very special, very specific."

Coll nodded.

"You're to go to La Palazzo de Sulla immediately.
You'll get your instructions there."

Coll went white.

La Palazzo de Sulla was the home of Lord Montif-
ero de Sepori, one of the most powerful noblemen in
Cerchicava. It was rumored that he was a Master of
Necromancy, but no one, not even the city's duc, had
ever had the evidence or the courage to accuse him.
Those who worked in the cutting trade knew he was
their ultimate master but it was never spoken of. Lord
Sepori had a long reach. He could pluck your thoughts
from the air as easily as he could snuff out your life.
If you were loyal and useful, he would insure your
safety; if you crossed him, or hesitated, you'd find

yourself on the receiving end of a spell too horrible to even contemplate.

Coll *had* contemplated it, and his blood ran cold as he approached the small side door of the palazzo an hour later.

Rumor had several cutters dead under terrible circumstances of late. One, a small, consumptive youth named Alfons, had been found by a dipper, his ribs staved in and one heart chamber sliced cleanly away. Like the others, Coll had simply assumed he'd tried to betray their powerful master. Now he wasn't so sure. Perhaps he'd only doubted. Perhaps he'd laid awake at night, listening for the faltering heartbeat of the dying, feeling their fear sink into his spirit and shrivel it up. Perhaps he'd hesitated, just once, as Coll had tonight.

His mouth suddenly dry, the young cutter rapped on the door.

Lord Sepori was a husky man in his late forties, his thick, black hair streaked with gray. He was seated by the fire in a book-lined study, the sleeves of his shirt rolled up to reveal muscular arms scored with the burn marks of years of spellcraft. Coll could almost feel the power radiating off him. He looked up as a servant bent to whisper of Coll's arrival, and the cutter could see the red shimmer of a magical spell over his eyes.

Sepori gestured. Hesitantly, Coll entered the room, pausing as the man stood.

"Gebhard speaks very highly of your work," he said, his voice a surprisingly warm baritone. "A man who might go far. A man to take notice of."

"Ah, thank you, My Lord."

"Walk with me."

Striving to hide the revulsion he felt, Coll followed the mage through a small door and blinked. Before him stretched a huge, glass conservatory filled with roses. Hooded lanterns hung along the stone sidewall illuminating the structure with a soft, yellow glow, and the air was filled with perfume and the odor of rich, damp earth. Coll could only stare about him in astonishment.

Lord Sepori's red-tinged eyes glittered in cold amusement. "Does this surprise you?"

An immediate denial died on the cutter's lips. "Yes, My Lord."

Showing his teeth, Sepori reached down to caress a peach-colored bud. "Such beauty," he murmured. "Beauty should be preserved, don't you agree?"

"Ah, yes, sir."

"And ugliness destroyed."

"Sir?"

Crushing a small insect between his fingers, the lord straightened. "Gino!"

A man working within the roses at the far end shuffled forward. The magical tattoos on his face glowed hotly, as did the stitching across his mouth and nose. Coll took an involuntary step backward.

Sepori took no notice of him. "These plants are infested," he said in disgust. "Destroy them and inspect the others at once."

The apparition bowed, and Sepori moved on.

"We're on the brink of tumultuous changes, Coll," he said, his tone conversational once again. "Changes which may snatch a man from the richest palazzo or raise him from the vilest gutter. Do you follow?"

"I think so, sir."

"Excellent. I require a very special item tonight, and I need a cutter of extraordinary skill and unshakable loyalty for the collection. One with the brains to rise in my organization as far as ambition may take him. I believe that you are such a man. Am I correct?"

The necromancer was very close to him now. Coll could smell the bitter odor of stale magic and preserving oil on his clothes. His chest grew tight, and he stilled the urge to inch away.

"Yes, My Lord."

"The specifications are most precise. You may not

take a marker, but the mark is young and ailing. He will not present a problem. His name is Lorenzo de Marco, the son of our *most benevolent* Duc Giovanni de Marco."

Lord Sepori's sharp gaze was on his face. Coll grew very still but dared not show any outer emotion. The mage continued.

"You will enter the ducal palazzo in the guise of a physician with the assistance of one in my employ. The boy has many; one more will not be noticed. You will be given ether to anesthetize him, and I require one square inch of liver. That is all."

Coll blinked, a sudden pressure against his temples causing him to flinch. When he opened his mouth to speak, no words emerged.

Anesthetize him.

"Yes," Sepori said calmly. "The mark must be alive."

Sound came finally. "But . . ." Coll struggled to find the words. "The flesh must be dead."

"We are no longer bound by such constraints. My scholars have discovered a new spellcraft with four times the offensive power of the old. It requires the flesh of the *living. I* require that you collect it for me."

There was a rushing in Coll's ears. All he could see was the face of the dying priest, screaming his denial of the desecration of his body. He began to shake.

Sepori raised one ironic eyebrow. "You've made many collections in the past. Why do you recoil now?"

Coll had never considered himself a brave man, but staring up into the glittering eyes of the necromancer, he could only shake his head.

"But they were dead," he whispered.

"Can you be so sure? How long does it take for the spirit to leave the body? Even the priests debate this issue to no conclusion." Sepori drew closer, towering over the younger man. "How do you know you've never collected from the living?"

Coll swayed, almost fainting, and Sepori moved away.

"I'll give you a moment to think on it," he said over his shoulder. "I'd hate for you to blurt out the wrong answer. Return to me when you've collected your thoughts."

The door closed.

Coll collapsed against the wall. The enormity of what he'd just learned was too much to take in, and all he could do was shake his head back and forth. As he crouched there, the light grew dim, and he looked up to see the silent gardener slowly extinguish each hanging lamp. The creature came forward.

His back pressed against the wall, Coll shrank from the undead thing. It reached out, and the building plunged into darkness. Coll screamed.

Cold fingers gripped his arms and dragged him to his feet. He heard voices, crying, shrieking, pleading for mercy, for death. Then he saw Alfons.

The dead cutter shuffled toward him, his opaque, yellow eyes finding him despite their blindness, the great wound in his chest open and bleeding a pale green mist. Alfons raised his hand, and Coll saw the glittering blade of a stiletto pointed at him. He tried to jerk away, but the apparition threw one cold arm across his chest and hauled him into the air.

"No!"

"*It's much too late for that,*" Alfons said in a flat, unemotional tone. "*You doubt; you betray. Submit. It's all you deserve now.*"

Coll kicked out and missed. The apparition raised him up until his chest stretched painfully forward. The knife came down.

The blade sliced through cloth and flesh in a single motion, and Coll choked on a scream. The dead cutter was so close that he could see the maggots in his cheeks; and then the blade cut deep, and he almost fainted from the shock of it. Grinning, Alfons held something up in one bloody fist, and suddenly Coll was alone, crouched in the lee of the conservatory doorway.

Sweat beaded his face and soaked his shirt. With trembling hands he scrabbled at his shirt to feel the flesh underneath. There was no wound, no scar. Looking up, he saw the silent gardener throw a rose plant into a cart, then raise one gray hand to snuff out the first lamp.

Coll bolted through the door.

Lord Sepori had returned to his chair, turning the pages of a leather-bound book with an even expression. He glanced up as the young cutter stumbled forward and fell, gasping, to his knees before him.

Sepori set the book aside. "You see," he said almost gently, "it's much too late to turn back now." He reached out to smooth Coll's sweat-tangled hair. "Better to embrace your future than to meet such a fate."

Coll could only kneel there shaking.

"I know you've had doubts and regrets," the mage continued. "That's normal for any man, but ..." He raised one finger. ". . . don't make the mistake of thinking that giving voice or deed to such feelings is at all forgivable. Serve me, and I will keep you safe. I will mold you and guide you in a world of power and wealth greater than you have ever dreamed of." His hand gripped Coll's hair and raised his head to meet his eyes. "Fail me and you'll be plunged into far worse horrors than those you've witnessed tonight."

Well beyond terror, Coll stared up into Sepori's face and saw the death the priest had seen in his. "I won't fail you, Master," he answered, his voice a cracked and ragged whisper.

"See that you don't."

Two unfamiliar markers accompanied Coll and Sepori's physician to the walls of the ducal palazzo. Refusing to meet his eyes, the physician guided him to Lorenzo de Marco's bedchamber, then departed quickly. Coll was left alone with the sleeping child, an ether-soaked cloth in one hand, his knife in the other. He took one step forward. He stopped. Tried again, and stopped again, the thought of cutting through the child's flesh making him ill.

"It's much too late to turn back now."

Jerking back, he looked wildly about the room. The glowering coals in the grate cast shadows across the room that he dared not examine. Breathing deeply, he willed himself to calm. The voice had been in his head, a residue of his ordeal in the lord's palazzo. A warning not to fail.

He took another step forward and forced himself to look dispassionately down at the young mark, noting the hollow cheeks and pale, purple bruising under the closed eyelids. Coll had seen enough death in his short life to know it hovered perilously close to this boy. *He'll probably die anyway,* the cold voice of survival sneered. *What is this child to you that you should risk losing everything for him? He's never had to fight for what he has. He was born to safety, warmth, and comfort. You have clothes on your back and food in your stomach only because you serve. Fail just once* . . . Fail just once and he would become like that apparition in the conservatory. There was no way out for him; it was indeed too late to turn back now.

Bringing the cloth forward, he touched it to the boy's face.

The child whimpered and Coll paused, tried again, and jumped as a half-burned log tumbled from the grate to send a shower of sparks across the hearth. Renewed, a tongue of fire leaped up, and Coll saw the face of the dying priest rise from the coals.

He stumbled backward, flattening himself against the far wall. The vision followed the motion, then swung its attention up to the young cutter's face. Coll's mouth went dry. The vision stared at him, compelling, and the young cutter suddenly knew what it wanted.

"No," he croaked out. "I can't. I have to go through with this. I have no choice."

The boy moaned in his sleep, and Coll snapped his teeth together. "He won't just kill me," he hissed. "He'll turn me into some rotting, undead . . . thing. I can't."

The vision merely stared at him, neither accusing nor absolving, merely waiting.

"I'd never get away with it. He'd know I betrayed him. He'd just send someone else, anyway," he added.

The vision made no answer.

To his surprise, Coll felt a faint sense of hope begin to grow from a place he'd thought long abandoned. So far Sepori had not detected his thoughts and sent some magical attack to crush him for his hesitation. Maybe the palazzo was protected; maybe the boy was. *Maybe you are,* the voice of survival answered. Coll stared at the motionless vision. Maybe. His eyes suddenly cleared. Maybe he did have a choice, a chance, but he'd have to move fast.

A word to the guards at the door brought the duc running to his son's bedchamber, but instead of a dying child he was met by a pale, desperate-eyed young man clutching a knife.

Duc Giovanni de Marco was known as a pragmatic man. He sized up the situation in his son's bedchamber in an instant, then calmly asked for an explanation. Coll's hysterically babbled response was not what he'd expected.

Lord Sepori was a powerful and respected member of the duc's own class. There was no reason he should have believed this ragged, young man but the duc had waited a long time for proof of Sepori's guilt, and he had no intention of letting this opportunity pass. Calling for his guard captain, senior mage and physician, he had his son removed to a safer room, then presented them with Coll's story.

The ensuing outrage was quickly suppressed as they realized the possibilities. Pressed against the wall, Coll listened to their plans to kill his master, his own thoughts in turmoil.

He'd always believed that to be safe was to serve the most powerful protector. If the duc could destroy Lord Sepori, then Coll would be safe—but only if the duc could destroy Sepori. It was begining to look as if he couldn't.

The duc's people continued to debate, the lord himself listening objectively. The captain was pushing for an all-out attack, the mage advising caution. Finally the physician, a wizened old man, cleared his throat.

"We cannot defeat Sep . . . the necromancer by secular means," he wheezed. "He's a powerful mage and will have powerful offensive and defensive capabilities. We must fight him with equal magnitude or we will lose."

"Are you powerful enough to do that?" the duc asked bluntly, turning to the mage.

The woman pursed her lips. "No, My Lord."

"There may be another way," the old physician continued. "Necromancy is a very precise and delicate spellcraft. One wrong . . . component . . . and the effect could be most devastating to the mage involved."

The duc frowned. "How do you know this?" he demanded.

The physician met his suspicious gaze fearlessly. "I do not know this for certain, My Lord, but one hears such things. Ask the boy."

The duc's gaze swung toward Coll, who nodded mutely.

"And?"

"And I believe that if we could substitute the collected . . . er . . . item, we might effect a magical attack against him which would put him out of commission long enough for a military attack to succeed."

"Substitute the collected item? Just what kind of a substitute are you suggesting?"

"Substitute flesh, My Lord."

"No."

The old man drew himself up. "This threat poses the greatest danger this city, this country, has ever faced, My Lord. If he gains the living flesh of the aristocracy, no one in power is safe. I strongly advise that, for the good of the realm, substitute flesh be delivered so that the necromancer might destroy himself in the spellcasting."

His eyes narrow, the duc glared back at his physician. "And who do you suggest that this flesh be taken from?"

"That is for My Lord to decide."

"No, it isn't. You're my adviser. Advise me. Whose spirit would *you* damn for this deed?"

"A criminal from My Lord's prisons?"

The mage was shaking her head. "There isn't time, My Lord. Most spellcraft must be done with fresh components. I'd surmise Lord Sep . . . the necromancer plans to work his casting directly."

"Then what would *you* suggest?"

She raised her hands helplessly.

In the corner Coll continued to stare into the fire. The eyes of the dead priest stared unwaveringly back at him, demanding atonement, expecting action. He stepped forward before the thought of what he was offering to do caught up with him.

"I will volunteer my flesh, My Lord," he said quietly.

The duc turned to stare at him.

"You?"

"Yes, My Lord."

"Why?"

Coll could give him no rational answer, but the physician leaped at the offer.

"He's perfect, My Lord, a nobody. His flesh would ruin the spellcasting."

"All my subjects are somebody," the duc grated. "Do you know what you're offering? What it might do to your body, your spirit?"

"I know, My Lord, but we haven't much time. This will work. I know it will. To substitute my flesh for a nobleman's would completely throw the spell. It might even kill him."

"And it might kill you."

"If this doesn't work, My Lord, I'll wish I were dead."

"But you're expected to . . . make this delivery yourself arn't you?"

"Yes, sir."

"How can you possibly do both?" The duc swung his attention back to his physician. "Can you guarantee his safety?"

Coll answered for him. "No, My Lord, he can't."

The old man opened his mouth angrily, but, confident now, Coll cut him off. "I'm the only one here qualified to collect the item safely."

"You can hardly perform surgery on yourself," the duc pointed out.

"No, sir, but your mage can overlay my will onto your physician's. Using his hands, I can do the cutting."

"That's coercion," the mage replied stiffly.

The duc turned. "Can you do it?"

Glaring at the cutter, she shrugged. "I can, My Lord, but it's highly unethical."

"I have no intention of allowing my will to be suborned by a defiling little corpse-cutter!" the physician snapped.

"Yes, you will!" the duc flung back. "You argued for this form of attack. Very well, you've convinced me. And if this boy can offer such a sacrifice, then you can give him what assistance he requires. Is that quite clear?"

The old man wilted in the face of his lord's sudden rage. "Yes, sir," he said meekly.

"Do it."

* * *

Once begun, the spell took less than a heartbeat to cast. There was a sudden bout of vertigo, and Coll found himself looking down at his own body stretched out by the fire. He was as pale as a corpse, his thin chest barely rising, his dark eyes blank and staring. The mage pulled his shirt up to expose the flesh underneath, and Coll swallowed against a rising bout of nausea. He had only one chance. He knelt.

Years of practice made the first cut for him. The second was harder. There was a sharp pain, and Coll felt the physician echo his body's sudden jerk. He almost dropped the knife, but somehow he had the urn filled and the horrible wound stitched up before the repulsion spilled through his self-control. Snapped back into his body, he began to vomit. Beside him, the old physician collapsed.

Somehow, they got him cleaned up and on his feet by forcing a narcotic infusion down his throat. Then, reeling from the effects of the spell and the surgery, Coll staggered from the palace.

The return journey was a nightmare. His abdomen ached horribly, and the bitter taste of the infusion made him want to spew again, but he clamped his teeth shut against it. He had to make the delivery; after that, he could be as sick as he wanted.

The markers brought him into the palazzo, but instead of returning to the lord's study, they took him down a flight of stone steps. At the bottom was an open door. They entered.

The odor of stale magic and rotting flesh almost made him faint, but the sight of Lord Sepori, dressed in a stained robe and leather apron, stiffened him as no infusion could have.

The necromancer set a thin chopping knife onto the grooved table and frowned at the cutter, his red eyes dark.

"You're late," he said coldly, holding out one imperious hand.

Coll stilled the urge to bolt from the room.

"Forgive me, My Lord," he choked. Not daring to meet the man's eyes, he passed over the urn.

Sepori pulled the cork and pored the contents out on the table. Coll paled. Picking up the knife, the mage indicated the door.

"I will speak with you afterward. Wait in the upper hall."

Coll stumbled from the room.

The upper hall was dark and deserted, the crescent moon barely illuminating a foot of tiled floor. Several times Coll made to run, but each time he drew back. Where could he go? It was much too late to turn back now.

Suddenly a white-hot pain scored across his abdomen. He fell with a cry, striking his head against the floor. As wave after wave of pain doubled him over, he shrieked in agony. He was on fire from the inside, and he began to tear at the bandaged wound, desperate to wrench the terrible pain from his body. The dead priest appeared before him, a promise of relief, but as he reached out, it became the stitched and tattooed visage of the silent gardener. Coll screamed.

Hands gripped him, raised him into the air. He almost lost consciousness then but somehow remained aware as he was dragged from the room.

There was mage-fire everywhere. Coll's clothes began to smolder with a dull, blue smoke. He cried out as the flames lashed against him, and then he was outside, gulping in the cold night air. He saw figures fighting in the courtyard, saw the duc's mage send a bolt of azure fire toward him, and before he could cry out, his undead bearer was slammed away by the force of it. Coll crumpled to the ground. Dragging himself to a corner, he watched with staring eyes the taking of La Palazzo de Sulla.

By dawn it was almost over. As the new sun touched the walls, Coll felt a sudden rush of frigid air and knew Sepori was dead.

He began to cry.

Standing with his physician in the center of the courtyard, his face smeared with soot, the duc turned.

"Help him," he said wearily.

The man knelt and examined the wound. Coll shuddered. "It's as I feared, My Lord," he said with a shake of his head, "the spellcasting has injured him internally."

"Then heal it."

"I can't, sir. I'm not trained to combat necromantic spellcraft."

"Then who is?"

The physician shrugged. "A priest?"

"Get one."

"They will not tend to the dammed, My Lord . . ."

The duc rounded on him. "This boy saved my son's life tonight," he growled, "possibly the entire city. You've never given me such service; neither has the church. You will find him a priest."

The physician looked into the savage face of his lord and acquiesced.

The duc turned away and gestured for his guard captain.

"I want this craft wiped out," he said grimly. "When you're finished here, spread out across the city. Anyone suspected of practicing, supplying or supporting necromancy is to be immediately put to death. I don't care how you discover their identities, I just want it done. Understood?"

"Yes, My Lord."

The duc glanced down at the young cutter again. Coll was staring up at him, his expression dull.

"Take him up."

Two guardsmen moved to haul him to his feet.

"Gently, damn you! Take him to the palazzo. The priest can tend to him there."

"Yes, sir."

Lifting him carefully, the guards placed him on a piece of burned door. The duc turned away.

Across the courtyard those who'd survived the fire were being dragged out and put to the sword. Coll blinked as the limp body of the gardener was hauled from the wreckage. Finally free of Sepori's spellcraft, it had an air of peace that reached out and touched the ex-cutter gently. Coll suddenly felt very tired.

The guardsmen moved off. Coll's last sight before sleep claimed him was of the duc standing in the courtyard, watching the blue smoke rise above the necromancer's home. He closed his eyes, knowing that all the spirits which had hovered about his bedside were finally laid to rest and that two of them, a priest and a gardener, guarded his dreams.

SOLO

by Robert Greenberger

"**I**can't do it any more," he said by way of greeting.
Old Grimface Nelkin looked old and tired,
worn from the service he proudly provided the Galway family but also tired of life it seemed. The deep
lines on his face allowed the candlelight to draw shadows that masked much of his expression. The slate-gray hair was kept untied, against current fashion, fanning across his shoulders and looking in need of a
trim.

Knowing better, I merely took the chair nearest him
so I could catch the dry words in his usually hushed
tones. Nelkin once sounded powerful in this way but
that night he sounded very, very tired.

He drank from his flagon and studied the intricate
carving of a manticore on its face. I recognized the
flagon as one he was given by Dorn on the occasion
of some famous battle, one no one ever spoke of and
one I never dared ask about.

"Dorn wants another hit, and I know I am done.
It's time for youth. It's time for you to solo."

Me? This went against form, and I knew it. I fully
expected to work alongside him for a time, making
sure my skill and technique were just right. But to solo
after just one hit together boggled my mind, which,
according to some, was not so hard to do.

"Things are getting ugly, and Dorn wants them hit
where it will hurt deeply. Wives, sisters, foot soldiers,
they don't mean a thing to Mickanton. He's in love,
the fool, and Dorn knows it. Lacey she's called, short

for something I forget. She's his mistress, and that's the target. Dorn figures hitting her may make Mickanton sit up and realize that this thing has gotten out of hand. And then maybe he can have a sit down and settle this."

Nelkin studied his cup once more and then drank for a time. I sat, still silent but listening to my heart race. This was not just any assignment but an opportunity with a purpose and a chance to make my mark with Dorn. It was obviously time for Nelkin to retire gracefully to the background, provide house security of some sort or whatever they do with aging warlock assassins. I can't recall any ever getting to this stage, and I suspect Dorn doesn't know what to do with Nelkin either, and surely that is a problem for another time.

This, of course, brought me to Deep Pockets Glim's, the best-supplied Arts shop. With only two days and two nights to figure it all out, I think I know what I want to do. Of course I am inspired by Old Grimface's success and I want to honor his lessons, but not by the same complex magicks of red and white. I prefer the essence of the elements, letting earth, wind, sea, or fire aid my work. I feel the strongest bond with wind and set to work devising the right kind of spell to whack that woman silly or, better yet, dead.

"Oh, it's you," Deep Pockets Glim says by way of greeting. This is a sign he knows and respects you.

I nod my head in greeting and let my eyes scan the shelves, a treasure trove of pretty arcane stuff, seeking out the crystal boxes and quartz containers that hold my ingredients. Deep Pockets Glim never offers to help, always waiting for you to ask. His expertise is amazing, and he always leads you to exactly what you need, which can be very helpful unless there's a dispute as to what kind of ear you need or which kind of mineral works best. No one has ever seen Deep Pockets Glim perform a spell, but he knows of what he speaks and has earned Old Grimface's respect; therefore he has my own.

Strolling through the well-lit shop, I begin ticking off the makings of my spell. Actually, it's spells since I have a plan and plans can be very good if they do not become overly complicated. Nelkin taught me that by revealing to me the reports of those that preceded him and how they failed. Some were trying to be too fine, others too cute, and all failed because they got caught up in the spellmaking, which prevented the hit from getting done.

With each ingredient, Deep Pockets Glim organizes the items on a countertop behind the main table. He never guesses what you are trying to do, and he's never been suspected of tipping off one family that another might be casting after them, which is another reason people continue to frequent his establishment. The first reason remains his inexhaustible supplies and keen knowledge of where to find the best of any ingredient the books may call for, although you can't find the books in his store since he feels you should know what you're doing before you buy the best. His thoughts are good ones, and I admire a man with high standards such as he holds.

My order complete, Deep Pockets Glim turns his back to me and begins measuring things out and fills my leather satchel with the finished items, which he has artfully wrapped in soft parchment or sealed within small glass bottles. This makes me think that now that I am a solo, I will need to buy my own crystal and quartz holdings so I could build a small inventory of those things which will not spoil with age.

He rattles off a price and I know not to even try to haggle, since Deep Pockets Glim has been known to throw such customers out of his shop.

We nod one final time and I am quickly out of his shop and am hurrying back to the center of the End, where I hope Salia the Dancer is still loitering. I think it might be nice to buy her a drink or two and talk

the night away. This may be nerves talking, but I cannot begin to mix my spells until the morning, and then
the stalking doesn't begin until after the noon meal
and, as everyone knows, Salia may not be able to
dance, but she has legs that are lovely to look upon.

My spells mixed and complete, I speak with Slither
York, Dorn's best snitch, and he tells me that Lacey
has not been seen on this sunny day. But, he tells me,
she is known to watch the small animals that scramble
for crumbs in the park that surrounds the Castle.
Slither York is a tall, thin man with a long nose and
a nasty profile, and he has been with the family for
thirty-five summers. We have not had much to do with
one another, but his word is law, and he has always
been good at knowing who has been found in foreign
beds or which family might be trying a new angle or
which four-footed beast might win in the evening race.
We chat about the weather, and he tells me which
carved wooden bench is her favorite. He wishes me
luck and then slides into an alcove, seeking out some
other nugget of information.

The walk to the park is not an unpleasant one although it is far from the Galway Keep. Since my
nerves have been getting the better of me, I figure the
walk will do me some good, especially since it lets me
remain solitary, away from those wishing me luck or
offering advice. I avoid both Dorn and Nelkin this
day, and they wisely have not sought me out. Nelkin
shows me respect with this action and for Dorn, this
is in keeping with his style of leadership.

At the edge of the park I slow my pace, ignoring
the chafing of my thick wool tunic as it rubs along the
sweat and ointments on my chest. The park is a circu-
lar affair with several entrances and pathways where
children, lovers, animals, and peddlers mix. Older folk
sit at ancient oak tables and play Spades & Angels,
moving their pieces back and forth, letting the shadows battle against one another. This being another

sunny and unreasonably warm day, there are a fair number of people out and about, which only helps me since I can spy my prey before I myself am spotted.

On the one hand, I am pleased that I see no one I know since I do not wish for the distraction; on the other hand, I wonder where all my acquaintances might be since this is the kind of place where they congregate to discuss the issues of the day, hoping to spy the young and pretties sunning themselves.

Walking about, I find a peddler selling small squirt tubes filled with sweetly spiced water. Feeling the thirst upon me, I buy one and wet my lips as I seek the woman. Lacey has been described well enough to me that I should know her upon sight. She has been said to be a tall woman, maybe even taller than Old Grimface himself . . . and yet she is not supposed to be gangly but full limned with her face framed with a cascade of crimson curls that end somewhere down her back. While many admire her limbs and others find her hair and face more than fair, it is said by those in the know that it is her eyes that have made her the most desired woman west of the Castle. The eyes have been said to cut through to your heart or could bring merriment or maybe even wake you from slumber with their intensity. Having never seen her myself, I can only imagine how Lacey's eyes will affect me.

Almost done with my drink, I have circled maybe a third of the park but have not begun to despair that Slither York may be wrong since I have never known his information to lead Nelkin astray.

Lacey is seated on the described wooden bench, with its high sides and carved images of clouds and sun, one hand low to the ground with crumbs of some kind in the palm. No animals are about to take advantage of the morsels, but the hand remains in place, perhaps trying to coax some shy animal out of the shrubbery. I let my eyes slowly follow the hand up the bare arm, and there are the first curls of that bright hair. She is in profile to me, and I can see only a finely featured half of her head.

It is indeed fair to look upon.

I strain to see what color the famed eye may be since Slither York has never mentioned that one fact. It seems to be of a copper color, which works to provide depth to the face.

And then, her senses working better than my stealth, she swivels her head and her full gaze is on me.

The copper eyes are full of light and life and something else, something mysterious that I cannot describe, perhaps because of my relative inexperience with women of this sort. Still, the stare has me standing stock-still and stupidly staring at her. My pretense is gone, and even though there remain yards between us, there is a connection, eye to eye, and I find this most unusual. The hand drops the crumbs, and a long finger wiggles in my direction, inviting me to come to the bench.

I try to remember if Nelkin ever taught me about such a direct approach, but my mind fails to find the memory or the lesson, so maybe it was a topic never covered. Maybe he did not care for the method, or perhaps this was something missing from his own experience. Regardless, I realize I am entirely on my own and must trust in my lessons and meager experience. With a few strides, I am at her side and she smiles for the first time, a wide, full-lipped smile that conveys warmth. Women have not found me hard to look at, but she seems to find me fascinating as I find her, and this confuses me for a moment.

Once at her side, I steal a moment to glance at her attire, which is of a deep ocher with chocolate-brown accents and designs. The designs are familiar, and later I will realize they are symbolic of the Mulvey family. But now I barely note them beyond their color and return my attention to her face. We are comfortably close but not yet touching, which is the way things should be upon a first meeting, even more important considering she's my target.

Yet, I cannot help but want to be closer and want to touch her with my hands. Her eyes continue to study me, showing little emotion beyond maybe some curiosity. Her lips part, and finally she speaks, her voice soft and pleasant, with a trace of accent I cannot place. "You study me. Why?"

"I was studying all of nature," I begin to reply. My throat, recently wet from the sweetly spiced water, is now dry and uncomfortable. Sweat continues to form, but sweat not from the sun. She is another man's woman, and she is the one I was asked to whack, so none of this makes any sense to me. Old Grimface taught me this much. "Never, never get too close to your victim," he warned me the first week I was apprenticed to him. It was advice repeated weekly ever since, so why am I suddenly a few finger-widths away from her?

"You're too kind," Lacey said. She seemed perfectly comfortable with me, not moving or inviting me closer to her. "What brings you to the park?"

"A day at liberty, and what better way to enjoy it than to be out here and search for my acquaintances so we may congregate to discuss the issues of the day, hoping to spy the young and pretties sunning themselves."

She laughed at that, and the sound was most pleasant. "So you were spying upon me, eh?"

That's not what I meant, and I felt my cheeks get hot at her teasing. Now I don't mind a little flush when bantering with a woman, but this felt all too different. "I guess I was at that," I say just to keep the conversation going. "Do you mind?"

Lacey shakes her head no and smiles once again. The warmth fades from my cheeks, and I try to think of the best way to get her away from the public so I may complete my job. While talking with Lacey was not part of my plan, it can only hasten me to its conclusion. "May I buy you a drink on such a warm day?" I figure at least we can get moving so eventually I may get her alone, or at least away from all these innocent eyes.

"You may at that," Lacey replies.

I realize we haven't even exchanged names, and maybe that's how she wants it. After all, she's involved with someone. I might be too for all she knows although I suspect she would not care. This way, there's less to be dishonest about, and that's just fine with me. In a languid motion, she rises from the deep bench, her skirt flowing around her sandled ankles and her hands smoothing out the wrinkles.

"I know a smart inn nearby where we can get a fine ale and the conversation is always sparkling," I suggest.

Again a shake of the head, and the loose curls bob up and down despite the bulk of the curls bound by coral combs. Her eyes once again tighten their gaze, and I feel entirely wrapped up by them, held by something strong and invisible, and it is not too unpleasant. "My apartments are nearby, and I have something a little more exotic for you than Inn fare. You do strike me as the kind of man who likes to try new things." Her smile says more than her words, and I can feel a tension in the pit of my stomach that was not there a moment ago. How she can have this affect on me has me baffled, but I pay it no mind since her apartment is a fine place in which to perform my task. Best of all, if no one sees me enter, then no one will know who took out Mickanton's mistress but only that the deed was done.

"I find that an entirely agreeable suggestion," I say.

"Of course you do," she says and begins to walk. I stay a mere half step behind her, walking as comfortably as I can. Together we look at the trees and their protective shade, or the children playing hop and skittles, or even other couples strolling hand in hand. For all they know, we could be newfound friends or re-

united relatives or even people tossing back and forth
the subjects of the day. Instead, we speak of nothing,
and I am not at all bothered by this.

As it turns out, her apartments are over a small row
of stores just a few minutes from a park entrance, and
it is with no surprise that I see we are now west of
the Castle. There's little doubt the current tensions
between the Mulveys and the Galways will pass, they
always do, and things will settle back into their routines. I find myself privately thrilled at the prospect
that I will actually play a significant role in the current
turn of events.

The apartments are spacious without seeming too
large for just one woman (and probably Mickanton,
but I'm not supposed to know about him being here),
and they show a taste for art from the lands of Sarony.
I do not know the style very well, but I have heard
tell their tools for making art are much desired. She
has perhaps too many pillows on her chairs, but she
also seems like a woman used to being comfortable
wherever she chooses to sit.

Right now, she is standing against a broad cherry
wood case, swinging open a door which reveals short
glasses on the left and tall, thin bottles on the right.
The bottles are identical and only the labels, in some
simple script, differentiate one from another. With little more than a glance, Lacey selects the third outer-
most bottle and sets it atop the case. The liquid within
is pale and pink, and she fills the glasses only a third
of the way.

I gently place my leather satchel by my side, keeping the top slightly open. I also realize that I should
not drink too much from this glass since she only fills
it a third of the way, which is a sure sign of the liquid's
potency. It would not do for me to miss my first hit
because I was less than sober.

Lacey walks over with the glasses and hands me
one, keeping the other in her right hand and studying
its contents. The liquid is clear, without sediment of

any kind, and it has no immediate aroma. Satisfied that it is of the right consistency, she raises the glass in my general direction, and once again I feel this unmistakable attraction toward her.

"You are not often with women like me, are you?"

Now I smile and hold the cool glass in my own right hand. "None who has ever invited me back to their home within minutes of meeting me."

"Ah, that is because I can tell you are very attracted to me."

"Of that, there is no doubt," I admit. "After all, you are very attractive, and a man would be blind not to notice."

"Yes, there is that, but I could feel we have something more in common. I can sense that you weave magic, and I wanted to talk to you about that alone."

My eyes must have gone wider than I felt them since she reacted with a small laugh. Lacey sipped from her glass and waved a firm arm toward twin chairs set facing out a large window that stretched nearly from floor to ceiling. This allowed most of the natural light to seep into the room and give it warmth.

"Don't be so surprised," she said gently. "We witches are supposed to be the more sensitive of the two, and I could feel the magic about you once you walked into the park. It was just a matter of time before you found me—or I you."

I sat beside her and allowed myself a glance out the window, noting that the countryside on the west side of the city was quite lovely what with the squatters and peddlers in other parts of the City. Things were well maintained and very, very quiet, which made me wonder how Mickanton ran things. I did notice that I had trouble taking my gaze away from the window and that I was having a little trouble staying focused. All this without having taken a sip from her fine stock.

"I must admit that while I have made many an acquaintance with a lady, I have never done so with a witch." I fiddle with the glass but manage to avoid drinking from it, mostly out of fear. Already, I could feel a heaviness at my feet. There was definitely a spell having its way upon my body.

Her eyes twinkled for a moment and their hold on me lessened. "Oh, I suspect you have had your share of ladies, but yes, we witches do not circulate much. Tell me, what kind of rank do you hold?"

"Third Star, Purple Circle," was my honest reply. Why lie when I wager she can sense just how much power I can wield. This is, after all, a witch who detected me entering the park from the north end. Maybe talking would slow down events, giving me a chance to figure out what was what with the magic being played upon me.

"Quite a rank for one of your youth. Now tell me," and with this she leaned close enough so that her bare left forearm touched mine. "What do you do with this power?"

"I am still studying," I say although the reply is not entirely true, and I wonder if she can sense that too. I begin to think that maybe I will find myself in over my head if I do not act soon and whack this Lacey. Too slowly, I begin to recall my spells, shaping syllables and images in my mind.

"Trying for the Sixth Star no doubt," she says with good humor. "And you may get there and then again, you may find yourself bested. After all, what good is magic if you cannot test yourself against those of your kind?"

"I have been tested, time and again," I tell her, which is true considering the number of bouts I have endured with Old Grimface, just to get from White Circle to Blue. "I have done well enough to earn my rank and not just with the books."

"Don't think too little of the books," she says, and now her other arm rests against mine. The warmth at the contact points has raised the hairs on my forearms, and I know there's ample magic in the air. This means I have to act and act somehow quickly before she makes me do things I might like but are certainly not what I came here to do.

"Whatever you want of me will not do you any good," she says after several long moments of silence. Lacey laughs again and this time there's an edge in the tone. "You want me and for some reason. Maybe to score with the Mick's woman, maybe to kidnap me and cause the Mick pain. Maybe, maybe, maybe but those maybes won't add up to a thing."

"You had no choice but to get close to me. You see, young swain, whenever I go out from these rooms, I always surround myself with a glamour spell." She pauses to see if I know what she means although such attraction spells are not taught until one reaches the Magenta Circle.

"You intend me harm, as other warlocks have in the past," Lacey says with a hint of anger in her tone. "I could not allow you to threaten me so I used the glamour spell to thwart your warlock's skills, bringing you close to me so my other spells could inhibit your skills."

And that explains the way I feel. Even though I now know this, I haven't the experience or training to ward off such an enchantment. Some debut this is turning out to be. Well, I had little choice but to act, and it meant completing my incantation.

I force out the last syllable of my spell, one that should have been completed much, much sooner, and watch as the container within my leather satchel shatters with the cracking sound of glass. Four balls of white hot light spring upward and then curve directly toward her, gathering the speed of a gale wind. They are small but deadly and should pierce her skin in a few seconds.

"*Qaliban thalos,*" she says quickly, and her body is sheathed in greenish magic. Without moving a muscle Lacey anticipates the impact, and I watch in amazement as the lightknives strike her aura of protection and break apart with a soft tinkling sound not unlike wind chimes. I hate wind chimes.

"You foolish assassin," Lacey says, anger definitely in her voice. "That is what you are, isn't it? A solo warlock, from Dorn no doubt. Right?"

"I cannot deny this information as it is true," I say.

Lavender dots of light form on her fingernails, slowly growing in intensity and size, as she once again summons her own magic, no doubt switching from something defensive to something truly offensive. I calculate that I have maybe a minute before there's enough power to unleash in my direction even though I have no clue as to how powerful she is.

"You don't understand, do you?" Lacey asks me. "You had no choice but to come to me. No choice but to fall under this spell I use to keep people like you at bay. It always works on the unwary, and you, young swain, are an inexperienced little boy who should never have been sent out after me."

Something within me snaps, and the sluggishness instantly fades away. I study her eyes and see no warmth or humor anymore. They are deep and fathomless, with malice hiding behind the copper hue. The lavender intensifies, and I may have twenty seconds left.

Everything is suddenly in a rush as I feel my pulse begin to pound and the words swimming through my mind. "*Volthoom,*" I say.

A force of ruby red energy leaps from my chest, its state of readiness having been concealed under my heavy tunic. The unleashed magic shatters her shield first and strikes just above and below the heart. Upon contact with skin and bone, my spell immediately fades, and I note the coruscating energy on her hands has dissipated as well.

"How," is all she manages to ask, recognizing she can now measure the remainder of her life in seconds.

I smile once more, a cold, calculating smile that hopefully shows some maturity mixed with my youth.

"I wouldn't be a very good solo if I didn't come prepared for my first hit to go uneasily. So I prepared two spells, either to make my mark in the world. The first was my preferred one—my lightknives—but you stopped me thanks to your glamour spell which dulled my reflexes. But I knew to seek you out with something ready in case of emergency, and I had Corbal's Lightning ready for a final gambit."

"Of course," she coughed, blood trickling down her chin and from the wounds to her chest.

"I could act more quickly once you tipped me off that I was in thrall to the glamour spell. By explaining yourself, I became wary, weakening your hold on me. I was made free, and I could act as I was trained."

The copper eyes, the ones I could have looked into for years on end, began to lose their light. The blackness behind them, the confidence they once held, was gone.

My first hit as a solo. Couldn't have done it without Old Grimface's first piece of advice: "Always have a spell up your sleeve." Or on your chest, which now itched something fierce.

Walking out of her apartments, our duel having attracted no one's attention, I wonder where Salia the Dancer might be right about now and whether or not she cared to take a walk in the park while the warm sun still shone and talk about the current affairs of our fine City.

CYCLE OF HORROR

by Mickey Zucker Reichert

A gooseneck lamp shed a glaze across Don
DelVeccio's desktop, and neat stacks of paper
glowed like ghosts in the meager light. A plume of
smoke wafted from the cigar between his fingers, adding grayness to an already dingy room. Across from
his boss, Kenneth Carney schooled his features to
aloof disinterest and sprawled casually across a black
leather chair.

DelVeccio leaned forward, bringing his jowly features and gray-splashed mustache into the light. He
went straight to the point. "They iced the Goblin."

Rage flashed through Carney, suppressed by years
of habit. The Goblin had joined "the family" more
because he fit in nowhere else than because of any
tendency toward crime. His short stature, bull face,
and missing neck had earned his nickname and caused
people to shy from him, but he had done little more
than serve as boxer or getaway-man for the "stop-at-
nothing" criminals, the S.A.N., like Carney. What the
Goblin had lacked in looks, he made up for in
personality.

Carney managed to keep his expression blank,
though his fingers winched to white-knuckled fists.
"Why?"

DelVeccio's only answer was a drab puff of smoke.

"Who?" Carney asked the next obvious question
and, this time, received a reply.

"One of Alano's boys."

The room blurred. Carney glanced at DelVeccio, at

the small dark eyes and the salt and pepper tufts above each ear. The familiar, coarse features seemed smeared, and Carney realized tears had filled his own eyes. He would miss the Goblin, and not only because he had been the only other Irishman in DelVeccio's gang. For years, Carney had found a willing and trustworthy ear, a man with whom he could share insecurities that the need for professionalism and apparent ruthlessness forced him to hide from everyone else. Only the Goblin understood the seemingly sourceless emptiness that had driven Carney from an upscale New York neighborhood to a life in Philadelphia's mob. He would never have dared tell another of his belief in reincarnation: his certainty that he had killed in previous personae that made his job so much simpler and his theory that some tragedy in a previous life left him forever frustratingly unfulfilled.

DelVeccio continued to study Carney. He sucked in a draft of the cigar and loosed it through his nostrils, looking for all the world like a dragon poised to attack. "I thought you'd want to be the one to . . . clip him."

Carney closed his eyes, gaining control as much from habit as intention, hoping his boss had not seen the tears. "He got a name?"

"Alberto Pizarro." The corners of DelVeccio's lips twitched, the closest he ever came to a smile. "But I meant Alano."

Catching himself staring with disbelief, Carney pursed his broad mouth, seeking to twist the unintended expression into a mask of impassive defiance. "You found an opening?"

"Salvy found an opening." DelVeccio balanced the cigar on an ashtray. "Meet him at the one-arm joint in a three count."

Three hours. Carney nodded. He wanted to handle the rival leader immediately, to expend his rage in a savage assault with a blunted ax; but he appreciated the time to gain his composure. Years of warfare, cen-

turies if he believed the snatches of others' memory
that sometimes assailed him, had taught him patience.
"I'll be there," he promised.

Six hours later, Kenneth Carney lay flattened on the
rooftop of Don Alano's favorite restaurant. Lights
from nearby businesses strobed blue and amber high-
lights through short black locks otherwise hidden by
moonless darkness. Cars wound through the streets
two stories below him, an angry horn occasionally
blaring over the patter of nightlife footsteps. According to Salvy, Alano would not arrive for at least
another hour, but Carney wanted to assure his position, his privacy, and his escape. Those things attended
to, he found himself craving the solace of his own
thoughts, seeking the origin of a cold, empty dread he
could not vanquish. Over ten years, the slow cadence
of anticipation that always preceded a hit had become
a welcome friend. Now that professional calm eluded
him. His soul ached within him, and he suffered an
eerie certainty that, whether or not he handled Alano,
the Goblin's death would herald many more.

An icy breeze wafted over Carney, ruffling his hair.
Sorrow caught him again, a dense tidal wave that
crumbled composure. He bit back a howl of outrage
with effort, but a sob still escaped him. He had not
realized how much his companion had meant to him,
would not have believed himself capable of such caring. Then a vague familiarity joined his anguish, as if
he had lived this moment a thousand times. His
thoughts seemed muted, overrun by something nameless; and he knew better than to attempt a hit in his
current state. Seeking the familiar, he closed his grip
around the butt of his suppressed 9 mm and sucked
in a deep breath of sulfur-tinged city air.

Gradually, Carney's mental haze cleared, admitting
strangers' thoughts that crowded upon him like nightmares. These were not wholly new, the recollections
of warriors whose lives he had previously embraced

as his own: a veteran of World War I; a survivor of the American Revolution, on Britain's side; a private with the Wild Geese, battling his way across Europe. In despair, he let their remembrances wash against him, recalling their names and shapes as his own the same way other men revived images of boyhood dreams. Losing the fight for composure, he allowed their thoughts to war within him, finally surrendering to Bradach O'Grada, a Gaelic renegade whose mindset took hold and demonstrated, in riotous detail, the cause of his unreasoning discomfort.

Lithe as a wolf yet heavily muscled and deep chested, Bradach O'Grada embodied a deadly combination of strength and agility. Dark-skinned, darker-haired and -eyed, he crouched on the sheer cliffs of Britain watching the smoke of a camp below curl lazily toward the horizon. He recognized the strangers as Saxons, on their own land and no threat to him.

Footsteps at Bradach's back tightened his fingers around the haft of his ax. He whirled to find Edwin running toward him, a Saxon fisherman who had taken a liking to Bradach as he passed through the last village. Loosening his grip on his weapon, the Gael nodded acknowledgment.

Panting, Edwin drew up beside Bradach. Each word seemed a great effort, "Vikings . . . attacked . . . the lower villages. Sorry, Bradach. Maolmin . . . was killed . . ."

Stunned to silence, Bradach could only stare. Carney recognized the same desperate dread that assailed him now. A friend like Maolmin, like the Goblin, came only once in a lifetime; but, oddly, it seemed he had lost his confidante a hundred times as a hundred different people in a hundred lives. Each time, that death foretold another tragedy, the nature of which neither Carney nor Bradach could remember.

*   *   *

Shock dragged him back to his other persona, a hitman dizzied by the same nameless, sickening horror that seized his previous incarnation. Many times before, Carney had become fully enmeshed with a past life, making it seem definitively and utterly real. Suddenly, he realized he had never envisioned the death of any of those who had used his soul before him. Though he had relived wars, battles, and skirmishes, his recollections always ended abruptly, long before each met his demise, his thoughts cut short by a mental barrier he could never seem to breach. *And this episode with Bradach had transcended that boundary.* Carney became abruptly certain that the source of his haunting emptiness, the reason why he had chosen a life of savagery over a steady accounting position like his father, lay with the event that repeatedly sundered his bonds with the past.

Carney gritted his teeth, weak with the frustration of coming so close to understanding and losing contact without an answer. He knew Bradach waited in his mind, at the exact same stage in his life. This time, he surrendered his thoughts to the Gael with eager violence.

Carney felt the change at once. Hatred warmed him like strong ale. Fury bucked against his control. He saw Vikings as children of the dragons that cursed their ships' prows, soulless demons who feasted upon the deaths of innocents. His hunger for blood grew as strong as those he condemned. "Edwin, in what direction did the Vikings flee?"

Nervously, the fisherman shifted from foot to foot. "Toward the lowlands and the walled city of Hengstby." He locked a steady gaze on the unadorned shield strapped to Bradach's left arm.

Bradach frowned. He held no love for Saxons, but the common enemy they shared might bring them together in the cause of war. He jammed his ax handle into the belt of his mail, adjusted his helmet, and started purposefully down the trail.

Edwin stumbled after Bradach. "Where are you going?"

"To Hengstby," Bradach replied with a growl. "Northern blood begs spilling."

The woods thickened on Britain's lowlands. Stands of pine broke to great forests of oak; and, where golden blades of sunlight penetrated their branches, the weeds grew knee-high. The Vikings left an easily followed trail of trampled foliage and wolf howls. Each time they gave tongue, war passion whipped Bradach to a frenzy he could scarcely contain. He beseeched the gods for stragglers to sate his ax; but, when he arrived at the city, he had taken no Viking lives.

Hengstby's stone walls rose to twice a man's height. Armored Saxon warriors perched atop the battlements, their bows empty despite full quivers and the mad press of Norsemen who frothed and bellowed beneath them. The Vikings crashed blindly against the wall, too engrossed to notice Bradach among the trees. Curious about the inactivity of the Saxons, he curbed an instinctive headlong rush at the blond reavers who had slain Maolmin.

At length, an escort of Saxons ushered a woman to their guard tower. Hair of burnished copper fell in ringlets to her slim shoulders and framed small but well-shaped breasts. Though too far away to study her face, Bradach knew it from primal memory: eyes gray and mystic as the heavens; round, well-set cheekbones; and a wide mouth clamped tight in sorrow. He had never heard her name nor seen her in this life, but he knew her. She was the woman of his dreams, the one who could fulfill his destiny through centuries. Spellbound, he watched, panting with eagerness, as she raised her arms in parley.

The Norsemen fell silent as she spoke, to Bradach's surprise. She used their language, and the nasal syllables belled from her tongue with unexpected beauty. "What do you wish of us, Vikings?"

A vulgar clamor rose from the offenders. Bradach would have leaped upon the entire press had the woman commanded it; but she waited, behind soldiers with drawn bows, for an intelligible reply.

On the ground, chaos gave way to order. One Viking stepped forward. Even from a distance, Bradach recognized him. His men called him Ragnar Battle Boar because he entered warfare in a rush of flailing steel and trampled dying foes beneath his feet. Bradach knew his face well; some of his scars were by the Gael's own hand.

"We want blood!" screamed Ragnar, and his voice maddened Bradach to murder. "Targets for our swords and death screams! We want gold and glitter and glory!"

Another Viking continued in the ringing wake of Ragnar's challenge. "And we'll have wenches like you to struggle and moan beneath us!"

Caution lost to anger, Bradach sprang from the brush with a roar. But his war cry died beneath the raucous din of laughter, and the woman's reply stopped him cold.

"Away!" She waved her hand as if to expel a bothersome insect. "You'll find no gold, no gems, no wine. We sent all our treasures away when warned of your attack. As for women, you'll find only myself; and I'd leap from this tower before I'd let any of your wolves take me!"

The Norse ranks erupted in riot. The Saxons hustled their woman from the ramparts. The archers nocked arrows and drew bowstrings taut. Ragnar hurled commands that his followers ignored until the Saxons' feathered shafts took down half a dozen. Then, reluctantly, the Vikings rallied around their leader. At his word, they marched into the forest to camp and prepare for battle.

Emotions warred within Bradach: outrage, desire,

hatred elemental as a summer gale. The hours dragged past while he struggled with his passions. His love for this woman he had never met was at least as strong as his hunger for vengeance.

Bradach forced his thoughts to other matters, but they returned to pain him until the sun sank into the blood-red expanse of sky. He knew the Norsemen would fall upon any Saxon troops that came to Hengstby as reinforcements and slay anyone who fled the walled city, but he hoped one swarthy Gael could pass unnoticed through the evening's gloom. He sneaked quietly toward the gates, nearly reaching them before a guttural cry sounded behind him. He whirled to face a Viking scout party and their six drawn swords.

Bradach laughed with savage joy. Wielding shield and ax, he leaped upon them with the fury of a starved beast. Steel flashed and whirred around him. Two swords crashed against his shield. One stuck fast, and his ax severed its wielder's neck. Then a blade clattered harmlessly from his armor.

Viking howls broke around Bradach. He blocked and swung like a mad thing, his ax all but invisible in the gathering darkness. He struck for a pale face. Steel cleaved helmet and head. The spilled red gore filled Bradach with a fierce pride that fueled his rage.

A sword thudded against Bradach, staggering him. He threw out an arm for balance, blundered into an opponent, and took the other down with him. Instinctively, he raised his shield. The motion saved his life. A blow strong enough to brain him dashed the shield against his helm. The Viking cursed as his sword shattered, then screamed as an arrow pierced his armor like cloth.

Bradach lost his ax in the fall. The Viking on the ground with him had dropped his sword as well, and they discovered it simultaneously. The Gael reached it first, but his hand closed over the blade. He withdrew, and both sprang for the hilt. Arrows from the city felled the two remaining Norsemen, silhouetted by torchlight.

The Saxons held their fire as Bradach grappled the last of his opponents. He locked a hand on the sword grip and thrust the other for the Viking's throat. Bradach's attack fell short; his fingers tangled in his foeman's beard. The Norseman locked both hands on the hilt and sprang back with a desperate strength that broke Bradach's hold but caused himself great pain.

Both men gained their feet. The Viking clutched the sword. Bradach grabbed for the dagger at his belt and raised his shield. The Norseman rushed Bradach. The Gael shifted weight to dodge, but the Viking fell at his feet with a shaft in his back. Grateful for the archer's aim, Bradach cast about in the grasses until he recovered his ax.

"Quickly!" A guard at the Hengstby wall gestured. Bradach ran to him. Four warriors held the gates wide while he passed through, then slammed the doors behind him.

Bradach nodded his thanks to two Saxons who blinded him with lanterns as they examined him. They exchanged knowing glances, which he took to mean they recognized his features. An outlaw by betrayal but still fiercely loyal to his tribe, he had earned a reputation as a Viking slayer in the skirmishes across Ireland. "Well fought, Gael," said one.

Bradach studied the damage to his shield; new battle scars striped the hide-covered wood. "Less so if not for your archers. I thank you."

"Any Viking enemy is a Saxon friend," the same man replied. "But what brings you to a town under attack?"

His words reawakened Bradach's purpose. Yearning sparked within him. "The chance to smash Viking skulls first. But no man could keep me from the woman I saw in your tower. Who is she, and where must I go to meet her?"

The Saxons exchanged glances and frowns, which

tried Bradach's patience. He could not explain the wild intensity of his love for a woman he had never met, but he could not suppress it. Neither a shipload of Danes nor one Saxon city could hold him from her. He would gladly cut down all the warriors in front of him to find the stranger he desired. Bradach understood, without right to question, that he could never continue his life without her.

The larger of the Saxons spoke. "Lurlei is our priestess and the only one who speaks the nuances as well as the words of the Vikings' language. She's our luck, chosen by the gods to inspire men to victory."

Bradach drew himself to his full six feet and twisted his features to a purposeful glare. "I must see her. Any man who stands in my way will know my wrath!"

The Saxon stepped behind his companion before answering the challenge, Bradach noted with some satisfaction. "Have you forgotten we fight a common enemy or that you stand among an army of our people? You shall see her, but not until she awakens come morning."

Masses of Saxons turned scolding eyes upon Bradach, who regretted his boldness. "Very well. The Vikings *will* attack. They worship slaughter more than gold. And I will aid your village as I would my own."

The man who first addressed Bradach strode forward. "I am Dunwolfe. I will take you to quarters where you can sleep. Follow me."

Bradach trailed Dunwolfe through the half-lighted gloom of cottages to a large stone building in the center of town. Nearby, sheep and pigs huddled in a paddock, food for the soldiers in the event of a siege. Dunwolfe led the Gael to a wide doorway in the central dwelling; and, after a brief exchange with the sentries, they entered.

Gael and Saxon trod the length of a corridor, plain except for a gaily carved walnut door that stood apart from its simpler oak neighbors. To further distinguish it, a pair of burly, gold-bearded Saxons stood guard

on either side. Bradach knew Lurlei slept beyond that
gilded portal, but he heeded the warning glower of his
companion and cast it only a passing glance. Dunwolfe
had promised a meeting in the morning. No man or
god could stand against Bradach should the Saxon
break that oath.

They continued walking to a narrow, stone-cut stair-
way at the end of the hall, then climbed to a short
corridor with only two doors, both open. Dunwolfe
passed by the first, a rough-hewn, empty chamber with
a domed window overlooking the city. He gestured at
the second room. It was square and small. Its win-
dowless, lightless interior seemed black as night, and
Bradach examined it with the help of Dunwolfe's lantern. It contained only an unsteady, wooden table and
a pallet of straw.

Dunwolfe drew a taper from his pocket and lit it
from the lantern. Stepping into the room, he let wax
drip to the tabletop and secured the candle on this
base. It held darkness at bay in a wide semicircle,
and the cheery dance of its flame made the remaining
shadows seem as grim as Bradach's thoughts.

"Rest," Dunwolfe said. "You'll need your wits
when the battle begins." He turned and strode to the
hallway. The door banged shut behind him.

Still fully armored, Bradach lay on the straw. His
lids felt heavy with fatigue, but excitement wrested
sleep from him. He rose and paced, without conscious
direction. He caught himself with a hand around the
door ring, preparing to break whatever trust the Saxons held for him. He forced himself back to the pallet
and squeezed his eyes shut. Somehow, sleep came to
relieve Bradach of his troubles.

Bradach awoke with a sudden rush of awareness.
Many hours had passed; the candle had melted to the
table. Alerted by an indescribable feeling of menace,
he snatched up shield and ax, groping through darkness to the door. When he threw it open, screams and

clashing steel assailed his ears; and he realized the thickness of the chamber walls had isolated him from the din of battle. He raced into the next room and stared through the window at the red carnage below.

Urgency thrilled through Bradach. Calling curses upon the Vikings, he sprang for the hall. A Norseman on the stair fell dead from his blade before he saw Bradach. The Gael swept down the steps and burst into a corridor littered with corpses. His mind was a dark fog of rage. He cut past Vikings like weeds, blundered around a hard-driven blow that his armor fended, and dashed aside gaping Saxons.

Bradach never recalled breaking through the walnut door, yet suddenly Lurlei stood in front of him, more beautiful even than he had imagined. At first, she shrank from him, and the lace of her dress swirled like sea foam around her ankles. Then her eyes went soft and starry with recognition. Her lips parted to reveal teeth brighter than the pearls at her throat. Abruptly, her gaze locked beyond Bradach, her hand shot up, and she screamed in terror.

Bradach whirled, and a broad sword crashed against his shield. He returned an upstroke that deflected from a shield edge. As he redirected the strike, he recognized his opponent as Ragnar. The cold scorn in the Viking leader's eyes revealed that he had recognized Bradach as well. Ragnar's sword swept for Bradach's arm. Bradach closed in and caught the stroke. Infighting rendered Ragnar's longer weapon useless. With a roar, he shoved the Gael back with sword and shield.

Bradach had forgotten the Viking's damnable strength. He would win this contest with guile or not at all.

The warriors sprang together in a frenzied hurricane of battle. As they hammered their weapons against armor and shield, Bradach lost ground to Ragnar's powerful strokes. Without warning, the Gael's shield strap snapped. Ragnar's blow dashed it to the floor. His sword blazed for Bradach's neck. With a desperate surge, Bradach caught the blade on his ax. Then the Viking slammed his shield against Bradach's ribs with a strength that stole his breath and drove him to his knees.

As Bradach fell, he noted Ragnar's confident grin of triumph. The attack did throw off Bradach's balance, but he overplayed Ragnar's advantage with a seemingly helpless stagger. Ragnar lunged for a death stroke, and Bradach's ax leaped upward to meet him.

"No!" screamed Lurlei. She hurled herself in front of Bradach like a sacrifice.

Too late, Bradach tried to pull his blow. His ax bit into her chest, and Ragnar's sword cut off her dying shriek.

It came to Bradach in a rush. He had killed her before. Countless times, in countless personae, he had met the woman who could fill all the desolate longings of his mind and soul. Each time, he took her life before they could unite. The pattern would endure through eternity, his soul pursuing hers, a continuum of failure. Grief dissolved to terror, then outrage filled him like a tide.

Lurlei's body pinned Bradach's ax. The sword sang for his head. He caught Ragnar's wrist, dodged his strike, and buried his fist in the Viking's face. Ragnar dropped, mouth twisted in pain and shock. Bradach seized Ragnar's sword and, with inspired strength, shattered his skull.

Kenneth Carney jolted back to reality on a restaurant rooftop. His heart pounded a furious cadence, and his fists clenched so tightly his nails left bloody arcs across his palms. He knew what fate held for him. It would all begin with the Goblin's death.

Memories swooped upon Carney again, this time of his own life and the private conversations with his friend. The Goblin was the only one with whom he could share the madness of past life memories and not worry about judgment. The Goblin had listened always without criticism, had understood the grim and terrible hole in Carney's soul that drove him to his current occupation. Each successive life became more desperate, and he more horrible. The Goblin, Carney realized, was Maolmin—and hundreds of other companions through millennia—with his own cycles and demons to suffer. Though malformed and sickly most of his days, the Goblin had maintained a gentleness so rare and precious in the underworld. Again fighting tears, Carney moved to bury his head against his arm. The sight of a woman on the sidewalk below froze him.

She was tall and slender, with copper-colored curls tied back from the heat. She moved with a grace from another era. Carney knew her at once, as Bradach had before him. But where the Gael's glimpse had filled him with longing, Carney's evoked self-righteous pity. He knew it was his destiny to meet that girl . . . and his bane to kill her.

As if in answer to this understanding, a black Mercedes glided to the curb. Alano and two bodyguards emerged from the car. The goons studied the area, but their gazes never found Carney. They headed for the door, even as the woman did the same.

Mechanically, Carney's hand locked around the gun, gaze trapped on the woman, spirit crying out in need. A crack shot, he could not miss Alano his mind assured him, could not possibly accidentally harm his eternal love. Yet, history told otherwise. Carney did not know if his now-trembling hand would fail him, if a bullet might ricochet, or if panic or an attempt to protect him might send her skittering into return fire. But he harbored no doubt that when he fired at Alano, she would die.

Chilled to the marrow, Carney shivered violently. He tore his eyes from target and soulmate to stare at his gun for the first time. A familiar world of bitterness and unfulfilled dreams paraded in front of him. Then, slowly, he put the barrel to his head and pulled the trigger, ending the cycle of horror that had cursed them all through eternity.

Gumshoes & Gangs

"That stupid dick just can't be bought."

Within the parallel universe of mob morality, the private detective, "the gumshoe" if you will, is usually cast in the unlikely role of rogue knight, a crusader responding to a higher authority on a divine quest which is usually in search of the truth.

. . . or, in simpler terms, he's a tough guy trying to crack a case.

Gumshoes come in all shapes and sizes with different clients and purviews. Simon Hawke's tough guy just happens to be a magically enhanced cat, while P. N. Elrod's Jack Fleming does all his prowling at night (he's a vampire). Max Collins' tale involves a case of possession/reincarnation, while Heidi E. Y. Stemple's is positively surreal.

MY CLAW IS QUICK

by Simon Hawke

It was raining like a Great Dane pissing on a flat
rock when she came in, dripping water from her
shiny black raincoat all over my nice clean floor. My
secretary would've made her hang it up outside, but
my secretary wasn't in. She goes home at five, like
normal people do. Me, I was already home.

I'm a simple kinda guy, and I don't really need a
lot. A clean litter box, fresh water in the bowl, some
kibbles or some tuna mix, I'm happy. There were
times I didn't even have that much. Those were the
old days, in the mean streets and back alleys, dumpster diving and scratching and clawing to survive. I lost
an eye that way. Food was scarce back then, and I got
into a set-to with what looked like a starving dog who
wanted what I'd scored for dinner. I didn't want to
share. I wasn't very street smart then, and it turned
out the dog was a coyote. I got chewed up pretty bad.
Well, live and learn. These days, things were a lot
better. I had a business of my own, an office with a
secretary and my name stenciled on the door—Catseye Gomez, P.I. The P.I. stands for Private Investigator. I have a license and everything. Sometimes I even
get a client or two. Like the slinky number standing
there in front of my desk, dripping water on the floor
and looking kinda uncertain about the whole thing.

I uncurled from the comfy leather chair where I'd
been dozing and hopped up onto the desk. "Evening,
Miss," I said. "How can I help you?"

She stared.

They always stare. Usually it's my prosthetic eyeball that captures their attention. It's rather special, made of turquoise. A Chinese, robin's egg blue stone with a fine vertical matrix running through it that looks sorta like a feline pupil. I think it makes me look dashing as all hell, but it also happens to be functional. I can't use it to see, but the stone is magical and draws upon my life force to hurl energy strong enough to stun a full-grown man. It could kill, as well, but a shot like that would take a whole lot out of me, and I'd need to lay up for a while and recover. Anyway, I figured she was staring at ole Betsy, but I was wrong, as it turned out. It was not my enchanted turquoise eyeball; it was me.

"Goodness. You're a cat," she said.

"What gave me away?" I asked, switching my tail back and forth in irritation. I hate it when people state the obvious.

"No, I mean . . . I . . . I didn't know," she said. "I thought you'd be a man. A human."

"Then I take it this isn't a referral," I said, giving her the once over. For a human female, she wasn't bad. If you like the type, that is. Long, raven-black hair which she'd kept mostly dry thanks to one of those tricky little collapsable umbrellas you can slip into a purse; a voluptuous, hourglass figure, the kind that had men doing double takes when she went undulating by; nice legs that went all the way up and made an ass of themselves; nice face, good cheekbones and wide mouth . . . I imagined she wouldn't be one to sit home by the phone on Friday nights.

"I got your name off the Web," she said. "I don't know, I . . . guess I liked the sound of it. I didn't think to take it literally. No offense, you understand." She had the decency to blush. "I mean, there wasn't a pic or anything."

"I tend to keep a low profile," I replied. "You didn't see the letters 'T.C.' next to the 'P.I.'?"

"I assumed it was some sort of license or degree," she said.

"It stands for 'Thaumagenic Citizen.' That means an intelligent, talking animal produced by thaumagenetic engineering, complete with equal rights of citizenship. Hell, I thought everybody knew that."

"I guess I've heard about it," she replied, "but it's all still very new to me. I'm from Mars. Bradbury City."

"I guess that would explain it," I said. Along with the accent I could not quite place. "How long you been on Earth?"

"About three days."

"So I imagine you're having a bit of culture shock. They don't have any thaumagenes on the Mars colony, do they?"

She scowled a bit at my calling Mars a "colony" and shook her head. "No. The idea is still regarded as a little . . . controversial. It certainly takes some getting used to. Every time the wolfhound who's on the door at my hotel nods and says, 'Good morning,' I jump about a foot." She looked concerned at my response. "Are you all right?"

"Yeh," I said. "I was just laughing. When a cat laughs, it always sounds like a hairball coming up. Not much I can do about it. It's the way I was engineered. So you're staying at the Plaza?"

"Yes." She raised her eyebrows. "How did you know?"

"They always use wolfhounds to work the door. That's Erich. I know him. He's big and scary looking, but he wouldn't hurt a fly. Pardon my manners; I should offer you a seat. Or would you prefer to deal with a human? If you like, I could refer you to an excellent investigator. She's expensive, but she's good."

"Oh . . . well, I'm afraid that expenses might be a consideration. Your ad said, uh, reasonable rates."

"I do work pretty cheap, but then I don't have much

overhead. I don't need a fancy sharkskin suit or trench coat or a fedora."

"Fedora?"

"Never mind. Before your time. Before mine, too, come to think of it. Why don't you take a load off and tell me what you need?"

She unbelted the raincoat, sat and crossed her legs in a way that seemed quite casual. Her skirt rode up pretty high. If I were human, I might've been distracted, but I'm not and so I wasn't. It was too bad, really. She did it very nicely. It made me think she must have practiced.

"My name is Sedona. Sedona Summers."

She waited. So did I.

"Aren't you going to make some clever comment about me being 'pretty hot?'" she asked, dryly.

"I seem to have managed to resist the temptation."

"Well . . . you're not a man."

"And you're no Persian pussy, lady. Get to the point."

"Sorry. I'm trying to find someone," she said. "My sister, Phoenix. She ran away from home about a month ago."

I closed my eyes. I was tempted to say it was no wonder she ran away from home, but I resisted that temptation, too. "I take it your family originally came from Arizona?"

"How did you guess?" she asked, wryly.

"Just a wild shot in the dark. Go on."

"She met a man . . . well, I guess you know how that story goes. I mean, you're a *tomcat*, after all."

"My, a little edgy, aren't we?"

"A bit. Is that a problem for you?"

"I'll live. Continue."

"The authorities on Mars managed to trace her back to Earth, and then the trail ran out here."

"They basically pulled the passenger manifest, tracked it through to the connecting flights and

couldn't be bothered to take it any further," I said.
"Not their jurisdiction."

"Exactly. And the authorities here were not particularly helpful, either."

"Is the girl a minor?"

"She's seventeen."

"Age of consent," I said.

"But not on Mars," she replied.

"Well, this isn't Mars," I said. "We're a bit more progressive here. We grant animals equal rights and everything. Besides, runaways are not exactly high priority with the police department. They've got much smellier fish to fry. They usually leave the runaways to private operators like myself."

"That's pretty much what they said. So . . . do you think you can find her?"

"Probably. I'd say the odds are good. A month is not a terribly cold trail. I've had much worse. The question is, what if she doesn't feel like being found?"

"That's up to her, I guess. I just want to know that she's all right. I want to see her, talk to her. If she doesn't want anything to do with me, then I'll accept that, but I want to hear it from her myself."

"I take it you were close?"

"We were best friends. We used to tell each other everything. But lately . . . I don't know. I just don't understand what happened."

"What about your parents?"

"They're both dead. It was a shuttle accident."

"I'm sorry."

"It was a long time ago. I practically raised Phoenix by myself."

"And this guy that she ran off with was an older man?"

"Yes." She made a face. "Is it really that obvious and trite?"

"I've found that human behavior is often obvious and trite," I said. "No offense, you understand."

"Well, I guess I had that coming, with my catty comments."

"Sure. Look, forget it. I must've got up on the wrong side of the cushion this morning. So what do you know about this man she ran off with?"

We batted it around a bit, like a mouse that couldn't get away. The scenario was not an unfamiliar one; just the players change from time to time. Sedona Summers and her sister, Phoenix, were best friends, I had no doubt of that. But then Sedona was more than just big sister. She was also the surrogate parent, and she took that role quite seriously. Protective. And, as little sister got a little older, that protective got to seem more like bossy and repressive. Phoenix started to rebel a bit. It's hard enough trying to be a single mom without your daughter also being your sister. And no, forget it. I saw that movie, too. And we're not gonna go there.

Individuation is an awkward stage in humans. With some people, it can take the form of piercings, green hair, brandings and tattoos. With others, it's affairs with older men. Or women. Or whatever. Like I said, the players change, the plot remains more or less the same. The story that Sedona Summers dumped on me was really a cliché. If I had anything to say about it, the ending would be a cliché as well. The happy kind. But there was no guarantee it would work out that way. I saw it as my responsibility to make sure Ms. Summers understood that. She seemed to. Good enough. From there on, it was simple and straightforward. She laid a small retainer on me, gave me a holo of her sister, told me what she knew about the guy that she ran off with . . . which was next to nothing, really . . . and from there on it was my ball of yarn. All I had to do was unwind it.

The first step was obvious enough. Find the guy that sister Phoenix ran away with. He had to have some money. Fares from Mars to Earth and back aren't cheap. Sedona Summers had blown most of her life savings on hers, and the little she had left, what she hadn't given me, was all that she was living on. And the Plaza wasn't cheap. There were lots of cheaper places in the city, but certainly not the kind a nice girl from Mars would want to stay in. Her funds weren't going to last forever. That kinda made me feel some pressure to make sure she got her money's worth.

Farron W. Richards turned out to be fairly predictable. Not the kind of human I had a lot of time or patience for. If I had been human myself, he probably wouldn't have even seen me, but his type tends to be more concerned with appearances than with the way things really are. And the way things really were was pretty simple. Farron Richards was a serious waste of human genetic material. He dearly would have loved to tell me where to go, or actually have his secretary tell me in his place, but his liberal sensibilities were of the hypocritical kind. In other words, he would just as soon have run me over with his car, but he didn't want word to get around he wasn't kind to animals.

Anyway, the secretary buzzed me in, after I let her scratch my head a bit. Personally, I don't like to be touched by humans very much. It's a casual sort of arrogance that presumes an intimacy they would generally never assume with one another on such a slight acquaintance. But I'll put up with a certain amount of the "What a cute kitty" crap if it'll get me what I need. I figure it all comes with the territory. I didn't like it, but I had a job to do.

"So . . . if it isn't the cat detective," Richards said, turning from his terminal as I came in. He did not bother getting up. I did not bother asking his permission to jump up onto the expensive, tufted leather chair. I just proceeded to make myself comfortable, doing that claw thing up and down on the nice, soft, nappa hide. He could not quite hide the wince as the leather made satisfying little scritching sounds. "Catseye Gomez. I've heard of you," he said. "Saw that interview on *Today*."

"I'm never at my best that early," I replied. "Look, Mr. Richards, you're a busy man, I'm sure, so I'll get right to the point. I'm looking for Phoenix Summers."

"I'm afraid I can't help you," he said.

"Can't or won't?"

"Can't," he repeated. "I haven't the faintest notion where she is."

"She came back with you from Mars last month."

"We were traveling together, if that was what you mean."

"I understand there was more than traveling involved."

"And if there was, why would it be any of your business? We were both consenting adults."

I could've given him the line Sedona tried on me, but I didn't waste my time. He knew the law as well as I did, I was sure of that. The minute they left Mars orbit, Phoenix Summers ceased to be a minor. The fact that she was young enough to be his daughter . . . well, that was not my business, either.

"You paid her fare," I said.

"No law against that, is there?" he replied.

"No, I guess there isn't. But I'm sure the employees would love to hear that over by the water cooler."

He stiffened slightly. Didn't like that. "I was polite enough to see you, Cat," he said, "but since you came in, you've done everything short of messing on the rug to tick me off. I take it you remember where the door is. Or should I call a guard dog to help you find the way?"

I didn't think I'd get much out of him. His sort, you never do. But I had to cover all the bases, just in case. "Tell me just one thing before I go," I said. "Did you at least leave her with some money, or did you just dump her like a load of dirty laundry when the thrill was gone?"

He commed his secretary. "Rachel? Call the dogs," he said.

"Just one or two more questions and I'll leave," I

said. "When was the last time you saw her? C'mon, save me some legwork and at least tell me where you dumped her. It might not be much, but it's a place to start. She must have been worth something to you. I mean, hell, you paid her fare to Earth."

"Chump change," Richards said. "She was pleasant company. A bit of fluff that livened up an otherwise dull and routine business trip. There was no more to it than that. She knew what she was doing. In a lot more ways than one, if you catch my drift."

"Oh, I caught it," I replied. "I'll stop by the clinic and get a shot for it tomorrow."

"Cute," he said, "very cute. You'll be meowing out of the other side of your mouth in about a minute, when the dogs get here."

"Don't scare me too much," I replied. "I might piddle all over your nice clean carpet."

"Look, Cat, the last time I saw Phoenix, she was getting into a cab outside El Morocco with the five hundred dollars that I gave her in her purse. Just to help her out, you understand."

"I'll bet she earned every single cent."

"You know, I've had about enough of you," he said, and right on cue, the door opened up behind me and security came trotting in. Three German shepherds, with radio-equipped collars and little blue jackets that said "K-9 Security" on them in gold letters.

"Get this flea-bitten furball outta here," said Richards.

Two of the dogs looked like they were ready to go for me right then and there, but the bigger, lead dog stopped 'em in their tracks. "Cool it, boys," he said, with a casual look in their direction. "I'll handle this." He turned to me. "Hello, Gomez."

"How's it going, Bruno?"

"Can't complain. I'm workin'."

"This is the best you could do?" I said.

Ever see a German shepherd look sheepish? It looks kinda ridiculous. But then, German shepherds are supposed to be smart, and Bruno kinda breaks the mold there, too. He used to be a police dog, but he took a few too many shots to the head with billy clubs. He was a pretty good attack dog, he just wasn't too good at letting go once he got his teeth into something. In other words, he wasn't all that bright, and with a temper that made a Doberman look mellow, that didn't make for a particularly stable combination.

"What is this, old home week at the animal shelter?" said Richards. "I told you to get this mangy alley cat the hell outta here!"

Bruno bared his teeth and growled.

"Hey, You work for me, you dumb mutt!" said Richards.

I closed my eyes. "Oh, mistake," I said, shaking my head. "*Big* mistake."

Bruno launched himself right over my head, and the leap carried him past me, across Richards' desk and right onto his chest. Richards screamed, and the chair went over backward as they crashed to the floor in a tangled heap. From the high-pitched squeal that came from the floor behind the desk, I had a pretty good idea what Bruno had his teeth into. Richards sounded like a woman as he screeched, *"Jesus! Get him off me! Get him off me!"*

The other two dogs looked at each other uncertainly, apparently feeling they should do something, and they started forward, but I stood in front of them and shook my head. "I wouldn't get involved in this if I were you," I told them. "Trust me on this one, guys. It could get real ugly."

Ever notice how goofy dogs look whenever they get confused? I just left 'em sitting there, whining softly to themselves and looking stupid, and walked on out the door. The secretary was sitting at her desk, reading a celebrity profile magazine.

"You might want to dial 911 and tell 'em to send down the paramedics," I told her.

"No hurry," she said, without lowering the magazine. "Mr. Richards said he didn't want to be disturbed."

The noise coming from the intercom on her desk made it sound as though someone was butchering a pig back there. She'd had it on, and she heard every word we'd said. She peeked out from behind the magazine and winked at me.

I gave her a little energy twinkle with ole Betsy. "Later, doll," I said.

"Take care of yourself, Cat. And hey . . . good luck. I hope you find her."

Finding the cab driver who'd picked up Phoenix Summers at El Morocco wasn't all that hard. I knew most of the dispatchers in town, and it didn't take too long, especially with a recent holo to flash around. With that face and body, Phoenix Summers was a pretty memorable girl, and the cabbie who had picked her up remembered where he took her because it was one of those addresses in town that cabbies tend to know about, the kind that traveling businessmen will pay a little extra for. A young girl fresh off the boat from Mars doesn't just happen to get an address like that out of the phone book. Richards must've laid it on her when he kicked her to the curb. I could just see him doing it, too. "Here, honey, go see Paco, he's a friend of mine. He'll fix you up. He owes me. Just tell him ole Farron sent ya."

Yeh. Right. It was all coming together, and the picture wasn't pretty.

I knew all about Paco and his operation. There are two things that all big cities have in common: roaches and characters like Paco. Come to think of it, that's rather redundant. I had a feeling I was probably biting off more than I could chew, but then, I kept thinking about Sedona Summers sitting in her expensive room back at the Plaza, worrying about her little sister and waiting for the phone to ring. What the hell, I thought, things had been a bit too quiet lately, anyway.

Paco and I had crossed paths a couple of times before. Neither one of us had enjoyed the experience
very much. It was inevitable, considering our respec-
tive lines of work, that we would run into one another
every now and then. It just served to remind me,
whenever I got to feeling cocky about my flamboyant
and independent lifestyle as a private eye, that I was
really nothing more than just another bottom feeder,
rooting around down in the muck and grime along
with Paco and others of his ilk. Except that Paco made
a better living at it than I did. But then, I had my
ethics. Which, along with about six bits, would buy me
an overpriced cup of coffee with steamed milk, some
powdered cocoa mix and a French name.

Paco was Connected with a capital C. He ran a
whole bunch of unsavory little rackets for the mob.
Drugs, gambling, loan-sharking, prostitution, Paco had
his measly little claws in all of them. And he was
pretty much untouchable. Protection money got paid
every month; lawyers with diamond pinkie rings and
custom-tailored suits collected fat retainers, and politicians happily accepted large campaign contributions
without ever asking where the money came from. Organized Crime, just another aspect of the modern business world. They liked to think of it as "dealing in
commodities." The only commodity that seemed in
short supply these days was truth.

Farron Richards was what you'd call a "talent
scout" who freelanced on the side for Paco. He took
his business trips to Mars and Luna City and the habi-
tats, and other more terrestrial destinations, and kept
his eye out for likely prospects for Paco's little stable.
Runaways like Phoenix Summers filled the bill quite
nicely. Take them out of their home environment,
bring them to a strange new city, dump them and get
them totally off balance, then steer them Paco's way.
And by the time he was done messing with their heads
and tearing down their personalities, they were totally
dependent on him, lacked any sense of worth, and felt

too ashamed to go back home. They'd become just another commodity, the oldest one in the world.

There were no door dogs at Paco's place, but an honest-to-God liveried doorman with gold braid, an admiral's cap, and epaulets on his coat. He called up and told 'em who I was and a moment later, got the all clear to let me in. He held the door open for me without an ounce of condescension and a polite tip of the hat. I padded across the ornate, plushly carpeted lobby of the brownstone, past the potted plants and velvet-upholstered furniture, pretending not to notice the security cameras discreetly tucked out of the way up by the ceiling molding. The elevator was all done up in burgundy leather tuck and roll upholstery, like a coach the Scarlet Pimpernel would ride in. The mirrors in there had that gold filigree stuff running through them, which I never saw the point of, anyway. But then, what do I know about interior decoration? I sleep on a blue foam cushion my secretary picked up at a yard sale in the suburbs. It's got a little palm tree on it and says, "Souvenir of San Diego."

The elevator stopped at the top floor of the four-story brownstone, and as the door slid open, I found myself looking at a slab of muscle in a sharkskin suit with a magnum-sized bulge beneath his left armpit. Why was it that muscleheads always liked big, shiny steel, long-barreled revolvers? There were little semi-autos that carried more rounds and did the job much more efficiently, but no, they had to have these cannons that looked like chrome-plated baseball bats. Humans had this size fixation I just didn't get. The males all wanted to be bigger, and the females all wanted to be smaller. Made no damn sense to me at all.

The steroid overdose escorted me to Paco's office, then knocked twice on the door. Another guy built like the Empire State Building opened it, filling the doorframe with lats that looked like batwings and arms the size of tree trunks. He stood there looking down at me until I said, "Well, you gonna let me in, or you just gonna stand there, blotting out the sun?"

"Let the cat in, Guido," a familiar, high-pitched voice came from behind him.

Guido moved aside with all the ponderousness of a tectonic plate shift and I stepped into the room. Paco had this thing about the color red. The carpet was dark red, like coagulated blood, and the walls were a dark crimson that was almost purple, like a bruise. The leather upholstered chairs were as red as cheap fingernail polish, with little brass studs all over 'em, and even the huge, handcarved desk was kinda red, one of those exotic hardwoods from Brazil or someplace with a name that sounded like a Latin dance step. Behind the desk stood two more bodybuilders whose combined weight had to be somewhere around six hundred pounds, and between them, underneath a black velvet painting of humans playing poker, sat Paco, four-and-half, high-strung, trembling pounds of malevolent Chihuahua.

His fancy red leather chair was placed on a dais, like a throne, so that he could look out across the desk and see whoever stood on the other side. When you saw how small he was, you started to understand this thing he had about surrounding himself with size. I hopped up onto one of the leather chairs placed before the desk and got myself a bit closer to eye level with the little guy. He gave a funny little yipping bark and one of the bruisers reached into a cut crystal dog bowl sitting on the desk. The bowl had the name "Paco" etched into it in a Florentine, gold-inlaid script. The bruiser took a small chunk of raw steak out of the bowl and hand-fed it to Paco, who gobbled it down, masticating like a starving rat.

"So, Gomez, long time, no see," he said. "What brings you all the way uptown? You lookin' for a little kitty, eh?" He chortled at his little joke, wheezing like a hamster with a hairball.

"There's a little holocube of what I'm looking for

in the pouch around my neck," I said, and waited while Paco jerked his ratty little head at one of the goons, who stepped forward to take the little cube out of my pouch. He placed it on the desk and the girl's hologram appeared, looking very pretty and a lot more innocent than she would probably ever be again. "Her name is Phoenix Summers," I went on. "And I happen to know she came here."

"People come and go as they please," said Paco. "What is that to me?"

"It's the going part that interests me," I said.

"And this is because . . . ?" said Paco.

"Her sister is in town, looking for her," I said.

"So, send the sister down," said Paco. "I could always use another girl." He gave his hamster-wheezing chortle again. "Good one, eh, Guido?"

"Yeh, good one, Boss," the meatbag said, feeding Paco another piece of steak.

"Just let me talk to her, okay, Paco? I'll pay the going rate."

"Tell you what I'm gonna do, Gomez, just because I'm feeling so magnanimous today. You can see the girl, no charge. Talk all you like, eh? What the hell, it's a free country, ain't that right, Guido?"

"Right, Boss."

I glanced from the meatbag to Paco. "You two oughtta take this act on the road. I hear the comedy clubs are dying for new talent."

"Now, you see how you are?" said Paco. "I try to be a nice guy, and you give me lip. You wanna see the girl or not?"

"Yeh, I wanna see her, Paco. I'm sorry. I'm just a wise guy at heart, you know how it is."

"Yeh, I always did say you were in the wrong business, Gomez. You oughtta come and work for me. There'd be a lot more profit in it for you."

"I'm sure of that," I said. "But you know me, Paco. I've always been the independent type."

"Cats," said Paco, with a sniff. "Who can figure 'em, eh, Guido?"

"Uh . . . right, Boss."

"Take Gomez here down to see our little Phoenix. And then make sure he finds his way back out, kapish?"

"Sure thing, Boss."

"You see that, Gomez? I'm being cooperative," said Paco. "No problems, right?"

"Uh . . . right, Boss," I said.

Guido looked at me and frowned.

"Go on, Guido," Paco said. "Take Gomez down to the third floor. And, Gomez, you ever decide to make some decent money, you just let me know, okay?"

"I'll do that, Paco," I said. "But I wouldn't stay up all night by the doggie door if I were you."

I didn't like it.

It was much too easy. I kept thinking about that as Guido escorted me back to the elevator and down to the third floor. Paco'd had Phoenix for at least a month. That was more than enough time for him to do a thorough tap dance on her self-esteem, which probably wasn't all that high to start with, especially after Richards tossed her aside like yesterday's paper. Paco had to be feeling pretty sure of himself. Maybe I was just wasting my time. And maybe Sedona Summers was just wasting her money. Maybe Phoenix didn't want to go back home again because she felt she never could.

The meatbag took me down a narrow, carpeted corridor with doors on either side that all had little gold numbers on them. There was laughter coming from behind door number four and moaning from behind door number six. I didn't know what the hell was going on behind door number eight, but it sounded like the soundtrack from *A Christmas Carol,* when Marley's ghost shows up, rattling his chains. Door number ten swung open to reveal a bedroom that was decorated like a little girl's room, complete with stuffed animals and dolls. Except the young woman who was reclining on the bed, reading a magazine, did not look like a little girl at all, despite the baby doll pajamas.

She looked up as Guido opened the door and I came in, then her eyes got wide with indignation and she sat bolt upright in bed. "No *way!*" she said. "You can just *forget* about it!"

"Relax, kid," I said, as Guido chuckled and closed the door behind me, "it isn't what you think."

"Yeh, well, it's not gonna be what *you* think, either," she replied, tossing the magazine aside. "I don't care if you *are* a thaumagene, there's no way I'm gonna do a cat!"

"Well, it's nice to know you still have some boundaries you won't cross," I told her. "Sedona will be relieved to hear that."

The girl's expression changed immediately. Her jaw dropped and, for just a moment, her eyes lit up with hope. And right then, I knew that she was not beyond redemption. It's when the eyes stay dead and flat, no matter what you say, that you might as well start shoveling on the dirt.

"Sedona?" Phoenix said. "You know my sister? You've talked to her?"

"I've seen her, kid. She's here, just a cab ride across town. And she's been worried sick about you."

For a moment Phoenix didn't say anything as it sank in, and then her eyes brimmed up with tears and she put her face into her hands and started sobbing. I couldn't just stand there and let her cry. I felt sorry for the kid. I hopped up onto the bed and started rubbing my head against her leg.

"It'll be all right, kid," I purred. "It's okay. Don't worry. We're gonna get you outta here."

"Oh, Kitty," she said, picking me up and hugging me, "what am I going to do?"

"Hey, hey, put me down," I said. "I don't like to

be picked up, okay? And I could do without the squeezing. Nothing personal, all right?"

"I'm sorry," she said, putting me down. "I forgot. You're not just an ordinary house cat, are you?"

"Bite your tongue," I said. "I'm a private investigator and your sister hired me to find you. She's come to take you home."

Phoenix looked away. "I can't go back," she said. "Much as I'd like to, I just can't. Not after what's happened. Not after . . . what I've done."

"Sure you can," I told her. "Look, Phoenix, everybody makes mistakes. It's what makes people human."

"Yeh, what would you know about it? You're a cat."

"What, you think cats don't make mistakes? You ever see a cat jump out of a ninth-story window, trying to catch a pigeon sitting on the windowsill? They say cats always land on their feet, but that doesn't do much good when you're traveling 190 miles an hour. You ever see a Siamese with its paws up where its ears should be?"

She stared at me and then began to laugh. That meant there was hope.

"Come on, kid," I said. "I'm taking you outta here."

"Paco will never let me go," she said. And then she shuddered. "At first, I thought he was kinda cute and cuddly, but he's crazy. And he's dangerous."

"Hell, you could knock him over with potholder," I said. "How dangerous can he be?"

"You don't know Paco."

"Yeah, I do. We've had a few run-ins before. And notice I'm still here. Come on, put some clothes on and let's get out of here."

She threw on some jeans, a pair of boots and a sweatshirt and we headed out the door. The coast was clear all the way down the hall and to the elevator. The laughter and the moans had ceased coming from behind door numbers four and six, but whoever was rattling the chains was working overtime. We took the elevator down to the lobby. Paco and the goons were waiting for us when we came out. Phoenix gasped and froze right in her tracks.

"Gomez, Gomez, did you really think that I was just gonna let you walk outta here with my investment?" Paco said, trembling with malice. "You didn't really think you could sneak out, did you? Guess you didn't notice the cameras, huh?"

"I noticed them," I said. "In the lobby, in the elevator, and in the corridors upstairs. I'm betting you got some hidden in the rooms, as well, so you can run a little blackmail racket on the side."

"Like I said, Gomez, you're in the wrong business. You oughtta come and work for me. You're too smart to waste yourself on being a shamus. But maybe not quite smart enough, eh?"

"Smart enough not to come here and try to tangle with you without reinforcements," I said.

The deep, rumbling growls coming from behind them made Paco and the meatbags turn around. Bruno stood behind them in the lobby, growling, fangs bared, saliva dripping from his muzzle. Erich, the big wolfhound from the Plaza, stood beside him, looking like a goddamn rabid nightmare from the Scottish moors.

Paco yelped and took off like a shot, scrambling straight up the trunk of a potted corn plant like a goddamn squirrel. I didn't even know Chihuahuas could climb like that. It was pretty damn impressive.

"*Shoot* 'em! Shoot 'em!" he yipped, from his perch up in the leaves.

Guido went for his gun first, but the problem with carrying a cannon with an eight inch barrel in a shoulder holster was that you couldn't draw it all that fast. He hadn't even cleared leather when Bruno landed on his chest like a defensive end sacking a quarterback. Meatbag Number Two at least managed to get his gun out, but big Erich snagged him by the wrist, gave his head a shake, and flipped him over on his back like an aikido master. Meatbag Number Three had a .45 Comp gun in a speed rig. He had already drawn a bead on Bruno when I let him have it with ole Betsy, blasting him with a blue bolt of thaumaturgic energy that singed his chest and threw him back against the wall, unconscious. I heard a sickening crunch, followed by a high-pitched scream, and realized that Guido was gonna be singing soprano from then on.

Erich was showing a bit more restraint. The big wolfhound looked down at the big goon he'd thrown and said, "Had enough, little fella? Or do you wanna play some more?"

You really don't want to argue when you're flat on your back and a dog the size of a Buick is sitting on your chest. The meatbag shook his head and remained perfectly still.

"You're not gonna get away with this, Gomez!" Paco yipped down at me from the potted tree. He was shivering like a leaf, shaking with fury. "I'm not gonna forget this! You hear me, Cat? You and I ain't through!"

"In case you forgot, Paco," I said, "cats can climb trees, too."

He shut up then, but I knew I hadn't heard the last from him. We had danced before, and I knew we'd dance again. The city was plenty big enough for both of us, but that didn't mean we had to like it.

The doorman in his fancy, braided uniform held the door open for us as we came out.

"Thanks, Abe," said Erich, with a nod at him.

"Anytime, ole buddy," said the doorman.

Phoenix stared at them, confused.

"Same union," I said.

"But won't he get fired?" Phoenix asked.

"Not unless that little rat wants his place of business picketed," said Erich. "That could tend to draw a bit too much attention."

"Thanks, Erich," I said. "I owe ya one. And you, too, Bruno."

"Hey, you bailed me outta the pound after I took a piece of Richards," said the shepherd. "You don't owe me nuthin'."

"What do you think, Erich?" I asked. "You got some work for this crazed police dog at the Plaza?"

Erich cocked his massive head. "How about an escort for our single guests who like to go jogging through the park at night and early in the morning?" he said. "Salary plus tips."

"Hey, works for me," said Bruno. "Thanks."

"Somebody had better warn the muggers," I said.

Then Phoenix let out a squeal when she saw the limo from the Plaza pull up to the curb with her sister, Sedona, sitting in the back seat. A moment later, they were in each other's arms, laughing and crying at the same time.

"I sure do love happy endings," Erich said. "Come on, Gomez. We'll give you a lift downtown."

"No, thanks, big guy," I said. "It's a nice night. I think I'll take the long way home and cut through some back alleys, just for old times' sake."

"Suit yourself," the wolfhound said. "Come on, Bruno. Let's go."

As they piled into the car, Sedona Summers looked over and said, "Thank you."

I gave her a little energy twinkle with ole Betsy. "Just doing my job, ma'am," I said. She gave me a dazzling smile, got back into the car, and then the driver shut the door, got in, and pulled away. I watched the car recede into the distance down the rain-slicked street and thought about what the big wolfhound had said. I liked happy endings, too. It was a cool, crisp night. I headed back downtown with my head up and just a bit of swagger in my step.

THE QUICK WAY DOWN

by P. N. "Pat" Elrod

Gordy Weems trudged up to my table, his phlegmatic face showing a muted combination of annoyance and disgust. "I got a stiff in the men's john," he stated.

I refrained from making any obvious jokes. He was too serious. The Nightcrawler Club, of which he was the manager, was a class operation; bodies in the toilet were not the norm for such a fancy joint. Sure, Gordy ran a very large hunk of Chicago's underworld territory, but he was too careful and smart to bump anyone on his own property.

"Not from natural causes?" I knew the answer, but had to ask just to be sure.

"A pill in the heart. I figure a .22. There's not much blood. When his tie's in place, it hides the hole."

I had no curiosity to ask how he'd determined that little detail. "Who?"

"Alby Cornish."

I was impressed. Alby was—or had been—an up-and-coming boxer being groomed for important fights. He could throw a right that would knock down a barn and knew how to take a dive and make it look real.

Gordy turned his head slightly, making sure no one was close enough to eavesdrop. "He was here all evening with that club singer, Ruth Phillips. They were living it up pretty good until about an hour ago."

"What happened an hour ago?"

"Ruth's boyfriend caught them."

No need to say more. Ruth Phillips was known to

be tight as a tick with Soldier Burton, a tougher-than-average mug who got the moniker for his uncanny ability to march from courtrooms free and clear of all charges, if not of all suspicion. He started out as an enforcer during Prohibition and now ran a ring of bookie joints. I could guess that he'd taken Ruth to the fights one time too many, and the sight of Alby's sweaty, well-muscled body had made an impression on her.

Gordy snorted. "The bouncers said everything looked okay. Nobody made a fuss. Ruth took off, leaving Cornish and Burton at the table. They talked and had drinks, watched the show, then went to the lobby. I figure they stopped in the toilet for a leak, and Burton popped him during the drum finale."

The club's band had a hell of a drummer. Between his work and the blare of the horn section during that number Burton could have fired off a cannon and no one would have noticed.

"I need help, Fleming," said Gordy.

Now I was surprised. "You got it, but what can I do? You must have ten other guys who can move a body just as easy as me."

"Yeah, but they don't need to know about this and be talking to the wrong people. Soldier Burton's ambitious. He's been trying to bite pieces off my territory for over a year now. It's no accident he left Cornish here. He wants to make trouble for me with the New York bosses. I'll lay you short odds he's already called the cops."

The drum finale had been about five minutes ago. "We better get the lead out, then."

He nodded once, and I boosted from my regular table up on the third tier overlooking the stage and followed him to the plush lobby.

"Where was the attendant when this happened?" I asked, pitching my voice low and casual.

"On break getting a sandwich. When a show's playing, nobody gets up to use the john, so he's usually away then. Tonight he comes back, finds what he found, and tells me about it."

"Will he spill to anyone else?"

"He'll keep shut, likes his job too much. He's taking another break. A long one."

The men's room was fancy: gold-veined black marble floors, gold-plated faucets. You half expected the water flowing out to be scented. There was only one patron left, and he was just drying his hands. We waited for him to clear, then Gordy went to the last stall and pushed the door wide. Alby Cornish was slumped on the toilet seat, legs splayed and arms dangling, looking asleep, but definitely not breathing. He had a fighter's beat-up face and was dressed sharp as a Broadway hoofer. Gordy had been right about the tie hiding the bullet hole, but ten feet away I could still smell the blood. It teased at me, as it always did, the way the scent of fresh-baked bread teases at a normal person. I'd fed earlier that night at the Stockyards, so my corner teeth stayed in place, but even if I hadn't, the sight of Cornish's pathetic remains would have killed all hunger.

"We pretend he's drunk?" I asked.

"Yeah."

"Where do we take him? The lake?"

"To Soldier Burton's place."

"Huh?"

"He wanted to make trouble for me. It's gonna bounce right back at him. If you don't mind helping."

I didn't mind, but I wanted more of an explanation. Unfortunately, there wasn't time to get one, not if the cops were on their way. We lurched from the john with Alby between us, his limp arms hauled chummily around our shoulders. A few of the regulars in the lobby bar saw us dragging him past and hooted at his inability to hold liquor. A couple of the bouncers looked our way, but Gordy headed them off and said he was handling things. We collected Alby's hat from the check desk and jammed it on his head. It made him look more like a foolish drunk than a dead man.

We took him out into the muggy heat of an early summer night. Even the breeze off the nearby lake was no help at clearing the close air. The bloodsmell rose thick from Alby's corpse, throwing me off my stride as we got him down the steps.

"Cops," I said, spotting a radio car as it turned onto the far end of the street. "C'mon, my buggy's just over there."

We moved steadily so as not to draw attention, but we got it anyway. Even as we shoved Alby into the back seat of my Buick, the prowl car pulled up and both uniforms got out. Apparently they'd been told what to look for.

Gordy straightened to his full height, which was considerable, and waited for them. He made no outward show of it, but I could tell he was dangerously tense. His heartbeat was loud to my sensitive ears. There was a chance he could buy these two off, but it would give them a hold on him.

"Lemme handle it," I said out of the side of my mouth.

His gaze flicked sharply at me, and he made a very tiny grunting sound.

"Evening, officers." I moved to the left so I was under the full glare of a street lamp. What I had planned for them required light enough for them to see me. "What's the problem?"

Two minutes later they were driving off, calling in to report a false alarm. It seems the dispatcher had sent them to the club to check on an anonymous tip about a body on the premises. Gordy and I got into my car and took a different direction away.

"How do you do that?" he asked, sparing a glance out the back window for the cops' receding taillights.

"Native talent." I'd hypnotized them faster than any stage magician and planted a few easy suggestions to make them forget all about us. "It comes with the condition."

"Along with the blood drinking and vanishing act?" Gordy knew all about me being a vampire.

"Yeah."

"Jeeze." He'd seen me do my special evil-eye whammy on mugs before, but he was still impressed by it. I asked for directions to Soldier Burton's place. He gave them, then settled back in silence for the rest of the ride.

We'd met last August, soon after my brutal demise at the hands of another mobster. Under the orders of his boss, Gordy had tried to beat some information out of me, but I didn't hold that against him. It's a tough world. Besides, after what I'd been through in the dying and the coming back from it, a couple of fists in the gut were a regular cakewalk to me. Over the course of a few rough jams we'd developed an odd sort of friendship and mutual respect for each other, so that's why I didn't think twice about helping him to move a corpse halfway across Chicago.

I parked in a dark patch by the service door of a swank building of ten or so stories and cut the motor. Gordy's plan was simple: Get what was left of Alby Cornish up to the penthouse floor where Burton lived, then call the cops.

"I know a homicide dick who's been itching to cuff Burton for years," said Gordy.

It sounded okay to me, and now I could see another reason why he'd wanted my company. He needed my other talent for vanishing and getting through the cracks around locked doors. I did just that to the service entrance, which would only open from the inside. Once in, I pushed on the bar and Gordy strolled past, carrying Alby's two hundred fifty pounds on one shoulder with ease. We found the service elevator and took it to the penthouse floor without encountering anyone.

"Wouldn't it be better if Alby were actually in the apartment?" I asked.

"It would, so long as you don't get caught."

"Fat chance of that."

I did my vanishing act again, this time slipping under the servant's entry to reappear in a fancy kitchen which was cleaned up for the night and empty. The place was quiet; Soldier Burton was probably off making an alibi for himself. I slipped the door open and told Gordy I'd take it from there.

"You don't have to."

"It's being practical. If someone walks in, I can get scarce, you can't. Go down to the car, wait a few minutes, then call your tame cop to come over. I'll be gone by the time he arrives."

A reasonable man, he handed the body over to me, along with the hat. If it weren't so damned macabre, the whole thing would have struck me as being like a frat house prank. Things were too serious for laughter, though. I could feel the dead man's weight right down to my soul. Not an hour ago he'd been leading a crooked but fairly harmless life, having a stolen good time with a pretty girl. Now he was a piece of meat headed for the coroner's knife.

Hurrying from the kitchen, I soon found what I wanted, a bathroom. I eased Alby onto the toilet and damned if he didn't lapse into the same sprawling posture as in the club's stall. I placed the hat on his head at a jaunty angle and told myself that his killer would pay—if Burton was indeed the killer, but I had no reason to doubt Gordy's line of reasoning or his word. Sure, he and Burton had a stew going between them over territory, but from what I knew of it, Burton was more annoyance than threat. This business had just upped the ante. Too bad for him that Gordy was a sharper player and had an ace like me in the hole.

Then I turned around and discovered a whole new change in the game.

Facing me was a blonde angel, all satin curves in

lavender pajamas but with a look on her kisser that declared her to be tougher than a keg of nails. Before I could fully register its presence, the revolver in her dainty pink hand gave a nasty snap in my direction, and something exploded above my left knee. My leg stopped working. I dropped, clutching the sudden burning wound and cursing.

She didn't say anything that I noticed, I was too busy trying to stay solid. For this shooting there was plenty of blood. The lead had gone right though my thigh. The holes were knitting up, though. The process was fast, but damned painful. My usual reaction to a bad hurt is to vanish, which would instantly heal things, but it didn't seem a good idea to give in to it while angel-girl was watching.

"Ruthie? What the hell are you doing?" A man's startled voice called from farther in the flat, accompanied by approaching footsteps.

"What do you think? I told you I heard something." Ruth Phillips, for I recognized her now, rounded on someone behind her. "You bastard! You told me you'd taken care of Alby!"

"I *did* take care of him, honey. What's—" The man came within my view of things and stopped short to stare at me lying wounded on his tiled floor and Alby at ease on the toilet. I took in a glimpse of a handsome, no-nonsense mug with about forty years' worth of strong-armed living behind it: Soldier Burton, in bathrobe and bare feet, but with his hair still combed and his razor thin mustache unblurred by stubble. If he and Ruth had been in the sack together, they'd been damned quiet about it. "Who the hell are you?"

I really didn't feel like talking just then except for profanity, which I kept to myself. Maybe she'd shot me, but I wasn't in the habit of swearing in front of women.

Ruth filled in the silence. "He's one of Gordy's insiders. Hangs around the club like he owns it. Dates their headliner, Bobbi. She's always talking about him like he's the Second Coming or something."

Burton glared down at me. "Did Gordy put you up to this?"

I assumed he meant my dumping Alby on the premises. I didn't feel like answering that one either and continued to hold my leg, plowing inch by inch through the pain. It slowly—far too slowly—receded.

"What do we do with him?" she asked.

"Lemme think." Burton frowned mightily.

I looked at Ruth and jerked my head in Alby's direction. "*You* wanted him bumped? Why?"

Her sweet-looking bee-stung lips curled into a sour sneer. "We both did, The dumb lug didn't dive when he was supposed to and cost us plenty in the—"

"Can it," said Burton sharply. "He don't need to know anything."

"Does it matter? You're not sending him back, are you?"

"Of course not. What's your story, ace? Bring Alby here, then ring the cops?"

"A favor for a favor," I said as cheerfully as I could manage, given the state of my leg. "They should be here pretty soon, too."

"Damn." But Burton didn't seem all that upset. He must have finished with his thinking. "Okay, doll, I want you to cover this punk while I carry Alby."

"Carry him where?"

"The roof. You—" he snarled at me. "On your feet and walk."

There was blood all over; Ruth's bullet must have clipped a good sized vein; I'd lost plenty. Had I been a normal human, I might have bled to death by now. Instead, I peeled myself off the floor, taking my time because I was dizzy. Another stop at the Stockyards later tonight would be necessary—if George and Gracie allowed me to leave. I didn't think they would. I speculated about hypnotizing them same as the cops, but there was a booze smell on their breath, lots of it, which would severely hamper any effort I made in that direction.

I limped out under Ruth's watchful eye. She looked more than ready to pop my other leg, keeping far enough back so I couldn't lunge for her. My condition allowed me speed enough to do that and more, but I was curious as to how they planned to get out of their mess. A body in the bathroom and a guy dripping red all over their floors would need a hell of an explanation.

Burton was powerfully built, but he grunted under Alby's weight. He took small fast steps to the kitchen, leading us into the service hall and hitting the elevator button. It was a long wait for the cage since Gordy had taken it all the way to the ground floor and not bothered to send it up again. The doors finally parted, and we crowded in. They hadn't noticed that my bleeding had stopped. I was healed up now, skin, bone, and muscle better than new. Too bad I couldn't say the same for my ruined pants.

The doors parted next on hot humid air blowing strongly from the lake. It was no cooler up here than on the street far below. Ruth urged me out, and I went, continuing with the limping gag. Burton dropped Alby, then got behind me and snaked his arm around my neck, pulling hard. I was taller, but he had the balance and dragged me backward toward the low wall that marked the edge of the roof. I let him get away with it for the time being. If my curiosity hadn't been up I'd have turned around and folded him in two the wrong way.

"Don't do anything stupid and I won't snap your neck," he told me.

"Grhg," I said agreeably.

"Ruthie, get the bullets out of the gun."

"What?"

"Just do it."

She grumbled but did it. "Now what?"

"Put the gun in his hand, I want his prints all over it."

She grinned, liking the idea. I reluctantly cooperated but made a mess of it, smearing my bloodied fingers on the gun's surface. Even the FBI would have a hard time picking up anything useful from it, but I planned not to have things go that far.

Ruth, holding the gun by the satin sash of her pajamas, was busy putting bullets back into their chambers. She clicked the barrel into place on the frame, and turned it so the two empty shells were in the right position for having just been fired. Smart, smart girl, but she'd forgotten about her own prints on the bullets. Interesting that Burton didn't remind her about them.

"What's this about?" I asked, when the pressure eased slightly on my windpipe.

"That's for the cops to figure."

"You want them to think I scragged Alby? Why would I do that?"

"As a favor to your boss, Gordy."

"The DA won't buy that as a motive," I said, hoping to hear more. "I'll walk free of this one."

Laughter in his voice as he spoke into my ear. "I don't think so." Burton hauled back, giving me an almighty spin and heave that yanked me from my feet, then he suddenly hurled me loose.

Right over the low wall.

I had time for a short scream, very short. It doesn't take but a few seconds for a grown man to drop a hundred feet.

In those few seconds flashes of things impressed themselves on my panicked mind: rush of air, windows tearing past, sidewalk coming up. The appalling, helpless agony of falling.

I would hit headfirst.

No!

An instant before striking the cement my world went gray.

I still fell but abruptly slowed.

Nothing to see, little to hear. I'd have held my breath if any had been left in me.

Then . . . impact.

A broad surface, flat. I seemed to spread out over a large portion of it. A larger portion than I had any right to take.

No. Pain. None.

That was important. Very, very important.

Some minutes—or maybe hours—later I started thinking again. In the shocky aftermath I got the impression that I was all over the walk like a pancake, inches thin, covering a wide area. It took no small amount of concentration to persuade my invisible and amorphous body to pull back into its normal shape—whatever that might be. I'd never seen myself in this form, only knew what it felt like, what was right and what wasn't.

When instinct told me I was ready for it, I cautiously resumed solidity. Everything seemed to be in place. I didn't have so much as a bruise for a souvenir, unless you wanted to count the stark terror that still shrieked around in my rattled brain like a tornado. Trembling uncontrollably, I let it run its course. There was no point in rushing things. It would wear off in time. Like a few years or so.

After a while I sat partway up and got my bearings. Side street, no one in sight at this hour. No sign of Gordy. He was probably waiting at the other end of the block wondering what was keeping me so long. I was glad to help a friend in need, but goddammit, he owed me a pair of pants for this little party.

The shakes gradually passed off, and I was able to crawl into a shadow in time to avoid being noticed by a passing prowl car closely followed by another vehicle. I thought I recognized its driver. If he was who I thought he was, then Gordy did indeed have clout in the city, and Soldier Burton had been a fool to challenge him.

But soon now I would be putting in my two cents' worth.

I waited and rested, giving the cops plenty of time to make their way up to Burton's penthouse. If Burton and Ruth were on the ball, they'd have cleaned up my blood by now and flushed it away. They'd leave it for someone else to find my body below, and soon after the one on the roof would be discovered. Though it would look like a setup, the intended conclusion would be that I'd shot Alby, then in a fit of remorse took a dive of my own. The gun, with my smeared prints, was probably still on the roof waiting to be slipped into an evidence bag.

I'd have to deal with it first.

The fastest way up was the way I'd come, and I wasn't too happy about that. My recent ordeal aside, I was afraid of heights even on my best night. At least by vanishing I didn't have to look down. I did feel the press of the wind on what should have been my back as I floated up the side of the building to reach the roof. It was with vast relief that I bumbled my way over the lip of the low wall and into the tar and gravel surface to go solid again.

Poor Alby—for I was feeling quite sorry for him by now—was exactly where he'd been dropped, and so was the gun. I picked it up and wiped it clean, adding a new handkerchief to the list of clothing items Gordy would replace.

Gun in hand, I went down the service stairs and eased around to the main hall. No cops in sight, but Burton's door was open, and I could hear voices. I'd been right: Gordy had clout. One of the voices belonged to Lieutenant Nick Blair of homicide. We'd had a few run-ins before, and he didn't much like me despite my whammy suggestions to the contrary.

Burton was all innocent puzzled resentment as he tried to determine what could have prompted such an invasion of his home by the cops. Blair wasn't sharing much with him, and from the shrill noises Ruth made the other men must have been making a quick, uninvited search of the premises looking for bodies. As it was unlikely Burton would make any mention of going to the roof, I'd have to arrange it myself.

Just floating upstairs again and making noise wouldn't be enough to get them all to investigate. Shouting was out as well, since there was a chance Blair would recognize my voice. I didn't want to fire the gun, either. Bullets have a nasty habit of going where they shouldn't, and the sound of a little .22 might not be enough to draw everyone's attention. I'd just have to get cute, then.

From my limited knowledge of the layout of the place there was a big window in the main room, and its curtains were wide open. I hurried back to the roof, leaned cautiously over the wall and checked. Yeah, plenty of light spilled out. With a gulp and grimace, I went partially transparent, and, fighting the wind, eased out over the edge. Lower and lower I went, until I reached the window and could see the tableau within.

Blair, another plainclothes man, and two uniforms, along with Burton and Ruth. Perfect. I rose high enough to grab hold of a decorative ledge, then went solid again and determinedly didn't think about the drop awaiting me if it gave way. It held my weight. I was stretched down far enough so that only my legs were framed in the window. I gave an experimental kick against the glass.

What a thud. But it didn't break. Maybe the noise got their attention; I couldn't tell. I kicked again, harder. They must have used extra heavy glass in case of birds smacking against the building. Another kick and another. I was losing my hold on the ledge and getting tired. The blood loss had taken its toll on me. One more toe-bruising kick, the hardest I could manage, was all I had left in me.

The glass suddenly shattered. I heard Ruth's surprised yelp and other sounds from the men and could figure they were rushing to the window to have a look.

Partly transparent, I let go of the ledge and shot straight up. They would have the impression of my dangling legs rising toward the roof. I waited to the count of twenty to give them all time to stampede up the service stairs, then floated down and in through the broken window.

The flat was empty, as I'd hoped. Solid again, I strolled to the phone and had the operator connect me to the local precinct. I got hold of the senior man and gave him Burton's number, making him repeat it back to me. He did so, but I could tell he was getting hot below the collar. He demanded my name.

I love the control that an anonymous phone call gives me.

"Never mind who I am, you just write this down. You know about that call Lieutenant Blair just went out on? Well, it's definitely murder. Yeah. They just found Alby Cornish on the penthouse roof. That's right, the fighter. Soldier Burton popped Alby tonight for not taking a dive. You'll find the murder weapon in Burton's sock drawer with his girlfriend's prints all over the bullets. That's Ruth Phillips. Call Blair back at this number in about two minutes and tell him what I just told you. No, I don't think so. I'm just an honest citizen trying to help Chicago's finest. You do your job right and we'll all be happy."

I put the receiver back and swiped the hem of my coat over it, then sought and found the bedroom and Soldier Burton's sock drawer. The gun fit neatly under his collection of argyles. If he had a good enough lawyer, he could just march away from this rap, but maybe not with Blair on the case. He was a cop who truly enjoyed the hunt; he'd make things plenty hot for his quarry on this one. Ruth's prints on the bullets would also implicate her in the mess in a big way. She might be turned against her boyfriend by a smart prosecutor.

But, it wasn't my worry anymore. My main concern now was finding Gordy and getting a ride to the Stock-yards for some fresh blood. He'd have a hell of a laugh over this story. I wondered how Blair would fit the business of my breaking the window into his re-port. It wouldn't be the first time I'd left him with an inexplicable mystery.

Someone was in the hall, Burton, arguing with the cops and cursing. As they approached the door, he protested he didn't know nothing about no dead body and almost sounded believable.

No way out for me except the one I'd taken in. Unpleasant but quick. I took it, slipping through the shards of glass like smoke.

The last thing I heard as I drifted down the building with the hot wind for company was Burton's phone ringing its urgent little jingle of doom.

A BIRD FOR BECKY

by Max Allan Collins

Sooner or later, in the life of a private eye in the city, a beautiful woman with a problem walks in the door; and two days before Thanksgiving of 1943, on a delightful fall afternoon in Chicago, a soot-tinged but nonetheless pleasant breeze breathing in the window riding the coattails of the elevated train rumbling by, that is exactly what happened to Richard Stone.

He just didn't expect her to be thirteen years old and the sister of his fiancée (and secretary).

"Katie isn't here, kid," the rangy, darkly handsome detective said. "It's her afternoon off."

He was twenty-nine years of age and fit as a fiddle but hadn't fought in the war; he was one detective who really did have flat feet. Moderately successful, he did mostly retail-credit checks, after finally getting disgusted with divorce work. A snappy dresser, his ten-dollar green-and-black tie loose at the collar of his brown double-breasted gabardine, he had just lit up a Havana cigar after finishing up a stack of reports when he heard somebody entering out in the outer office, followed by the little knock at his inner office door.

"I know it's Katie's afternoon off," Becky said, peeking in the barely opened pebbled-glass-and-wood door, her voice as tentative as it was sweet. She was a cherubic child, china-doll pretty, round-lensed wire glasses perched on her button nose lending her an air of studiousness, honey-blonde red-ribboned hair brushing her shoulders. "I was with her—I . . . I'm afraid I ditched her at the department store."

"That's no way to treat your big sister," he said, trying to put a little scold in his voice, but liking her spirit—and, like any good detective, curious as to her motives.

The child entered the room—and she was a child, a slender teenaged beauty barely touched by puberty's hand—and he felt almost guilty noticing how nice her legs were as they flashed toward him under the blue pleated skirt. Her blouse of blue with white stripes had parallel rows of tiny white buttons that gave her a naval air.

Her expression was military-severe, too, as she positioned herself before his desk; so was her posture. An ex-soldier might have said, "At ease."

Stone said, "Sit down, honey. Take a load off."

She pulled up the client's chair and sat, but she remained troubled, a furrow digging into that smooth, smooth brow. "I need your advice, Uncle Dick. Your help."

"You know you can come to me for me anything, dollface. Unless you've gone and found another guy on me?"

Now she smiled. "No. You're still my best beau, Uncle Dick."

"Good. So what's the trouble? What's got you shakin' off your sister in the middle of Christmas shopping?"

Becky and Katie lived with their widowed mother in a northside apartment. The child was on Thanksgiving vacation break.

She was frowning in thought. "I think I need to see an alienist. Or is psychiatrist the more accepted term now?"

He resisted the urge to smile. If anybody was well-adjusted, it was this kid; if any thirteen-year-old didn't need a headshrinker, it was her. She used proper English, went to church (and Sunday school) with perfect-attendance-pin regularity, wore no makeup despite peer pressure, was a voracious reader, and earned straight As. Her nastiest habit was buying movie fan magazines and taking in two picture shows every weekend.

He played it straight, however; didn't kid her.

"What's troubling you, sweetheart?"

Her eyes lowered; they were darting, as if she were following a mouse scurrying around down on the floorboards. "It started last . . . last month. I was doing research at the library."

Some wild kid, this Becky.

Now the big long-lashed eyes raised and locked onto him, unblinkingly blue and beautiful. "You remember . . . that gangster picture you took me to?"

"Oh, hell's bells, kid—you didn't tell your sis we took in that matinee, did you?" He had told Katie they were going to a Disney picture. "She doesn't like that violent nonsense. She'll kill me if she finds out—"

"Remember how you told me," Becky said, rolling over his words, "that *this* city, *our* city, had *real* gangsters a lot, lot worse than anything in that picture."

"Sure. Right. I told you that movie was a laundered, Hollywood version of a real story. About a real gangster—Moe Kingman."

Fourteen years ago, the city had been rocked by gang wars, and Morris "Moe" Kingman had been in the thick of it; a daring, innovative gangleader, King Moe had worked to form alliances with the Capuzzis, Greenbergs and every criminal faction from Cicero to Gary, then doublecrossed them and wound up in a ditch riddled with lead.

"Well, I went to the library to do research," Becky said. "I read all the old newspaper accounts. And there were magazines articles, too, in the national press, and even a couple books on the subject . . ."

"Don't tell me you did a term paper on it."

She nodded. "Yes. For Social Studies. 'Diplomacy in the Criminal Underworld: The Failed Reign of King Moe.' I got an A minus."

"Minus? That's not like you."

She shrugged and her blonde locks bounced. "The 'minus' was for 'inappropriate subject matter.' "

"Ah. So blood and guts doesn't play in eighth-grade Social Studies."

"No. You can get away with it in History, better. You should read my Genghis Khan paper."

"Becky," Stone said, grinning, shaking his head, "you have hidden depths I knew nothing about."

"You can say that again, flatfoot."

Stone blinked; not only were the words inappropriate, coming from that sweet kewpie mouth, but the voice itself was suddenly of a new, deeper, rougher timbre. Almost, not quite, a male timbre; but still, it was a little girl's voice, it was Becky's voice all right. . . .

"Becky?"

"Not Becky," Becky said, and her eyes had narrowed, and her mouth was a sneering smirk. "Name's Moe. But you can call me Mr. Kingman."

Stone's breath drew in, involuntarily; he might have been hit in the stomach.

"Becky . . . what the hell kind of talk . . ."

"Watch your language, dick," Becky said, the lack of capitalization on the word apparent in her rough, mannish tone. "Don't ya know you're talkin' to a damn kid?"

And Becky chortled. She squinted in irritation and removed the wire glasses, tossing them onto the desk. Then she reached for the brown wooden humidor to the right of his blotter, popped the lid and selected a Havana. Stone's jaw dropped as he watched her use the horse-head lighter on his desk to fire it up.

The child's quick puffs developed into a long draw on the cigar that, finally, made her cough. "Lousy brat's lungs ain't worth beans," Becky said, then seemed to settle down, puffing on the luxurious smoke, easing back in the chair and crossing her legs in a most unladylike manner, an ankle resting on a knee.

"You know, Beck," Stone said, sitting forward, "I like a good laugh as much as the next guy. But you're pushing it. If your sis . . ."

"She ain't gonna show up here," Becky said. "It's her day off! Why would she comin' look for the brat here, anyway?"

Stone stood. He pointed a scolding finger. "Put out that damn cigar. Now!"

"Tch, tch, tch," Becky said, cigar buried in a corner of her mouth, bobbling; the kid's face had transformed into something you might see in a pool hall. "Language! A child is present."

"You're not too big for me to lay you over my knee . . ."

"I think I am," Becky said, looking herself over. "A little flat-chested, maybe, but this is definitely not a body you wanna be 'layin' ' over your knee . . . particularly if your secretary fools us and *does* show up."

That froze Stone: not just the threat but the nasty adult knowledge this kid suddenly had.

"You wanna keep your distance from me, dick," Becky said. "Hands off. Dirty old men go to jail, you know, for takin' advantage of sweet young things. Word 'jailbait' ring a bell?"

Stone was reeling. He stumbled back behind his desk and lowered himself into the swivel chair. "Becky . . . what's this about?"

The sweet kid's face grimaced around the cigar. "I told ya, knucklehead. The name's Moe Kingman. Yeah, yeah—and you can call me Moe. Be my guest."

She had come to him talking about a psychiatrist; and as he looked into the cold narrow eyes in the child's face, Stone knew this was not a joke. This was something. Something strange. Something terrible. Something real.

Becky was batting the air with a hand in which the cigar was propped, making smoke trails. "Listen, I don't know much about this mumbo jumbo . . . ask

the kid, when she comes back. I know *she's* got a
theory. Jeez, kind of an egghead, don't you think?"
Becky gestured to herself. "Good lookin' kid like this,
and no boyfriend? She oughta be hangin' around the
soda shop lookin' for partners to play post office—not
hauntin' the library, researchin' dead gangsters."

"Like you."

"Like me. Look—here's where the kid comes in.
For whatever reason, she's the door I found to come
through. I been asleep for God knows how long . . .
or maybe the damn devil knows. Anyway—I'm back.
I'm in her head and talkin' through her mouth. Get
the picture?"

"Starting to."

"I'd rather have my old body back, but last time I
looked, it was full of holes. Worms are crawling in and
out of them holes about now, and makin' new ones."

"Probably not, Moe. You're dust and bones by
now."

"Rub it in, why don't you? Now here's where you
come in—you're gonna find my killer."

"What?"

Becky's grin was in no way girlish. "Find my killer,
and I'll give you the kid back. Or at least, I'll try
to. I'd be lyin' if I said I was in complete control of
this situation."

"Don't you know who killed you?'

"Sure, in the who-pulled-the-trigger sense. It was
Duke Mantis. That bum still around?"

Stone nodded. "Sure. Running your old club, the
Palace . . . only it's called the Chez Dee now, after
the current owner, Danny O'Donnell. Only, Duke
doesn't get his hands dirty anymore."

She snorted. "He was a cheap gunsel back when I
knew 'im. Smalltimer, freelance, not aligned with nobody. And before he plugged me, the slob didn't do
me the courtesy of tellin' me *who* hired 'im—and who
framed me.

"Framed you?"

"Yeah. I had a counsel meeting organized, bringin' every outfit together into one big syndicate. And somebody made me out a doublecrosser. Some damn Judas in the woodpile. *That's* who really killed me . . ."

Becky touched her chest; her face seemed greenish.

"Jeez Louise," she growled. "Maybe this thing's a little strong for me, after all that time away . . ."

She rested the cigar in his glass ashtray and then, like a child at school resting her head on her desk, rested hers on his. Stone rose, came around and stroked the sleeping child's head.

He stood there watching her slumber, her breathing building to a gentle snore, and wondered how he could help her. She was his client, after all. Wasn't she in his client's chair?

The door in the outer office opened and he heard Katie call out: "Richard! Richard, I need your help!"

He went out to her, Katie Crockett, his sandy-haired secretary (and fiancée), her lovely dark eyes brimming with tears, her high-cheekboned model's features clenched with worry.

"I can't find Becky anywhere," she blurted. "We were shopping and I just turned around and—"

"She's right here, sweetheart," he said, taking her by the arm; the young woman wore a gray wool coat with shiny brass military buttons over a white blouse and navy skirt. "She got lost and was pretty worried, herself . . . and when she couldn't find you, she came here looking for me. Knowing you'd check here eventually."

By this time Katie, listening as she went, had moved into the inner office where she could see the child sleeping, head on the desk. The smell of cigar smoke hung like a nasty curtain, however, and Katie's face—which had gone from worry to relief in a heartbeat—now turned to a frown.

"Richard, were you smoking one of these in front of her?"

"No. No, sweetheart . . . I just happened to be smoking when she came in. I put it right out."

"That awful smoke. So strong. Bad for her."

"I couldn't agree more."

Now Katie clung to his arm, fell against him, her coiled worry having turned completely to loose-limbed relief. "Thank God she looks up to you so. And thought to come here."

"She's a great kid."

"The best. But lately . . ."

"What?"

"I don't know," Katie said, and her shoulder-length locks bounced on her shoulders, much as Becky's had earlier. "She just . . . hasn't quite been herself lately."

Private First Class Ben Crockett, Katie's younger brother, Becky's older brother, had died in the war. The news had come last Christmas—a Christmas Day telegram that had brought anything but good cheer— and now with the holiday season upon them again, Ben's family would have bittersweet memories to deal with, with the bitter almost certainly outweighing the sweet. Stone knew that Becky had adored her brother and was hardly surprised the girl was troubled.

But for those troubles to emerge in such a bizarre fashion was unexpected, to say the least.

He took Katie and her sister out for supper, to the Bismarck Hotel's dining room, where the menu was "Bavarian" (before the war, it had been German). Dark wood, rich carpet, glittering glass chandeliers, mirrored walls that made the large room huge, and, of course, linen tablecloths provided an elegant evening-out atmosphere that he hoped would soothe both his girls. And anyway, the chef was a client and a pal and the bill would be on the cuff.

But nobody—not even Stone—finished their fancy meals. A gray cloud hung over the table: Katie's stomach was "nervous" from the scare of losing Becky at the department store; and the child and the detective stole furtive glances as they shared their terrible secret.

When Katie went to the powder room, way off in the hotel lobby, the detective and his client were finally alone.

"When did this start?"

"Today was the first time, Uncle Dick. The first time he . . . came out."

"What do you mean, 'came out'?"

She shrugged helplessly. "Before this, he was just a voice in my head. Talking to me. Sometimes out loud, in the mirror, but with nobody around. Except for, well . . . several times he . . . he took over and pretended to be me."

"Pretended?"

She nodded, blonde locks bobbing, blue eyes bright and worried behind the round lenses. "But he wasn't very good at it. He used slang words I wouldn't. Sis gave him . . . or me . . . some awful funny looks."

"You know . . . your idea about seeing that certain kind of doctor. It ain't a bad one."

Another nod, the eyes widening. "Hearing voices is a symptom of certain mental illnesses. I did research on a paper for . . ."

"I'm sure you did. But this isn't school, Beck. This problem isn't . . . abstract."

She sighed a world-weary sigh beyond her years and stared into her crystal glass of shaved-ice and water. "Joan of Arc heard voices," she offered, just a little bit defensive about it. "And she was a saint."

Or a screwball with religion, he thought. But he said, "That's right."

"It was his idea, you know."

"Whose idea to what?"

She pointed to her head. "Him. To come see you."

"Moe Kingman sent you to see me? See, there's proof this is your imagination at work, your whadyacallit . . ."

"Subconscious acting up."

"Yeah, that. I wasn't a detective back in Moe Kingman's day—I was a kid, like you. He wouldn't know me from Adam—"

She was shaking her head. "He knows everything I know, Uncle Dick. He has my memory to look things up in—like the card catalog at—"

"The library, I know. Where you get all your great ideas."

She used a fork to traces lines in the tablecloth; quietly, almost pitifully, she said, "I hope I *am* crazy."

"Don't talk nonsense."

She looked up and the eyes were wet, now. "I do. I hope I'm fruity as a cornucopia basket, Uncle Dick. I don't wanna be some reincarnated gangster!"

People at nearby tables were looking at them; he shot them glares, sending them scurrying back to their food as he scooted his chair closer to the kid.

"Moe *said* you had a theory," Stone said quietly, almost whispering. "Is that it?"

She nodded. "Mr. Kingman died about the time I was born. He came back as me, only usually in reincarnation, you don't remember former lives . . ."

"Ah. So you're an expert on reincarnation, too."

"That History paper I did on King Tut last year? It kind of got me interested. And I also did one for Science called 'Psychic Phenomena: A Factual Basis for the Supernatural.' And then in Geography my term paper was on 'Religion in India' . . ."

"Oh, brother . . ."

"That movie you took me to, and the research . . . must have triggered it. Woke him up, kind of."

Stone humored her. "Well, then, how do we put your former self back to sleep?"

She reached a small delicate hand out and gripped his hand with strength worthy of a steelworker. The eyes behind the glasses were narrow again.

"Find the rat bastard that killed me," Becky said harshly, "and you can have the damn kid back."

Stone blinked and was looking back into the wide eyes of his future sister-in-law.

"I'm sorry, Uncle Dick," she said, and she began to cry.

He handed her a linen napkin. "It's okay, baby. Don't worry about it. I'm on the case."

Katie was approaching, and Stone told the kid to dry her eyes and pull herself together. Their red-jacketed waiter soon arrived to offer dessert, but Becky wasn't interested.

"You two have some if you like," she said. "It's my turn to use the restroom."

And as she scurried off—maybe to finish off that cry of hers—her older sister said, "You see that, Richard?"

"What?"

"No dessert. She really *isn't* herself."

"The question is," Stone said over a beer in a booth at the Blue Spot, "do I tell Katie?"

"Why wouldn't you tell her?" Hank Ross asked, over his own beer. The heavy-set homicide sergeant, ten years older than Stone, was probably the detective's best friend and could be counted on for no-nonsense advice.

"I don't know if she can handle it," Stone said. "I've caught her at her desk, bawling over her brother's picture, half a dozen times the last three or four weeks."

Hank smirked, making his bulldog puss even more wrinkled. "You figure Katie's too fragile."

"Something like that."

"Hell, if she can put up with a selfish lunkhead like you for a boss—and a boyfriend—she can take almost anything."

"Thanks for the vote of confidence. But there's something else."

"What?"

"Becky came to me not just as her 'uncle,' but seeking my help in . . . a professional capacity."

"As a client, you mean."

"Yeah. And she deserves her privacy."

"Client confidentiality kinda thing."

"Right."

Hank's eyes rolled like slot-machine lemons. "Are you completely nuts? Katie's thirteen-year-old sister thinks she's a dead gangster, and you wanna respect her privacy? She needs help, Stoney. Medical help."

"She did bring up the idea of a psychiatrist herself . . ."

"Right. Cook County has a good man on the staff I can refer ya to; it's who the p.d. uses when any of our own starts developin' belfry bats."

"Hey! This is a normal, well-balanced kid, Hank—"

"Yeah, yeah. Who just happens to think she's the late Moe Kingman. King Moe! That pipsqueak pretender."

"You knew him?"

"I knew him. Five-feet-six with an ego bigger than a battleship. Pinstripe suits with black shirts and white ties, thirty-dollar Florsheims, puffin' cigars longer than pool cues and costly as a porterhouse."

"Any extra charge for the mixed metaphors?"

Hank laughed over the rim of his beer mug. "Who taught ya that word, that bookworm kid? She's broke up over her brother's death, her overactive imagination is brimmin' with all that hooey from books and movies, and she's a candidate for the laughing academy if you don't get her some help. Client! Jesus!"

"Who murdered Moe Kingman, Hank?"

"Whadda you care? It's ancient history."

"I'm doing research. And I ain't the library type."

Hank let some air out. "Well, the way street scuttlebutt had it, it was Duke Mantis—he was a trigger back before he became a nightclub entrepreneur, y'know."

"But who hired him?"

Hank shrugged, took a gulp of suds, and said,

"Could have been any one the major mobs—the Capuzzis, the Greenberg boys, O'Donnell's faction. They were all at that damn dinner."

"You mean, there's some truth in that old wives' tale?"

"Yeah, yeah, I know it sounds like a skyscraper of a tall story, but I was in on the investigation with the county coppers, myself." He shook his head, staring down into his empty beer like he was looking for tea leaves to interpret. "Funny. It was just about, what? Fourteen years ago this month."

Stone nodded. "Thanksgiving dinner for the boys."

The story, which Stone had always dismissed as so much malarkey, was that Moe Kingman had invited a high-ranking rep from every mob in the city out for a Thanksgiving peacemaking dinner at a back-country roadhouse. They were all sitting around the back room at a banquet table, big-shot tuxedoed thugs swimming in a haze of cigar smoke, pounding down booze, flirting with scantily-clad B-girl waitresses, waiting for Moe, when a waiter placed before them a silver platter with the biggest, most succulent-looking roast turkey anybody ever saw.

According to the much-passed-around yarn, the waiter had presented Mr. Kingman's apologies for his tardiness and said it was Moe's desire that they not let the bird get cold. To go ahead and carve and eat the steaming, fragrant fowl.

Legend had it that the representative of the Capuzzi gang was the one who began carving the bird, whose stuffing was a delicate mixture of sage, bread crumbs, and TNT.

Hank was holding his empty mug up; a passing waitress took it for refilling. Then the homicide sergeant said, "It was the biggest mess I ever saw. Blood. Guts. Not to mention turkey meat. A real slaughter."

"Then how does anybody know what really happened?"

"Duke was there. Sole survivor. He stepped out into

the parking lot to get a pack of smokes outa his glove compartment, and the whole damn place blew up behind him."

"Convenient."

"Maybe. At any rate, King Moe's efforts to consolidate the city's underworld factions into one mob blew to smithereens when that turkey exploded. Any gangleader in town mighta put that contract out on him."

"Moe . . . or Becky . . . thinks somebody in his own mob betrayed him."

"Coulda been. His partner, Sam Parr, took over the mob, for all the good it did him. Parr's a crack bookkeeper but no kinda businessman. When the Prohibition plug got pulled, the Kingman mob under Parr kinda crumbled."

Parr worked for O'Donnell now.

Hank accepted his refilled mug from the waitress and had a sip; his eyes turned sly. "Of course, maybe . . . if it was Parr who framed him, if Moe *was* framed . . . maybe Parr's motive wasn't strictly business."

"Oh?"

"You are young, aren't ya, Stoney. Moe had a beautiful chorus-girl wife . . . Linda LaRue, real name Selma Horshutz, a blonde with curves in places where most dames don't even have places. Least she used to. I hear she's kinda blowsy now, and's back to using 'Selma.' But Parr stuck by her. They even had a kid."

"Greed and love. The two big motives."

Hank leaned forward. "Stoney, you can't be serious. You're not really gonna look into the murder of Moe Kingman . . ."

"Why not? You cops never solved the case, did you?"

"Tell ya what, Stoney," Hank said, and he dug out a small notebook and stubby pencil from a suitcoat pocket. "I'm gonna write down that head doctor's number. Whether you take that kid there or sign on for some help yourself, that's up to you . . ."

* * *

"Richard," Katie said, hugging him by the arm, "I'm so pleased you've taken such an interest in Becky."

They were in the reception area of his modest two-room suite of offices, waiting for the child to come back from the washroom off his inner office.

"No big deal," Stone said. "She wants to pick out a Christmas present for her big sis and needs a little help from Santa."

Katie's big brown eyes were lavishing love on him; she was a beautiful girl under any circumstances, but Katie seemed especially radiant today. "Since Ben died . . . and of course Poppa died when Becky was only four . . . having a strong father figure for her to look up to—well, it's very important."

"Hey, she's a cute kid. My pleasure."

She kissed him, a sweet, long kiss, then smiled slyly at him. "It will be . . ."

Becky came out from the inner office; she wore a light blue wool winter coat with a hood and a belt that cinched around her not unlike that of the trench-coat Stone was wearing. It was an adult-looking garment, but her doll's face was that of a child younger than her thirteen years.

"Thanks for the list," Becky said to her sister, referring to a wish list Katie had given the girl to aid her in shopping.

"You hold down the fort," Stone advised Katie as he took the younger girl by the arm and guided her out the door. "We'll be back in time for dinner."

"Let's eat light," Katie suggested, taking her position behind her desk. "Mom's planning a feast for tomorrow, and you two better build up an appetite."

Tomorrow was Thanksgiving, of course, but the thought of a roasted turkey only reminded Stone of a certain banquet Moe Kingman had once thrown.

"Do you feel guilty?" Becky asked him as they walked toward the parking lot where his Chevy coupe was parked, down the block. The air was fall crisp, with more than a hint of winter to come.

"About fooling your sis? Heck, no. I think we're in agreement we don't want to worry her. We'll see what the doc thinks."

Becky had been eager to take an appointment with the psychiatrist over at Cook County, the one Hank Ross had recommended.

"If the doc advises informing your sis," Stone said, opening the rider's side door of the Chevy for her, "we'll fill her in. Otherwise . . ."

"What she don't know won't hurt her."

He looked at her sharply.

She smiled, and giggled, like the kid she was. "Just pulling your leg, Uncle Dick. That was me talking."

He sighed, smiled back, glad that she was feeling good enough about this to joke a little but not feeling very much like joking himself.

He was cruising through an industrial district when he felt a small hand on his sleeve.

"Hang a right, shamus," Becky said.

"You kidding around again?" he asked, smiling over at the child.

But the smile froze. Becky, wire frames on the seat between them, was training Sadie at him. And Sadie was no lady: she was Stone's .38.

"I got this outa your desk drawer," Becky said, "when the kid wasn't payin' attention."

Stone's hand tightened on the steering wheel, but he kept any reaction out of his face. "Hiya, Moe. Thought you two shared all your secrets."

"We did. But I'm gettin' stronger, pal."

That wasn't good news.

He turned right, into a rundown area that had never recovered from the Depression. Dead warehouses loomed like an industrial Stonehenge. The gun looked huge in her hand, its snout an awful empty eye that stared at him.

"What do you want, Moe?"

"What I *don't* want is my head shrunk. I ain't a mental condition, dick. I'm an old soul in a new carton."

"So you do buy Becky's take on this."

Becky shrugged, sneered; the .38 was steady in her small hand. "Maybe we're just starting to blur into each other, a little. You want me out of her life, and yours, then get crackin' on the case."

"Why don't you keep Becky's appointment, then, and let an expert hear both you *and* the kid talk." Stone kept his voice calm, reasonable. "If you can convince that shrink you're not a mental condition, then I'll gladly take your case."

Becky's chuckle came rumbling out of depths she didn't possess. "No. I know what makes dicks like you tic. Money."

"How are you gonna manage that, Moe? Becky gets thirty-five cents a week allowance, and she pays for her meal ticket out of it."

"Pull over."

"Where?"

"There!" She waved the revolver toward a warehouse labeled ACME STORAGE, a mammoth brick structure with boarded-up windows.

Stone pulled up near the front entry. The street was as empty as a Western ghost town; the fall breeze, unable to find any fallen leaves to blow around, settled for scraps of refuse. At Becky's command, Stone got out of the car, and then she was behind him, the steel nose of the rod digging a hole in his trenchcoat, at the small of his back.

Stone, prodded by the girl's gun, headed for the front door.

"That discolored brick to the left of the number," Becky said. "It's loose. Work at it and it'll pull out."

He did as he was told—and the brick *was* loose, and when he removed it, he found a key in a recess on the other side of the brick. The key opened the front door, and soon the detective and the little girl with the big gun were standing in a huge open space, broken up only by the posts that climbed to the high open-beamed ceiling and a small wood-and-glass-walled office opposite where they came in.

"Ran a lot of booze outa here in my day," Becky said, her small harsh voice careening off the cement floor and frightening birds nested high in the rafters, sending them flapping. She nudged him with the gun and their footsteps echoed.

"Okay, dick," Becky said. "Step into my office."

No key was required for that. Any furnishings that had once been here were long gone, though an old frayed green carpet covered the floor.

"Yank the carpet back," Becky demanded. "Over in that corner."

Humoring the kid, not wanting to try to take the gun away for fear it might go off and hurt her (or, for that matter, him), Stone pulled back the carpet. A chunk of wood was fitted down into a recess in the cement floor.

"Lift that outa there," Becky snarled.

He did. It revealed a small cast-iron safe with a combination lock.

"Seven right, one left, four right," Becky said.

He turned the dial as directed; and he heard the tumblers fall into place, and the lock clicked open.

Inside the safe were stacks of greenbacks. The hundred-dollar variety.

"Should be a cool hundred Gs in there, flatfoot," Becky said. "Twenty-five of it's for you if you take my case. Another twenty-five if—*when*—you solve it."

Stone was lifting the bundles of bucks reverently out of their little basement. He piled them neatly on the floor and sat staring at the stuff, legs crossed like a kid playing Indian.

"What about the other fifty Gs?" Stone asked.

"That's for the kid's college education," Becky said. "I mean, if she's right and this is my new life, I gotta look out for myself, right?"

* * *

Library research hadn't led Becky to that warehouse, that loose brick, not to mention that loose cash. Stone could not quite bring himself to believe that his fiancée's kid sister was a reborn mobster; but he was capable of believing that hundred Gs, all right.

As far as Stone was concerned, Moe Kingman had a client.

They were in the Chevy again, heading out of the industrial district.

"Let's drop in on my old flame," Becky said, lighting up one of Stone's Havanas with a match off a Blue Spot matchbook from his glove compartment; she had apparently pilfered several cigars at the same time she'd lifted his .38 (which she had returned when Stone accepted the twenty-five thousand dollar retainer).

"Linda LaRue, you mean? Mrs. Sam Parr? That's a good place to start, Moe, but I work alone."

"No," Becky said, and puffed at the cigar, getting it going. "I wanna see her. I gotta see her. See, I loved that dame, and that dame loved me. She'd know me anyplace."

Stone gazed at her, agape. "She'll look at a thirteen-year-old girl and see her years-dead boyfriend?"

"I got a distinctive personality," Becky said, cigar tilted upward like an FDR cigarette-in-holder, "no matter what the package."

He couldn't argue with that. "You're going to make yourself sick with those things."

"Naw. The kid's gettin' used to me as a house guest. You know where my old partner and ex-girl live?"

Stone didn't, but a stop at a phone booth and a quick look in the book was all the detective work it took. Mr. and Mrs. Sam Parr and their grade-school-age son lived in an upper-middle-class neighborhood in the northwest suburbs—a story-and-a-half oversize bungalow on an oversized well-tended lawn. A driveway rose to a one-car garage; shrubbery hugged the house; a swing set guarded the rear.

"Not exactly a gangland hideout," Stone said.

"Sam's a bookkeeper," Becky said. The tamped-down cigar was in the car ashtray, for later refiring. "If Sam killed me, it was for love, not money."

"You don't think your 'old flame' could've been in on it?"

"Never," Becky said, with a flounce of her blonde locks. "I got a way with dames."

"Yeah," Stone said, and headed up the walk.

He knocked at the front door but got no response; listening carefully, he could hear a mechanical whine from inside. Somebody was doing something in there that was a little noisy—vacuuming, maybe.

"Let's try around back," Stone suggested.

The back door stood open, letting out baking smells. The unmistakable aroma of pecan pie tickled Stone's nostrils. He knocked on the open door, sticking his head in.

"Excuse me," he called, over the thrum of the electric mixer.

She heard him at once—the mixer was only on a low speed, as she blended the pumpkin and spices and milk and eggs and sugar—and in the plainly attractive housewife's face remained echoes of the pretty chorus girl she'd once been. She stood at a counter in a moderate-size, very modern kitchen, gleaming white with electric appliances, electric refrigerator, gas range, white-and-black checked linoleum.

"I'm sorry," she said pleasantly over the mechanical whine, "we don't buy from door-to-door salesmen."

Selma Parr, the former Linda LaRue (née Horshutz), was pleasantly plump but pushing it; she wore a white-and-blue checked tablecloth of a housedress with a frilly white apron, her dark blonde hair pinned up. The only powder on her face was some stray flour on one cheek.

"I'm not a salesman, Mrs. Parr," Stone said. "I'm a detective . . ."

She frowned, turned off the mixer; she pointed toward the outside with her wooden, pumpkin-mixture-moistened mixing spoon. "My husband is a legitimate businessman. If you don't have a warrant, I must ask you to—"

He stepped tentatively inside, hat in his hands. "I'm not with the police, ma'am. I'm a private investigator. It's about something that happened a long time ago."

Her eyes—big brown, long-lashed chorus-girl eyes in the matronly face—tightened. "I . . . I don't really care to talk about the past. Please go."

Stone sighed. "There's somebody who wants to see you."

Becky stepped inside, looking sweet and innocent in her blue winter coat, the smell of cigar smoke masked by that of pecan pie.

Selma Parr smiled, the automatic response of a mother to a child, any child. "Why, what do you want, little girl? Or should I say 'young lady'? Are you with this gentleman?"

"You still got that tattoo with my name in it, baby?" Becky asked. "The heart-shaped one where the sun don't shine?"

And Selma Parr—the former Linda LaRue (née Hurshutz)—fainted dead away, in a pool of her white apron on her black-and-white checked linoleum, mixing spoon limp in her hand.

The detective helped the housewife up from the floor and was guiding her to the kitchen table when they both noticed that the girl was already seated there—and was in that same, folded-arms, asleep-on-her school-desk posture as in Stone's office.

"What . . . is this about?" Selma asked.

"I think the kid gets worn out after a while," Stone said matter of factly. "Being Moe must take a lot of juice."

Selma's eyes were wide. "Being Moe . . . ?"

Becky was slumbering peacefully, gently snoring.

"There's no way to sugarcoat this," he said.

"Sugarcoat what? How could that . . . child know what . . . she knows?"

"I can only tell you what *I* know," he said.

And as the child slept, Stone told Selma the entire story—well, almost the entire story; the part about the money he kept to himself. Old habits die hard.

It took a while, and Selma listened quietly, nodding in interest (if not acceptance) of the bizarre tale, and gradually began interspersing housewifely duties during the telling, rising to tend her pecan pie, removing it from the oven and out to cool, filling a pie crust with pumpkin filling, putting that pie in, finally serving herself and Stone cups of coffee.

"You think this poor kid is a nutcase?" Selma asked. She was on her second cup of coffee and smoking a cigarette now, and the chorus-girl side of her was mingling with the mom.

"She's a brilliant child, and she's been troubled over the death of her brother. It was just last year—Christmas—that the telegram came."

"But—how does she *know* these things?"

Stone shook his head. "I'm not sure. Somehow I don't think she read about your tattoo at the library."

Selma winced. "I wasn't a tramp, Mr. Stone. I was with a handful of men in my day and with only one man after Moe—my husband. Nobody but Sam and my personal physician ever saw that tattoo . . ."

He sipped the coffee; it was rich and black and good. "Who knows? Maybe there's something to it. Maybe Moe really was reborn as this sweet kid. Whatever the case, he says he'll leave her alone if I can solve his murder."

"Is that how you intend to address this problem, Mr. Stone?"

"At least in the short term. The way she's acting, if

I take her to a shrink, they'll lock her up and throw away the key. Hell, they'll bury it."

Selma seemed genuinely concerned as she gazed at the girl. "With this . . . delusion, she might hurt herself. You say she's smoking already. Maybe drinking will be next . . . Moe was a heavy drinker, you know. He's bound to start in again . . ."

"Listen to yourself, Selma."

She shook her head. "I know. I know. I'm talking like I believe this, myself."

"Do you know anything about Moe's murder, Selma? Anything you didn't tell the cops?"

She seemed more hurt than alarmed by this question. "Moe . . . that child . . . doesn't think *I* had anything to do with it, does he? She?"

"Moe says you loved him."

Her eyes went half-hooded and wistful; cigarette smoke curled lazily up from her fingers. "I did. He was a little guy, but he had a big heart. He came up hard, from the streets, and got involved in the only line of business that was open to him. He was trying to stop the gang war, trying to bring about an alliance that could end the killing and pave the way for the rackets to give over to legitimate business. That's why they killed him."

"Why *who* killed him, Selma?"

"Only Duke Mantis knows the answer to that question." She laughed, hollowly. "Funny—Moe's death did bring about a truce, if not an alliance. All the mobs had something in common: They'd all been betrayed by that 'little dirty doublecrosser.' "

"Which you don't think Moe was."

"No. He was a straight-up guy, and I loved him."

"You married his partner."

She lifted her chin nobley. "Sam loved Moe like I did. Sam and Moe came up on the same hard streets together; they mighta been brothers. Sam only took me under his wing 'cause Moe wasn't there to do it anymore."

"Love makes good men do bad things, Selma."

"Not Sam. He's a gentle soul. Ask Moe. I mean, ask her."

Becky was stirring. "Oh . . . where . . . are we, Uncle Dick?"

"You don't know, honey?"

Rubbing her eyes, she tried to shake the grogginess off. "No. When he . . . he takes over, I'm starting to . . . black out. Oh, Uncle Dick—I'm frightened!"

He gathered the girl in his arms and was soothing her as she sobbed into his chest. Selma came around and patted the child's shoulder as well.

"Could I get you a glass of milk, dear? The pecan pie's for Thanksgiving, but I have cookies."

Becky's smile was warm, and embarrassed. "No, thank you, ma'am. I'm sorry if I caused you any trouble."

Then the girl stood, straightened her blue coat and said, "Take me home, Uncle Dick. Please."

"Hey, Mom!"

It was a boy's voice, just outside the door, and then he came in, in a hurry, a fresh-scrubbed freckle-faced kid of twelve with a full head of reddish brown hair, a flurry in dungarees and red-white-and-blue plaid shirt, blurting words out on the run.

"Can I go over to Larry's and play trains? His dad just got him this great Lionel . . . sorry. Didn't know we had company."

This is Mr. Stone, Morris. And this is Becky . . . what was your last name, dear?

"Crockett," she said, quietly.

"They're old friends of the family," Selma told her son. "Is it all right with Larry's mother, you coming over?"

"Sure!"

"Then go ahead. Just be back for supper."

And the boy was gone.

"Morris?" Stone asked Selma.

"Yes," she said.

Stone nodded, gathered Becky up and soon they were back in the Chevy.

She was putting her glasses back on. "Who was that, Uncle Dick?"

"Selma Parr. You know, Linda LaRue."

"Moe's old girlfriend! Is she a suspect?"

"I don't think so. Not her *or* her husband, either. You don't name your firstborn after a guy you killed."

He dropped his thirteen-year-old client off at her family's apartment. No sign of Moe since Becky fell asleep at the Parr place.

"Bring your appetite tomorrow," Katie's mom said. She was an attractive woman in her fifties who might have been Katie's sister but for the snow-white hair.

"You bet, Mrs. Crockett. Is that mincemeat I smell?"

"Certainly is," she said sweetly. "Bet that brings back childhood memories."

"Certainly does." He had hated his mother's mincemeat pies.

But he left the apartment house thinking about Thanksgiving and about Thanksgiving banquets, and an idea merged with a hunch, becoming a full-blown scheme by the time he got back to the office.

He dialed Sergeant Ross at police headquarters.

"You think you could fix me up," Stone asked his friend, "with the private numbers of the top mob guys in town?"

"You mean Danny O'Donnell himself? And Gus Greenberg?"

"And Papa Capuzzi, too. All of 'em. I don't want to talk to secretaries, either."

"Well, sure, Stoney . . . what kind of party are you thinking of throwing?"

"A surprise party."

"Who's the honored guest?"

"The host."

*   *   *

The Chez Dee had been a fixture on bustling Rush Street since speakeasy days; in fact, back when it was called the Palace, the restaurant/nightclub had been renowned for hidden doors, sliding panels and secret staircases that gave prohibition agents fits. The Palace had been King Moe's domain; after his death, Sam Parr had sold the joint to Danny O'Donnell.

Sandwiched between a flower shop and an all-night barbershop, the Chez Dee boasted a canopy, a uniformed doorman and a facade of translucent glass-brick behind which glowed the pulse of night life. Its vertical neon sign glowed, as well, a beacon in the pleasantly chilly night, attracting the upper crust of the city's riff raff—the richer gangsters, the more corrupt politicians, gamblers, show people, industry captains with their shapely "nieces," and even occasional tourists looking for color.

Stone handed the hat check girl his trenchcoat and fedora and got a celluloid token in return; he paused at the velvet rope and waited. It was fairly early—just before six—and the sleek, glass-and-chrome *art moderne* dining room, with its indirect lighting and stylized murals of slender men and women in tuxes and evening dresses, was sparsely populated. The orchestra hadn't taken its position on the stage yet, and it would be hours before scantily clad showgirls began their "Broadway" revue.

"May I help you, sir?" the dinner-jacketed head-waiter asked. He was a burly guy in his thirties who looked more like a bouncer than a waiter, but his diction was good and he was polite enough.

"I'm Mr. Stone. I made the reservation this afternoon, for your private dining room?"

"Ah, yes, Mr. Stone. We're ready for you. Your guests should start arriving, when?"

"Seven. It was a last-minute invite for them, as well."

"Our kitchen is ready for you, although our chef wanted to apologize because he couldn't accommodate your request—it's a little embarrassing that you had to have the main course catered in."

Stone smiled, shrugged. "Well, Thanksgiving dinner just wouldn't be right without a turkey. Luckily, the chef at the Bismarck Hotel's a client of mine, and you know, roast turkey's their specialty. Here's my guest list . . ."

Stone handed the man a folded sheet of paper.

"This is certainly an, uh . . . elite group," the astounded headwaiter said.

A Who's Who of the city's underworld is what it was.

"I would appreciate it if Mr. Mantis would stop in and say hello around seven-thirty," Stone said. "I'm sure my guests would appreciate it, too, as I know a lot of these gentlemen are business associates and friends of his . . ."

"I'll be sure to tell him. I'm sure he'll stop in." His smile was nervous. "You want me to have a man show you the way?"

"No," Stone said. "I can manage."

He wound through the Chez Dee's dimly lighted oval bar, which was doing considerably better business than the dining room; well-dressed men and women were huddled here and there at tiny tables and in snug booths, as the bar's waitresses—in the Chez Dee's trademark French Maid outfits, including mesh stockings—served up pulchritude and cocktails.

He checked out the private dining room. A big banquet table dominated the spartanly appointed area, the only decorative touch another mural—this one a cityscape, in the same stylized deco manner—with a door that connected with the kitchen.

Satisfied with the layout, he returned to the bar and found a stool to park himself to wait for his guests to start arriving. Feeling a little nervous and perhaps a tad smug about his plan, he noticed a slender, attractive waitress working the other side of the room, and felt a chill.

"Want somethin', bud?" the bartender asked.

"Yeah," Stone said hollowly. "A double."

"A double what?"

"A double anything. I'll be back for it."

He crossed the room and walked over to her, and when she turned, he almost collided with her.

With the dim lighting and her heavy makeup and well-padded bra, not to mention those nice slender legs, Becky made a nice-looking barmaid, for a thirteen-year-old.

"What the hell are you doing here?" they whispered at each other, simultaneously.

Then he guided her by the arm across the bar and into the private dining room; she was still carrying her drink tray, though it was empty except for some change. Kid was making pretty good tips for a beginner.

"What's this about?" Stone demanded.

"I'm doin' your job for ya, flatfoot," Becky said. "This is Duke's joint, so I figured I'd look him up."

"Does your sister know you're here?"

"Yeah, sure. Like she knows I stole her makeup and one of her brassieres and half the toilet paper in that dump to stuff it with. Hey, she's kind of built, your girlfriend."

"Don't talk about your sister that way!" Stone's head was spinning; his gangster guests would be arriving shortly, and here he was with a pubescent racketeer in mesh stockings on his hands. So to speak.

"Aw, she thinks I'm at the library. And, hell, I know my way around this joint better than anybody alive. I planned this club, designed the place. I know ways in and out of here the cockroaches don't."

"And you sneaked into the dressing room the waitresses and showgirls use, and appropriated a costume, and just blended in."

"That's right. I didn't get to the top of the rackets without brains."

"Your brains were found in a ditch out in the country, Moe, scattered around what used to be left of your head."

"Tell me about it! Just let me get that Duke alone, and I'll get who hired him out of him!"

"How?"

Becky shrugged. "I'm pretty, ain't I? And young. And Mantis is a dog, like all men. One way or another . . ."

Stone grabbed the girl's arm. "If you compromise this innocent kid—"

"Hey! I'll just get him in a compromising position and lower the boom. . . . So what the hell are you doing here?"

Stone quickly told her his plan. And his theory.

Becky's eyes were wide with disbelief. "*That's* who you think killed me? Are you kidding?"

"No. You want in on this, to see for yourself, then I'll tell the bartender we want a couple of waitresses to work the room and request that the cute kid with the nice legs who walks like a dockworker be one of 'em."

"There's nothin' wrong with the way I walk!"

"You got to promise to behave yourself."

Becky grinned. "I'll be a good girl. Got a cigar on ya? It's about time for my break."

By seven-fifteen the room was filled with hard men in black tuxes, the air a blue fog of cigarette and cigar smoke, drink glasses clinking with ice, boisterous conversation forming a cloud of noise. The chair at the head of the table was empty, but the guests had the first course—salad—without the man they assumed was their host.

When he called to invite them, Stone had told each of his honored guests that he was calling for Duke Mantis. So each of these underworld figures—Danny O'Donnell, his associate Sam Parr, Gus Greenberg, Papa Capuzzi, and half a dozen others—understood that this Thanksgiving dinner was being thrown by their old friend, Duke.

Along the walls stood the baggy-suited armed guards of the evening, several bodyguards from each of these rival gangster contingencies; right now, an unspoken truce existed between these men. But behind their raucous laughter and confident talk lurked an uneasiness. Perhaps they were all remembering another Thanksgiving dinner, with an exploding main course.

But Duke wouldn't try anything in his own joint; that would be suicide. Wouldn't it?

Nonetheless, the first bodyguard in—one of O'Donnell's men—had positioned himself at the door and patted everyone down as they came in. No one objected to O'Donnell setting this ground rule of no firearms, and even the bodyguards themselves had willingly given up their rods, which lay on a small table in the corner, revolvers, automatics, piled on a linen tablecloth like a bizarre centerpiece.

Stone's gun wasn't among them; he hadn't packed it. But he knew where it was—this time, Sadie wasn't in Becky's pocket, that was for sure. Becky, one of three underdressed barmaids working the banquet room, didn't have pockets in that satin scrap of a getup.

"What are you doin' here, Stone?" Danny O'Donnell asked. His tone was cordial but his eyes were ice.

"I don't know this guy," Greenberg said. "I know everybody here but this guy. Who *is* this guy?"

"Leave him alone, he's a good boy," Papa Capuzzi said. "Him and Jake Marley were partners."

"Oh yeah," Greenberg said. "Marley was a good man. Used to help us out when he was police chief in that little burg out in the boonies. Are you the kid who caught his killer?"

"One and only," Stone admitted.

"Good for you," Greenberg said, and lifted his

bourbon glass in a casual toast. "Now, where's our host, and where's the goddamn food? I'm hungry."

It was another five minutes before Duke Mantis picked up on that cue; understandable, considering he didn't know he was the host.

Duke was tall, rail-thin and angular, sharp sticks well-arranged in the sheath that was his tuxedo; his dark hair was slicked back in the George Raft manner, his eyes pinpricks of bright black in slits beneath slashes of eyebrow, his nose thin and sharp, mouth a wide cut in a long, narrow, high-cheekboned sunken-cheeked chalk-white face.

"I'm sorry, Mr. Mantis," the bodyguard at the door said. "Host or not, I gotta frisk you. No firearms at the table."

"I never pack in my own joint," Duke said contemptuously, but stood for the frisk. "Whadaya mean, 'host'?"

Danny O'Donnell rose. "You had one of your people call this afternoon, didn't ya? We all got calls like that. Ain't this your party?"

Mantis moved slowly around the table; for such a bony-looking guy, he had a dancer's grace, and his smile was calm, cool. Without sitting, he positioned himself at the head of the table, leaning both hands on the back of the chair.

"I couldn't be happier havin' you here at the club, boss," Mantis told O'Donnell. "Same goes for the rest of you gents—but I didn't invite ya."

"Then it's some kinda setup!" Greenberg said, and suddenly everybody was getting up, chairs scraping on the floor, fear in the air.

"Gentlemen!" Stone called out, still seated. "Please sit back down, and take it easy. Mr. Mantis didn't throw this shindig. *I* did."

All of the deadly eyes in the room were on him; it wasn't a wonderful feeling. But soon everyone of these hard-faced men had taken a seat—except for Mantis.

"You?" Papa Capuzzi asked. "But why do you misrepresent yourself?"

"What the hell are you doing," Mantis said, "usin' my name?"

"I invited everyone here," Stone said, quietly, "and said that Duke Mantis would be your host. Well, he is. It's his club."

"But you rented the hall," O'Donnell said.

"Yeah."

"Why?"

"Because fourteen years ago, another Thanksgiving banquet was held . . . and many of you in this room lost close friends and business associates . . . even loved ones. You lost a brother, didn't you, Mr. Greenberg?"

Greenberg nodded solemnly.

The door from the kitchen opened, and Stone's pal Rico from the Bismarck brought in the steaming, aromatic turkey on a silver tray. He put in the midst of the table, nodded at Stone and went out.

"I can guarantee you this bird isn't stuffed with dynamite," Stone said, as the men stared at the main course, contemplating that terrible night fourteen years ago. "I had this catered in from the Bismarck, and you know how great their stuffing is."

"Forget the holiday banter," O'Donnell said. "What's the point of *this* banquet?"

"I was hired by an old friend of Moe Kingman—"

"That bastard!" Greenberg said.

Becky, standing just behind Greenberg, frowned and seemed about ready to conk him with her drink tray; Stone shook his head at her, and she let out a breath and faded back into the woodwork.

"I was hired," Stone began again, "to clear Moe's name."

"He was the lowest murderer that this town ever saw," Danny O'Donnell said, so softly it might have been a prayer.

In the background, Becky winced.

"I don't think so," Stone said. "You think Moe gave every mob in town the bird, fourteen years ago, right? Who alone survived that night?"

Mantis slammed a fist on the table. "What are you sayin'?"

Stone said, "I'm asking: Who killed Moe Kingman?"

Shrugs and little smiles around the table made it unanimous when Moe's old friend Sam Parr, a small sad-faced, bald man, said, "Everybody knows Duke did it."

Stone looked at Mantis, whose white face had reddened.

Mantis said, "I did it, all right. And that's all I'm sayin'. Back when I was a freelancer, when I took a contract, it was between me and the client."

"Very admirable I'm sure," Stone said, "and I won't ask you to betray your sense of integrity, Duke. But I will ask the question: Who hired Duke Mantis to kill Moe Kingman? That's the question I want to ask *you,* gentlemen. *Did* anyone in this room hire Duke to kill Moe Kingman? If not, Duke took it upon himself to do that little deed. And if so, why would he do that? Only because he engineered the entire slaughter of your friends, associates and family to make Moe Kingman someone all of you would want to kill—and himself a hero. Once word got out Duke was the trigger on that job—with everyone of you assuming one of the others hired it done—then Duke was aces with everybody. He went from smalltime freelancer to running this fancy club for you, Mr. O'Donnell."

Face white again, the blood drained out, Mantis said, "You're dead, Stone. I'm comin' out of retirement to take care of you personally."

"Unless," Stone said, "I'm wrong, and one of you did hire Duke, here. Maybe you hired him, Mr. O'Donnell. I mean, you're the one who set up him so sweet."

O'Donnell shook his head, no.

Stone nodded. "I didn't think so. I mean, I'm sure you felt, Mr. O'Donnell, as did so many of you in this room, somewhat indebted to Duke . . . and perhaps because he was the sole survivor of that awful massacre, felt even a certain . . . loyalty to him."

Becky was taking all this in with eyes that were wide and yet tight, her lipsticked mouth open.

Mantis said, "I was hired by somebody in this room. But I don't rat out my associates. Rest assured."

Stone said, "We're all friends here. No one in this room has any reason to deny hiring you to kill Moe . . . unless no one here did. Did you, Mr. Capuzzi?"

The white-haired patriarch of the Capuzzis shook his head solemnly, no. So, one by one, did the representatives of every organized crime group in the city.

"I don't have to take this in my own joint," Mantis said, and he walked quickly to the door.

But the skinny one-time hitman took a quick detour to that table of rods and helped himself, filling his hands. Every man at the table, every bodyguard along the walls, turned their eyes on the wild-eyed club manager. The three barmaids—one of whom was Becky— were equally rapt in giving Duke their attention as he stood with his back to the closed door between the banquet room and the bar, a .45 automatic in one hand, a .38 revolver in the other.

"You guys give me no choice, do you?" he said. "Stone, you son of a bitch, you signed my death warrant tonight. So I'm the only one who can leave this room alive . . ."

Stone dove for the turkey, shoved his hand between the bird's legs and found Sadie, where Chef Rico had tucked her. He didn't bother taking the gun out, just lifted his hand off the table, turkey and all, and fired between the seated O'Donnell and Greenberg, the bullet blazing out from where the bird's head used to be.

Mantis slammed back into the door, nailed in the shoulder, dropping both guns as he did. Bodyguards had the guns in hand before Mantis could even think of retrieving them, and the skinny tuxedoed hood slid down the door, a pile of bleeding bones, whimpering. There was noise out in the bar—shouts, and patrons fleeing the gunfire; but nobody tried to come in. A gangland conference in the back room where gunplay had broken out was not a party anyone was anxious to join.

It was over—or so Stone assumed.

Becky was heading over to Mantis, and she was reaching inside her neckline and coming out with a little .32 that Stone recognized as the purse gun he'd given Katie for protection. Becky's bra, like the turkey, had been stuffed with firepower.

She stood above the moaning gangster, pointing the gun at his head.

"Now you pay, you rat bastard," Becky said.

Mantis looked up, astonishment mingling with his pain and self-pity. "What . . . what did I . . . ever do to you?"

She crouched and placed the nose of the gun against Mantis' skull. "I'm about to show you."

"No," Stone said.

Becky didn't take her eyes off Mantis. "Stay outa this, dick!"

The detective crouched beside her, placed a hand on her shoulder. "You don't need to do this. The men in this room, in their own sweet time, will take care of this problem."

"It's *my* problem."

"You pull that trigger, you're bequeathing an innocent kid a stigma she'll never overcome. And, Moe— you *are* that kid."

Becky turned away from Mantis, though the nose of the rod stayed put. The beautiful blue eyes might have been Becky's, but Moe still seemed to have a hold on her.

"Moe, give this kid a break . . . give yourself a break. Live a little."

Becky smiled; her eyes teared up. "You did it, didn't you, dick? Found my killer. The other twenty-five Gs you'll find in your bottom desk drawer, by the way."

"Thanks, Moe."

Becky's laugh was deep and hollow. "How the hell was I to know that the guy that killed me . . . was the guy that killed me?"

And Becky collapsed in a little puddle of skimpy satin and mesh stockings.

When he turned, the room was empty. There had been a shooting, after all, and even in a joint like this, the cops would eventually come and there would be questions. So the gangsters and their retinues had gathered their guns and gone out the kitchen way.

Not a bad idea.

He gathered his fiancée's kid sister in his arms, and she was slumbering like a baby when he found his own way out through the kitchen and into the night.

The next afternoon, after Katie's mom served them a sumptuous dinner that included a far more savory turkey than the shot-up bird he'd left behind at the Chez Dee, Stone was relieved to be given a choice between pumpkin pie and mincemeat.

Katie was helping her mother in the kitchen and Stone was kicking back, so full from the feast he was nearly in pain, wondering if the girls would mind if he turned on the radio to hear the game (he had twenty bucks on St. Simon's), when Becky came over and gave him a hug.

"Thank you for everything, Uncle Dick."

"You know, I'm not going to be your uncle, sweetheart. I'm gonna be your brother-in-law."

"I can use a brother."

He hugged her. "I know."

Her eyes, behind the lenses of the wire frame

glasses, were bright and a little sad. "He's gone, isn't he?"

"Ben?"

"No. I . . . I mean Mr. Kingman."

"I think so. Though if you're right about reincarnation, the good qualities he had are still with you."

"You know, I think he left me something. A keepsake."

"What?"

"I'll show you."

She went off to her room and came back with a turkey—a cloth one, a stuffed animal, a toy, a comical-looking gobbler like something out of a cartoon. She plopped it on his lap. "Unless *you* bought it for me, Uncle Dick."

He examined the cloth bird. "Can't say I did. You don't remember getting this for yourself, when you were him?"

She shook her head. "No. Toward the end, he just kinda took over. It was like I was . . . asleep."

He examined it; the thing wasn't sewn together very well. In fact, he could see where it had been opened up at its professional seam and then clumsily, hastily resewn. And he saw the corner of something. Something green. Something paper . . .

"I'm gonna have to open this up, honey," he said. "But we can get it sewn back up."

"Okay," she said. She seemed curious, too.

With a two-handed tear, he opened up the bird, and its stuffing was green, entirely green: hundred-dollar bills.

"Uncle Dick!"

"This is yours. He wanted you to have it."

"It's so much . . ."

"If I'm not mistaken, it's fifty thousand dollars, and we'll get it into a college fund for you, right away."

"Is that from Mr. Kingman?"

"Yes, Becky."

"He wasn't such a bad man, was he, Uncle Dick? Looking out for me like this . . ."

Stone nodded and hugged her again, the bird full of money between them, the bills crackling like fall leaves.

He was grateful to the late gangster, whether a reincarnation or just a figment of this child's imagination; but he didn't see Moe as such noble guy.

Like the gangster had said, sending this kid to college was the best way for King Moe to look out for himself.

THE DREAM JOB

by *Heidi E. Y. Stemple*

As Detective Danetti pulled off a pair of bloody latex gloves at the crime scene, Ivan—aka the Terrible—stretched the last bit of sleep out of his body and put a bare foot on the floor by his bed. The sun was just topping the toothy skyline of New York City when both men looked out the window, each in a different apartment separated by seventy-two long blocks, but each thinking of the other.

"Ivan." Danetti scowled. The one word spoke volumes, but not to the body of Tiny Joe Jerome on the bed. His ears would never hear another word.

"Good morning, Danetti," Ivan sang, voice thick with Czech vowels. No one was there in person to hear him either; the ears in his home were all electronic. He was alone in his bedroom, as he had been for the last seven hours.

"Enjoy your day, Danetti," he added as he stepped into the shower.

Danetti wasn't expecting any evidence to be recovered, but he sat at his desk willing the phone to ring, or the fax to spring to life. Mindlessly he flipped through the file in front of him. Tiny Joe was a small-time player like the others, now just another entry in a list that read like a bad mob movie: Jack the Knife, Tony the Tyrannical, One-Eyed Sly, along with eighteen others who had all done a stint in the morgue before being released for burial.

Instinctively, Danetti knew this would be the same

as the rest in other aspects as well. No prints, no weapon, no suspects—officially. The M.O. was identical: killed at night in the bedroom, a single clean knife wound to the heart. No sign of forced entry. No sign of a struggle. No weapon left at the scene. A perfect hit. A perfect job. It was a mob hit all right, that was easy to guess by the victims' common occupations, but—rumors aside—there was no way to prove anything else without a doer.

Still, Danetti knew who had done the hit.

Ivan. Ivan the Bloody. Ivan the Terrible.

The evidence, or lack thereof, proved it.

Danetti would stake his life on it. Which was exactly what he intended to do.

When a call finally came, Danetti answered it before it finished its first ring.

"Danetti," he half yelled into the phone.

His boss's cigar-deepened voice began without preamble, "I'm pulling the surveillance on Ivan's penthouse. The job that went down last night, it wasn't him. He was holed up at midnight. Lights out at one twenty-seven. No movement after that until you were half way through the crime scene this morning. Then it's the usual, him singing to you. Bugs is bugs, Danetti. We got the best up there, and he didn't move. It's not him, Danetti. Find me another suspect."

The dial tone sounded before Danetti could say a word. Not that he could think of one to say. He slammed down the phone and reached for his bottle of Tums.

"Pizza!" The intercom had buzzed and the doorman announced the delivery as Ivan was scanning the paper. No news interested him.

He opened the door and accepted the pizza box, handing the delivery man a twenty. Both men nodded silently, and Ivan closed the door carefully, knowing that the snick of the latch would be recorded on Danetti's bugs.

"Snick for you, snack for me, Danetti!" sang Ivan.

Back in the kitchen, Ivan put a forkful of scrambled eggs in his mouth and lifted the pizza box lid. Atop the stack of crisp bills sat a note reading, "For a job well done." Ivan put the note on the newspaper and picked up the money. He put the top three one hundred dollar bills in his pocket and walked with the rest to his wall safe mounted behind a gold framed Salvador Dali. An original, not a print.

He didn't bother to count the bills. He knew they would all be there.

Then he ate the note.

Turning toward the kitchen counter where he'd found one of the many police bugs, be belched loudly and laughed. He had what he called a "dream job."

Literally.

Danetti looked across the dimly lit table at his snitch. He was disgusted, as usual, by the sight of this scruffy little weasel of a man who stayed out of jail only as long as the free-flowing stream of information he fed Danetti was correct. Today the weasel was scared. Danetti played with his handcuffs as a reminder of the ever present threat of jail. He was angry.

"Tell me something useful," he demanded of his snitch.

"It was him, Danetti, I swear it on my mother's life and the life of my sisters, all six of them, and well not my brother, 'cause he'd kill me if he heard me swearing, and I don't know how The Terrible did it without leaving his place, he's like scary like that, can be at two places at one time and I don't know, but I know, because my brother delivered the money to him personally, thirty Gs, and it was brought there just this morning, but you wouldn't tell my brother I told you would you, because jail would . . ."

Danetti silenced the weasel with a cold stare. He stood, threw two bills on the table and turned to leave.

He didn't look back, but he knew his voice would carry.

"You'd better be right . . ." and he left the threat to resonate in his wake.

Ivan had time on his hands. Standing at his balcony railing, he sipped some dry sherry from an ornate crystal goblet and watched the stars over the river.

He sighed. His life seemed perfect. He wanted for no material comforts. He had a string of gorgeous women who were at his disposal in a moment's notice. His job was secure because no one could do it better than he could. And his alibis were provided by the NYPD and their handy little critters discreetly planted in every room of his house.

"To bugs," Ivan said, lifting the glass in a mock toast.

But Ivan was not completely happy. He had no one to share his successes with, no one to brag to. He longed for an intellectual equal, and a challenge of some sort.

He threw the glass over the railing and went back inside, not even waiting to hear it shatter in the courtyard thirty-six floors below. The sherry glass had been part of a perfect Edwardian set of crystal brought over from England. But what did he care? He could always buy more.

Easy.

That was the problem. It was all too easy.

Ivan sighed again. Though it was early still, he retired to his bedroom and slipped into bed in his handmade teal silk pajamas. Three hundred dollars, shipped in from the Orient. Silk on the silk sheet.

To dream.

"No more, Danetti. Go home." The direct order from Jake behind the bar left no room for discussion.

Danetti was soused. He knew it. Jake had confirmed it. Nothing to do but stumble home. It was a good thing he could find the way home with his eyes tied behind his back, or something like that.

It took him a couple of minutes to get the key in the lock. His hand was shaking, and he had to close one eye and aim for the middle key hole. One lock. One small lock. He had nothing left to steal. Mary Katherine, his good Catholic wife who hadn't believed in divorce, had taken everything in the settlement.

It took him another long minute to drag his body to the pull-out sofa which served as his bed. It was lucky he hadn't folded it up earlier since he had neither the desire nor the dexterity to unfold it in his current state. He slumped down onto the bed and fell into a whiskey-induced sleep in the middle of untying his shoe.

Ivan was in bed when Danetti woke him. He sat up slowly in his perfectly creased deep blue Armani suit and thin burgundy tie. Danetti was wearing his dress blues with his gold shield prominently displayed over his heart. His hand was at ready by his weapon.

"I've been waiting for you, Danetti," Ivan said. His voice mangled the vowels. He raised one perfectly manicured eyebrow. "I've been waiting a long time."

Danetti drew his gun and trained it on Ivan. His hand was rock steady.

"How do you do it, Ivan?" Danetti spit the words out and watched them spatter and fall to the ground at the feet of the impeccably dressed Czech.

Ivan's laughter started like ice tinkling on the sides of a glass, but increased in volume and intensity until it rang in Danetti's head.

Danetti looked around as if to see where the surreal noise was coming from and in that brief momentary loss of concentration, Ivan reached up and caressed the gun in Danetti's hands. His hand went over the top of the barrel and under it. He ran a finger down its length and sighed.

All the while, the laughter bounced off each of the

bedroom walls, seeming to chase itself and splinter into a dozen voices.

Desperate to stop the source of the noise, Danetti closed his eyes and squeezed the trigger.

Silence.

"It's over," Danetti thought. Maybe even said it out loud.

But something was wrong.

There was no more laughter, but there had been no clap of gun fire either.

He opened his eyes slowly.

Ivan was standing in front of him. No wounds, no blood, but at least no more laughter.

"Until you believe this is my reality, you cannot stop me," Ivan stated. He reached behind him to the antique claw-footed nightstand and opened its single drawer.

Shaking his head just slightly as if to clear the fog, Danetti leaned toward the table and peered in the drawer. A glint of light caught his eye, and he saw a knife partially wrapped in crimson velvet.

The knife.

Danetti knew it was the murder weapon. He could feel his certainty in the cold fingers that ran up his spine and danced on the back of his neck.

He looked up at Ivan.

"Until you believe this is my reality, you cannot stop me."

The repeated statement came again and again, as if they were in some sort of cave or echo chamber.

Danetti reached for the knife, and Ivan made no move to stop him.

Just as Danetti touched the cold steel of the blade, the knife began sinking in upon itself, growing farther and farther away from Danetti's outstretched hand.

Danetti gasped in a huge gulp of air and sat bolt upright. Instinctively, he tried to jump to a defensive position, but his shoe lace—still half untied—had wound itself around the arm of the couch, and Danetti hit the floor shoulder first. All the air rushed back out of his body in a great "humph!"

He was stone cold sober.

Ivan also awoke with a start. A bead of sweat etched a line from his temple to his jawline. It was still dark out.

He lay wide awake staring into the darkness for hours. When daylight finally came, threading its way through the city high-rises to knot itself in Ivan's room, he stood. His silk pajamas were badly creased, but he didn't notice.

Pulling open the drawer in the antique claw-footed night table, he lifted out a crimson scarf and brought it to his nose. He took a deep breath as if he could smell something, some clue, in the velvet. A smile crept from his eyes slowly, ever so slowly, down to his lips.

"Challenge," he said simply to the ever listening electronic ears of his bedroom. "Made. Accepted." There was hardly any Czech accent in the three words.

Danetti thought a shower would clear his head. But it didn't. The dream's intensity did not diminish in the jets of steaming water.

He even tried to go back to sleep, lying prone and rigid on the pull-out couch. But sleep wouldn't come.

He arrived at his office two hours earlier than he was scheduled instead of his usual twenty minutes late. If anyone was surprised, the scowl on his face discouraged questions. The red lines that looked badly stitched across the whites of his eyes kept the others silent.

He had pulled his file on Ivan and was well into it when his captain shuffled up to his desk.

"Find me a suspect on the Jerome case?" It wasn't the question that bothered Danetti, but the tone.

"I have a suspect." He shot back. A little too hostile. A little too quick.

His captain ignored him and shuffled away with not so much as another word.

Danetti continued looking through the transcripts of the tapes from Ivan's surveillance recordings. He knew them by heart and nothing was new to him.

His own name played prominently on every page.

"Good morning, Danetti."

"Come and get me, Danetti."

"I expect more from you, Danetti."

All statements made by Ivan in his heavily accented singsong voice.

"I'm coming, Ivan." Danetti said aloud. "I'm coming."

He turned to the photos. Twenty-two bodies in a variety of rooms. Rented rooms. Hotel rooms. Bedrooms.

And a picture of a bedroom without a body—Ivan's bedroom. Taken while the tech team had planted the bugs.

Danetti had never been in Ivan's penthouse, but the image on the page in front of him was not new to him. It was etched in his mind from hours of studying the computer photo. There were red grease pencil marks where the bugs had been placed, but that's not what interested Danetti. What caught his attention in the picture was off to the unfocused corner of the shot. One very fuzzy, but familiar piece of furniture sat next to the bed. Danetti squinted and stared until he teared.

He just couldn't be sure.

He picked up the phone and punched in an extension.

"O'Reily, I need an image enhanced."

Ivan wandered the gallery in search of a new piece for his collection. He had called ahead to arrange a private showing, as was gallery policy. He had his eye

THE DREAM JOB

on a particularly interesting piece. It was a Dali sketch, one which the artist had done well before his surrealist period. The clean lines of the pencil on parchment interested Ivan almost as much as the famous melting clock of Dali's later works. He couldn't get his hands on that one, of course. It belonged to a museum in Florida.

Ivan appreciated Dali's work not so much for the art or the value. There were far more beautiful and expensive pieces in his collection. But Dali, in Ivan's opinion, was a man who clearly understood the mechanics of dreams.

Maybe even understood Ivan himself.

Perhaps someday, he thought as he counted crisp bills into the gallery owner's palm, I'll have the clock painting, too.

Danetti could hardly believe the picture in front of him. It had arrived in a mangled envelope overused for interoffice mail. O'Reily had done a superb job in enhancing the image. Once the object in question had been an almost imperceptible dime-sized smudge. Now, mouth agape, Danetti looked down at a full eight-by-ten picture of an antique claw-footed bedside table with a single drawer. It was the twin of the table he had seen in his dream.

"How could I have known that?"

Detective Fernandez at the desk next to his looked up. "Huh?"

"Nothing, man," Danetti silently cursed himself. He must be crazy, he thought. He'd been talking to himself far too much lately.

Ivan sat down on his leather sofa and unwrapped his bundle. The sketch in its heavy frame looked even better, he thought, in the subtle lighting of his home. He studied it for a long minute, whistling an aria from *La Bohème* loudly.

Then he flipped the picture over and pierced the

brown paper on the underside with his thumbnail,
whistling *La dona è mobile,* which masked the slight
noise of the ripping.

Carefully he removed a small handwritten note that
was folded once.

"Brooklyn Friday Sam Castanetta" was all it said.

Ivan came to the end of the aria, took a deep breath
and swallowed the note.

"Friday it is," he said, directly challenging the bug
in the lamp to his right. He would have disappointed
if he had known no one was listening.

Danetti stormed out of his captain's office letting a
puff of cigar smoke escape with him. He was so angry
the fumes could have been his own. All his surveillance had been cut. Everything. Even the bugs. Danetti hadn't even had the chance to show his captain
the blown up picture, not that he was sure even *he*
believed his own story. And how would he bring it
up? "I had this dream. . . ." Not the stuff of organized
crime investigations.

"You're on your own, Danetti!" His boss called out
after him. Danetti just kept walking. Past his desk. Out
the door of the station. Past his car. Down to Jake's.

"You don't know how right you are, Captain." He
raised his first glass. "You don't know how right you
are."

Danetti awoke in the closet. It wasn't unprece-
dented for him to wake up in a strange place. He'd
come to in the bathroom more times than he could
remember. And once in a great while in a strange
woman's bedroom. In the hallway in front of his door.
On a bar stool. And even once in an alley, badly
bruised from a fight, or a fall, or both.

But, in a strange closet? This was a first.

He could recall Jake throwing him out of the bar.
"Enough, Danetti. Time for bed." That much he could

remember. But not much more. Was he home? He shook his head.

But, it wasn't the alcohol he'd consumed that was confusing him. He was disoriented, not drunk. He was sure that he would be able to see straight if he could see.

As his eyes adjusted to the darkness, he made out a strained light coming from louvered doors. He could feel clothes hanging above him. He was definitely in a closet, but the one small closet in his apartment had solid doors.

As if by instinct, he felt for his weapon. It was there, holstered under his arm. He drew it soundlessly from its sheath. *Security!*

A new noise startled him. It was subtle, but in the quiet of the closet it seemed to scream.

Gripping hard to the cold steel of his gun, Danetti strained to recognize the foreign sounds. All his energies focused on what he could perhaps recognize. The slide of a lock. The opening of a door.

He put both hands on his weapon and gripped hard. The gun felt strangely malleable. He looked down at the object in his hand. In the semidarkness, he could the outline of what he was holding: a lethal tasseled loafer!

He dropped the shoe and darkness closed over him, a palpable darkness, as warm and soft as a baby's blanket. He was unarmed in an unrecognizable dark closet. A cry of desperation, like an infant's cry in the night, almost escaped his lips.

Ivan had become accustomed to the surreal nature of his dreams. Though he had been taken in by them as a child—floating above the stairs, landing in fields that should not have been under him—it had been many years since he had learned to control the dreams. Now he could block the sounds and concentrate on manipulating the realities.

Upon opening the door of Sam Castanetta's apartment, he barely noticed the flying lights and the other odd aspects. All he saw was the man on the bed—the sole reason for his being in this place.

Crossing to the sleeping man's bed, he stepped over seven stones and waded through an orange river that might have stopped someone less accustomed to the language of dreams.

He drew a cloaked crimson object from his jacket pocket.

Danetti was still swimming in confusion.

"It's just a dream." He repeated his mantra. He might have been saying it out loud or under his breath. He no longer knew. He might have been screaming. "It's just a dream!"

How long had he felt around blindly for the weapon he was sure he had dropped, mistaking it—somehow— for a shoe? A minute? An hour? Two weeks? He had no idea.

Another sound brought him up to his knees, and he saw that light was once again seeping through the louvers. He put his face up close and squinted. Through one eye only he could see a figure moving.

Danetti moved even closer to the louver, and it hit him over the eyebrow.

"Damn," he whispered.

The moving figure turned at the sound and was suddenly haloed in a kind of green light, like the light of an aquarium.

Danetti froze. The face was Ivan's.

Another sound, this time from behind Ivan. It was something like a rushing river and something like a snore. Ivan turned and raised his arm. Once, twice he struck something; then, whistling a bit of a song that Danetti recognized vaguely, Ivan turned and walked through a door.

Not out. *Through.*

Danetti opened the closet door, and found himself on the banks of a stream. In the middle of the water, which was a wash of red, lay a casket.

He peeked in.

Sam Castanetta lay grinning up at him out of two red mouths. One was in its proper place, the other was five inches beneath.

Danetti held his breath, closed his eyes, and turned.

Behind him was a door. It was shut.

Remembering what Ivan had done, and expecting any moment to be knocked silly, he walked straight into the door.

And through.

Ivan was washing his hands in a magnificent bathroom off the bedroom when Danetti came into view.

"Who would have thought the old man had so much blood in him," Ivan remarked to the mirror.

Danetti looked puzzled. "Castanetta wasn't all that old."

"It is Shakespeare, you yobbo," Ivan growled, turning.

"Yobbo?" Danetti was puzzled. The whole deal was puzzling. Like a dream. It *had* to be a dream.

But before he could figure out what kind of dream, Ivan had lifted something from the sink. It hadn't been his hands he was washing after all, but a knife. A big, bloody knife.

Ivan flung himself, knife first, at Danetti.

Danetti reached for his gun, remembered it was a shoe on a closet floor somewhere, and stepped aside.

"My dream," he cried, "not yours! So I can't die!" He put his foot out and tripped Ivan.

Ivan fell forward, the knife flipped over, and he landed onto the blade, which filleted him as if he had been a prize salmon. His eyes opened wide and his mouth, fishlike, opened and shut. Not a sound came out, not even a whistle.

Danetti sat down hard on the floor next to the dying man. For a moment he could scarcely breath himself. His heart was pounding much too quickly. He willed himself to calm down. "After all," he whispered, "it's only a dream."

He heard a sound beside him and looked. It was some kind of hospital equipment. The sound was that of the image going flatline. He closed his eyes, sighing.

When he opened them again, he was lying on his own bed. Something hard was digging into his armpit. He sat up and felt it. It was his pistol in its holster. The noisy thing by his ear was not a hospital machine at all but the telephone.

He picked up the receiver. "Hello?" He was amazed at how calm his voice sounded.

The captain bellowed in his ear. "You are never in your wildest dreams gonna believe who showed up dead this morning."

Danetti sighed. "Don't count on it," he said. "You have no idea how wild my dreams can get." He pulled up his pants and reached into his jacket pocket for a stick of gum.

A tasseled loafer fell to the floor.

Dons & The Damned

*"One owes one's Don a certain
amount of tribute."*

Some overly optimistic friends of mine say that
there is a little bit of magic in everything we do. I
can't help but look at this as both a blessing and
a curse, as do the other writers in this section of
contemporary tales of mob magic. Jody Lynn Nye
examines the complex web of power upon which a
family's influence is based, while Randall G.
Thomas examines the role an enchanted charm
plays in a mobster's quest for power. The section
is then rounded out by two very different fish stories, with Roland Green sending his gangsters to a
watery grave, while I prefer to have my contract
executed in a slightly tastier manner.

Bon appetit!

POWER CORRUPTS

by Jody Lynn Nye

"Carboni?"

Michael sprang to his feet and shook down his pants legs. The stone-faced man in the thousand-dollar navy wool suit beckoned him to follow and strode off down the hall. He stepped aside to let Michael pass into the mahogany-paneled office and pulled the door behind him. Michael felt the wards close tight, too. The wizened little man in the ten-thousand-dollar suit behind the black marble desk came around and ceremoniously kissed Michael on each cheek.

"Michaelangelo," he said. "How's my good little soldier?"

"Don Amici," Michael replied, bending over to kiss the ring on the small man's right pinkie. The big diamond had grown significantly in size in the two years since he first came to ask a favor, a sign that the Don had added to his dominion. Michael had been important in that growth, but still, a part of him shook with nerves. How dare he come to demand a reward for what was no more, after all, than loyal service?

"So what do you want, boy?" the don asked, settling back in his russet leather easy chair. It tilted back, and the don flicked a finger. The springs froze silently in place. Michael envied him his absolute ease with magic and swallowed nervously. He straightened his tie.

"With respect, Don, I've been thinking—I've got my territory out east under control. We're channeling covert immigration, the gambling houses, the person favors, all at a nice profit to the Family. I think I can handle more."

"You want what, then?" the little man asked, impatiently.

Michael stiffened his back. "I'd like to move up. I'm ready. I want a bigger piece of the action, Don Amici. I can do more for the Family if I get it. I work hard—I think it would be a good thing." The old man lowered his eyebrows, still black although the rest of his hair was iron gray.

"What are you, Martha Stewart? I decide who gets upped. I told you, boy. I told you two years ago, when you first came to me, you couldn't resist asking for more, and here you are." He chuckled. "I shoulda made a bet on it. Don't be too greedy, sonny. If you make the angels jealous, they'll bring you down."

Michael was ashamed, but the old man was right. He *had* told Michael so. The power was intoxicating. It was that which drove him, far more than the thought of doing good for the Family or obedience to the lieutenants and captains above him. He'd had a taste, and he wanted more. He *had* to have more.

He'd come to the Don on Fat Tuesday two years before. At the time, he'd believed it was an auspicious date, but it turned out to be the last good time before he felt as though he were living in a perpetual state of Lent.

To become a member of the Family web meant getting power, real power, magic like he'd heard about in fairy tales as a baby. He'd always seen guys on the street using it, according to their place in the Family hierarchy. The lower-downs used little spells, such as making a flatfoot look the other way when some deal was going on, or fixing a hole in a tire. The upper-ups had a lot more. They could sweep a showgirl right out of the chorus line and into their hotel rooms. They could empty any unwarded bank vault or shop window with a mere flick of the finger. They could change computer files or wipe them clean. Weak-minded politicians were nothing but meat to them. Michael craved *that* kind of power. To get magic in the first place meant taking an oath of allegience to his lieutenant, his Uncle Fabio, in front of the Don, as their senior capo, the highest power on this continent. The moment that vow was spoken, Michael felt—no, he *knew* he had done something irrevocable. But the rewards that had come with his vow were undeniable, and addictive.

Like every new soldier, his magic was the lower-down, hole-and-corner stuff. He could change the print on a letter, unlock doors without keys, and, in one moment that he would never forget as long as he lived, vanish the bullet out of the chamber of a gun that a rival gang member was aiming at him just a split second before the guy pulled the trigger. The weird thing was how good it felt to use the power. He found excuses to cast little spells, wallowing in the tingle that went through him as the magic rushed out of his fingertips. The big guys told him he had an aptitude for it, and he was proud.

The Family, too, benefited from having another soldier on the line. Every new guy, even one on a low rung, added to the linked power of the magic web. Every addition caused all the guys above to become even more powerful. All new magic was shared out up the line in proportion to rank. In a way, it wasn't a fair deal. Nobody's whole strength belonged to him. Only the person at the center of the web had all his own marbles, and a piece of everyone else's into the bargain. The capo, Don Amici, occupied that place and had all that power at his fingertips. Michael wanted it, but it was out of his reach. The moment he'd taken that vow, he was stuck in the hierarchy where it placed him. He had to find a way to climb the ladder and take control. If he couldn't do it with permission, he had to do it without. And he had an idea how to make it work.

Respectfully, he took his leave of the don. "I'm sorry if I wasted your time, capo."

"Never wasted," Don Amici said, rising from his chair to pat Michael's cheek. "I like to see ambition like yours. One day, it'll take you places."

"I hope so." Michael bit his tongue to keep from saying more. He would never leave the room alive if the magic monitors that guarded the don from invasion could read his thoughts.

"Don't be such a stranger," Don Amici called, as the blank-faced sentry walked Michael down the hall.

"What did he say?"

"He said no, what do you think?" Michael said peevishly, brushing aside the round-cheeked man with tight-curled red-gold hair, then turned to catch his arm. "I apologize, Samel."

"No problem, boss." Samel Borovets was a good guy. So was Joey Biggs. Both of them had come from the bowling team of a friend of a friend. Untraceable and trustworthy.

"So we go ahead with the plan?" Joey asked, grinning with his big teeth in his narrow face. He didn't have it all upstairs, but he was loyal.

"Yeah, we go ahead. But don't tell me anything, you understand?" Michael said, pointing a finger at each of their chests. "Nothing."

Samel grinned, his wide eyes guileless. "It'd be like we never met, boss. We're not doing anything, personally, right?"

"You can't," Michael said automatically. It was the oath talking.

"Of course not. I can't. I won't. I promise you."

"Me, neither," said Joey, his sincere, silly face nodding.

"Good enough," Michael said, climbing into the back of the big, black Lincoln. "Drive me somewhere. I have to think."

The power worked like a one-way valve. You could

"use" someone below you, take their magic and bend it to your own will, but you couldn't use anyone above you without their permission. That meant the upper-ups had plenty more power than lower downs. If you recruited more soldiers, your power was increased, but so was that of the people above you, in proportion to their position on the totem pole. You had to share the benefits of your work with so many people that any single increase felt minimal. Michael wanted his voltage upped. Not just one soldier at a time but a big increase. The power gave him a high, almost sexual—almost better than sex because there was no guilt afterward. He wanted desperately to know how it felt in the highest ranks. But, no, he couldn't move up, because he couldn't get past anyone above him. Without permission, they were inviolate, and nobody would give consent to a pass. This wasn't golf. He had to keep recruiting people to increase his share, and it hurt when he found someone good and they had already been sworn by another lieutenant. He became compulsive about looking for more. The Family web was the perfect pyramid scheme, entirely self-perpetuating and unbreakable. No one ever quit, not that they could. The magic was too good to leave behind. For five hundred years the chain had continued unbroken.

The person at the center of the web controlled it all, had the world at his fingertips. Michael had thought deep and hard about his dilemma. The only way to be at the center would be if you started the mob in the first place. Day one. If he built himself a little empire now, it would still belong to the people above him. And even with a thousand soldiers, he couldn't do a thing about the upper-ups. It was like slavery. Once they were sworn in, that was it.

The American web was independent because all the capos over Don Amici in the old country had died. Michael could be there in that center office. The position of absolute power was just sitting there waiting for him, and he couldn't have it until he moved up four more ranks. Which was taking far too long. He had to make room.

The way he saw it, his problem lay in a straight line. Not everyone of a higher rank was directly connected with his chain of command. The other upper-ups working for Don Amici were captains who had grown big empires not connected to Michael's captain, a man named Dan Moko, who was right underneath the capo. Moko's lieutenant was a guy called Peter Montmorency, who had sworn Michael's Uncle Fabio, who had sworn him. Four steps to the top of the heap. They might as well be chasms because of that one-way valve.

At first, Michael thought of going to outside forces to bust the levels above him, but he dismissed the idea without hesitation. There was no way he'd involve law enforcement. The cops rousted Family members every time there was an unexplained death or a mysterious robbery. They tried to act as though they had so much on him. Penny ante. He'd do time for nothing, for squat. They couldn't get him behind bars or even in front of a grand jury. Even with his minor-league spells he could wipe out their files on him. But they pushed at him, fishing for information about the web. They knew about it. They'd tried to break it up more than once. There were task forces out studying it, trying to find the weak places. They were curious about it. It was seductive. The Feds had a little magic, stuff cobbled together from hereditary witches and computer wizards, but nothing as big or as organized, or as powerful, as the Family. They wanted data, and they figured he'd blab what he knew about how it worked in exchange for their help. Michael turned them down every time. If they started interfering with the web, there'd be nothing left for him when he finally got where he was going.

The cops and the Feds had tried to infiltrate the Family before. They'd sent undercover agents, but the instant the moles took the oath to the Family, they blew their own covers. Michael called it the pentathol spill. The second the power hit them, new inductees always blabbed about everything they'd ever done against the Family. The dons were always careful to have recording devices in place when a guy took the oath, or they'd miss all the good stuff. The Family would never have known where Greg Berber had been moved if it wasn't for the Fed who tried to infiltrate Carl Fredrickson's branch. Berber had once been a captain, a position of trust below Dan Moko, a place of real power, until he got into debt with someone who turned out to be an agent. Once the agent was a part of the Family, he ratted out all his accomplices, er, fellow agents, and put the Family on the trail to California, where Greg and his bimbo had moved. Greg still couldn't act against them, but he'd told, and that was bad. Michael's last promotion had been when Greg was removed permanently from the picture by the guys above him. The Feds knew, and they couldn't do a thing. Their little bitty magic couldn't hold a candle to the Family web.

Then Michael had his really brilliant idea. He started to enlist men, good men, without making them take the oath. It took a lot of self control to keep from grabbing their hands to bring them in, since he was a touchy-feely kind of guy, but it worked. He made them swear a different kind of allegience, pledging their honor and blood. Without the vow, the new soldiers were free of the strictures of the Family. No promise, no problem—but no magic, either. They wanted it, once they started getting around, what with the magic peep shows, the lap dances that never failed to get a rise out of the patrons, guaranteed; the endless streams of lucky dice rolls, liquor, women, and cash that seemed to fall into the hands of the Family. In return for their abstinence, Michael swore to his men that once he made the center of the ring, they'd have it all. They'd be his captains, and they'd have the best, the most magic, the hottest spells. The whole

damned country would be theirs. Everyone but him
would be under their jurisdiction. All it would take
was a few well-placed accidents. It wasn't like Michael
had to wipe out everyone above him, just the ones in
a straight line to that mahogany-paneled office. The
don was old. He might die soon, and if Michael was
just underneath him in the organizational chart, having
shown a real aptitude for business, ruthlessness and
that ambition the don had praised, he ought to get
the top spot.

In the meantime, he had to keep guys in check without resorting to pulling strings in the web. An unfamiliar exercise, it took real creativity. A few of the new
guys wanted to cut loose, and would have gone to a
brother lieutenant to swear the oath and get the
magic . . . if they'd lived. Those examples were good
for maintaining loyalty, too. Michael was amazed at
how easy it was to keep the other lieutenants from
knowing what he was up to. All he had to do was
pretend his secret force were sworn soldiers. You
couldn't tell if a man was a part of the chain just by
looking at him. It was what was inside that made the
difference. The Family was used to magic. They'd
grown lazy. They had no defense against this newfan-
gled organization. But the unsworn men witnessed everything, saw how the Family worked, and saw the
magic that they couldn't do.

"What's it feel like?" Samel had asked, the first
time he watched Michael unlock a door, at the back
of a rival's casino they had been about to knock over.
Michael wanted to tell him it felt good, but he didn't
want Sam getting too antsy. He, like the rest of Michael's soldiers, was waiting. Not so patiently sometimes, but Michael wasn't just the man with the magic,
he was a tough bastard who punished as easily as he
rewarded, and he was a hundred times more devious
than anyone who worked for him. Sam wanted the
power bad, but he didn't ask all the time, as some
people did. He just went about his business, and Mi-

chael asked him no questions. They both knew that if things went right, they'd both benefit. Joey was different. He went along with things. Michael was never sure if he understood the things he heard, but he did his job, too. Michael was glad to have both of them. They'd be good captains one day. Michael knew his time was limited by their patience. Soon. It had to happen soon.

He was sitting down to brunch in his father's restaurant that Sunday when the first news hit. His mother came to sit beside him and Uncle Fabio and a couple of the old man's cronies in the booth way in the back, where they could see everyone coming and going, and no one could see them. Michael looked curiously at her, at the fuss going on at the front of the restaurant.

"It's bad," she whispered. "Somebody just ran over Dan Moko. He's dead."

Michael schooled his face and made the same noises of regret as the others. He sat back in the booth and waited. Sure enough, just as when they'd whacked Greg Berber, the verification came. Slowly, but unmistakably, the thrill of the power surrounded Michael. In the inner ear that was attuned to the magic, he thought he could hear voices and music, while his body was caressed by velvet forces that enveloped and penetrated his skin like an all-over electric massage. When it was all over, his heart was beating fast, and he knew he had that damned silly smile on his face. He and Uncle Fabio had just been promoted.

What happened after that was totally unexpected. Uncle Fabio clutched his chest and collapsed back in his seat. Michael sprang to get the old man a glass of water. By the time he turned around again, Fabio's lips were blue and his eyes were rolled back in his head. Michael tried to use magic to hold the spirit in the body until the paramedics arrived, but there was no one left to pull back. He looked for help, but the moment the sirens had started wailing, Fabio's two companions melted away into the crowd.

The heart attack had been perfectly natural. Michael thought that the strain of promotion must have been too much for Fabio. The paramedics couldn't save him, not with medicine, not even with modern magic. Michael was left kneeling at the side of a corpse, feeling a painful hole in his own heart. He would never have attacked Uncle Fabio even if he could have; he was his mother's own brother, and he loved him. Of the targets above him, he was waiting for his uncle to die normally. He was an old man in poor health. It couldn't have been a long wait. Michael was livid that the old man's so-called friends had taken off, but he suspected that maybe someone else out there didn't want Fabio around any more. But it meant another step up for him. Two steps up in one day. Only two to go. He walked away from the restaurant in a haze of magical feedback.

The high of being two rungs farther up the ladder was so overwhelmingly good that Michael hardly wanted to leave his apartment the next day. He did little things, such as making a fresh cup of espresso appear on the table from a restaurant halfway across the city. The coffee tasted good, but the buzz on the side was fabulous. He started to see visions. He'd never been capable of clairvoyance before. If the common solider on the line ever knew what was above him—! But he couldn't do a thing about it, because the common guy was not as smart as Michael Carboni.

Though officially he was in mourning, people came and went as they always did. The only real difference was that he wore a black suit instead of his usual charcoal gray. Michael saw the usual people asking for help, trying to get his backing for schemes, pleading for spells in exchange for desirable favors. Now he could see who was good for it and who was stringing him. Some he helped himself; others he sent to his lieutenants, who were all enjoying being two ranks higher and were bringing him new soldiers every day. So this was what it felt like to be a don, he thought with satisfaction, sensing his share of the power coming in steadily. People did for him, and he could sit at a distance, keep his hands clean and reap all the benefits.

Sam and Joey and their men were on orders to stay away from his apartment, and keep at their jobs. He didn't want anyone to see they weren't feeling the psychic feedback with everyone else. He felt bad about that, but he'd be making it up to them later, with interest.

With his new powers of prescience, he made a call to his lawyer and opened the door an hour later to the detectives standing on the mat before they'd had a chance to ring the bell.

"Sergeant Percher?" Michael said, ushering the chunky uniform inside. He turned to the muscular plain-clothes. "And you're Lieutenant Witkin, FBI. Right?"

The detectives were taken aback. "Uh, yeah," said Witkin. His clean-shaven, tanned narrow face wasn't accustomed to wearing a dumbstruck expression. He schooled his features back into smooth impassivity. "Sir, we're investigating the death of Fabio Carboni. He was your uncle, we understand."

"That's right," Michael said. "It was a heart attack. The man wasn't in the best of shape. He ate too much, and he didn't exercise much any more. It was perfectly natural."

"Sir," said Witkin, "in this neighborhood, a bullet in the back is listed as natural causes. We have to look into it."

Michael shrugged.

"So," said Percher casually, taking out a notebook, "do you know anything about the death of Dan Moko?"

"Sorry," Michael said, with an air of finality.

"You've got to know more than you're saying," Witkin urged. "We know all about the web stuff. You can help yourself. Come on, talk to us."

"Sorry," Michael said, without heat. This was an old argument. Not only wouldn't he tell any Fed a single secret if he could, any treason of this kind would get back to the Family. They had ways of knowing. Roswell, hell. The government couldn't keep a secret like that, they couldn't keep anyone safe who'd ratted on the web.

"That's enough, gentlemen," the lawyer said, shuffling the officers toward the door. "You're on a fishing expedition now. Mr. Carboni's told you what he knows."

Witkin paused to aim a finger at him. "We're watching you, Carboni. Remember that. We're on the side of the angels."

"Yeah, yeah," Michael said. It was a hollow threat, same old, same old. The Fed's piddly squat magic couldn't see through Family security, Nothing could.

Late that night, Michael woke up screaming with pain. It felt as though lightning were racing through his veins, blasting him. He tried to block it with a warding spell, the first magic he'd learned as a soldier. To his horror, it didn't work. His attacker was much stronger than he was. It was the capo, he thought with horror. Don Amici had found out about his plot. This was the end. But he wouldn't go without a fight.

He climbed out of bed and crawled across the floor, reaching out with his mind for the light switch. The light didn't go on. His magic was gone. He was being punished. Before he died, he was going to lose everything he prized. Power bursts came from within, hurting, aching, but not ripping him apart. Michael started to think. He knew what a real hit looked like, had participated in enough of them. This was not personal. It wasn't aimed at him.

He wasn't being attacked, he was being *drained*.

Someone above him was in trouble, and stripping every underling for defensive magic. Michael called out for his men. No one answered. The sworn soldiers were certainly in the same condition he was, and the unsworn were under orders to stay away. He laughed weakly. This was the way the Feds would like to see him, helpless. He curled into a ball on the floor.

Sleep was impossible. He fought off imaginary monsters that came through the walls, batted at a hail of bullets that wasn't there. Rain pounded on the roof, and Michael could feel every drop hitting him like a hammer. But near dawn, he started to feel all the fight was worthwhile. The pain continued, as if his magical muscles were badly bruised, but the stream of power started to come in stronger and stronger. By the middle of the morning, when Sam and Joey found him, he could levitate himself back to bed and grab a doctor from a nearby hospital to look him over.

The men looked wiped out.

"We got some news for you," Joey said.

The funeral was a majestic event. People came from practically the moon to honor Don Amici's memory and to kiss the ring of his successor. None of the other captains or lieutenants had challenged Michael's early claim to the mahogany-paneled office. They were all sure he'd been responsible for the capo's death; none of them wanted to find out how. All they knew was that the old man was found sitting dead as a stone in his fancy leather chair, with the body of Peter Montmorency stretched out like a footrest under his feet. There wasn't a trace of magic anywhere in the office. The Family was baffled.

As the longstanding custom went, the captains swore a new oath to the new capo, promising to serve Michael as they'd served his predecessor. Michael felt the pride of 500 years of history coming to rest upon his shoulders. He tried to feel unworthy, but he couldn't. He tried to feel guilty, but he was too pleased with himself. This moment was exactly what he'd schemed for. Michael's soldiers escorted them in and out of the fancy office one at a time, enjoying the procession. He stood in front of the fancy desk, arms folded, legs planted four-square on the floor. This was his room now, his place, his pride. The magical rush was building in him. It ought to take a few days to set in all the way, but in the meanwhile, it felt good.

When they had all gone, Michael sat down for the first time in the leather chair behind the desk. At once, the bespelled padding folded itself comfortably around his posterior. All his, forever, like the power. He beckoned to Samel.

"I've waited a long time for this," he said. "You've waited, too, my friend. So have the others. It's time for your reward. Bring them in. All of them."

He was surprised at how many soldiers there were. Michael did a quick head count and came up with fifteen. He looked to his two captains for explanation. "We had to recruit a lot of guys," Joey said. "We couldn't tell you nothing before, boss. Some of these guys is, uh, specialists."

"Pleased to meet you," Michael said. There was a general murmur of respectful thanks. "Samel, you first. Come here." He took the man's hands between his. Sam had a nervous half grin on his face. "Repeat after me. I, your name, solemnly swear to be a bondsman to you, and all my power that comes to me belongs to you. Every bondsman I take will serve you through me, body and soul, until you or death release me."

Obediently, Samel chanted the oath. It felt like no other swearing-in Michael had ever experienced before. The power built in the ground below their feet, and spread up into their bodies like a heatwave. Michael enjoyed it, but he really had to smile at the look of delight on Sam's face as the magic took hold in him. It was a captain's share, perfectly apt and fair for such a good man.

"I keep my promises, right, Sam?" Michael said. Sam nodded dumbly, still smiling, and shook hands with him. Hastily he remembered, and bent to kiss his ring. The little diamond grew just a trifle. One day it'd be huge. "Now you, Joey."

If anything, Joey looked more nervous than Sam. He hesitated before stepping forward, and almost cringed when Michael touched his hands.

"I'm not going to eat you!" Michael said, fondly. "I owe you, my friend. Now, repeat after me."

"Can we do this another day?" Joey asked.

"No. Now," Michael said. Sometimes Joey could be so dim. "Come on, you've been waiting for a long time for this. I, your name . . . "

Haltingly, Joey repeated the oath. When he spoke the last words, Michael waited for the glorious rising of power out of the earth, but instead, with a crash and a flash of light, the two of them were knocked apart. Michael was picked up out of his seat and hurled almost clear across the room. Michael's lieutenants hurried to help him. Joey climbed to his feet, looking apologetic.

"What the hell was that?" Michael asked. "I never felt anything like that before."

"Boss," Joey said, looking really ashamed of himself. "I've got something to tell you."

Michael signaled for one of his men to turn on the recorder.

"I work for the FBI."

When the sun went down, Joey had been talking for hours. Michael was appalled by everything that had come out of his new captain's mouth. Joey was one of Agent Witkin's men. ("I thought he was smart," Michael had said.) When Michael had gone recruiting, Joey had been transferred from another undercover assignment.

"Thanks to you, we had access to the Family web. From observing your organization, we got information we never had been able to get before. The government saw how well it worked and started their own web. They never anticipated you being able to detect the FBI oath. Or boot it."

"What? You were sworn to them?"

"Yes, until you pulled me loose," Joey said. He no longer looked vacant. Michael realized that had been an act. He wore an expression of panic. "I've got to tell you all about it."

Michael sat back in his chair, no longer at ease, but interested, and listened to a catalog of his own blunders. Because of his ambition to be at the top, he had kept from swearing in his secret force. His great loophole had put the Feds right into the middle of their operation. He himself had taught the Feds who, what and, most specifically, *how*. They had dates, names, grimoires, all of it. He'd been so busy trying to climb the ladder, he'd forgotten to check behind him. The oath not only gave the Family magic and protected the upper-ups from attack, it made the lower-downs trustworthy. With no pentathol spill, he couldn't know he was harboring agents.

"But I've got you now," Michael said, when Joey paused for breath.

"Yes. But we've got you, too, on all the racketeering, weapons violations and black magic charges you'd like to name. Conspiracy to commit three murders, to start with."

"You were in on them." Michael pointed out.

"I tried to prevent them," Joey said unhappily. "Sam did it all. We've got indictments against all of you." He clapped his hand over his mouth, but it was too late. Now that Michael knew they existed, he could find out where they were and wipe them clean.

"But you, personally, can't act against me," Michael said, matter-of-factly. "Not now, not ever. It's a one way valve. And anyone *you* swore in is mine, too. I don't know how many there are, but *you* do."

"For now," Joey said, although his face registered

horror as he realized Michael was right. "You just proved that one oath can supersede another. And if you can take defectors, so can the FBI. There's a lot of people afraid of you, capo. Some of them will be willing to trade information for immunity, and they'll take their soldiers with them."

Michael gaped at him for one second. "*If* they find out about oath-swapping. They're not going to hear it from you. Take him," he said to Samel.

"The Feds are getting ready for you," Joey said, as the others surrounded him and pulled his arms behind him. "It'll be war. Your organization is older, but there are more of us. Them," he said, as the oath corrected him. "Every day. You could turn states' evidence and lessen the time you'll spend in the pen. Help us help you. We're on the side of the angels."

"I'll never spend a day in jail," Michael said, but he no longer believed it. Sadly, he signed to Sam to take Joey away. He realized he had engineered his own punishment. He had thought it would be so easy once he was in control of it all. It would have been so good to be at the top, but not if his power base was going to be chipped out from under him a man at a time. He remembered what Don Amici had said about angels and jealousy. Too late, he wondered what else the old man had known that he didn't.

WHADDYA SEE?

by Randall G. Thomas

The kid looked familiar somehow. But something wasn't right.

Miguel "the Wire" Franzoni set his fork on the table, wrinkled his brow and squinted, an ugly facial twist that made him look whiny and irritable, like a man with a nasty toothache. A dollop of marsala sauce squeezed out of the corner of his mouth, hung on his full black mustache, and dropped a single brown spot onto the bib napkin that curved its way toward his ample belly. A waiter caught the pained expression, stopped replenishing Valpolicella into Don Franzoni's wine glass, and turned to find out what the hell had seized the great man's attention.

Rocco and Johnny had already escorted the kid all the way up to the ornate corner booth. Now they were basically holding him there, doing a great job of rumpling an Armani suit that was so black it shone. The Armani, that wasn't right. White T-shirt, no tie, moussed-back jet-black hair, who did this little creep think he was, a waiter in some fern bar? Not from the look on his face.

The kid showed no fear whatsoever. He was giving as good as he got, not struggling at all, absolutely ignoring Rocco's wiry coolness and paying no attention to Johnny's hulking frame and black eyepatch. He was staring straight ahead at the most powerful sanitation executive in Brooklyn, standing in front of Don Miguel Franzoni's own second course in his own private dining room in his own social club and regarding the

Wire as though he were nothing more dangerous than a high school truant officer.

Lean, angular features curled into a little smirk, an eyebrow lifted, there was even the beginning of a sneer as the kid looked away disrespectfully for an instant. He did have balls. Something about him wasn't exactly right, but Don Franzoni definitely paid attention. Because there was something else about him, something familiar. Like maybe he should know this little creep.

"Kid walks up to me at the plant," Rocco reported. "Says we should bring him to see you." Johnny gave the kid's wrist a hurtful little twist and daydreamed about creative ways to whack him.

Strike one, you don't give orders to a Franzoni capo at the Franzoni recycling plant, thought the Wire. Strike two, you don't even *be* at the fucking plant in the first place, because there are things over there that you don't see and also do things like walk around and wear your Armani suit and breathe air.

The kid mumbled like De Niro. "I hear you're the big dog."

"Shut up," barked Rocco.

"Rocco!" Don Franzoni stopped him, then oozed greasy warmth. "This kid doesn't have long with us today." He stared meaningfully. "Let's enjoy our brief visit."

"Thought you and me, maybe we work together." The kid stared. Balls, balls.

The Wire swallowed the mouthful of veal that had been muffling his speech, sipped from the glass and napkined his mouth foppishly, never taking his eyes off the kid. He balled the napkin and stood slowly, importantly, like the captain of industry that he was. He stepped out of the booth, and both Rocco and Johnny were stifling smiles of anticipation by the time the Don was nose to nose.

"I . . . don't . . . work . . . with . . . *nobody*." He

punctuated each word with a finger to the kid's chin. A little showmanship.

"You'll like this," the kid said cagily. "A lot."

He made a move for his pants pocket and Rocco and Johnny tightened. One head-flick from the Don, and the kid was free. He shrugged his suit straight, fussed with his cuffs, and waggled his fingers grandly, like a magician. Then he reached into his right-hand pocket and pulled out a ring.

A ring was all that it was. A golden ring with a crest on it. A big one, sure. Like the Super Bowl rings the Wire had fenced twenty years ago. Like the ones the kings wore at the Lincoln Center operas Don Franzoni adored. Like the ring Rocco and Johnny kissed every morning of their lives. "Watch this," said the kid, and he slipped the ring onto his left hand. There was a little shimmer in the air, and the Don had to steady himself for a split second.

Then, all of a sudden, the kid got it right.

His shoulders rounded a bit, as if he had suddenly relaxed a rigid stance and allowed his body to slump. But it wasn't just posture; the kid's body was really changing in front of Don Franzoni's eyes. He was developing a belly while Don Franzoni watched, like a quick-time film of a pregnancy carried to term. His cheeks slowly puffed, his neck slightly retracted like the recoil of a jack-in-the-box, his eyebrows bushed and nearly joined. He smiled up while his body was still shifting, and all of a sudden Don Franzoni made the connection that had been just out of reach this whole time.

This kid was turning into *him*.

But not a carbon copy of the well-stuffed capo that stood before him now. The kid was shifting into the spitting image of the Wire maybe twenty, thirty years ago. That's what Don Franzoni had been trying to remember: This whole situation reminded him of the time long ago when he was working as a bagman, and he'd been taken before a big, big Manhattan boss. Just

like this, as a matter of fact, complete with the goons.
The guy thought he'd been skimming off the top of
the insurance payments he was collecting. But young
Franzoni had stayed cool, calm and collected, just like
this kid. Even fingered an accountant for good measure, got the guy a permanent vacation at Club Dead
while the Wire spent the extra pocket change. This
was the same thing. Same no-fear attitude, same sneer.
Don Franzoni was looking at himself, that's what the
kid reminded him of. Himself. The kid was a dead
ringer for himself, down to the mustache.

Mustache.

The kid had been clean-shaven a moment ago.

That wasn't all: the Armani had disappeared, and
now the kid wore a gray double-breasted suit, spats,
and, cocked rakishly just over the eyebrows, Don
Franzoni's favorite black fedora. The one that was
packed deep in a closet in the guest bedroom of the
Wire's Long Island estate. The one he hadn't worn in
more than twenty years.

The kid had gained several pants sizes, lost several
inches of height, and changed his clothes, all before
their eyes. Rocco and Johnny were staring at the kid
with identical looks of confusion.

"Jesus, kid, how'd you do that?" For one moment,
the Wire forgot to maintain his unfazable public
demeanor.

"Jesus," Rocco and Johnny echoed in agreement.

"How'd you change clothes so fast? Where'd you
get that hat?"

Rocco turned slowly. "What hat?"

Don Franzoni's cheerless eyes flashed. "The fuck
you mean, what hat? Fucking fedora on his fucking
head."

Rocco glanced at Johnny, then back at the don.
"Uh, I don't see no hat, boss."

"The fuck you talking about?"

Rocco stared back at his captive. "He changed
clothes, boss, but he ain't got no hat."

"Sure he does," offered Johnny, adjusting his eye-patch and beginning what for him was the equivalent of a major address. "He's put on an Army uniform. He's holdin' the hat under his arm. I swear he looks like my big brother the night he got shipped off. Hey, kid, you know Sal Mancini? You look exactly like him."

"Are you crazy?" Rocco blustered. "Kid looks like a fancy rich boy. Got glasses, sweater with the arms tied in front, Cole-Haans, a real fruit. I'd love to beat the shit out of him right now." His fingers curled at the beautiful thought of whamming a completely defenseless egghead against a hard floor for a long, long time. Same kind of guy used to make trouble for Rocco in high school, get them all laughing at him. "Try it now," he said out loud. "Just try it, you gimp."

"Shut up." Don Franzoni leaned in and squinted. "That ain't what I see. This kid changed, and I wanna know how."

"Didn't change nothin'," mumbled Don Franzoni's younger self in a soft voice that sounded like De Niro. "It's this ring. You put it on, people see what they wanna see. What they're thinkin' about. What they remember."

"I don't get it."

"Everybody sees somethin' different. They make it up themselves. What's on their mind. Sometimes I can even feel it too." He scratched his upper lip. "Some-body put a mustache on me, didn't they?"

"He's nuts, boss." There was just a trace of a shudder in Rocco's voice.

"You know I ain't lyin'," the young Don Franzoni stared down the old Don Franzoni as defiantly as if he'd just been caught with both hands in the bag. "Don't ya?" With another grand gesture, he removed the ring and stuffed it in his pocket. A slight shimmer made the Wire feel a little disoriented, but when his head cleared, there stood mousse-hair in his Armani and T-shirt again. Rocco and Johnny were both slack-jawed.

"So you're Mandrake the Magician." The don fidgeted with the knot on his tie. "Very impressive. I don't understand this trick any more than I understand how my grandson makes his handkerchief appear to change color. He is a good grandson, however, and I enjoy indulging him."

"No trick. You know it isn't," the kid insisted with confidence.

"All well and good. Now be kind enough to tell us why the fuck you are standing here."

For the first time, the kid's face betrayed a bit of concern. "Don't you get it? Don't you understand what this means? I can go anywhere. Do anything. Hit a bank in broad daylight. Whack a cop in the middle of the precinct house. I can't get nailed, cause nobody can ID me, nobody can finger me in court."

"Why come to me? Why do I deserve this . . . generosity?"

"I hear you're the big dog around here. I can't do anything by myself. I need backup, mouthpieces, money. Maybe they can't nail me, but I can't help but get pinched. I figure you and me, maybe we work something out. Fifty-fifty."

Don Franzoni picked at a spot of lint on the kid's jacket. "So you are new to the city, my magic friend?" He motioned to the waiter, who handed him a small brush, and the don began straightening and grooming the Armani's black sheen very deliberately. "Surely you got your own associates for such unglamorous but necessary tasks."

"My associate where I got this ring, he's not doing so good right now. Me and him, we parted ways. Him and his other associates too."

"I'm beginning to understand." Don Franzoni moved to the kid's side to brush his right sleeve. "And do you know where the ring came from in the first place?"

"Frankie musta rolled somebody for it, he never would say. Who cares? He got it, it works, and now I got it, capische?"

"Young man, I think we got a deal. Let's celebrate our new partnership." Don Franzoni walked around behind him to brush the jacket in back, as the waiter brought two glasses of grappa and the kid reached out for one. "You are a man who is wise beyond your years. You showed excellent judgment, and proper respect, by coming to me. Now what kind of sums would you want for the loan of your unusual method of disguise?"

"Ah, no," the kid called over his shoulder, "I'm the only one who uses the ring. That's not negotiable." He downed the drink.

Don Franzoni's reply came in a whisper: "Everything is negotiable."

The don's motions were jerky, nonthinking, insectlike. The foot of piano wire was around the kid's throat and digging into his neck before he even had a chance to cough from the grappa. He was halfway gone before he reached for his throat in shock and panic, but there was no room for his fingers; the Wire kept up the pressure from behind, his knee pressing into the small of the kid's back. The kid continued to flail and even pulled the clothes brush out from under the wire in Don Franzoni's left hand, waving it stupidly behind him until Rocco pulled it away. The kid kicked and hocked, his face beet red; his bowels loosened, and his gyrations lost all meaning, like a toy whose battery is nearly dead. Finally the kid stopped struggling altogether. Rocco and Johnny let him go, and he slumped toward the floor. Still the Wire exerted himself at full strength, a glistening patina of sweat dotting his forehead, a slight quiver betraying his physical effort. It was a full minute later before he began to relax and finally stood up, still breathing heavily. There had never been a single bullshit miraculous recovery in the long history of Franzoni garrotings, and there never would be. And as usual, no screaming, no pleading, no crying. The Wire was an expert in a manner of execution that smelled terrible but barely made a sound.

Don Franzoni reached into the corpse's pocket and retrieved the ring. He held it up to the light and twirled it around for inspection. He lifted the second glass of grappa to the kid, and threw the clear stinging liquid down his throat. He turned to Rocco and Johnny and began their responsive ritual that happened about this time, every time. "Whaddya see?" he barked.

"Loada garbage," Johnny recited dumbly.

"Whaddya do?" the don boomed.

"Pick it up," Rocco fell in.

They moved toward the kid's body as Don Franzoni pushed the ring onto his finger and waited. Nothing. He began the second verse. "Whaddya see?"

Johnny stopped in horror. Standing before them in the boss's place was his father, belt in hand, sweaty with booze, hyperventilating, ready to kick ass on either him, Sallie or their mom, most likely all three. "L-loada garbage," he squeaked in a trembling little voice that he hadn't used since he was twelve.

"Whaddya do?" Johnny's father asked in a voice that sounded a lot like the boss's.

Rocco saw the same wealthy preppie snob he'd seen before. But this time, the fruit was breathing hard and blood was dripping from both his hands. The preppie sneered, looked straight at Rocco, and asked again, in a booming voice that didn't quite belong: "Whaddya do?"

"Pick it up, boss." Rocco turned away.

Dan Franzoni took the ring off. In an instant he was himself again.

"Hey," he said. "I gotta idea."

SCARED STIFF!
Crowded Brooklyn Bank Robbed In Afternoon

Witnesses Offer Conflicting Descriptions of Only Un-
masked Man;
Strange Case of Mass Hysteria
Security Guard, 58, Strangled to Death
One Franzoni Lieutenant Arrested
Franzoni: I'll Talk to Cops, No Subpoena Necessary

Don Franzoni kept one of the most magnificent lim-
ousines in New York: snow-white, long as a city block,
satellite dish, fully stocked bar and Jacuzzi inside. The
monstrous car made everything nice and simple: You
could pick up a broad and have anything you wanted,
do anything you wanted, without ever getting out of
the thing. Just find a driver who knew how to take it
slow. In the limo's cavernous rear compartment the
Don had enjoyed some of the city's finest professional
hostesses and more than his share of freebie soap
opera starlets and lounge singers. And all that was
before he had the ring.

The last few nights, all he'd had to do was slide
down the opaqued window and watch as the next
beautiful, scrubbed face registered Omar Sharif or
Sean Connery or whatever particular limo-oriented
fantasy this one nurtured. She'd put a tux on him
maybe, erase the lines on his forehead and the wattle
on his neck, perform one-second liposuction. Whatever she wanted, he became—and within half an hour,
champagne would be spilling from her flute glass and
flowing past her naked breasts as she leaned back in
the hot tub to look at the canyons of midtown or the
brownstones of Park Slope through the moonroof of
the whitest car she had ever seen, with the finest man
she could ever imagine.

But now was not the time for such frivolity. The
limo would not become broad bait again until evening.
In daylight hours it sent the same signals of power
and importance but to a different end: Now it said the
owner of this vehicle was a successful businessperson
of taste and erudition whose time was so valuable that

his appearance anywhere was an imposition—and in connection with a capital crime, a virtual impertinence.

At least that's what it seemed like to most of the hundred-odd gawkers outside the precinct house as Mr. Franzoni grandly stepped forward to do his duty as a citizen. Being so close to a man accused of ties to organized crime was thrilling, almost dangerous, but without any real risk. They had to see this celebrity for themselves, and he didn't disappoint, with his barrel-chested carriage, pristine Italian suit, perfect white carnation in the boutonniere, black overcoat draped over broad shoulders like a cape, and dozens of individual variations on that theme; to most of them he looked like the noble, principled family patriarch they had gotten to know in the movies. This was a man accustomed to leadership, striding through the sea of cameras and microphones with a bearing that was almost military, no, royal, as one large, eye-patched subject kissed the ornate ring on his left hand; now he leaned forward to hear from someone carrying a briefcase, it must be his attorney, yes, a hunched, rodentlike little man whose eyes darted guiltily around the throng. There were a few, mostly police and prosecutors, who saw two weasels, equally venal save that one was much fatter than the other, but those were people who had already dealt with Howell Josephs III, Esq., Don Franzoni's mouthpiece.

"What, is DiCaprio here?" asked Josephs, who saw the don through a very clear pair of eyes.

"Just about," replied the Wire. "I'm a hero."

"A reckless hero," the lawyer cautioned. "As your attorney, I want to repeat the advice I already gave you. This is a stupid thing to do. I don't like that you're here. I don't like that you told the press in advance when you were gonna show up. I don't like that you're saying anything to the cops. They've got nothing on Rocco, they pinched him just to bait you.

You shut up and leave everything to me, and Rocco will be walking out of here in a day or two."

"I know what I'm doin'," Don Franzoni said as he slipped his new ring into his pocket while the lawyer held the door open for him. A cop headed outside felt dizzy for an instant, but his head cleared and he let the fat guy in the black coat pass ahead of him and on through the metal detector, followed by a little guy with a briefcase and the biggest valet the cop had ever seen.

Two hours later, they told Rocco he had some visitors. They took him past the regular visitor cages, dumped him into an interrogation room, shut the door and sat a guard outside. Johnny already sat there, crunching on a nice biscotti his mother had made, and he had just offered the bag to Rocco when in walked his mouthpiece and his boss.

Don Franzoni was as smug as ever, but Josephs' face was white with shock.

"Rocco, sit down," said the lawyer. "We gotta talk to you."

"When do I get outta here?" Rocco asked.

"Well, that's just it," said Josephs, without looking up. "The don wants to explain."

Don Franzoni removed his overcoat and spread it over a folding chair. "Rocco, that bank job we did, it was what you call an experiment. I had to find out if that ring worked in combat. And it worked, all right. Like a charm. Nobody was able to ID me because they was all describing somebody different. Some of them scared as hell, too. Told the cops they saw an Arab terrorist, a Nazi, a fucking devil with horns, like that. I even hopped in a lineup a few minutes ago." He met the lawyer's rueful glance. "Against counsel's advice. And nobody picked me out. Nobody."

"The job was going great, boss. You didn't have to ice that guard."

"But you see, that was all part of the experiment, Rocco. For the Family. I had to find out how far I can go now that I have the power. And it turns out I can get away with anything."

"Great, boss, now let's go home."

"There's one problem, Rocco. This new D.A., he's a young guy, he wants to be governor some day, senator, president, who the fuck knows. He wants to get me. He wants to get me bad, Rocco, it'd make his career. He said he's going to keep this case open until they get a conviction, no matter how long it takes. It'll never blow over. So he's gotta find somebody guilty, and it can't be me: Who'd take care of the Family then? You understand."

"What?" Rocco's voice began to shake as he slowly figured out what the don had in mind.

"Rocco," interjected Josephs, "the guard was hit with Don Franzoni's M.O."

Rocco knew that perfectly well. He had watched the man kick and splurt.

"So?"

"So I just told the D.A. that the only guy I knew good as me on the wire was you."

Slowly it sunk in. Even to Johnny.

"You set me up!"

Don Franzoni walked behind Rocco and patted him on the shoulder. Rocco stood immediately to face him. "Don't worry, I ain't got no wire. Listen, the D.A. needs a conviction. I need the heat off while I figure out what to do. The D.A. and I both get what we need. And one of the things we don't need is you. Besides, you do your time and we'll take care of you later."

"A lifetime, boss. I'll get life! You're using me like you used that fucking kid!"

Don Franzoni leaned back in his chair. "Only thing I used was this," he said, pulling out the ring. "You just happened to be standing there."

The Wire smirked, and to Rocco the expression looked just like those rich preppies used to. One more fuckover, that's all it was. Maybe the last one. God-dam that fat man.

Johnny could stand it no more. The big man stood and faced down his boss for the first time in his life. "You can't do this to Rocco! We was partners!"

"Shut up, Johnny!" The don's smirk turned ugly and he slammed the table. "You sit down and shut up, or next time I might experiment on you!" Johnny seemed to shrink and resumed his seat. The don's voice became calm but the threat was still there. "And don't you ever oppose me again." Johnny thought he heard an echo of "young man," and smelled a rancid whiff of bourbon and sweat, but he decided it was just his imagination. He sat. And he seethed.

"Howell understands. Don't you, Howell?"

Howell Josephs had been unusually quiet through-out the don's whole rant, but his mind was working several chess moves ahead. If Franzoni kept it up, it wouldn't be long before the D.A. would grow impa-tient with the small potatoes the don was serving him while the main course was still running free, and then the next step would of course be to isolate him. To take away his defenses one by one. And the very first isolation technique would definitely be to gut his attor-ney like a deer, drag up every instance in which Jo-sephs had bent the law so that Don Franzoni wouldn't bend a wire around his neck, and there were plenty of them. It's one thing to be an idiot, thought Josephs, even an idiot bully. But this is worse: You found a way to drag me down with you, and there's nothing I can do about it.

Don Franzoni pantomimed yanking the slack from a piece of wire. "Don't need this, boys," he said, slid-ing on the ring, "when I've got *this*."

The ring passed the second joint on his finger.

The Wire's eyes went wide.

His tongue lolled out of his mouth crazily, and his hands went to his throat, but there was nothing there to fight against. He tried to send air up a violently crushing windpipe but couldn't make a sound. In a panic, he looked from Rocco to Johnny to Josephs.

"Jesus in heaven!" said the lawyer. "I gotta tell ya, Don Franzoni, I really didn't believe you before. But that thing must really work!"

The don kicked at the table and tried to stand but couldn't find the strength.

It finally dawned on Rocco. "Yeah, boss, you put on that ring, people see what they wanna see. What they're thinking about."

Johnny said, "I'm thinkin' about him with a wire around his own neck."

"We all are," said Josephs with a satisfied smile. "We're all thinking the same thing. And he can feel it too. Can't you?" The don rocked from left to right. "Like they say in show business: just give the people what they want." The lawyer moved close enough to whisper: "It's the *ring*, you moron."

The don took his hands away from his throat to pluck off the ring, but Johnny was already there, ripping the Wire's right hand away and crushing the fingers of his left hand in a powerful grip. "No, boss," he said with chilling calm as tears rolled down Don Franzoni's face. "It looks better on you."

The three men continued to stare with the intensity of starving animals. They were breathing hard, enjoying this, teeth clenched, pulling the imagined wire tighter and tighter with the force of their will. It wasn't long before the Wire slumped over for good. He had barely been able to make a sound the whole time.

Testily, Josephs pulled the ring past Don Franzoni's bruising fingers. There was a slight shimmer, then the room righted. They inspected the body closely: The don was definitely deceased, but there were no marks on his body, no blood at his throat, nothing except for the darkening left hand. And the smell.

It was Rocco who spoke first. "Whadda we do now?" The others stared blankly. Then Howell Josephs III began to think.

"Johnny," said the lawyer. "When I open the door, take this guard down very quietly. But only temporary, right? I want him to wake up. Cause when he does, he's gonna get a promotion."

"OK, but . . . "

"Rocco, get the don's overcoat and put it on. Then get ready to put *this* on." With a tiny ping, something golden twirled across the room.

Rocco caught the ring in one hand. As he shrugged on the great black coat, he began to understand.

"Johnny? Now."

Josephs opened the door. "Officer? We're ready to return the prisoner."

Two minutes later, the press corps parted before Mr. Franzoni's mammoth security man as he led his dapper employer back to the limo. The businessman himself had no comment and walked briskly, still being careful to smile and wave with the great generosity of spirit that was his hallmark; to him, photos were always flattering, and if anything he looked even grander than when he had entered the building more than two hours before.

Josephs stopped briefly before the forest of microphones. "We're confident that justice will be done in this case, and we will continue to do our part as citizens to help our law enforcement agencies in that process. We have no further comment at this time." The others were already inside the limo by the time the driver opened the door for him, intent on the live feed showing their very automobile. They watched themselves pull out into the street on television.

The Don spun the ring around on his finger. "Whaddya see, guys?"

"We see *you*, Rocco," said Josephs. "Be careful we still like what we see."

Rocco pulled the ring off. A little shimmer, and all of a sudden the Don's overcoat looked ridiculous on him. Johnny grinned and gave Rocco a poke on the arm. "What happens when they figure out he's gone?" he asked.

Josephs stared out the window. "They got the Wire now. That's who they wanted all along. Rocco, you woulda been out in two days anyhow, and the D.A. knew it. They're gonna forget all about you. Dismiss the charges for lack of evidence." He stretched. "I'm gonna call up some friends over there and make sure they do."

"And this?" Rocco turned the ring in his hand.

"Meal ticket, my boy," the attorney grinned evilly. "Can you imagine a ballbuster like Johnny on a job with this thing? Can you imagine a lawyer in a courtroom? We're gonna do something with this ring the Wire never dreamed about, and it's gonna make us the richest mugs in history."

"What's that?" Rocco lifted the ring up to his eye.

"We're gonna share it."

"Right." Rocco stared at the lawyer through the fingerhole.

And ring or no ring, he just didn't like what he saw.

SASHIMI

by Brian M. Thomsen

Whit Costa sat back in his chair and breathed a sigh of relief as he read the bank's confirmation of the transfer of the funds to cover tomorrow's payroll run. He never liked it when any of his three hundred employees (formerly four hundred and soon-to-be two hundred) were mad even though that was a necessary hazard of being a company's president and founder, and nothing ticked off the employee ranks more than having their paychecks bounce like so many rubber balls. The money from the Pacific Rim had arrived safe and sound and in the nick of time.

Whit would have said "Thank God" had he not previously publicly declared that such expressions of religious partiality had no place in the working environs of a forward looking politically correct corporation that practiced diversity, and thus instead just satisfied himself with a simple yet, in his own mind, eloquent "Woo" while breathing yet another sigh of relief.

"Whit," hailed the voice from his desk intercom, "Sondra Boyle wants to know if her meeting with you to discuss the art issue is still on."

Whit looked down at the list of employees in front of him and noted that there were three stars next to her name: two hollow (signifying gender minorities—female and lesbian) and one dark solid (signifying racial minority—Asian). *Nope,* he thought to himself, *there's no chance that she will be on the layoff list,* and then replied aloud to Helga, his secretary at the other end of the intercom, "Of course. Please e-mail her back and confirm."

"Certainly, Whit, and Sal Torres is here to see you, and he doesn't have an appointment unless you forgot to tell me that he does."

Whit thought for a moment and tried to remember, scratching his pale and balding pate that was reminiscent of an illustration of the famous monkey Curious George when he was puzzled (that is, of course, provided that George was played by a short, pudgy, pale-faced gnome of an executive who confused a dress-down style with just plain sloppiness), shrugged, and replied, "Send him in."

Sal had been a close friend for the last few months and had helped to arrange the deal that had bailed out General Neutron Electra, Inc. (G.N.E., Inc., affectionately known as "GENIE"), from the financial woes that had been brought about by the corporate expansion that far exceeded the potential of the market, as well as a premature plateauing of product sales and licensing. Contrary to "GENIE corporate mind and way of thinking," it appeared that there were a finite number of applications for even the best-constructed coin-op video game, and no amount of marketing dollars were ever going to change that. If Sal and his silent friends had not arrived . . .

"Whit, how's it hanging?" Sal boomed with a belch.

"No longer by a thread, thanks to you and your Pacific Rim associates," Whit replied, not bothering to get up since Sal had decided to park his designer-jeaned ass on the corner of his desk.

Sal waved his finger in a shame on you gesture and corrected, "Not associates, acquaintances. I told you that. Not that there is anything wrong with the guys. Tanaka and I are soulmates."

"Soulmates," Whit replied, already beginning to lose interest and wishing that he didn't feel self-conscious about playing with his Gameboy in front of others during office hours.

"Yeah," Sal continued, enjoying the sound of his own voice, "I knew we had a lot in common the first time we shook hands."

"You can tell a lot from a person's grip, I guess."

"Sure, but I meant from his fingers. They were working men's fingers, just like mine."

"Like yours."

"I could tell that he must have been a machinist. That's how I worked my way through college. I guess I was just a bit luckier than him. I mean, I got through my tenure at the blade with all ten digits intact."

By this time Whit had already ceased to listen to the facilitator of the corporation's salvation and had started to read the papers that Sal had placed in front of him.

"Do I really have to read this stuff?" Whit asked impatiently.

"Well, you should," Sal answered, "after all, Tanaka is under the impression that you agreed to all of these terms prior to accepting the bailout funds. Too bad he didn't ask you to sign anything up front."

"Too bad," Whit repeated.

"I guess he thought he was dealing with a gentleman."

"He was," Whit answered with a scowl, "but desperate situations can drive even a gentleman to accept desperate measures and occasionally do ungentlemanly things."

Sal let Whit's comment pass despite the falsity of his claim. Sal knew that Whit had no conception of a gentleman's behavior. He frequently went back on his word, was more than willing to trade employee dedication for fiscal or social expedience, and had all the sense of fair play of a spoiled child. Still, he had to hand it to him. Whit had managed to take a simple coin-op video game and turn it into a multimillion dollar corporation with eyes on joining Boeing and Microsoft as the financial jewels of the Pacific Northwest. Pumping money into PR and the myth of the

corporation's dedication to social awareness, GENIE
had become the darling of the business mags for
awhile, until reality intervened and everyone (outside
the company, of course) realized that they were a fad-
driven industry and would soon have to accept a vastly
smaller consumer base, as had the comic book and
collectible card game companies that had migrated to
the same region before them.

Whit's whine-filled squeal interrupted Sal's contem-
plation.

"He wants to use General Neutron for gambling?"
the CEO said incredulously.

"That was his basic idea," Sal conceded. "General
Neutron's minions wipe the other guys out and make
you, the player, big bucks . . . provided you can pay
for the ammo, power-ups, and first aid. Given the success of that Star Trek casino, it's not an idea without
merit if you know what I mean."

Whit knew what he meant and filed it away for a
time later on down the road, once the matters at hand
had been cleaned up, and said, "Agreed, but we have
more pressing matters at hand, the reorganization."

"The bank is willing to sign on now that the debt
and operating cash on hand are under control, but it
still means a substantial reduction in personnel."

"The list is already compiled," Whit volunteered,
handing a copy to his co-conspirator.

"Good," Sal replied; he took a quick look at the
list of names, shook his head and chuckled, "One hundred new recruits for the ranks of the unemployed.
How did you put the list together so fast."

"The computer did it for me. I set the departmental
quotas and had it cross referenced with the personnel
files, and voila: a list of employees with the least
chance for successful litigation of a class action suit."

"White heterosexual males between the ages of 20
and 40 with traditional religious group affiliations,"
Sal volunteered.

"For the most part, exempting family members and the Pippin's gang."

"The Pippin's gang?"

"The six guys I used to game with at Pippin's Pub. Loyalty counts for something."

"Oh," replied Sal softly, making a note of Whit's definition of loyalty. "Of course, you included job performance reviews, contributions to corporate productivity and profitability, and such in the program's decision making."

"No," Whit answered, "such things aren't in keeping with our team spirit mentality. Excellence has to be group determined. Performance reviews might get in the way."

"Of course, what was I thinking?"

"Now, how do you think Tanaka will take the news?"

"Poorly, but he's powerless. All he has is an unsecured loan, which GENIE will obviously repay subject to its corporate reorganization. It's his word against yours as to whether he is a partner or not."

"Good."

"By dinner tonight the reorganization will have been filed with the necessary protections in place."

"Good. You can break the news to him then."

"You mean *we* will break the news to him then."

Whit caught the warning tone in Sal's voice and quickly conceded the point. "That's what I meant."

"Of course."

Sal slid himself off the side of the desk and headed for the door.

"I'll have Helga make reservation at Toshiro's. You know, the raw fish place."

"Fine," Sal agreed, and then paused and returned to the desk for a moment, removing a lapel pin from his pocket. "I almost forgot. Here's a gift from Tanaka. He gave me one too. We should probably wear them tonight. He and his people are a little touchy about gifts, if you know what I mean. We wouldn't want to offend them."

Whit looked at the pin and at the three Japanese characters engraved on it's face. "What's it mean?"

"Who knows," Sal replied, quickly hastening off for an appointment to lay the ground work for another shady deal.

In the recession of the late 1990s he was never long between clients who needed help with his own special kind of financial planning and debt avoidance.

Sondra was ten minutes late for her meeting with Whit, but he didn't mind and was more than willing to cut one of his favorite employees a little slack. It was hard to believe that she had started out as a student intern at Wizcom, one of the small companies that GENIE had devoured in the past three years, and had in just that short amount of time managed to remove, step-up, and replace four of her immediate supervisors. No wonder her coworkers called her Dragonlady behind her back (quietly, of course, since it could be misinterpreted as an ethnic slur, which was grounds for dismissal).

Whit shared with her the list of employees who would receive their dismissal e-mails in the morning, and she once again pledged her loyalty to him.

"You don't have to worry about me, Whit," she assured him "GENIE is very important to me."

"Good," he replied, careful to avoid direct eye contact with her, and quickly changed the subject by showing her the lapel pin he had just received. "Pretty cool, huh?"

"Way cool," she replied. "Very Japanese."

"Any idea what it symbolizes?" he asked carefully, not wanting her to think that he thought that she should know just because she was Asian.

"Oh, it's just the symbols for three numbers, *za, ku,* and *ya.* Three, nine, and eight. A losing hand in a card game whose name escapes me. My grandfather used to play it."

"Oh," Whit replied, thinking to himself that tonight Tanaka would find out that it was himself who held the losing hand. *Too bad.*

"Here," she volunteered, leaning in close to him in a manner that would have been completely unacceptable had their sexes been reversed, a hint of jasmine seducing its way to his nose, "let me put it on your lapel."

"Thank you," Whit replied awkwardly, averting his eyes from her ample cleavage and noticing that one of her fingertips was bandaged. "What happened?"

Sondra quickly drew back, having finished affixing pin to lapel, and tried to hide her fingers in her fist. "Oh, nothing," she replied, "just a nasty paper cut."

"Too bad. I bet it hurts like the dickens."

"There are worse things one can do to one's self," she offered enigmatically.

For a fraction of a second Whit contemplated going home to change into something a bit more professional before the dinner meeting but then quickly dismissed the idea. A GENIE T-shirt with General Neutron on it under a sports jacket and khaki pants was who he was after all, and he had no desire to buck the traffic back to Tacoma from their overpriced Bellevue offices when dinner was in Seattle on the sound. Besides, the time he saved would allow him to stop by New Video to review the latest releases.

New Video was filled with the usual college types and middle-aged nerds who were overpaid by either Microsoft or Wizards of the Coast or some other "cool" company. Needless to say, Whit felt comfortable, in his element.

"Yo, Captain Neutron," hailed Silent Tod, the slacker son of the often absent proprietor, "real cool pin on your jacket, man. *Yakuza* rules, man."

"Yakuza?" Whit queried, vaguely recognizing the word.

"Yeah, *Yakuza*," Silent Tod repeated, pointing to each of the tiny Japanese characters, "*ya, ku, za.* Yakuza, the Japanese gangsters. I know all about them. I've seen every film John Woo has done. He deals mostly with the Chinese Triads, but sometimes he has the Yaks in there as well."

The Yaks. Whit couldn't help but visualize a bunch of hairy goats playing hitman, was mildly amused and decided to correct the young video hound. "You're wrong. They're numbers. 398."

"You mean 893, man," Silent Tod corrected. "A losing hand of the *bakuto.* Loser is just one of the translations for the yaks, man. Personally, I prefer 'the men who walk in the shadows.' Cool, huh?"

"The men who walk in the shadows?"

"Yeah, man. You and I are *katagi,* that's short for *katagi no shu,* 'people who walk in the sun,' like you and me. They walk in the shadows. Gangsters, cool. Hey, you want to play some pachinko? I know this guy I met at the Woo film festival and . . ."

Whit had seen Silent Tod this animated before. When he latched onto something new, there was no stopping him. Whit remembered when he went off on a Bab-5 jag and espoused the virtues of being a member of the psy corps to him for two whole hours; he quickly glanced at his watch and hightailed it towards the door, not wanting to be late for dinner as Tanaka would probably be pissed enough by meal's end as it was.

"Gotta go," he signed off, passing through the sensors and out the exit empty handed.

"Wait, man," Silent Tod called after him. "I thought you were going to get me a job in your MIS department. I'll lend you my copy of *Hardboiled.* It's Woo at his prime. Maybe we can like do a latte or something, huh?"

*   *   *

Toshiro's was located along the base of Queen Anne hill, and its second floor 'reserved' room afforded a decent view of Puget Sound. Whit recalled that they prepared a wicked California roll as well as several other palatable concoctions of raw fish, rice, and seaweed. Personally, he would have preferred Burger King, but there were certain hostly obligations that he felt appropriate to the situation, and Whoppers were not really a suitable serving for the occasion. Who knows? They might be vegetarians, and just because he had to inform them of the change in their business expectations was no reason to offend them.

Whit was surprised to find a "closed" sign outside the restaurant and a big and burly Asian gentleman in a dark suit standing by the door.

"Excuse me," Whit said to the imposing figure, who reminded him of Oddjob in that classic James Bond film, "but I had reservations for tonight . . ."

"Yes," the human wall said curtly. "You must be Mr. Costa. Mr. Tanaka is upstairs waiting. He prefers his privacy and has taken the liberty of reserving the entire restaurant for the evening . . . at his own expense, of course, as it is his preference."

"Of course," Whit replied.

"You mustn't keep Mr. Tanaka waiting," the human wall urged. "It is not good for him to become impatient."

Whit seemed to sense a touch of fear in the human wall's voice. *I guess no one likes to see their boss pissed off. Oh well, it can't be helped tonight,* he thought to himself, and decided to hesitate for just another minute with a question. "Has Mr. Torres arrived yet?"

The human wall thought for a moment and said, "He is not inside. I believe he is already late."

"Figures," Whit replied, entering the dim sushi bar (closely followed by the human wall). He went upstairs to the room that had been reserved thinking, *Damn that Torres, always ready to share in good news and duck out on the bad. I wish we could trade places.*

Tanaka and his boys (five plus the human wall) had rearranged the table placements in the private room so that all of the food was on two long side tables with two smaller tables set for four each. One of Tanaka's associates, a slightly smaller version of the human wall, had taken a place behind the bar, his jacket off and sleeves rolled up to reveal what looked like the beginnings of an intricate tatoo on each forearm.

Tanaka barked something in Japanese which was instantly translated by one of his aides, a smallish fellow of slight build who was probably a lawyer or accountant or some other personal administrative type.

"Mr. Tanaka welcomes you and thanks you for picking such a pleasant place, and he apologizes for any lack of respect that he may have shown you by taking control of the evening's privacy and invites you to have a drink and unwind before we dine and take care of the matters at hand."

"Sure, no problem, thanks," Whit replied with a doffing gesture as if he was wearing a hat, as his eyes gradually grew accustomed to the dimly lit room. "I'll just get something to wet my whistle, so we can sit down and get to it."

Whit ordered a rum and coke from Tanaka's barman, commenting, "Nice tats."

The burly barman placed the drink in Whit's hand, nodded, and rolled his left sleeve up further to show off more of the intricate skin art that seemed to reach up the entire length of his arm and perhaps beyond. Whit was impressed and thought he might offer to introduce him to the biker drag queen his ex-wife took off with who had a weakness for body art; but then he thought better of it, just repeated "nice," and headed back to the table where Tanaka was seated, first making a quick stopover at one of the food tables for a few pieces of sushi.

Whit offered Tanaka a piece of California roll off his plate as he sat across from the shadowy Japanese business man, saying, "Sushi? They make a wicked California roll here."

Tanaka barked another response in Japanese which his slightly built lackey quickly translated as, "No thank you; he prefers sashimi."

"Whatever," Whit replied, wishing that Sal would arrive and take some of the burden off of him. "Guess we just have to wait for Sal to arrive and . . ."

Tanaka barked again.

"Mr. Tanaka says that that will not be necessary. Mr. Torres is late, and besides he has already spoken to him, and further conversation with him is not required. Mr. Tanaka wishes to talk to you about the use of your machines in his casinos and his purchase of the majority share in your company."

Whit took a swig from his drink, and asked the lackey, "What exactly did Sal tell him?"

"It is of no consequence," Tanaka barked in perfectly accented English, then added something else in Japanese, whereupon the lackey removed himself from the table to stand next to the other aides in a phalanx of readiness that quite coincidentally blocked any access to the staircase downstairs. "It is time for you and me to talk without an intermediary."

Whit took a breath. He had never heard Tanaka speak in English before and had always assumed that he didn't understand it. Score one for the Japanese businessman. He waded in to the matters at hand.

"Undoubtedly, Sal told you that we have a problem . . ." he began, pausing a moment for a response and, not sensing any, continued, ". . . a few problems actually. To begin with, it is our feeling that the use of Captain Neutron for gambling purposes might get in the way of the franchise . . ."

"The franchise?" the shadowy Asian gentleman queried evenly.

"The potential for movies, theme parks, books . . ."

"Ah, yes," Tanaka replied in the understanding tone of a Confucian scholar, "those things which you felt would save your company from financial ruin in the past. Those things which you have failed to make work in the past. The great nonexistent franchise opportunities. They did not save your company. My and my associates' money did, and in exchange we were promised the opportunity to utilize your little blasting man in our gambling establishments and a share in your company so that we may share in your *great* franchise potential opportunities."

Whit felt a quiet rage build within him as he listened to the Asian's remarks, sure that they were dripping with sarcasm at *his* expense.

"Now see here," Whit blustered with self-importance, "if you have talked with Sal, you no doubt know that the deal is off. GENIE will survive on its own with federal financial banking protection, and you will get back some of your losses as soon as restructuring is complete."

"We don't understand restructuring," Tanaka said in a measured tone, still having yet to raise his voice in English, the barking of orders in Japanese a thing of the past.

"It's a money thing," Whit said haughtily, "and unfortunately for you . . ."

"Fortune is capricious. I do not let it bother me."

"How nice for you," Whit replied dripping with sarcasm. Obviously this guy didn't understand the way things worked in the good old US of A.

"And it is not what we agreed to."

GENIE's lawyers, of which there were many, would eat him alive; relying on a verbal handshake was definitely a thing of the past.

"I also never allow myself to be taken advantage of." Tanaka snapped his fingers, and the lackey placed a set of papers in front of Whit. "Kindly sign these papers," the Asian instructed, "and please do so of your own will. We had a deal. You must honor it."

"Or your goons will work me over."

"No," Tanaka replied. "I am not some mob boss gangster. I took you to be a man of virtue."

Whit laughed, leaving the pen that had been lain with the papers unlifted, his guffaw and inaction an insult to the foreigner. The arrogant little CEO just didn't care.

Tanaka shook his head in what might have been disgust and stood up, revealing a true size that even dwarfed that of the human wall.

Whit became worried and tried to stand, but he found himself unable to as soon as Tanaka held up his hand as if summoning a force of some sort to hold him in place.

"Enough! You are no better than that gaijin Torres," the Japanese giant said in a tone of resignation. "I had heard many unflattering things about you but could not assume that they were true before this moment. I have heard that you are two-faced, weak, cowardly, and stupid. You are pale and scared like the underbelly of a blowfish whose inflated actions mirror your own expressions of self-importance."

Whit tried to respond but found himself incapable of forcing any words out.

"You have engaged in disreputable business practices, have victimized partners and clients, and have hidden behind a hypocrisy of social tolerance akin to that practiced by the Spanish Inquisition. True, the affiliations are different, but the results and crimes are more or less the same . . . but I was willing to forgive such silliness as errors of youth.

"Perhaps you are surprised at my knowledge of western history, let alone my knowledge of you and your company. Did you think that I would pursue my business blindly? One picks up much over the centuries. Much knowledge, many allies, and many vassals."

Centuries? Whit thought in horror.

"Despite the management failure of GENIE, the inattention you pay to getting the job done and the people who do it, the concerns of yours that were more akin to some adolescent social club than to a business with, as you say, *franchise potential,* your appetite for humiliating your competitors as you take advantage of them, your disdain for your retail partners in the marketplace, I was willing to overlook such things and extend you a hand up, a chance to better yourself, an opportunity for respect. You were to be one of my vassals, though another had already informed me of the deceitful shell game you were playing and made me an offer to take your place in our negotiations . . . but I am a man of honor. I owed you the chance to make obeisance to me, to show me the proper respect, but you have obviously declined. Another hasn't."

Tanaka slowly removed a very small object from his pocket. It was something bloody wrapped in a handkerchief. Slowly, the Asian gentleman unwrapped, and held it out for Whit to see . . .

It was the bloody tip of a human finger.

. . . before the Japanese giant popped it in his mouth and swallowed it.

"I add another to my fold."

It was at that moment that all the mishmash of facts came together in Whit's head. *Gangsters, fingertips, tatoos,* Yakuza—*this guy is a killer, a madman, or worse!*

As if reading the CEO's mind, Tanaka volunteered, "Yes, I am *Yakuza,* but not the way you may be thinking. If I were one of those killers from so many bad films, you would be dead already, like your friend Mr. Torres."

Whit gasped.

"I am sorry," Tanaka replied icily. "I was sure that you were told that before you came in. Perhaps you misunderstood when my associate made reference to his being *late.* He was *gaijin,* without *giri.* He did not understand honor or respect. He was merely a necessary facilitator, a panderer of other people's money. Like the spineless sea leech, he will not be missed."

Whit struggled, but he could not regain control of his body. He was consumed by fear.

Then, quite surprisingly, Tanaka removed his jacket and began to take off his shirt to reveal his illustrated chest.

Tanaka approached his prey slowly, Whit imagining that the tattoos on his chest seemed to be moving in ways that did not correspond with Tanaka's body.

"I am one of the true *Yakuza*. I am a creature of the shadows . . ."

Whit began to make out the moving illustration of hands armed with daggers, mouths brimming with razor-sharp teeth, and jungle cats with slashing claws bared. The Asian's chest was miasma of fear-inspiring illustrations, one more exotic than another, all savage and awe-inspiring, like so many denizens of a hellish inferno.

Tanaka was standing above him now, and the tattoos seemed to be stretching closer as if they were ready to spring from their pectoral home.

". . . and you, my puffy and pale little blowfish, are unsuitable for anything else but my dinner . . ."

Silently the illustrated horrors pounced on their helpless prey like so many sharks and devilfish, rending his flesh as they sliced him into bite-size chunks of human tuna. Whit's momentary agony seemed to last an eternity before his corporeal pains were replaced by greater ones as his soul was ripped apart to satisfy the hungers of the creature of the shadows.

The last thing the former CEO would ever recall hearing before surrendering to the unending eternal torment of the damned was:

". . . and as I said before, I have always preferred sashimi to sushi."

The next day Sondra Boyle, formerly known as the Dragonlady, issued a revised list of corporate layoffs that included all of Whit's family and friends and reinstated various necessary personnel.

Sondra was immediately hailed via e-mail as being a much more benevolent, perhaps even competent, despot than Whit, who had mysteriously disappeared on the night before with Sal Torres and was rumored to have been under investigation by various groups about matters such as embezzlement, fraud, and such.

One of the people who was not reinstated was Sondra's supervisor, who had reported directly to Whit, thus allowing her clear access to the executive suite with the backing of Mr. Tanaka, the shadowy shareholder from Japan who just happened to be on hand to announce his acquisition of General Neutron Electra, Inc.. There were a few details still to be worked out with various other financial concerns to which GENIE owed certain sums, but Mr. Tanaka assured the corporate body that they would be taken care of quickly by his very capable legal and accounting associates.

In an era when the Germans controlled American publishing and the government looked the other way at the foreign acquisition of the automotive industry, no one would care about the transfer of ownership of a simple coin-op game company.

Sondra's still-throbbing fingertip once again made itself known to her despite heavy doses of painkillers when she noticed the sharklike smile of her new corporate master.

A fingertip was not too much to lose up front for the control of a company.

She had made her offering for his respect and he had accepted. The company was now his, and she would run it for him until she too joined Whit and many others as food for the creature of shadows. She was his for all eternity and beyond.

She was a very competent shark, but she too would one day be sashimi.

LIVE BAIT

by Roland Green

It was the screaming from below that really got me scared. I wasn't surprised, because Patron was like that. I knew what he'd planned for the girl the minute he saw her. But I hadn't been scared before. I'd been worried, because I'd begun to suspect that for the money I'd gotten into something pretty dumb, with nasty bits. But being worried is a long way from being scared the way I was all of a sudden, because the screaming reminded me of what my old lady said when I told her I was in for this job.

"I got a bad feeling about Patron and that Lund bodyguard of his," she said. "There's something followin' them, for all the killin' they did. You be around when they kill again, maybe it's goin' to take you."

Now, Gloria was from New Orleans, which I've always taken as enough reason to listen to her bad feelings. In that city, you can just about scrape the other world off the walls, or dig it out of the mud, or fish it out of the river or sometimes even the birdbaths along with the mosquito larvae and the Big Mac containers. She came by it naturally, even if she didn't come very far.

You say you knew Patron's rep and you wouldn't have worked with him for ten times the deal? You FBI or DEA, maybe? Sorry, that's dumb. You don't need to get in my face. Matter of fact, a lot of this story is going to be about my being dumb, so if you don't like what that English professor last month

268

called "idiot plots," you don't have to go on listening to this idiot.

By the way, the deal was a hundred big ones, that's how much. Now do I sound so dumb? You look like you've been where that much would save your ass, too. I was in the same kind of mess. I needed to get a way farther from Texas than I was, and I wanted to do something for Gloria, like put us someplace where we could have a kid.

So the deal was running enough cocaine to zonk everybody in Biloxi for a week, using a boat that nobody would suspect until we'd landed and that wouldn't cost us so much that we couldn't just scuttle it when we were done. The Coasties were beginning to lean hard on drug smuggling around Florida by then, but they hadn't really set up their choke points deep in the Gulf.

When was "then?" Unh—the statute of limitations hasn't run out on some of what happened. I'm telling as much as I am because I'm not sure it's over in other ways too, and I want to warn a few people about—well, it'll be faster to tell the story from the beginning to as close to the end as I've come.

The idea wasn't original with Patron. It probably wasn't original with Captain Kidd. Hijack a trawler yacht or a big motorsailer, something with plenty of space below to hide the cocaine. Do this by putting a couple of people in the passage crew who would send out a signal that let a smaller boat carrying the drugs home in on it. The drugs and the rest of our people, with the guns.

That way, even if somebody suspected the first boat, the stuff would be aboard a second, unsuspected, boat before the narcs caught up. Then we'd have a good chance of being ashore in the Gulf Coast before anybody picked up our new trail.

So far, it didn't look so dumb. I wasn't too worried about what would happen to the people aboard the boat we pirated, either. I'd killed before—yeah, in

Texas—and it's no big deal, though I wouldn't say I
got my rocks off on it, the way Lund did.

I should have started thinking "dumb," or even
"bad," when we divided up the gang. Patron's bodyguard, Lund (yeah, he looked like a big Scowegian,
but *not* a dumb one and with a mean streak wider
than he was), and a guy called Iron Fluke because he
had a prosthetic hand were going to get into the crew.
I would be with the others and the cocaine.

The others were Patron himself, a wizened little guy
named Crinky who was our best shot and looked like
the kind of teacher who enjoys beating up on kids,
and Joel. The minute you saw him, you suspected Joel
was Jamaican, and the minute he opened his mouth
you knew. Or at least you knew that he was from
somewhere down in the English-speaking Caribbean,
and I suspected Jamaica because the rumors were getting out that the island boys wanted into the big-time
drug business. I figured that Joel was working for
somebody Patron wanted to go partners with, so we'd
be big enough to take markets away from the Colombians and then defend them.

I think now that Patron was *way* too optimistic. The
Colombians aren't so big any more, but back then
they could have bought their own country if they
needed it, or more muscle than anybody in the Caribbean except Fidel Castro.

Another time I was dumb, if you're keeping score.

So one thing followed another, and after enough
days went by, we had our cocaine aboard an old Baha-
man fishing boat, and the four of us were sitting and
waiting for the signal from Lund and Iron Fluke. We
knew they were crew aboard a fifty-five foot trawler
yacht named *Orpheus* that somebody was ferrying
back to Galveston after buying it in Puerto Rico.
They'd said the rest of the crew was an older guy,
probably the new owner, a college kid, maybe his son
or nephew, and the kid's girlfriend, who didn't know
shit from shinola about boats. Patron wouldn't have

minded knowing more about the people and if they had any guns; ditto for me, Joel, and Crinky. But if our people talked too much and the two men on *Orpheus* had guns, things might get hairy, Lund and Iron Fluke might get dead, and we wouldn't get anything except some dealers with an attitude on our tails.

Maybe this was more of being dumb, either us or the guys on the yacht. But we couldn't chatter back and forth much without tipping off everybody from Grand Cayman to Tampa, and Patron wasn't dumb that way. He knew you had to let the guys on the spot make the quick decisions without leaning over their shoulders on an open circuit.

I also think that by then Patron knew somebody or something was after him. He'd as good as said that he'd picked a bunch of different guys so we wouldn't get together against him. And I think not everybody he was afraid of having listen in was the Coasties or the narcs.

Anyway, there we were, waiting for the signal. After a while Joel got tired of sitting and went up forward to stretch his legs. I was about ready to follow him, when the clouds let through enough moonlight to let me see that he was wearing earrings. He sometimes wore one, but tonight he was wearing two, and these were a pair I hadn't seen before, white and curved, looking more like ivory than metal or wood.

He didn't like being looked at, so I was trying to figure out what the earrings were without eyeballing him. I couldn't have done a good job, because suddenly he said, "You got a hard-on for my ears, mon?"

"Not so's you'd notice. Only thing I've got a hard-on for is getting this job done."

"You be lucky, maybe that's what you get."

All this time Joel hadn't moved, but I just *knew* he was ready to take me down if I moved wrong, talked too long, or even thought about getting out my Magnum Python. I didn't know what he would have used, because nobody ever saw him with even a Swiss Army knife. But then, he was that big, maybe he thought he didn't need a weapon.

I sometimes had the feeling that Joel wouldn't have needed a weapon if he'd been the size of an African pygmy. Other times, I had the feeling that when he looked at me, he was looking through me or inside of me too. After a while, I was *sure* that even if he was working for a Jamaican posse, he was also working for himself most of the time,

I'd just decided that the earrings looked more like teeth—not human, thank God—when the radio made a frying-egg noise. Crinky slipped on the earphones, listened for a minute, then gave us a thumbs-up. Patron and I went aft to light the oil drum that would make us look like we needed help. We risked getting the wrong people's attention that way, but radio would have been even worse. Joel stayed up forward, which I didn't mind.

Orpheus showed up about twenty minutes later. She slowed down until she was just drifting, both diesels idling. The man was on the bridge, along with Iron Fluke, and the college kid and Lund were on the fantail, ready to throw us a line. The oil barrel had given off a lot more smoke than flame, so aboard the fishing boat all the coughing wasn't an act.

That pretty much kept the trawler people off-guard. They came right up alongside us, and suddenly we had guns on them—my Python, Crinky's Ingram, and Patron's M-16.

The owner on the bridge had more guts than sense. He grabbed for Iron Fluke, I guess figuring to either get his gun or use him as a shield. What happened then, I think, is that Iron Fluke punched the man in the stomach with his prosthetic left hand and went for his own gun with the other. On our boat, we couldn't shoot because Iron Fluke was too close. He probably was too close from where Lund was, but that didn't stop the man.

He and Iron Fluke fired just about the same time.

Iron Fluke gut-shot the man, who screamed, and Lund blew the back clean off Iron Fluke's head as well as grazing the man's scalp. Iron Fluke sort of slid down the man, who had one hand on the bridge railing and the other over his stomach.

This gave us a clear shot at the man, and Patron hit him in the chest with a three-round burst from the M-16. Then the college kid, who had been sort of paralyzed until then, jumped Lund.

I was ready to shoot the kid myself just to make sure he was dead before Lund got hold of him. Lund would have been right at home in Bosnia, with what he liked to do to prisoners or anybody who pissed him off.

Instead, Joel leaped over the railing—and some people do jump like big cats. I saw him do it that night. He landed on the fantail of the yacht just behind the kid, grabbed him by his long hair, and pulled him off Lund like he was peeling a Band-Aid off a blister. The kid went down on his back with a thump, and Lund pulled out that big long knife of his that he said was Waffen SS (except that even Nazis didn't have that bad taste).

He looked like he was going to carve on the kid some before killing him. Patron was ready to let him. I wasn't. I jumped over to the yacht just as the kid spasmed. When I knelt to feel his wrist for a pulse, I was incredibly *not* surprised that there wasn't any.

"He's dead," I said.

"Shit," Lund said.

"I didn't pull that hard," Joel said.

Then we heard "Oh my God" from the girl in a blue bathrobe who'd just stuck her head out of the companionway. When she saw everything more clearly, including the bodies and the look in Patron's eye, she went down on her knees. I don't know if she was praying or starting to faint.

I saw the look in his eye too, and didn't like it. I also thought that what would happen to me if I got

between him and the girl was something I would like
even less. I didn't think we could afford to lose anybody else, but that might not stop Patron and it certainly wouldn't stop Lund.

So Patron grabbed the girl by the hair and dragged
her backward down the companionway. She didn't say
anything I could hear before she disappeared, but her
lips were moving. Then as I said at the beginning, she
started screaming, and I started getting seriously
scared.

It looked like I was the only one. Lund was pretty
clearly thinking about when he'd get his turn. Crinky
didn't show much on his face, as usual. Joel was looking out to sea, so I couldn't even see his face.

The girl screamed a long time. That probably made
Patron happy. He was as bad as Lund that way. When
he finally came back up, I couldn't hear anything, but
the screaming started again when Lund went down. It
sounded kind of ragged now.

When Lund came back up, Patron looked at Crinky,
Joel, and me. "You fellows aren't going to pretend
you're better than me and Lund, are you?" He had a
hand in one pocket while he said that. I decided that
I'd been right about Patron not caring if we lost somebody else. I only hoped Gloria was wrong about somebody following Patron.

Joel turned back toward the rest of us, frowned,
then said, "I'll go."

For a second, that was a relief. But as Joel started
down the companionway, Crinky started to draw. "I
won't take seconds to a ———— ————!" he yelled.
He used a word I wouldn't have used around a col-
ored guy the size of Joel even if I hadn't been raised
not to use it at all. Then he started for the companionway before any of us could move to get between him
and Joel.

It turned out that Joel didn't need any help. He did
one of those big-cat jumps back up the companionway
and punched Crinky hard in the stomach. The Ingram

went *clank* on to the deck, and Crinky's head went *thunk* against the railing. Then we heard a really weird sound from below, sort of a cross between a sigh and a laugh. I'm pretty sure it was the girl.

Only pretty sure, because I was the only one looking down the companionway, and I saw Joel standing at the foot of it. At the same time the real Joel, or the other Joel, or whatever you want to call him, was standing on deck over Crinky crooning something Jamaican. I don't know what it was supposed to do, but it kept Patron and Lund from looking at anything except Crinky until I looked back down the companionway and didn't see anybody there.

Before I could tell anybody that we had too many Joels aboard, Lund went below; then he started cursing. "The ——— is dead!"

"More my problem than yours," was the first thing I could say. I decided not to mention the two Joels, particularly after Patron said that Crinky was dead.

He was quiet for longer than usual, then said, "All right. Look on the bright side. It's now a hundred fifty big ones each. Let's move the stuff, put the bodies in the fishing boat, and send her down."

We tied the bodies in place aboard the fishing boat, set off a couple of pounds of C-4 in the bilges, and watched her sink. We were in four hundred fathoms, so I figured that was enough to hide everything.

I took the yacht's wheel and turned on to a course into the Gulf. Then I nearly jumped overboard when Joel suddenly loomed behind me. If there'd been more than one of him this time, I *would* have jumped overboard.

"You see anything funny, mon, like around the girl or Crinky?" he asked.

"Crinky was going to cut loose with that snubgun. I wouldn't call that funny. You know anything about what happened to the girl?"

"Bad heart, mebbe," Joel said, with a shrug. "The kind that kills you, not the kind that makes you kill."

I didn't like that, but I figured that as long as we had only one Joel aboard, he could say damned near anything he pleased.

As the old trucking song goes, we had "a long way to go and a short time to get there." But *Orpheus* could do fourteen knots if you didn't care about saving fuel, which we didn't. The more we burned, the lighter she got. Also, we dumped a whole big crap pile of extra weight overboard, like booze and spare parts. Lund wanted to save things like the radar, to sell, but Patron said they could be traced. He was smart about that kind of thing, just as he was smart about dumping all the booze except a couple of cases of beer.

Before we dumped the paint, though, we painted the flying bridge and the forward deck green instead of white. It might not fool anybody close up, but we figured that if a search was on, it would start off with Coastie Herky Birds or Navy Orions for a while. We did enough to fool people in a cockpit three thousand feet up.

We slowed down the last day because we wanted to run in to shore at night. Between Coasties, yachts, oil rigs, and rig-supply boats, there'd be a lot more eyeballs running around loose over the last fifty miles. So we wanted to be inshore, maybe even high and dry, before dawn.

We were heading due north at about eleven knots when the radar went down. Patron swore a lot, mostly at Crinky for getting himself killed. He'd been our best troubleshooter for the electronics, as well as our best gun.

What I don't know about fixing radars would fill a book. Ditto Lund. So Patron and Joel started to work. About two minutes after they did, something shorted out, and all of a sudden we had a serious fire.

Lund emptied a fire extinguisher on to the fire, which didn't do any good. By then I'd gone from being scared to whatever is the next stage beyond that—terrified, maybe. At least *Orpheus* was diesel-fueled—no gasoline to blow up. But if we had to abandon the cocaine or get it ruined, we were in trouble. Not just from losing our money, either. People who deal in ton lots of cocaine get pissed when the stuff doesn't arrive.

We didn't have much time to argue. We agreed that Lund and I would inflate the Avon raft and put it over the side on maybe fifty yards of line. Patron and Joel would stay aboard and try to fight the fire. If the fire got out of hand or somebody suspicious showed up, they'd go over the side and swim to the raft after setting the scuttling charges. Then there'd be nothing to connect us with the yacht if we were picked up, and if we got ashore safely, we could at least hike.

Lund wouldn't have been my first choice for a companion on a raft or anywhere else, but I didn't have to put up with him long. We'd just paid out the whole fifty yards, when something bumped the raft hard. Too hard to be floating debris, even though there's a lot of that in these waters.

I remembered that the Gulf also has sharks and drew my Python. I looked at every ripple, sure that I was sooner or later going to see something under one of them. I wasn't going to shoot until it came up, so the bullet wouldn't ricochet off the water.

So I had my back turned to Lund when it came up and grabbed him. I say "it," because I don't know what it really was. Imagine sort of a cross between a tiger shark and a manta ray, and you'll have a rough idea. But the big rays don't have the kind of teeth this thing had clamped on Lund's right hand, gun and all, and right shoulder.

I got off two shots, and I don't know where they went except that they didn't bother the creature. It tightened its grip, then flapped its wings, thrashed its tail, and pulled Lund overboard. His head came up once, long enough for him to scream, then he was gone for good.

By then Patron had seen that something bad was going down and cut loose with the M-16. He punctured the raft. He punctured my left thigh and my right calf. He didn't do more to the creature than he could have done by throwing pingpong balls at it. I yelled because I was hurting and worse than terrified. When you're bleeding and one leg is out of action, you don't want to be in a leaky raft right over something with the table manners of a shark.

Then Patron started yelling in a very different way. I thought the fire was spreading, then I saw that he and Joel were fighting. It wasn't much of a fight because Joel threw the M-16 overboard and then held Patron over the railing. What happened next didn't surprise me. The thing that took Lund popped up out of the water like a missile. Suddenly Joel was holding only the top half of Patron. Then he dropped the rest overboard; I saw a lot of foam alongside the boat, and Joel grabbed the towline to haul me in.

I wouldn't be telling this story if Joel hadn't grabbed me off the raft just as it sank and pulled me in over the transom. He banged my leg so that I screamed, then I said something else as I saw a "Point" class Coastie heading for us with a bone in her teeth.

Joel didn't say anything. I think he was bleeding, he was breathing hard, and I suspect he had other things on his mind. All he said was, "Sorry, mon. The rest of this be family things."

Then the—*jumbie*, I think is what the Jamaicans call it—jumped right out of the water and over the boat. It grabbed Joel with both wings and teeth, and for a moment I thought it was going to fly away with him. But he was too heavy, or maybe he *made* himself too heavy. They went overboard just as the cutter turned a searchlight on us.

I heard a big splash, then the cutter's engines slowing to come alongside. Then everybody for miles around must have heard the explosion, like two or three depth charges all at once, with a magnesium

flare thrown in on top. I mean, the ocean around the
yacht and the cutter *glowed* for a whole minute.

It shook even the Coasties. The young woman at
the head of the boarding party asked, "What the hell
was *that*?" before she said, "You're under arrest."

All I could say then was, "Joel told me it was family business."

Since they found the cocaine and I'm doing twenty-
five to life, I've had a while to come up with a better
answer. I think Gloria was right, although I haven't
heard from her in about eight years, so I guess I'll
never have a chance to tell her.

The jumbie was after Patron. But Joel was after the
jumbie. Maybe he and his family had some sort of
feud with it. Or maybe they were spook chasers, Anyway, Joel teamed up with the rest of us because we
were good bait for the jumbie.

But by the time it came, Joel had too much blood
on his hands himself. He'd killed the two kids to end
their suffering and Crinky to save his own life. So the
only way he could take it out was to let it kill him.

You can believe as much of this as you want to. All
I can say is, I believe enough of it to be glad that this
prison is a long way from the Gulf—and if I do live
to get out, I'm going to move someplace even farther.

Crimes & Corporations

"In a few years we'll be completely legit."

One of the motivations that continues to come up in all post-Puzo gangster novels is the desire for the organized crime family to finally go legitimate and become law-abiding citizens without losing any of the perks and bennies of the mob way of life.

There is even a popular myth that a bootlegger's son could one day become President of the United States.

Things can't always stay the same; they have to change.

The mob of today will have to be replaced one day by an even more ruthless and bloodthirsty group of criminals.

Gangs, mobs, triads, and "families" make way for your heirs—the corporations of tomorrow (or maybe of today—only time will tell).

In the long run, the more things change, the more they remain the same, and Mike Resnick & Ron Collins', HR Directors and Tom Dupree's benevolent supercorporation are just as criminal as the Medicis, the Corleones, and all the other "moustache Petes" put together.

Welcome to the future.

STAN

by Mike Resnick and Ron Collins

It figures to be a piece of cake. I go to Engineering, lay down a little muscle, do a job on the chief engineer, they give me the new system, and everyone lives happily ever after.

Nothing to it. At least, that's the way it sets up.

Me, I'm Vinnie Caladina. A hit man.

I work for Jane McCracken in Human Resources, but everyone in the organization just calls her Da Boss. If she has her way, HR will be running this company by the end of the month. About time, sez I. Mickey Carlyle's boys from Marketing have made a royal mess of things lately, if you know what I mean. Ain't much moolah going around, and people are getting kinda antsy.

I finish my second cup of java and take a walk.

The engineering wing might as well be Pluto for all I can tell. It's a three-story building about the size of Rhode Island, made of yellow brick and glass that's been stained black so nobody can look in. Or out.

The floor plan is pretty much open. Managers' offices line the outside wall and block off most of the light. A rat's maze of soft-partitioned cubicles fills the floor space and is littered with trip wires, laser beams, radar systems, and other contraptions that can come to life with a flip of a switch.

Personally, the whole damned place gives me the willies.

Anyway, I walk through the maze and eventually

find what I'm looking for. The door is open, but I can still spot the nametag: *Everett P. Cohen,* the chief engineer of the Series 8000.

"Good morning," says Cohen before I made it to the doorway.

"Good morning," I reply as I step into the engineer's office and close the door behind me. "Just out of curiosity, how the hell did you do that?"

"Do what?"

"You know, the thing with the Good Morning before you even laid eyes on me?"

"Oh, that," he says, smiling like a kid in a funhouse mirror. He's sitting behind a curved desk, leaning back in his chair with his hands behind has head. A thin mustache rides his upper lip, and his hair is cropped short on top but pulled back to a small ponytail. "Stan told me you were coming."

"Who?"

"Stan."

I try to place who Stan might be. No luck. "I don't know anyone named Stan," I say at last.

"Stan's not a person."

"Huh?"

Cohen runs his fingers over a black box that is sitting on a rolling cart next to his desk. "This is our baby," he croons. "The Series 8000 Threat Analyzer and Neutralizer—STAN for short."

Did I tell you I hate engineers?

The system looks heavy, like an old-time VCR. Looping wire connects three subassemblies to the main box. One is a radar system like the cops use on interstates, and the others I can't place for all the world.

"Very impressive," I reply. "Let me not elude the point. Jane McCracken wants this device."

"That witch?"

"Uh, yes," I say, clearing my throat uncomfortably. "That witch."

"Tell her we need to pass a PV test prior to releasing it."

"PV?"

"Production Verification."

I scowl. Every part of me screams to just do the job and get out. But Da Boss wanted details, and I don't aim to disappoint her. So I fight back the urge to whack him out and point to the black tarantula-like machine. "No engineering gobbledygook. Just tell me: Will this one work?"

Whether it was personal insult or pure indignation, I can't say. But suddenly Cohen draws himself up and looks me straight in the eye. "Certainly! STAN has a broad array of sensors and prognostic routines to monitor the area and determine what steps it needs to take to resolve any particular threat. It's built on an MTPP, er, many-times parallel processing, architecture and the motherboard includes the latest in polytech . . ."

He drones on and on, speaking a language half acronym and half Sanskrit.

"Da Boss wants it delivered to HR immediately," I break in when he finally pauses to take a breath.

"Impossible." Cohen's voice is bold and assertive, almost rebellious. It raises hackles along my neck.

"Might be impossible. Might not," I say. I pull my heater from its holster and slowly attach the silencer, watching the expression on Cohen's face. "Are you planning on testing me?"

The engineer folds his arms stubbornly. "Might be."

Enough is enough.

Engineers are a dime a dozen, you know? And Da Boss didn't really care much if there was a little mess to clean up afterward. The man has ignored a direct order and is taunting me in the process, and this can't be allowed. I figure I am now justified in doing whatever is necessary.

I press off two shots. The bullets run true, straight

for his chest. Cohen doesn't even flinch. The black box hums, and the smell of ozone fills the room.

Then—so help me Big Al—the bullets stop in their tracks, maybe an inch from his chest. I just stand and stare, my jaw hanging open.

He reaches a hand out, plucks the bullets from mid-air, and places them slowly on his desk. "Got any more tricks up your sleeve?" he asks with a cocky, shit-eating grin.

Well, I may be dumb, but I ain't stupid. I look at Cohen and return the gun to my holster. He looks so fucking smug, sitting there protected by the Series 8000, or STAN, or whatever the hell it is called, but he has a reason to be.

Now me, I know that Da Boss won't put up with failure. Letting the organization down is a very unhealthy habit and not conducive to a long and happy life. Suddenly, I find myself hating Everett P. Cohen with every ounce of my body, which if you have ever seen me is a lot of ounces to hate anybody with. I decide he is a slimy, disgusting, overeducated pinhead with bad breath and a cluttered office. Maybe his stupid machine could warn the jerk. And maybe it could stop a bullet.

But it couldn't stop me—not Vinnie Caladina.

I lunge, arms outstretched, fingers ready to curl around his throat.

The STAN unit emits a blue ray.

Suddenly ice runs along my spine, and it feels like my muscles will peel from my bones any second. I fall to the ground, cracking my head on the corner of the desk.

The pain finally goes away and I stand up, regarding Everett P. Cohen with newfound respect.

"That's quite a machine you've got there," I say, gasping for breath.

He replies as if nothing unusual has happened. "As I was saying, STAN monitors everything that occurs, then takes whatever action it finds appropriate to protect its client."

Now I see why this machine was so important to Da Boss. With STAN working for her, she'd be invulnerable. She could take chances she wouldn't normally take, and who or what could stop her?

I slip away then, but there's a sense of panic rising inside me. All I can think of are Jane McCracken's fingers closing like a noose around my neck. She plans to run the company by the end of the month, and her plan is based on me taking care of this little detail.

And there is less than a week left in the month.

Magnum, Incorporated, is a giant in the security industry. We keep a pretty low profile, though, so I'm sure you haven't heard of us. Our lack of brand recognition is actually one of our strongest sales ploys. If we can turn a profit and employ the thousands we do while still remaining anonymous (or so goes the sales pitch), think what we can do for you.

As for me, I'm just a working stiff trying to get ahead. I hired on four years ago when Da Boss called me up out of the blue. I always wondered how she heard of me, but I figured I shouldn't ask too many questions. I mean, talk about your offers you can't refuse.

So I became a numbers runner for the HR gang. Before long I was doing muscle jobs, then a few shakedowns. Wasn't two years later I got my first hit job. Now I'm entrenched.

It's not a bad gig, you know? I'm trusted, and I'm good at my job. People know me (though I make sure the cops don't.)

I avoid office politics and jockeying for position inside the organization. Besides, ISO-9000 doesn't have anything that applies to the hit department, and Da Boss likes it when I stay *away* from e-mail, *capisce*? I take my annual two-point-three percent raise with a smile and accept whatever bonus Da Boss deems fitting without comparing it to anyone else's.

After all, it's the work that counts.

Life is good.

Life is steady.

Sometimes life is a little too short, but you have to take the bad with the good.

And, if I stay the course, maybe McCracken will find me my own division to run some day.

But Da Boss runs a tight ship, you know? Last month she found Calvin "The Weasel" Smith having lunch with a broad from Finance and passing a little more than affection, if you get the picture. (And there are magazines that would pay *plenty* for the picture, if you know what I mean.) Anyway, they found The Weasel the next night in a car that had somehow wrapped itself around a telephone pole. Accident, the coppers said.

But we all knew better.

Da Boss expected Everett Cohen would be dead by now and that STAN would be installed in her office.

Which meant I had to do something, or I'd be seeing a telephone pole close up. *Real* close.

If the engineering building is strange in the daylight, it's enough to make a man wet his pants at night.

Some men. But not me. I slip through the main security system by keying in the skeleton code and soon find myself in the middle of the wasteland of the rat's maze. The lights are off, but computer screens cast neon shadows that move like ghosts across the wall and ceiling.

Cohen's office is locked, but Vinnie Caladina never met a lock he couldn't pick.

You ever feel like Big Brother was watching? Well, you ain't never felt nothing like I feel right then. The room is eerie and somehow *evil*—and trust me, I know evil when I see it. Or do it. Anyway, it smells of dusty paper and warm computer components. STAN

crouches in the corner like a big mechanical crab, red
and green lights flashing silently. So maybe it could
stop a bullet, and maybe it could determine when
Cohen was under obvious attack—but I've figured out
a new approach.

I mean, how good can this machine be?

I go to the coffee machine and pull out the compartment where the grounds are normally held. I remove
a small packet filled with processed cyanide from my
back pocket. All it will take is a thin coating. Cohen
will actually administer it to himself and will croak
in minutes.

I smile smugly, growing more pleased with myself
as I slide the compartment back into the machine
without any intervention.

How about *them* apples, STAN?

A bank of red lights suddenly flash on STAN's console. A laser pen illuminates the coffee machine with
a green beam, and the printer beside Cohen's desk
spits out a sheet of paper. I pull the page from the
printer and see that it's a full chemical breakdown of
the substance in the compartment.

I crumple the page and throw it in the trash.

STAN prints another copy.

I throw this one away, too, and remove all the paper
from the printer's tray. From outside the room, I
heard another printer power up.

Shit! STAN can access the network.

I stare at the machine, feeling my blood pressure
shoot through the ceiling. STAN blinks at me and
keeps illuminating the coffee machine. I have the sudden urge to put a bullet right through its processor.

Then I change my mind.

A bullet is too good for it. Instead I want to give
the contraption a good whacking with a baseball bat.
Smash its resistors and its circuit cards. Crumble its
capacitors. Kick it in the balls.

I stand still for several seconds, just breathing.
Anger is unsafe in my profession. It causes mistakes.

Then I see the answer to my problem. A thick black power cord runs along the wall and up to STAN, and I realize that it's that goddamned simple. Pull the plug and STAN will die just as dead as if he were a man shot through the heart.

I glance sideways at STAN.

Will the machine see pulling the plug as an aggressive act? Probably. I try to put myself in the machine's position. If I were STAN and someone went to pull my plug, I would see that as a major problem.

Okay, so I'll have to be tricky.

I step around the desk slowly, trying not to draw attention to the outlet. I drop to one knee and make as if to tie my shoe. The power plug is only inches away. I undo my laces and tighten the knots, waiting for my nerves to calm. As I rise, I figure I'll grab the cord and pull, and STAN will go catatonic.

I give a last tug on my laces and stand up, reaching for the cord at the same time.

A blue-white spark arcs from the outlet. The whole of my arm feels like it's on fire. Someone screams, and I realize a few seconds later that it's me.

I find that I'm lying flat on my back. STAN blinks, a whole row of green and blue lights flashing in some arcane code that maybe only Cohen could have interpreted. I feel like it's laughing at me.

That's when I realize that the machine may be a coldhearted bastard, but it's no killer, no hit man.

And *that* will be its downfall.

Somehow I manage to crawl out of Cohen's office. Talk about embarrassing. Thank God no one sees me.

STAN probably doesn't realize it, but he's just raised the ante. Now it's *personal*.

"Are you ready?" Mugsy Bartholomew says as he eases off the accelerator.

It's amazing how the feel of an Uzi in a man's hands can raise his spirits. I grin maniacally and heft the machine gun. "Ready and willing."

The Chevy slows down. Outside, the yellow walls of the Engineering building ease by. When in doubt, go back to the basics, I always say. Cohen, it turns out, is a creature of habit. He always blocks out two hours around lunch to get things done in his office. Sure, STAN could stop a couple of bullets. But I figure a good drive-by shooting should overload the computer's processors. I mean, how the hell could it protect anyone from fifty rounds a second?

With any luck the damned computer will die with its maker, too. Da Boss can always get another one made from the blueprints once we get our hands on them.

Cohen's office draws near. I point the gun and let fly. The Uzi roars and spits fire. Bullets spray the area. Glass shatters. Bricks splinter. I hear Cohen's scream. A feeling of glorious power fills me as I imagine circuit cards ripping and integrated chips flying through the air.

I pour it on, remembering the powerless feeling I had as I crawled out of Cohen's office under STAN's watchful LEDs last night.

We drive away, leaving behind a bombed-out shell of an office.

Eat that, STAN.

We stop at a burger joint for lunch. Mugsy gets out to pick up our order while I sit back and enjoy the feeling of a job well done. This one is important, a big deal for me. It might mean a promotion, maybe even that little division of my own before it's all over.

It feels great to have it finished.

It's springtime, and the clean air fills my lungs with the scent of a fresh start.

But Mugsy is white as a ghost when he returns. "We got troubles," he says as he sat down.

"What's the matter?" I say. "Give it to me straight."

"I called the office to get a report."

"Yes?" I say, my heart sinking.

"You killed the wrong guy."

"No way," I say with a nervous chuckle. "I planned this job too closely for that. I couldn't have missed the office."

"You got the right office, Vinnie," Mugsy replies. "But Cohen and Fred Johnson switched places this morning."

"That can't be!" I scream.

I plug in my laptop data master and call up the company's network. There it is: an emergency work order requesting an office shift. The signature at the bottom stands out.

STAN.

Suddenly I don't feel like eating.

Over the next of couple days, I try knives and ropes and gas and bombs. I shut off the power to the whole building, but STAN's emergency battery unit kicks in and keeps it running. I use black mamba venom, hoping to find an exotic substance STAN can't recognize. (Do you know how hard it is to get black mamba venom in Manhattan? In *July*?) I cut the brake lines in Cohen's Z-99. I booby trap his house and even cover the bar he goes to on Wednesday nights. But it turns out that that underhanded son of a bitch has another version of STAN, smaller and portable.

Did I mention I hate engineers?

With every failure, my situation becomes more hopeless. With every miscue, my career goes further into the dumpster. I stop eating, and every time I doze off, I wonder if Da Boss is going to let me wake up. My dreams are filled with images of mechanical spiders with flashing red and green lights and gnashing silver teeth like the pins that curl out of computer chips.

The deadline looms. Emphasis on *dead*.

Finally, I realize that it doesn't matter.

This job is beyond my abilities. I'm a walking

corpse-to-be, but by then I hardly even care. STAN has beaten me, and I can't go on living this way. I wish I could quit, but you don't just resign from Magnum, Incorporated. There's more than one reason why no one's heard of us.

I decide there's nothing else to do but throw myself on the mercy of Da Boss.

Not a confidence booster, let me tell you.

Da Boss is a leader in every way. She dresses the part, acts the part, talks the part, and—above all—thinks the part. Quick as a whip, she is. And deadly as a black widow.

I walk into her office prepared for the worst.

She's sitting behind her desk with a pair of contract thugs, "Three Scar" Jenkins and "Gomer"Johnson, at her side. Her makeup is smooth, and her strawberry-blonde hair is perfectly coifed, as usual.

"Boss?" I say.

"Yes?"

"I might as well lay it on the line. Cohen's not dead, and I can't get STAN for you."

"Who's Stan?"

"It's the prototype Series 8000 system that engineering owes you."

The room temperature drops twenty degrees. Maybe thirty.

Jane McCracken sits back and lights a cigarette, drawing on it in a slow, self-absorbed fashion. She levels her ice-blue eyes and blows a gray cloud at me.

"Without that unit I'm still vulnerable, you realize?"

"Yes, Boss, I know."

Visions flashed through my head, visions of Da Boss pushing a button and having me fall through the floor to a gator pit, or something filled with all the black mambas that aren't in labs.

Instead, she grabs her purse.

"Follow me," she says, stubbing out her cigarette. "I'll show you how it's done."

I follow her in total silence, an underling being taken along for hands-on training, figuring that any comment I make will just increase my punishment. I contemplate my position as we go, but I don't see much future for myself, so I settle for trying to guess what Jane thinks she can do to overcome STAN. I keep coming up blank.

We reach the engineering building. It's late Friday afternoon, and most of the techies have already left. The area seems graveyard quiet. The skeletons of electrical equipment sit silently on engineers' desks, and my mind starts playing tricks. Did the box with the legs move? Did the strange assembly blink an infrared sensor at me?

I shudder and focus on the situation.

Light shines out from the crack under Cohen's door.

Da Boss pulls a pistol from her purse and opens the door without bothering to knock.

"I'm Jane McCracken, Director of Human Resources," she announces.

And that's when it happens.

A light blinks on STAN's console. It assesses the presence of the director of HR, and takes appropriate action to neutralize the threat. Valves click in the ceiling. The sound of water hisses through the pipes, and the pipes rattle throughout the building. The sprinkler in the ceiling begins spewing.

Da Boss raises up her hands, a look of horror on her face. Her suit becomes soaked. Water trickles through her hair and down her face, taking all three layers of makeup with it. Below the blush and the powder and the foundation, her skin is *green*. A wart shows on her nose.

"Help me!" she croaks. "I'm *melting!*"

And sure enough, she is.

Within a minute she's nothing but a mat of women's

clothes and a cloud of noxious gas. Who would have thought the Director of HR was a *real* witch?

I look at STAN in a new light. It killed her before she even fired a shot.

"What happened?" I ask.

Cohen glances at me with a sheepish grin. "I made a software code change this morning. Apparently it worked."

I stare at the limp pile of Da Boss's clothes, the truth of my situation slowly dawning. Thanks to the machine I have sworn to kill, my skin has been saved.

Of course, I am also out of a job.

No more apartment. No more two-point-three percent raises. No little division of my own. I might even have to go legit.

A shiver runs up my spine as I look up Cohen. "Uh, I'll just be moving right along," I say, backing toward the hallway.

"No, wait," the engineer replies, holding his hand up. He moves around his desk and sidesteps Da Boss's clothes. A calculating expression crosses his face, and he shoots me a sideways glance. His arm slides over my shoulder, and he turns me gently toward the doorway.

"I've been impressed with your attitude," he says as he leads me away. "You're no quitter, that's for sure."

"So?" I replied.

"I've been thinking about how this place is run, and how it could be improved. With STAN's help, I figure I can swing a few deals—if you know what I mean."

I knew exactly what he meant.

"Do I get a STAN of my own?" I ask.

"I don't see why not."

It was an offer I couldn't refuse. Could you?

WITH A SMILE

by Tom Dupree

There was a little game we used to play with fortune cookies, a cheap series of guaranteed laughs among a group in a Chinese restaurant. Everybody read their fortune aloud and added the words ". . . in bed" at the end. "Your life will be filled with rich achievement . . . in bed." "Your luck will change dramatically . . . in bed."

Elias said that's where Microdiz got the idea.

Funny, the things you forget. But he was absolutely right. The Microdiz twist, of course, is a happy twist. And these days, for a guaranteed laugh, everybody I know adds three words to the end of a phrase.

"With a smile."

I believe *The Goodmans* was the first TV sitcom family to use the vocal smile. People have been imitating TV families ever since the days of "To da moon!" and "Dy-no-MITE." It isn't hard to coin a phrase when there are 300 million people watching your every family foible. That was the top show back then, not Microdiz's first hit, but its biggest by far. So big it could actually affect the culture. Before long, *every* TV family was saying, "Go to your room, Norman. With a smile." "I lost my job today, Madge. With a smile." You even found the vocal smile in sleazedramas on HSC, I hear, though I'm proud to say I've never turned the Home Sex Channel on. Does it really keep the pervs occupied? Well, better in their rooms than on our streets.

It wasn't long before the vast audience picked up

on the vocal smile. Elias said he started seeing it on the nets almost immediately: "w/:)." He said it started on MDNet. Duh, he said. With a smile.

Elias has hated Microdiz ever since he was born. I mean it. When he was just a baby, he would start squalling the moment Michael Micro, the computer-animated mouse, came on to introduce the *Li'l Microdiz Block* in the morning. I don't know what set Elias off. I thought the program was very nice, very sweet. After all, no cartoon animals beat the hell out of each other. Instead, they immersed the kids in good citizenship, good hygiene, good etiquette, the whole thing. When Elias got old enough to talk about it, he said Michael used to scare him because Michael acted like a machine.

Elias's generation wasn't around before the Microdiz merger, but back then the separate companies were intimately interested in the future of our nation. One outfit provided the innards for every computer worth the money, the other one controlled the cuddliest family-oriented characters ever invented. Put them together and you have tremendous global synergy, the newly united company announced, a force for the family, a bold technological empire with America and apple pie calling all the shots. For example, we soon learned, you have a hellacious theme park. I'd love to have a dime for every dollar we spent at Microdiz Nation to get Elias to relax and enjoy himself. Heh, heh, they'll bet I would. Elias had managed to overcome his fear of Michael Micro by then, but looking back, I guess it burned down into sarcasm, and a little later into anger.

Microdiz was a corporate hero to lots of people, me included. It was the last remnant of the American Century, the finest example of the two things we still did better than anybody else in the world: make software and entertain the troops. Microdiz Nation was such a smash that the company founded Microdiz Neighborhoods in every decent-sized shopping mall in the country. The smart thing was, they did presentations to parents before they opened, and I admit it, they sold me long before the ubiquitous "Head for the Hood" advertising campaign put this destination at the top of kids' whine-lists nationwide.

They preconvinced us parents that this was a great place to drop kids off while you did your business. Every person who worked at a Hood was a federally licensed Micrositter, and the company's reputation was so immaculate that most people frankly felt better about leaving children here than with their neighbors. There were no towering rides like the Nation had, but besides the animations and the gift shops, the main fascination was the same one as in the full-sized park: Kids could sit down at one of the screens in a roomful of cubicles and talk to Michael; ask him questions about family, friends, citizenship, hygiene, etiquette, you know. The computer database, or whatever they used, was just amazing. Michael had the answers to thousands of kid-sized questions, wholesome advice on scores of topics provided by the best professionals available. And most thrilling of all for the kids was that the dialog was two-way: Michael retained names and faces somehow, so punch in your code and he actually recognized you after the first session. He could ask you how the math class was going, or if you'd made up with your best friend.

Even Elias took perverse delight in his sessions with Michael. He would pose a stumper like "Where is air?" and see how long he could keep Michael talking by following the mouse's every answer with the ultimate kid's question: *"Why?"* Michael, of course, had nearly infinite animated patience, at least until the topic-string wound down and stalled on the response, "Why don't you ask your parents?" Then Elias would move onto another bizarre topic. He spent hours at home dreaming them up. He was a bright kid. The Micrositters said Elias was a walking beta test.

However, that wasn't a very good way to win Microbux to spend at the gift shop. The kids did that by learning, by letting Michael know they had retained whatever good citizenship, hygiene or etiquette tidbits Michael had dispensed last week. Microdiz itself was golden, because of course the Bux actually came out of our admission fees, but to the children the mouse on the screen pointed the road to riches in the form of T-shirts, hats, pajamas, you know. I don't think Elias ever earned a Microbuk in his life, but I know he didn't care. That infant instinct to recoil never allowed him to develop an emotional attachment to Michael or any of his animated friends. To him, Michael was still just a machine. In point of fact, a machine to be broken.

Most kids weren't like that. Most kids loved Michael. They didn't mind at all when the little mouse followed them to school, w/:).

The Microfams program was a stroke of genius. Because tormenting the Michael Micro program in the Hood had become Elias's main pastime—Michael recognized Elias after a session or two and, from then on, always began by asking him, "What's today's brain teaser, Elias, ol' pal?"—our son was spending a good two hours in the Hood cubicles every Saturday morning while I did the shopping. One night I answered the phone and was astonished to find myself talking with Michael Micro. Well, to be exact, a recorded message from the actor who provided Michael's lovable squeaky voice. Michael told me he enjoyed being with Elias so much that he was offering us a special flat monthly rate: It would cover all our Hood fees and put a gleaming leased Microdiz Kompumax Youngbytz machine on Elias's desk at home. I started objecting here and there, as you do to any vox solicitation: Elias was too young, this would force us to use hours of Hood time every month, we couldn't afford it. But the same muscular database that so fascinated Elias and all the other Hood kids was pumping here too. Michael said that MKY's hardwired pro-

grams were designed for average second-graders and
even younger; you could adjust the bias for recorded
I.Q., even test for intelligence on the spot. The
monthly fee was flexible depending on the actual
hours we'd use, but Michael had been counting on his
fingers and toes, and he'd figured out we would have
saved an average of $14.78 a month over the last six
months if we'd been a Microfam when we started, so
how could we afford *not* to join? We had to face it:
The mouse made sense.

I looked over Elias' shoulder frequently after his
MKY arrived, and damn if it wasn't incredible. Very
simple mouse—natch—controls, digital real-time ani-
mation, stereo, lots of bright graphics and kiddie noise.
I have to admit that the machine taught Elias to recognize rather complicated groups of letters and numbers
very efficiently. He soaked it up like a paper towel.
He was counting and writing in no time, because the
voice recognition routines let him dream of a word
and then see it in a flash. "Spell *cat*." "Spell *computer*." "Spell *Microdiz*." It was that simple for Elias
to conjure the correct spelling on the screen, just that
easy to drink in a new vocabulary and then learn it
himself. Elias was aping the words on the monitor
and typing his own crudely meaningful "letters" to
me before he ever started communications courses in
school. MDNet went online about this time too, and
their interface fit our MKY like a white cartoon glove.
It was as trifling a task to e-mail Bangkok as it was
to find it on the spinning digital globe. Before long,
Elias' epistolary career had moved onto the network,
and his halting written letters began casting to and
from some jaw-droppingly faroff climes. What Elias
couldn't read, he could ask the voice synthesizer to
speak for him—after MDNet screened the content for
appropriateness, of course. We soon realized there
wasn't much need for a parental gatekeeper: Microdiz
was doing that for us. And after Elias' father died, I
needed all the help I could get.

Elias and I still went down to the Hood every week, like lots of other Microfams, because even our spiffy new family computer couldn't fence with devious discussion questions like "How many animals have become extinct?" and "Why isn't there any blue food?" They hadn't even bothered to place Michael's image on the Microfams and MDNet systems; guess they figured the rodent itself needed to play harder to get, to force that all-important trip to the mall, a weekend treat for paying customers only. But he soon came back for free, for real.

When the overloaded Jackson, Mississippi public school system, without a cent to hire sorely needed teacher-keepers, officially went bankrupt and sent its kids home, the Microdiz corporate thinking cap shot up in the air like a cartoon factory whistle at quitting time. Suitably somber at the news, Microdiz's educational brass flew to the symbolic disaster site with a modest proposal.

They produced an armload of studies—originally commissioned to help Microdiz expand the Hood program into smaller communities—which suggested that early elementary students from Microfams were achieving more, faster, than kids with no MKY educational system at home. Not just traditional knowledge either, said the suits, but also emotional intelligence and social skills: citizenship, hygiene, etiquette and the like. The Microdiz educational parser was the result of person-decades of effort, it could handle a classful of students for a fraction of the cost of real teachers. Each Micrositter could govern multiple classrooms with ease, since the basic position of the average student was bent over a computer screen. And without too much trouble, the existing set of interlocking data could be made to cover an entire elementary curriculum—heck, said Michael in the animated presentation, lots of it was in there already! Microdiz would rescue the Jackson, Mississippi Secondary School District, one grade level at a time, in exchange for a per-head fee that was less than half the tax burden the district was then paying. With a smile.

Of course, Jackson, Mississippi wasn't the only municipality that was all but tapped out. Other communities watched the great experiment in drooling stupefaction. When, after the inaugural year, the first grade's cumulative scores had risen an incredible 23 percent over the previous, non-Microtaught kids, prospective municipal clients stampeded to the Microdiz campus in Des Moines. There was a new, sudden demand for qualified teachers to encode knowledge at the campus, with huge salaries and Microdiz stock options as the bait. Des Moines ran a tremendous budget surplus and built a massive infrastructure for several years; it still boasts the nation's largest electronic library. The student guinea pigs in the Microskool testing laboratories were chosen by lottery and came to Iowa from all over the country. But even the most naive teachers, or "educational champions," as their corporate employers now called them, eventually had to look up at the sky through their new sunroofs and realize they had been digging the graves of their colleagues. After such a profound interlude, most of the nouveau riche teachers just shrugged and clicked their automatic garage door openers.

One inevitable day, of course, the mighty task was finished, and Microdiz was thus finished with ninety percent of its educational champions. I especially feel for the poor new graduates who came on last and essentially did nothing but mop up before they were tossed into the great ether of unemployment after a couple of fat paychecks and some fancy-sounding stock options they couldn't yet cash in. Teaching had become a bait-and-switch game. The flood of intense and driven college students studying secondary education halted like a Keystone Kops brigade once the latest set of glistening graduates found that not only were there no new positions in Des Moines, but furthermore the few remaining Luddites who were still clinging to pre-Microskool local jobs at earthbound wages guarded their rare and precious stations as if they were atomic bomb shelters. Even these dinosaurs weren't able to hang on for long. There were some backwater holdouts, but they were either slowly blackmailed by the velvet gloves of kids who were finding out on TV that Microskools had the funnest classes ever, or the parents in those communities simply turned their backs, marched off to the woods, and joined the rugged, eccentric nonelectronic home schooling movement, viewed as hopelessly backward by almost everybody else. "Skool's Out!" read the business magazine headlines. The teaching profession shriveled like a prune, and entertainment law returned as the hottest college curriculum. Before long, Microskools were everywhere. They were teaching Elias himself by the eighth grade.

By the way, I read that the Microdiz executive who came up with that idea for Jackson, Mississippi was only twenty-four at the time. He's retired now. He plays electric guitar in a band. They're terrible.

Meanwhile, the part of Microdiz that was built for entertainment was blowing hard, too. Microdiz movies were huge events, and not just for kids, either. Microdiz also produced serious dramas, like Shakespeare adaptations with teenage stars so people would want to go see them. Microdiz published books, both comic and otherwise, and multimedia disks; it owned cable TV networks, casinos, theaters, stadiums, and sports teams. The first sport it owned outright was professional cricket. Microdiz created Major League Cricket during the second year of the final baseball players' strike, at a point when stadium lessors and concessionaires were desperate for someone, anyone, to use their facilities. Microdiz hired enough players from Europe to put together two eight-team leagues in the largest cities. It promoted the new sport on TV, in the movies, in the theme parks and Hoods. Over the MDNet, e-mailers from around the world e-chatted with their

American e-friends, prepping them for cricket's arrival and debating the American rules changes: one-day matches, cheerleaders, colorful uniforms, acrobatic team mascots, "live" balls, a halftime show. Some people think baseball will be back one day. Fair enough, but where will they play?

One thing Microdiz believed in was diversity. That's why they bought more than one national television network once the Congress contained enough concerned and grateful members—most of them elected in grassroots efforts from Microskool communities—to relax the ownership regulations. As far as movies and TV shows go, movie and TV actors and writers and producers have been attracted by one thing since time immemorial, a thing which Microdiz had plenty of. At first Microdiz purchased its stars. Before long, of course, it was able to create them. Rod X. Pender and Janey Austin are just two examples of the return of the old studio-as-plantation system. There are lots more.

Some people originally thought it was foolish for Microdiz to create the Home Sex Channel, really not Michael's image at all, but the little guy's PR suits went on afterburners to explain that sex was a wonderful, normal adult function, and the more we knew about it, the more we could help the country's sociological problems and slow the spread of the exotic viruses that were pouring out of the forests of Africa and South America. You needed an access code to unscramble HSC, and only the parents in Microfams were awarded this secret. Some educational shows were specifically geared for kids, or so said the literature, so you could schedule a time to watch together and then answer the few tough questions which HSC left unplumbed. There were supposedly entertainment shows for us grownups, too, pitched as tools to keep parents together by enhancing their private satisfaction with each other, but I really couldn't say for sure. As I said, I've never turned the thing on. Elias had lost interest in TV altogether by the time HSC was launched, and what I don't know about sex already, I don't want to know.

It became gradually harder and harder for other show-biz types to compete, and easier and easier for them to simply shrug and join the Microdiz team, which is how Hollywood was conquered by the little cheesechomper. There was no war. The enemy was simply co-opted. There were still local-access shows, but nobody watched them. HSC effectively preempted the renegade hardcore pornography industry, the only facet of the entertainment business which Microdiz chose not to enter. Log on to network TV, you're a body for Microdiz advertisers. Subscribe to the premium channels, you're paying money to Microdiz, with a smile. As if they needed it.

The Microdiz school curriculum was such a success that it was easy to take the next logical step and privatize some other functions that municipalities couldn't afford to do properly. All of them were demonstrated first in Microtown, a planned community raised in an Iowa cornfield. From the Midwest out, Microdiz communities soon dotted the country, promoted by endless "soft" features on the TV news. Life here, reported the TV crews, was great. Trash collection and recycling? The streets in Microdiz towns looked like Microdiz Nation. Utilities? Power outages became a thing of the past, and Microdiz repair crews swarmed over disaster sites like so many ants; in fact, in the spirit of public service, Microdiz helped restore utilities many times after ice storms, tornadoes and floods even in places which weren't their municipal clients. But which typically had feverish town meetings a few weeks later and joined the team. Altruism does have its rewards, Microdiz-style.

And soon enough, even law enforcement was added to the Microdiz portfolio. Once Elias's class had graduated from high school—and earned a special discount on each graduate's next visit to Microdiz Nation—one of his best friends earned a spot in the inaugural class of Microcops, instructed by a buttoned-down security force from the Nation. Unlike Elias, Henry had been a Microdizzer all his life, and he felt this was his chance to give something back to the community. But he didn't join the Microcops for his health, either. Microdiz promised a guaranteed retirement after 20 years of service, even put the entire career's earnings in a draw-down escrow account up front—letting Microcops instantly earn interest on the whole amount and collect the bonus wad on retirement day. With a gigantic smile.

Henry never was able to understand why Elias didn't join him as a Microcop trainee, just as they'd done everything else together all their lives. Elias was hardly a Buddhist; he and Henry had both taken personal protection as an elective in Skool, and he was very happy to get his handgun license, even showed me how to use the pistol he bought for the class. It wasn't as though he was afraid of violence or confrontation. Henry called Elias a "cultural fascist" for *assuming* that the Microcops program was only there to produce an army of jackbooted thugs; wasn't it just possible that this was a force that could really do some good for the community? Then do it yourself, was Elias' answer. He even refused to attend Henry's graduation ceremonies. He sent over a bottle of whiskey instead and told me to take his pistol and put it in a museum.

Honestly, I thought Henry was right. Microcops were trained to protect and serve and promote citizenship, hygiene, etiquette, all that stuff. They did a great job getting rid of drug problems and such. To the average citizen, this blessing was only apparent when you concentrated on thinking about it, just like the work of the sanitation squad. You just put your garbage out on the street and forget about it, and the next morning it's gone. Same thing with crime.

There are still organized crime families in the larger

cities, but the prognosis is not good; Microcop special tactics teams are chipping away. Individual morally challenged entrepreneurs really don't have a chance any more. Even the president of Colombia asked Microdiz for a proposal. At least that was the rumor after his residence was firebombed last summer. Most people think that's *why* it was firebombed.

I think the key to the dramatic reduction in violent crime and sexual assault was, you know, swift and efficient prosecution and all, but Microcops also had some terrific hardware, and I don't just mean weapons. For example, the legal code began to recognize and accept new kinds of evidence, like defendants' Home Sex Channel viewing patterns. They could even extrapolate specific sexual perversions from these records, with the help of a battery of court-appointed Microdiz psychoanalysts.

About that time Elias quit coming over. I don't mean he disappeared with the raping and dope-smoking trash. Elias wasn't like that when he was teenaged and college-aged. Not a mamma's boy, either, I never wanted one of them. Believe me, he gave us plenty of trouble while he was growing up. But never the kind of trouble that lands you in front of a Microcop. Elias had wanted to be a writer ever since Michael taught him how to pound out e-mail to Burma, but I don't think it was for money. I mean, he never cared in the slightest about trying to get into the TV business or the movies. It wasn't wealth Elias was after; I believe it was simply the thrill of communication.

His first job was at our daily newspaper, and he was proud to get it, because he felt he had joined a noble cause. He said newspapers had been diagnosed in critical condition way back when radio was invented. They'd survived that and later made it through movies, TV, multimedia and MDNet; but no matter what came along, people would always like the feel of pressed ink on their fingers, even if it did come to them now on flash paper that combusted instantly when it fell inside a Microkleen receptacle. He lived here with me about a year or so, until he got the promotion that let him get his own place, and even then I still saw him just about every week when it was laundry day. He was writing his own humor column, stuff about other potential Microdiz animals and their private lives, behind the scenes at Microcop etiquette class, the world as seen by what he called "Microdizzies," you know. Some of it was funny, I thought, but a lot was just raunchy. I believe the word is "sophomoric," but what do you expect from a kid just out of college? I enjoy a joke as much as the next woman, but locker room humor should just stay there, if you ask me. Others disagreed with me and made Elias' column wildly popular, and he used to torment me with his latest concoction whenever we'd have dinner together on laundry day. I think he liked to see my mouth twist in embarrassment; he certainly cackled loud enough every time, and before long I was always laughing too.

When Elias' local paper joined the Microdiz-operated syndicate to get national and international news, it proved Elias right about the tactile need we still have for newspapers. Even with every up-to-the-minute bit of news available over MDNet, it's still important to have a printed document that gives you an overview without sitting down at a screen. The publication survived and even thrived. But Elias' relationship with the paper changed. He quit his column, stuck to editing the news sent by the syndicate, and started his own little publication on the side. Started doing his own laundry, too.

Elias had found a way to continue to bedevil Michael Micro all these years later. *Microzine* was full of satirical pieces about the Microdiz way. Phony test questions from the Microskool curriculum, are we men or mice?, new and far more arcane "mousetraps" for kids to use on the animated figure in the Hoods, that sort of stuff. What he didn't write himself, he gathered from like-minded correspondents over MDNet, other people who didn't necessarily think Michael hung the animated moon. Elias and his internationally farflung corps created *Microzine* over the net but insisted on distributing it to the outside world in hard copy only. To them, that was a statement in itself; *Microzine* was proud to be the printed equivalent of a shaving cup or a kerosene lamp.

My copy showed up in the monthly solid-mail packet, and later it began appearing on the doorstep. I read it pretty faithfully for a while. It had to serve as my visit from Elias, since the in-person ones were coming less and less regularly. I whined and complained, as any mother would, but privately I was just happy he had found something to throw himself into. So many kids nowadays are doing nothing but turning up as perps on the *Microcop Real Live Hour*.

But gradually Elias' visits slowed, then stopped altogether. And I began to lose my sense of humor over *Microzine*. The stories became heavier, darker, angrier. Elias and his correspondents were all but raving—they sounded like those poor people you see walking the streets delivering loud sermons to the sidewalks; the volume is turned up so high that you don't listen to anything. Dissolve the Microskools, disobey the Microcops, trash the Hoods, destroy Microdiz once and for all. There's absolutely no hilarity about someone who's foaming at the mouth. Or a son who never comes to visit any more. I'm sorry, I can't help it. He said it wasn't safe to be seen with him. He thought he was the target of a huge conspiracy. But most people raving about the end of life as we know it feel that way, don't they?

Then one night I was watching a bust on the *Real Live Hour*. As the video camera hovered, the Microcops kicked a door down and burst into a room occupied by five or six young people, all working at a desk with a couple of old-timey typewriters, scissors and paste pots. The camera was adjusted to spot dope, and when it moved in for a closeup, the full-screen viewfinder blinked bright red and howled a siren. The cops yelled at the kids to put their hands behind their backs. One young man was hauled up from a nearby computer console and shoved against the wall, but instead of covering his face like most perps do, he whirled toward the camera and began shouting.

I knew who it was before he turned around. I knew it was my Elias.

His face was fever-red, veins extended, features distorted, as he shrieked that this was the *Microzine* office, it was a setup, there were no narcotics here, the Microcops were illegally censoring the publication, they controlled everything we saw and heard. A burly Microcop pulled Elias back as the *Real Live* announcer stepped into the frame and told us that the susperps would be given the full benefit of the legal system and would have the opportunity to state their case in a court of law.

I went down the next day to the Microcop precinct. I had done everything right, made an e-appointment first, verified my Microfam status, the whole works. Everyone was drenched in helpfulness and utterly useless. Come back tomorrow, we may have more information. Clearly there's been a mistake. No case can possibly be adjudicated without prior notification to the family. Visits with susperps are not allowed before the hearing date, because that might taint the testimony. Go home and wait for the solid-mail notification. One thing that hasn't changed is the glacial pace of bureaucracy, and it made me mad, and it even made me scream at them. But screaming doesn't affect the attitude of bland respectful concern that must be hardwired into every career Microcop at that precinct, and after a while they calmed me down.

I've always tried to do the right thing. So I went home and waited for the next packet, and in two weeks I found out that my Micropals hadn't been lying. Elias' case was listed, and all I had to do to find out more was head for the nearest Hood.

I got to the mall, logged in and said hi to Michael, and there was Elias in a postage-stamp-sized video still frame. The superimposed title said this was a Susperp Response. The video began moving jerkily, with clean, crisp audio, and Elias started talking to me.

He said he was sorry for hurting people's feelings with *Microzine* and hadn't meant to cast any aspersions on the hard-working Microfolx around the country, it had just been a little bit of fun for him and his friends, he hadn't meant to cause any trouble at all. Since nobody had actually been hurt, nothing stolen or vandalized, and since good old Henry had spoken up for him at the post-bust hearing, the judge was giving Elias a chance to enroll in the new One-Strike Program. Either that or jail. So he'd made a deal.

Elias was shutting down *Microzine*, he'd make a special video to be shown in the citizenship classes at Microskool, and he said that after he'd had a chance to blow off his own steam for a while, he realized that they could have put him *under* the jail if they'd wanted, and quite easily under the law. But this closeup look at their fairly worthwhile community work, and the officers' even treatment of him, had given Elias a change of heart. He was entering the training program immediately with Henry as his sponsor. Six months of intense instruction in a dormitory with other recruits, a boot camp for the modern age. He'd send me a message every week, and he'd see me again in a few months as a full-fledged Microcop. Elias waved, the image winked out, and Michael's cartoon hand pointed to the disk dispenser, which spit out a disk that would replay Elias's message on our home MKY unit whenever I wanted. Nobody had mentioned dope at all.

I was thrilled. Talk about reintegration into society. The Microcops probably didn't know it, but convincing a hardcase like Elias had to be one of their greatest achievements in their short history. Of course, the threat of a jail term hadn't hurt, either, a prospect that was as terrifying to me as it must have been to Elias. I got back home and ran the file on the disk again and again.

And again and again, I watched Elias' progress during my weekly visits to the Hood. He'd talk to me and show me sample videos of his physical training sessions, target practice, susperp rights classes, advanced instruction in citizenship, hygiene and etiquette that would qualify him to dispense this stuff on the street. He was specializing in communications—perfect for a boy with his background—and said he was looking forward to working on the narrowcast nexus, helping to link and coordinate all the local Microdiz services. Later, I'd run the video on each disk at home a couple of times, too. I had never seen the kid so happy.

You can't stay perfect for long, I guess. Systems that are working fine when they're brand new have a way of naturally testing their restraints and finding the weaker points. Just as Elias was finishing his training, a few chinks began appearing in the Microdiz armor, and the glow of success dimmed by a few watts. We went without trash collection for a whole week once; when a few of the neighbors and I complained, the Microdiz dispatchers told us that the collectors had shown up right on schedule. Then what's this stuff all over the street, we insisted w/:), and it took a special on-site inspection team to establish that we weren't crazy. We found out that we weren't the only ones with vintage garbage problems; there had even been some brownouts in parts of the city, and the newsfeed reports quoted Microdiz spokespersons as saying this was the normal and expected result of dramatic growth in the number of people depending on city services. That might have been the Des Moines party line, but it didn't stop anybody from mumbling that Microdiz had just plain gotten it wrong. It's only human nature; I don't care about your record, what have you done for me lately?

Cobble together a solution and you only cause a mistake somewhere else, like forcing toothpaste out of a blocked tube: It's going to go somewhere, but probably not where you intended. When the Microcops ticketed the whole block the following week for environmental misdemeanors, they used as evidence the videos shot by the on-site inspection team during our sanitation crisis. It took us nearly a month, and some frantic e-mail to Elias, to get them to tear up the tickets.

While those tickets were in force, I wasn't able to use the Hood, as I discovered to my extreme irritation, but during these same few weeks the infrastructure was really creaking. One day, five Microcop cars screeched up to an innocent little bakery on what turned out to be a phony officer-down call. That Saturday, the cable system mistakenly switched signals between the *Li'l Microdiz Block* and the Home Sex Channel. Every traffic light in the city turned red for ten minutes one afternoon. The Microskool computer system declared an all-day recess. Outbound e-mail replicated itself several hundred times over and kicked itself back to the sender, hopelessly clogging the system. I thought about the endless trouble this was undoubtedly causing for Elias, gamely completing his Microcop training with the bad fortune of drawing communications duty. These incidents were nothing more than confusions, annoyances, embarrassments, and nobody was hurt, thank God, but at least on our street the Microdizzers were almost starting to look like morons.

Elias came through on the environmental misdemeanor debacle, like I said, and we were released from our privilege suspensions. The first thing I did, of course, was head for the Hood.

I logged in like always, and Michael Micro went through his usual wacky bootup dance while the system powered on. But at the end of the sequence, just as the tiny video message window was about to resolve itself, the whole screen went black, and a disk squeezed out of the dispenser. I cursed and tapped keys furiously, but nothing. No power. In fact, as I noticed when I looked up, the whole damn Hood had lost power. Not now, you mangy rat, I thought. Please, not now. Couldn't Microdiz do *anything* right these days? I tried stuffing the disk back in the machine, but without juice, it wouldn't seat itself. I could hear the wails of children all through the Hood.

I pounded the console and waited. Nothing. After a few minutes, with the kids' cries becoming steadily louder, the lights ratcheted up to half-power, and the amplified voice of a harried and evidently over-whelmed Micrositter announced that the Hood was shutting down temporarily until they could isolate the problem; would we kindly evacuate? Then Michael's cheery voice asked all unescorted kids to report to Michael's Playroom to wait for their parents, and bet-ter hurry, 'cuz free Microbux were waiting there for everybody! There was still no response from the con-sole, so I dumped the disk in my bag—at least I'd leave there with something useful—and headed for home, wishing poisoned cheese on Michael all the way.

It took twice as long as usual; every traffic light along the way was blinking amber, making each inter-section a de facto four-way stop, and more Microdiz security cars and fire prevention vehicles than I'd ever seen before were also inching their way past the end-less bottlenecks, the din of sirens spiking my stress level off the scale. I'd never been so glad to see my driveway.

I guess it was simply force of habit, the unthinking ritual of many weeks of activity, but when I got inside, I just idly powered up our MKY as I usually do, and fed it the blank disk before I realized my mistake.

Not blank.

It was Elias.

He was speaking sharply, rapidly, his eyes narrow with determination, into an MDNet multimedia sensor. This was the end of Microdiz's domination of our daily lives, the moment he'd been training for all these months. Sabotage routines of his own design were jamming commercial communications all over the city and being transmitted online to Microtown control facilities across the country, bicycled from one to the next, even and especially to the Microdiz campus in Des Moines. Along with a group of fellow rebels, he had created a maelstrom of data loss, power outages, traffic bollixes, and false alarms, an electronic Black Plague that would take years to repair. They did this, he said, not to destroy, but to create—the sense of responsibility and self-determination we had given up when we ceded it to Microdiz. Outside, I heard sirens and gunfire.

A disk routine ground into life. The image shimmered into Michael's log-on dance and suddenly we were online. A real-time feed winked in. Now Elias was at his communications station: disheveled, sweating, framed by a wall of blinking warning indicators, screaming over the sound of a klaxon. Thank God I'd made it home. Message all over MDNet. Cellular-triggered explosives. Command stations. Every Microtown. Evacuation warnings. Never let him live after this. Get out now!

Suddenly, Microcops poured in behind him. He turned, then back to me and waved with a sickly small smile. I could see Henry clearly. He stepped toward the screen with a revolver, pointed it at Elias' head, and pulled the trigger. As Elias slumped forward over the console, the screen first went red, then hot-white with the light of a mammoth explosion. I lurched forward as the power failed, the sound and picture died, and Elias was gone forever. I clawed the monitor and screamed for a long time, louder than the sirens outside.

It's been hours now and I'm quiet again. Some people are running hysterically through the street. Nobody knows anything. They're cut off. No power anywhere, no way to communicate. Is it like this in every Microtown? I can smell smoke and ozone. Microcop patrol cars go by now and then, I can hear the amplified voices. But there are just too many terrified people, and nobody's listening.

Just keep them away from me. I know what those vicious bastards did to my boy. I saw it. I saw it all. I've got Elias' pistol and I've got his ammunition. And I swear I'll spread Microcop guts all over this kitchen if they try to come in. I swear to God I'll do it.

With a smile.

THEY'RE COMING TO GET YOU. . . .
ANTHOLOGIES FOR NERVOUS TIMES

Don't Miss These Exciting DAW Anthologies

SWORD AND SORCERESS
Marion Zimmer Bradley, editor
☐ Book XV   UE2741—$5.99

OTHER ORIGINAL ANTHOLOGIES
Mercedes Lackey, editor
☐ SWORD OF ICE: And Other Tales of Valdemar   UE2720—$5.99

Martin H. Greenberg & Brian Thompsen, editors
☐ THE REEL STUFF   UE2817—$5.99

Martin H. Greenberg, editor
☐ ELF MAGIC   UE2761—$5.99
☐ ELF FANTASTIC   UE2736—$5.99
☐ WIZARD FANTASTIC   UE2756—$5.99
☐ THE UFO FILES   UE2772—$5.99

Martin H. Greenberg & Lawrence Schimel, editors
☐ TAROT FANTASTIC   UE2729—$5.99
☐ THE FORTUNE TELLER   UE2748—$5.99

Martin H. Greenberg & Bruce Arthurs, editors
☐ OLYMPUS   UE2775—$5.99

Elizabeth Ann Scarborough & Martin H. Greenberg, editors
☐ WARRIOR PRINCESSES   UE2680—$5.99

Prices slightly higher in Canada.   **DAW 105X**

FANTASY ANTHOLOGIES

☐ **HIGHWAYMEN** UE2732—$5.99
Jennifer Roberson, editor

Fantastic all-original tales of swashbucklers and scoundrels inspired by Alfred Noyes's famous poem.

☐ **ZODIAC FANTASTIC** UE2751—$5.99
Martin H. Greenberg, and A.R. Morlan, editors

Find your own future in these compelling stories from Mickey Zucker Reichert, Jody Lynn Nye, Mike Resnick, and Kate Elliott.

☐ **ELF FANTASTIC** UE2736—$5.99
Martin H. Greenberg, editor

Stories to lead the reader into the fairy hills, to emerge into a world far different from the one left behind.

☐ **ELF MAGIC** UE2761—$5.99
Martin H. Greenberg, editor

Fantasy's most beloved beings, in stories by Rosemary Edghill, Jane Yolen, Esther Friesner, and Michelle West.

☐ **WIZARD FANTASTIC** UE2756—$5.99
Martin H. Greenberg, editor

This all-original volume offers wizards to suit your every fancy, from sorcerers to geomancers to witch doctors to shamans.

☐ **THE FORTUNE TELLER** UE2605—$4.99
Lawrence Schimel & Martin H. Greenberg, editors

All-original tales of the mystical and malicious from authors such as Tanya Huff, Brian Stableford, Peter Crowther, and Neil Gaiman.

Buy them at your local bookstore or use this convenient coupon for ordering.

PENGUIN USA P.O. Box 999—Dep. #17109, Bergenfield, New Jersey 07621

Please send me the DAW BOOKS I have checked above, for which I am enclosing
$_____ (please add $2.00 to cover postage and handling). Send check or money order (no cash or C.O.D.'s) or charge by Mastercard or VISA (with a $15.00 minimum). Prices and numbers are subject to change without notice.

Card #_____ Exp. Date _____
Signature_____
Name_____
Address_____
City _____ State _____ Zip Code _____

For faster service when ordering by credit card call **1-800-253-6476**

Allow a minimum of 4-6 weeks for delivery. This offer is subject to change without notice.